D0277408

COPYRIGHT

This book is a work of fiction. The characters, incidents, locations, and dialogue are drawn from the author's imagination and are not to be construed as real. Any resemblance to actual persons, living or dead, is entirely coincidental.

FIRST EDITION

First Edition © April 2013

Surviving the Dead Volume III:

Warrior Within

By:

James N. Cook

Also by James N. Cook:

Surviving the Dead Volume I: No Easy Hope
Surviving the Dead Volume II: This Shattered Land

Part I

Today is victory over yourself of yesterday; tomorrow is your victory over lesser men.

-Miyamoto Musashi
The Book of Five Rings

Chapter 1

Black and Blue

The first light of dawn was just creeping over the horizon on a clear, cloudless morning. Rays of sunshine pierced the gloom, illuminated like diamonds on a carpet of frost-covered grass. In the distance birdsong filled the air, flittering through the tall, majestic trees that surrounded the field known, not affectionately by those familiar with it, as the Grinder. The morning would have been idyllic if not for the grunts, muffled curses, and dull thuds of flesh hitting flesh from the people struggling around me.

There were sixty-six in all—mostly men, but a few women as well—dressed in a motley assortment of outdoor wear as they punched, kicked, heaved, and grappled with one another. Thick wisps of steam rose from their heads like ghostly flames as they worked up a sweat in the chill September air.

As I had done every day for the past six weeks, I spent an hour teaching them new techniques both in striking and in groundwork, before turning them over to Gabriel for drills and sparring. It was the last week of their first phase of training, and Gabe was pushing them hard in preparation for phase two. I glanced at my watch, counting down the last few seconds of the round. The readout ticked down: three, two, one…

"Time," I said.

Gabe grabbed the whistle dangling from a cord around his neck and blew three shrill notes. The recruits fell out of their fighting stances, released holds, and untangled themselves as they got up from the ground.

"Sixty seconds. Hydrate and switch partners," Gabe called out, his deep baritone washing over the field. He turned his flint-eyed gaze toward me and reached out a hand for the stopwatch.

"Rotate in on the next round, Eric," he said. "Take on Sanchez first, then Flannigan. Hit 'em hard and put some heat on them. I want to see how they react."

I nodded, feeling the muscles in my jaw tense. Flannigan I wasn't too worried about. She was tough but lacked experience and was only about half my size. Sanchez was a different matter altogether.

The recruits finished drinking from their canteens and began returning to the sparring area in twos and threes. Some of them lingered by their packs a bit longer than Gabe felt was necessary and, never being one to tolerate laziness, he let the offending parties know that if they didn't hustle their asses up, *he* would be their next opponent.

That got them moving.

After slipping on my old six-ounce MMA gloves and washing off my mouthpiece, I called out to Sanchez and motioned him over. He frowned, his ink-black eyes darkening, and complied.

Sanchez didn't look like much. He stood a shade over five-foot-seven, and was maybe a hundred and fifty pounds soaking wet. Lean and wiry, he had narrow, boyish features that reminded me of every surly kid I had ever seen busing tables at a crappy restaurant. He was an unassuming guy, not the kind of person who would ever start trouble. But someone, somewhere, had taught him the sweet science of boxing, and had taught him exceedingly well.

Gabe knew Sanchez's story, but despite my frequent inquiries he had refused to share that information. His reasoning for this was that he didn't want it to affect the way I trained Sanchez, or any other recruits for that matter. Consequently, the first time I sparred with Sanchez, I had learned the hard way just how quick and accurate he was with his fists. It was not a pleasant experience.

Sanchez trotted to a halt in front of me. "You need me, sir?"

"Yeah, you're with me this round."

He narrowed his eyes slightly, fists tightening in his gloves. It had been a week since we'd last fought, and I had gotten the better of him then. I could tell he was itching for a rematch.

Gabe called out, "Touch gloves, get your hands up. Protect yourself at all times."

I assumed a fighting stance, as did everyone else on the field. Hands up, chin down, elbows tucked, knuckles just below my line of sight. My feet separated shoulder width apart, weight distributed evenly between the balls of my feet—pure muscle memory.

Sanchez took a similar stance, his base narrower than mine. Where my footwork tended to be precise and deliberate, not wasting any motion, Sanchez was animated and bouncy. Constantly moving and shuffling, never staying in the same spot for more than a second. He was an annoying opponent, but that was a good thing. As his trainer, I wanted him to be dangerous.

Gabe signaled the start of the round and, as always, Sanchez lit into me before the piercing note of the whistle had faded into the air. I backed off and circled, giving ground and absorbing shots on my forearms and elbows, amazed again at the kid's speed. I'm not slow by any stretch, but Sanchez is in a different league. I managed to snap off a few counter-punches, but the kid either slipped them or simply batted them aside. If this had been a boxing match, I would have been hopelessly outclassed.

Lucky for me, it wasn't a boxing match.

Sanchez overextended on a jab, blew the timing on a follow-up cross, and gave me the opening I needed to close the distance and clinch with him. I slipped an overhook around one of his arms, grabbed him by the back of the head, and started launching knees rapid-fire into his midsection. His breath went out of him with the first strike, but his expression never changed. He accepted the blows without complaint and started working to improve his position.

Just as I'd taught him, rather than instinctively dropping his arms to block the knees—which would have only made things worse for him—he postured up and stepped closer to me, closing the gap that allowed me to throw knee strikes in the first place. Now the fight had become something similar to a Greco-Roman wrestling match, albeit without rules.

Using a jiu jitsu technique called *pomo*, which I had drilled extensively with him and the other recruits in previous weeks, Sanchez started fighting his way out of the clinch by reversing the hold I had on his arms. He managed to work one arm loose, backed off enough to avoid the hip toss I attempted, and twisted away from the clinch.

In a surprising bit of innovation, he faked a jab-cross combination, stepped back, and launched a Muay-Thai kick at my midsection. It was a good kick, with the right amount of snap behind it. But it was also a mistake.

One of the worst things that can happen to you in a fight is for your opponent to know what you're going to do before you do it. The moment Sanchez dropped back from that lazy cross I knew what was coming next. When the kick came, I simply hopped back. His boot whipped past my midsection close enough to tug at my shirt. The momentum spun him around and exposed his back, taking him off balance for a second. That was all the time I needed.

Keeping my head low, I executed an old wrestling trick called a drop-step and shot in for a takedown at Sanchez's legs. The only counterattack he had available was a spinning back-fist, which he sent whistling over my head. I ducked the blow and committed my weight to the takedown. My shoulder hit his upper thighs, my arms hooked around behind his knees and, with an explosive lifting, twisting motion, I swept him up from the ground and planted him on his back, landing with me in side-control.

From there it was only a matter of time. It's hard enough to fight a skilled grappler under the best circumstances, but when said grappler outweighs you by fifty pounds and has seven more years of training than you do, it is simply impossible. Less than a minute after we hit the ground, I had transitioned from side-control into the full mount, softened him up with a few punches to the face, isolated an arm, and rolled into an armbar.

With his arm stretched out straight, caught between my legs and hands with my hips threatening to dislocate his elbow, he had no choice but to grit his teeth and tap out. Tap or snap, as my old sensei used to say. Not that I would have actually finished the technique and broken Sanchez's arm, but I could have if I'd wanted to.

I released the hold, rolled away, and stood up. Sanchez ignored the hand I extended to him, the wooden brown of his face darkening into an angry shade of purple, and got to his feet.

"Again," he said.

"Again, what?" I challenged, glaring.

He glared back for a few heartbeats. "Again, *sir*."

I motioned for him to step back, and he fell into a stance.

"Go."

The word was barely out of my mouth before he was on me again. The second bout went even quicker than the first; the kid was pissed off and making dumb mistakes. My own temper began heating up at his recklessness, and I started turning up the pressure, hitting him harder and using my strength to my advantage.

It was frustrating—I had taught him better than this, and he should have been able to put up a better fight. He knew not to let his temper get the best of him, but he was letting it happen anyway. As the round went on, he continued to fight well below his potential, so I continued to make him pay for it.

All too soon, Gabe blew the whistle. I had taken Sanchez's back and was applying a chokehold when the round ended. The kid glared sullenly when I reached down to help him up, but this time, he took my hand.

"Listen, man, you have got to get that temper under control," I said as I hauled him to his feet. "I know you can fight better than that. I've seen you do it."

He paused, searching my face for sincerity. After a moment, he let out a sigh and ran a hand through his dark hair.

"*Tienes razon, señor. Disculpa.*"

I shook my head. "Apologies won't keep you out of a pine box, Sancho. Get it together."

He nodded tersely, glancing up. "You're bleeding, sir. Want me to get a medic?"

Just as he said it, I felt something drip out of my nose. My hand came away red.

"No, don't worry about it." I waved him away. "I've had worse."

As he jogged away to get some water, I pulled a tissue from my shirt pocket and ripped it in half, stuffing the two pieces into my nostrils. Gabe came over to check on me while I pinched my nose to stop the bleeding.

"You all right?" he rumbled.

I nodded and jerked a thumb toward Sanchez. "I'm fine. We need to work on his ground game."

Gabe glanced in his direction, frowning. "There's no time. We only have three more months to train, and weapons and tactics are more important right now. Just do the best you can."

The big man patted me on the shoulder and walked back to the Grinder, hustling recruits along as he went. My nose didn't start leaking when I pulled the tissues out, so I figured I was good for another round and called out to Flannigan. The blond spitfire looked at me, touched knuckles with someone she had been talking to, and began jogging in my direction.

A former marathoner, Flannigan was quite possibly the most physically fit person I had ever met. Her remarkable endurance, paired with a sharp mind and a relentless appetite for training, had quickly made her one of my favorite students. She stood a little taller than Sanchez, albeit with a much lighter build, and had short hair that stood out at odd angles, framing her freckled, oval face.

"I got you figured out, sir," she said with a smile as she took her stance opposite me. "You're going down."

I fought the urge to smile, and kept my expression neutral. "Don't sing it, recruit. Bring it."

The whistle blew, and for a couple of minutes, I began to wonder if Flannigan's bravado was just her way of psyching up for the fight. Things certainly weren't going any better for her than they had for Sanchez. But unlike the fiery Mexican, rather than getting frustrated when I caught her in a choke (and it was always a choke; I hate hitting girls), she seemed to learn a little something, always making the next bout harder for me than the last. Even so, I wasn't having too much trouble handling her. I relaxed and trusted my long-ingrained technique to carry the fight.

And, as is usually the case, that was when I screwed up.

When I stepped into an outside reap that I had taken her down with many times before, Flannigan slipped out of it, making it look easy. I had half a second to realize that she had been baiting me before her elbow slammed hard into my shoulder, knocking me off balance. Gripping my lapels, she twisted her torso into a throw called the *uchi mata*. The throw was nearly perfect, but she had left too much space between us and was trying to muscle my weight over her shoulder instead of relying on technique. Had she been stronger, it might have worked, but the laws of physics bend for no one.

I dropped my weight and slipped to the side, forcing her to release my shirt and abandon the throw. She turned back into me, closing the distance until we were face to face in an over-under clinch.

Using my weight to my advantage, I started shoving her side to side with my shoulders trying to open up her stance. Flannigan, rather than trying to fight her arms free, stepped closer, pressed her chest against me, arched her back, and touched her lips to my ear.

"I like it when you choke me," she whispered, making me break out in goosebumps. "It makes me wet."

I froze up, cheeks burning. I must have blushed from my toes, all the way up to the tips of my ears. It only took me a second to get ahold of myself, but it was a second too long. Her mouth curved into a carnivorous grin just before her knee hit my solar plexus with all the gentleness of a car crash. Breath whooshed out of my lungs, hunching me over and opening up my neck. Flannigan followed up with a hammer-fist strike to my brachial nerve that turned my legs into limp noodles and forced me to lean into her to keep from falling down. This time, when she spun into the *uchi mata*, there was no slipping out of it.

My view went from earth to sky as she flipped me straight up and over, pulling on my lapels to make sure that I hit the ground with as much force as possible. Thankfully, there was no air left in me when I landed, otherwise it would have been driven out all over again.

Relentless demon that she is, Flannigan planted a knee into the bottom of my sternum, slid her fingers down through the neck of my shirt, and twisted the tough fabric into a collar choke. Even though my back was in agony, I was still cross-eyed from the brachial strike, and my lungs were too stunned to draw a breath, I somehow had the presence of mind to cross my forearms between hers, bridge upward with my hips, and break her grip. She pitched forward when I did so, allowing me to shimmy out from underneath her, throw a leg over her hips, roll on top, and pin her face to the ground.

She let fly a stream of curses as I flattened her out, pulled up on her head, and slipped a forearm over her throat. Normally I felt bad about cutting off her air supply in such a manner, but today, I found myself a little less than sympathetic toward my star pupil. Just as I began to squeeze, Gabe blew the whistle.

I got off her and struggled to my feet, hands planted on my knees, hauling in deep draughts of air. Flannigan's eyes held no sympathy as she got up and dusted herself off.

"I almost had you that time, sir," she said, spitting the words out.

I rasped a wheezing laugh. "Flannigan, you didn't have shit. You hurt me that last bout, but I seem to recall choking you out four times before that. Almost only counts in horseshoes and hand grenades. Next time, if you have a plan to beat me, do it on the first try. Marauders do not observe the fucking tapout rule. Got it?"

She opened her mouth to say something, hesitated, then bit down on it. "Yes sir."

I watched the anger and defiance drain from her face, a smoothing of expression that left her looking small and disappointed. I felt like a shithead for pushing her so hard, but

I wouldn’t be doing her any favors by going easy on her. She needed to learn how to fight, and she needed to do it fast.

“Go on and get some water,” I said, motioning toward the others. “Get ready for the next round.” She nodded wordlessly and left.

As she went, I wondered how many other recruits she was going to try that particular trick on, assuming I was the first victim. Thinking about it, I came to the conclusion that I probably wasn’t. Flannigan likes to plan ahead and set traps for her opponents. She had probably tried it out a few times, and when it worked, decided to use it against me. The only problem I had with that strategy is that she didn’t use it at the outset of the fight.

As I had told her, marauders don’t give second chances.

Chapter 2

Whirly-Bird

The walk home from the camp was more painful than usual that morning.

Flannigan's throw had done something unpleasant to my back, and one of my eyes had swollen nearly halfway shut. I touched the tender skin around it and wondered how that one had happened. I didn't remember getting hit there.

Not that this was surprising. The adrenaline rush of fighting often kept damage from registering until long after it had been inflicted. Over the past six weeks, not a day had gone by that I had not noticed a bruise or a cut in the mirror and wondered where the hell it had come from. The damage was beginning to take its toll, but I figured if the recruits could take it then so could I. Youth was still on my side, at least for a few more years.

I reached the north gate and stopped at the guard shack to check in my weapons. Judging by the guards' wide-eyed expressions and stiff posture, I must have looked even worse than I felt.

"You all right, mister?" one of them asked, a younger guy that I didn't recognize.

"I'm okay," I said, smiling through swollen lips. "You should see the other guy. I wrecked the shit out of his fist."

He shook his head and motioned for me to follow him, leading the way to one of the small, hastily built shacks just inside the gate. As a safety precaution, anyone returning to town from outside the wall had to undergo a strip search to check for signs of illness or infection. Two buildings had been constructed, with sniper stations on overwatch, to allow people to do this in privacy. Brett Nolan, one of the nurses who worked at the clinic with Allison, was on duty when I came in.

"Jumping Jesus Christ, Eric," he said, looking me over. "What happened here? You get run over by a truck?"

I let out a sigh. "Nope. Just reaping the fruits of my labor."

"Taught those kids a little too well, did ya?" He grinned through his bushy red beard. "They kickin' your ass now?"

I held up my arms so that he could look them over. "You know, as much as I love a little banter with another dude while I'm standing buck naked in the cold, I've got stuff to do. Maybe you can keep the jokes yourself and get this exam over with so I can go home?"

"Don't get your panties in a twist," he said. "I'll be done in a minute. Spread your feet."

I grimaced and did as he asked. After shining a flashlight over my legs and nether regions he pronounced me clean of infection, snapped his gloves off into a waste bin, and left me alone to get dressed. When I stepped outside, Mike Stall was waiting for me with my weapons, a cup of shitty instant coffee, and three ibuprofen tablets. God love him.

"Tough day at the office?" he said, as I downed the pills.

"Brutal." I managed a smile. "Thanks for the coffee."

The caffeine and the pain meds did their jobs and, by the time I got home, I felt almost human again. I got a fire going, heated up some water, and scrubbed off the dirt and grime from the morning's work. Checking out my injuries in the bedroom mirror, I could see that I was going to have some nasty bruises for the next few days, but that was nothing new. The swelling over my eye was an annoyance, but thanks to the anti-inflammatory effects of ibuprofen, it was already starting to go down. By tomorrow, it would be just another black and yellow stain on my face.

I had a few hours to kill before guard duty that afternoon, so I brewed some tea and sat down at the kitchen table with a hot mug and a John D. MacDonald novel. Allison was at the clinic looking after a woman who had just given birth to a healthy baby girl, so I had the house to myself.

The two of us had practically moved in together, but I still had a room at the house that Gabe and I had shared until a few weeks ago. The big guy never said anything about it, but after being cooped up together in a cabin for nearly two years, I don't think he was sad to see me move out. He was finally getting some well-deserved peace and quiet.

I was halfway through my tea and just turning the page to chapter two of *The Green Ripper* when a knock echoed from foyer.

Son of a bitch, I thought. *I never get a moment's peace around here*. I got up to answer the door, and when I opened it, Steve stood on the front porch wearing a mischievous grin.

"You know what today is?" he asked.

I blinked. "Uh. … Saturday?"

"Yes. But more importantly, it's market day."

"Okay, and what does that have to do with anything?"

Steve's smile widened. "I have a surprise for you. Come on, you're gonna love this."

I stood there staring at him for a moment, noticing that his uniform was different than usual. Normally, he wears Army ACUs with no insignia, something to do with him being a Special Ops guy. Today, however, he had on a more traditional-looking uniform. He was wearing his beret, which he never wore, claiming it didn't breathe worth a damn and felt like wearing a wet sock on top of his head. The captain's bars on his collar were self-explanatory, as were the nametag and the 'Special Forces' rocker on his shoulder, but the rest of the ribbons and shiny metal things pinned to his chest were a mystery to me.

"What's with the fancy duds?" I said, pointing.

"That's part of the surprise. Come on, we're wasting time."

I sighed. It was a mile out of Steve's way to swing by my house, so I figured there was no way I was getting out of this one.

"Let me grab my coat."

I walked with Steve toward the corner of Mill Street and Duncan, where the local farmers and tradesmen sold their wares every Saturday morning. Money was a distant memory, but the barter system was still alive and well.

Bullets, toilet paper, soap, hygiene products, and any kind of alcoholic drink had become valuable enough to be a form of currency, but just about anything was fair game if you could find someone willing to trade for it. Most of the trading on market day was just the locals selling food in exchange for valuable items, or more commonly, hours of labor.

Although trade goods might have been scarce, something everyone around town had plenty of was free time. 'Will work for food' no longer held a negative connotation. The local farms were productive enough to feed the entire community and then some, but they lacked personnel. Without gasoline to power their machinery, the farmers had to do everything by hand. And with the massive amount of work that goes into tending crops and raising animals, there was no shortage of openings in the fields.

Since most of the local farms were outside of the twelve-foot protective wall encompassing the central part of town, security was a major concern. Wandering ghouls were bad enough, but raiders from a rogue militant group calling themselves the Free Legion had been harassing those brave souls who provided their community with its livelihood.

In response, Walter Elliott, the local sheriff and one tough old son of a bitch, had recruited people to provide security for the farms in exchange for a percentage of everything they produced. Part of it went to the municipal emergency supply, and the rest was used to compensate the guards. Although it cost them a chunk of their harvest, the farmers had gritted their teeth and taken the deal. Unless they wanted to end up captured or killed, or have their livestock stolen and their fields burned by the Legion, they had no choice but to accept.

Even with the extra security, the Legion's raiders were still doing a fine job of making themselves a pain in the ass. Recently, they had begun a campaign of hit-and-run attacks on farms in broad daylight and had started taking potshots at guards along the wall. Usually, they fired off a few shots and then melted back into the trees before we could go after them, but on one occasion they made the mistake of shooting at a certain Marine Corps scout sniper of my acquaintance.

Gabriel often volunteered his services to the night watch in the hopes of catching the troublemakers in the act, and always brought along his .338 Lapua magnum sniper rifle. Capable of taking a man's head off at over a thousand yards, the powerful weapon was the stuff of nightmares—especially in the hands of one of the most highly trained snipers in the world.

On the night in question, Gabe had taken position on the westernmost guard tower and was watching the hills in that direction, just under the setting sun. He knew the raiders liked to use that time of day to attack because, with the sunset in the guards' eyes, it was when they would be the hardest to see. Gabriel had used the same technique himself many times.

He didn't catch any movement—they were too far away for that—but when they started firing, Gabe got a lock on their position. They were shooting unsuppressed rifles and, even from that distance, Gabe could make out the muzzle flashes. He estimated the range at about five hundred yards, made a quick scope adjustment, and sent three rounds downrange as fast as he could work the bolt.

They were dead before they knew what hit them.

When a team went out to retrieve the corpses, two of the gunmen were nearly headless. Afterward, I asked Gabe to remind me never to piss him off.

Other than that incident, the town's security forces, such as they were, had not made any headway against the Legion. They had enough people to man the wall and keep the farms safe, but going after the Legion in the hinterlands simply stretched them too thin. This meant that the Legion could operate with impunity as long as its members kept their distance, giving them control of the caravan routes between Hollow Rock and the Mississippi River. This had caused trade—the life's blood of Hollow Rock—to grind to a halt.

Obviously, something had to be done.

Determined to take the fight to the Legion, the mayor of Hollow Rock had asked Gabe to help build a small but well-trained expeditionary force to reopen the trade routes and eliminate anyone that got in their way.

Well ... to say that she asked him to do this may not be entirely accurate. My presence in this town was precipitated by a skirmish with the Free Legion and a rather nasty bullet wound in my side. I was unconscious by the time my friends hauled me through the northern gate and put me on an operating table. My girlfriend, Allison, who also happens to be the town's only medical doctor, operated on me while I was in a near coma and saved my life. Save for a big ugly scar on my side, I made a full recovery.

The buoyancy I had felt at surviving my first foray into the world of gunshot wounds was tragically short-lived. It turned out that the mayor charged a fee for any non-resident taking advantage of the town's services, like visits to the doctor. One might call it a visitor's tax. Once I was on the mend, the mayor had called Gabe to a meeting and laid out our payment options. Either we could give the town a third of our medical supplies, which were considerable, or we could stay and help defend the place until the threat posed by the Legion had been eliminated.

I should take a moment to mention here that Elizabeth Stone, the duly elected mayor, just so happens to be a pretty, doe-eyed brunette who is single and close to Gabe's age. I should further mention that Gabe has not gotten laid in a really long time.

Like, years.

Not surprisingly, he chose the second option.

"Looks like they're already here," Steve said, bringing me back to the present.

I looked up. "Who is?"

He pointed ahead to the square at the center of the market. Mayor Stone and Sheriff Elliott were mingling with some of the farmers at their wagons, smiling and doling out handshakes. A small platform had been erected at the intersection where the largest stalls met, visible to everyone in the market. Someone had even pinned a few red, white, and blue banners to it like the ones people used to hang from balconies and windows on Independence Day.

"What's going on with that?" I said, gesturing to the podium.

"All part of the surprise my friend, all part of the surprise."

I glanced over at him, and his grin had simmered down into a little self-satisfied smirk. *Smug bastard.*

The sheriff saw us coming and motioned us over. He was a tall man, well into his sixties but still hale and strong. He cut quite an impressive figure with his wide-brimmed hat, uniform, and pearl-handled Colt Python in a polished leather holster.

"Glad you could join us, Captain," he said, reaching out to shake hands with Steve. "How are things at Central Command?"

"As of about nine this morning, everything was running on schedule," Steve said. "Bird is inbound. Should be popping up over the horizon any time now."

"I'm sorry … bird? What are you talking about?" I asked.

Elliott jerked his head in my direction. "There any particular reason you decided to bring him along?" He didn't bother looking at me.

"Eric here has been helping Mr. Garrett train the new militia," Steve said. "I thought it would be a good idea to have one of the instructors on hand for the supply drop."

The sheriff eyed me up and down, clearly not liking what he saw. "All right, fair enough. Mayor's gettin' ready to make her speech. You might want to go ahead on up there."

"Will do." Steve turned and clapped me on the shoulder. "Hang out here for a few minutes. It's gonna be a hell of a show."

As he walked off toward the podium, Elliott continued to stare silently at me. From his expression, one would think that I had just pissed on his children. I turned and stared back.

"Something on your mind, sheriff?" I said, letting irritation bleed into my voice.

I had been putting up with the sheriff treating me like something he'd scraped off his boot for nearly two months now, and his condescending, dickhead attitude was starting to wear on my last nerve. He glared wordlessly for another moment, then turned on his heel and stalked away.

"Always a pleasure, Walt," I called out to his back. He kept walking, not bothering with a backward glance.

Prick.

I wandered over to a stall not far from the podium. A guy that I had seen before, but whose name escaped me, was selling baskets of eggs and live chickens in wire cages.

“Nice mornin’, eh?” the farmer said cheerfully. I nodded, feigning interest.

“You have any idea what that’s all about?” I said, making a vague gesture toward the podium.

He pushed back his straw hat and squinted at the mayor. “Not sure. Mayor said she had some kinda important announcement to make today. I reckon it has something to do with that treaty we voted on.”

A brief squawk of feedback sounded from the stage. Mayor Stone was testing the microphone on a PA system connected to a car battery. She was wearing a sleeveless white dress with an intricate blue pattern swirling down the sides that clung to her figure and emphasized her ample curves. Her arms were covered by a light blue cardigan, and tastefully applied makeup brought out the warm darkness of her eyes. It struck me how much of a contrast she was to Allison.

Allison is a petite little thing with small, delicate hands and a cute pixie face. The mayor was tall and athletic, her shoulders broad for a woman, and she had a generous curve to her hips. Not fat at all, just bigger than average. Carefully curled hair cascaded down her shoulders and framed her face, all high cheekbones and a broad smile. Looking at her, she could have been in her late twenties, but in truth, she was actually pushing forty. Whatever she was doing to take care of herself, it was working.

“Can everybody hear me okay? All the way in the back?” she said.

A scattered round of acknowledgments sounded from the tents as throngs of people wandering among the carts stopped to listen.

“All right, fantastic,” she went on. “Now folks, I don’t know how long the juice on this thing is going to last, so I’ll have to make this quick.”

She paused for a moment, allowing the crowds to go silent. I noticed that the mayor was letting a little bit more of her Southern accent creep through than she normally did. Curious.

"As y'all know, we've been requesting federal aid from Colorado Springs for a number of weeks now. Captain McCray here has been working diligently to obtain supplies, equipment, and reinforcements to help in our ongoing efforts to protect our community. It's been slow going, and I know things haven't been easy, but today I'm happy to announce that our patience has been rewarded, and that help is on the way."

The mayor beamed as the crowd broke into enthusiastic applause. She directed her smile at Steve for a moment, who flushed ever so slightly and smiled back, giving a single nod.

The mayor continued, "As we speak, there is an Army transport helicopter coming this way to make the first of several supply drops we'll be receiving over the next few days. It should be getting here within the hour, and Sheriff Elliott will be organizing a volunteer work crew to help sort everything out and get it where it needs to go. Now I know y'all are honest folks, but I still have to remind you that everything in those transports is city property and should be treated as such. Once again, I want to thank each and every one of you for your support and hard work, and I hope you enjoy the rest of the day."

The mayor stepped back from the microphone, flashing her dazzling white smile and waving at the applauding townsfolk. I didn't know if the warmth and sincerity she radiated was genuine, or if it was an affectation, but the townspeople certainly bought it. Her charisma was undeniable, and I could certainly see why she inspired confidence. But I was still reserving judgment.

She was, after all, a politician.

*****

When the helicopter arrived, it was every bit as spectacular as Steve had promised. A massive twin-rotor CH-47 Chinook, machine guns bristling from the side ports, and two impossibly large bundles of cargo dangling underneath, it roared over the treetops in a maelstrom of wind and flying debris to deposit its cargo before flying away and touching down in an open patch of field.

As it landed, I walked over to where Steve stood near the now empty podium. His expression was placid, as though watching a gigantic helicopter flit delicately about the market square was the most normal thing in the world. For a guy like him, maybe it was.

"Question for you," I said.

"Shoot."

I pointed at the helicopter. "Where the hell did they get fuel for that thing?"

"Strategic reserves would be my guess," Steve said. "Treated and stored properly, just about any kind of aviation fuel can last for over a decade."

That shook a memory loose, and I vaguely recalled something I read in college about strategic oil reserves. Possibilities began to swirl.

"Any idea where they keep it?"

He shrugged. "The government had about as many doomsday plans as Washington had lobbyists. There's shit stashed all over the country. Supposedly, the President and the Joint Chiefs know where all of it is, but they've only recovered a fraction of it."

I paused to consider that for a moment. If the government could provide us with tanks and air support, what did that mean for the fight against the Free Legion?

"Come on," Steve said, motioning me forward. "Got some people I want you to meet."

The drone of the helicopter's engine had faded from a high, keening whine to a lower, more tolerable pitch. The massive twin rotors slowed, no longer kicking up blinding clouds of dust and debris. Six figures exited from the open door on the side facing us, marching purposefully toward Steve.

From the corner of my eye, I saw Sheriff Elliott and Mayor Stone break off from the crowd and trot to catch up with us. Steve set a quick pace, and we managed to reach the newcomers before they caught up.

Three of the men looked like regular Army grunts, but battle-hardened ones. They strode forward with the casual confidence of veterans, handling their carbines with practiced ease. Walking in front of them was a tall, stone-faced man with eyes like granite and a shiny silver star pinned to his hat. Strangely, he looked familiar. I could have sworn I'd seen him before.

Behind him, quietly blending into the background, were two men in black fatigues with large, square cases strapped to their backs. One was tall and lean, with a nose like a hawk's beak and sharp, vaguely Asian features that spoke of Native American ancestry. The other man was shorter, broad shouldered, and had a face like a cinder block, all square lines and blunt angles.

Steve snapped a salute to the man with the star on his hat, who returned his salute and reached out to shake Steve's hand when he drew near.

"Good to see you again, McCray," he said.

"Good to see you too, General. How was the trip?"

The older man grimaced. "I thought the 'Ghan was the shittiest shit I'd ever have to suffer through. Fate has once again conspired to prove me wrong."

Steve grinned. "Sir, this is Eric Riordan, the man I spoke to you about earlier. Eric, this is General Phillip Jacobs. He's in charge of Special Operations Command."

The old soldier snorted. “Such as it is these days. Pleased to meet you, young man.”

I shook his hand and looked him in the eye. General Jacobs had a strong grip and a firm, steady gaze with just a faint glimmer of mischief hiding in the background. I liked him immediately.

“Likewise, general,” I said.

“Call me Phil.” His eyes shifted to a point behind me, and I turned to see the sheriff approaching with Mayor Stone close behind. The mayor’s body was doing all kinds of interesting things under her low-cut dress as she jogged toward us, and the effect was not lost on the men around me.

“Welcome to Hollow Rock,” she said, stopping in front of General Jacobs and flashing that heart-stopping smile. “I’m Mayor Elizabeth Stone, and this old fellow here is Sheriff Walter Elliott. I’m so glad you could make it.”

The general took her hand, simultaneously trying to rip his eyes up from her cleavage. “Well, Mayor, it’s nice to finally put a face to the name.” he said.

“You must be General Jacobs.”

“That’s right.”

“I’m sure you gentlemen must have had a long trip. How about we all head over to the VFW? We’ve set up a nice lunch for you there.”

The general smiled. “That’s sounds like the best idea I’ve heard all day. Lead the way, ma’am.”

Her dress swirled around her as she took the general by the arm and turned to walk toward a horse-drawn wagon waiting at the edge of the market. I pointedly ignored the sheriff’s disapproving glare as Steve and I followed the general’s entourage.

I glanced over at Steve as we walked, and the yellow-eyed bastard was still smirking. When this dog-and-pony show was over, he had some explaining to do.

*****

Lunch was everything the mayor had promised. Fried chicken, mashed potatoes, gravy, biscuits, black-eyed peas, and an assortment of cooked garden vegetables—a traditional Southern meal. My mouth was watering before I even made it through the door of the VFW hall.

Thankfully, the sheriff had stayed behind with the two guys in black combat fatigues to organize the work crew sorting out the supply drop. The sheer mass of the stacked crates that the Chinook had carried to us was staggering.

During the reception, the mayor mingled among the newcomers, taking time to talk to each one and learn a little bit about them. Occasionally, she would shoot a glance my way, and then look meaningfully at Steve. I began to get the impression that it wasn't her idea to invite me along.

While the mayor and General Jacobs were at the bar getting a shot of scotch from the mayor's personal stash, I grabbed a plate and got in line next to Steve at the buffet table.

"Were you planning on at some point explaining to me why the hell you dragged me out of my house this morning?" I said, keeping my voice low. "I mean, I appreciate a free meal as much as the next guy, but I get the feeling I'm not exactly welcome here."

"Eric, I promise that all will be made clear, just not right now. Don't worry, everything's cool."

"You sure about that? 'Cause the mayor wouldn't piss on me if I was burning, and the General's bodyguards keep looking at me like I'm fucking Scarface."

Steve chuckled. "I told you, everything's fine. Just eat your food, keep your mouth shut, and be patient. Trust me, it'll be worth it."

Against my better judgment, I did as he said. The food was good, which made staying quiet an almost enjoyable task. Once everyone was settled down at the banquet table, the mayor gave a short speech about how grateful she was for the government's help, how humbling it was have earned Central Command's trust, and blah, blah, blah. General Jacobs stood and gave an equally insincere and meaningless speech, but delivered it with less affected verve than the mayor had. Nevertheless, everyone gave him the same polite little golf clap that we had given the mayor.

After lunch, the volunteers who had put our meal together brought peach cobbler around to everyone at the table, and even topped it off with a dollop of fresh whipped cream—a rare treat indeed. It would have been great, except for the fact that I detest peach cobbler. The Army grunt sitting next to me devoured his in less time than it takes to say the words, so I offered him mine. He seemed to hate me a little bit less after that.

Just as I was eyeballing the side exit, and seriously mulling over how I could make my escape without drawing too much attention to myself, General Jacobs stood up and motioned to his men.

"Well mayor, I certainly do appreciate the hospitality," he said, "but I need to get back to the chopper and get on the horn to Central Command. Is five o'clock this afternoon still a good time to for the conference?"

"Absolutely."

The mayor smiled, stood up, and walked the General and his men out to the parking lot, where a wagon waited for them. She said a polite round of goodbyes as the horses strained at their tethers, and the wagon creaked off down the road, leaving me, her, and Steve all standing out in front of town hall. Once the wagon had disappeared over a hill in the distance, both Steve and the mayor turned and regarded me silently.

"So. Someone mind telling me what's going on?" I said.

The bright enthusiasm that Mayor Stone had displayed all morning dissipated like a fog under the noonday sun. She swiveled her gaze over to Steve.

"You really think he's the guy for the job?"

Steve nodded. "I'm sure of it."

"Okay people, I'm standing right here," I chimed in. "Could you please explain to me what the hell you're talking about?"

Steve suppressed a smile and gave me a warning look. "The mayor has asked me to help her out with a special project, and to pick someone qualified to take the lead on it."

"What kind of project?"

"The kind that saves lives and makes this town a safer place," the mayor said.

I stared at her for a moment. I was pretty sure it was the first time she had ever spoken to me directly.

"Okay," I said. "What did you have in mind?"

"We should go into my office. This is a matter best discussed in private."

She turned and walked into the town hall without a backward glance. I looked at Steve. He winked at me.

"What are you getting me into, man?"

"Come on, let's go inside."

I shoved my hands in my pockets, cursed under my breath, and followed him in. One thing I had to give this town. Life was never boring

Chapter 3

Trojan Horse

The mayor's office was exactly as Gabe had described it to me. Small, with floor-to-ceiling windows overlooking the front lawn, bookshelves, the requisite collection of college degrees and plaques hanging on the walls, and a massive oak desk that looked like it had been there since the Taft administration. The mayor sat down behind it and motioned to the two chairs in front of her.

"Have a seat, gentlemen."

I sat down in a comfortable leather chair next to Steve and watched while the mayor sorted through a few pieces of paper. She kept me waiting long enough to let me know she was keeping me waiting, and then slid two forms side-by-side on the desk in front of her.

"Captain McCray tells me that you've had extensive paramilitary training. Is that correct?"

I glanced over at Steve. "Yeah, I guess you could say that."

"At his behest, I spoke to Mr. Garrett about you. He told me that in addition to possessing significant unarmed combat skills, you're an expert rifleman, you have a strong grasp of combat tactics and wilderness survival, and that you're a serviceable sniper. Is all that true?"

'Serviceable' sniper. That sounded like something Gabe would say. "I'll have to defer to Gabe's judgment on that."

She smiled then, slight dimples forming at the corners of her mouth, white teeth showing through full lips. It was a practiced smile, and she knew exactly what kind of effect it had. But that didn't stop it from being charming.

"If Mr. Garrett's assessment is correct, then it seems there's more to you than appearances would suggest."

I wasn't sure quite what that was supposed to mean, but found myself smiling back anyway. "Thank you. … I think."

She looked over at Steve. "Captain?"

He turned his chair to face me. "I've seen what you can do Eric, and I have confidence in your abilities. The reason you're here today is because we need someone to infiltrate the Legion, and I think you're the man for the job."

I went still, and blinked at him a couple of times. "I'm sorry, you want me to do what?"

"Think about it," he went on. "We've been spinning our wheels against these assholes for months, and what do we have to show for it? The last thing this town needs is a prolonged fight that will use up resources and cost lives. If we can get someone on the inside, feed us intel on where they hide and how they operate, we can use that to pick them apart."

I stuttered, stammered, and held up a hand. "Whoa, wait a minute. Here's the thing—I'm not trained for that. I can hold my own in a firefight, but I know jack shit about espionage."

"I can work with you on that."

"Really? When? You spend ninety percent of your time running around in the woods looking for Legion raiders."

"And for all that, I've accomplished next to nothing. I think it's time to switch tactics."

I waited another beat, trying sort out all the reasons why this was a bad idea. There were a lot to sift through. "Okay, what about the militia? They still have three months of training ahead of them."

"This plan won't go into effect until they're finished. I'm bringing it up now so that we have time to get you ready."

"Steve, what makes you think I'm even willing to do this?"

"Because I know you, Eric. You're nosy. If there's one thing you hate, it's being out of the loop."

I frowned at him, and fought the urge to smack that goddamn smirk off his face. The mayor stayed quiet at her desk, watching.

They had planned this, the two of them. They had set up an ambush, and I had walked right into it. This, in and of itself, did not bother me. What did bother me was the fact that Steve was right. I do like being in the middle of things, sticking my nose where it doesn't belong, and generally getting myself into trouble. Damn him.

"Okay." I sighed. "One more question. Why me? I mean, fighting ability aside, what makes you think I'm the guy to do this?"

"You've read my intelligence reports," Steve replied, "so you know that the Legion is growing. What those reports don't say is that some of those people are survivors from the small towns around Hollow Rock and Bruceton."

"How do you know that?"

Mayor Stone interjected, "He showed me photographs. I recognized some of the people in them."

I turned to stare at her, suspicious. "How is that possible? You're telling me you recognized people from all over the county?"

Her eyes narrowed. "I grew up in Hollow Rock, Mr. Riordan. My family, those who are still alive, all live here. In my first election, I did my campaigning door to door. I've been the mayor of Hollow Rock for eight years, and I'm on a first-name basis with over half the households in Carroll County. I know the rest of them by either their tax records or their rap sheets. So yes, Mr. Riordan, I recognized people from all over the county."

I nodded, getting the idea. "Okay then, why aren't these people joining on our side? The Legion isn't exactly known for their fairness and hospitality."

"That's the problem," the mayor said. "We just don't know. It's not as if we wouldn't welcome them here; we need all the help we can get. But ever since the last election when Ronnie Kilpatrick defected, no one has attempted to join our community. Not one single person."

"Until you, that is," Steve said.

Now we were getting somewhere. "So you need me to find out how the Legion is sourcing their troops."

Steve nodded. "That, and we need to know where they're operating from. There has to be somewhere, or maybe several locations, where they take shelter from the infected and store their supplies. If we can find these locations, then that will be the first step toward defeating them."

I sat back in my chair and let the weight of what they were asking me to do sink in. Warm sunshine filtered in through the tall windows and framed the mayor as she sat at her desk, waiting.

"So let me see if I have this straight. Since some of the people in the Legion are from around here, or at least within a couple of days' walk, if someone from Hollow Rock or Bruceton tried to infiltrate them, then there's a good chance they would eventually be recognized. Good so far?"

The mayor nodded.

"Right. So what you need is someone who isn't from around here. Someone with enough of a Southern accent to blend in. Someone who wouldn't be suspected of being a spy from Hollow Rock. Someone with paramilitary training. Am I tracking here?"

She nodded again. "That's right."

"Told you he catches on quick," Steve said.

I shook my head, wondering, not for the first time, how I always ended up getting myself into these messes. I turned to look at Steve. "I'm not making any promises, but I'll give it a try. If you can teach me what I need to know, I'll do it. But I'm reserving the right to back out if I don't feel ready for it."

I turned back to the mayor. "And that's a take-it-or-leave-it offer."

Mayor Stone smiled again, and this time, the warmth seemed genuine. "Fair enough."

Steve reached over and patted me on the shoulder. "Good to have you on board. Now, there's something else we wanted to talk to you about."

Of course there is. Why wouldn't there be?

"And that is?"

The mayor said, "I understand that other than teaching two classes a day to the militia, you don't have anything else occupying your time."

"Well, there is guard duty."

She crossed her hands on the desk in front of her and leaned forward. "I think guard duty is a waste of your talents, wouldn't you agree?"

Uh-oh.

"That depends on what you have in mind."

She tucked a stray lock of hair behind her ear and leaned back in her seat. Her talent for making the slightest movement seem alluring was quite a thing to behold.

"The infected have become a serious problem."

I stared at her for a second, and then I laughed. Loudly. The mayor frowned, the corners of her mouth pinning down against her chin.

"Is something funny?"

"Oh no, nothing at all, mayor. Being that civilization is destroyed, and ninety-nine percent of the world is dead, and there are about three hundred million flesh-eating ghouls out there, then yes, I would venture to say that the infected have indeed become a bit of a problem."

Her warm brown eyes had gone hard and cold. "This is not a joke, Mr. Riordan," she said flatly. "We've lost six people in the last month."

That wiped the grin off my face. I held up a mollifying hand. "I know mayor, I heard about it. It's a tragic loss, and one that this town can ill afford, but what does that have to do with me?"

"Captain McCray says that you are exceptionally good at fighting the infected."

I looked over at him. "Does he now?"

"I saw you come up with some impressive ideas back in North Carolina," he said. "And Sarah told me about the swarm you fought outside of Morganton. You have to admit, you've got a talent for dealing with the walkers."

"Yeah, I don't know about that."

"I do." Steve leaned closer. "Listen, instead of having you stand around all day doing nothing on guard duty, why don't you work with your friend Tom to come up with better ways to defend against the infected? Don't sit there and tell me you don't have any ideas rattling around."

Again, he was right. I did have a few ideas I wanted to try out. I just hadn't said anything because I didn't think anyone would listen. And hell, at the very least, it would get me out of boring-ass guard duty.

"How much manpower and resources are you willing to commit to this?" I asked, looking at the mayor.

"As much as you need, within reason."

I nodded. "Okay. Let me talk to Tom, and we'll take a look around and see what we can come up with."

“Put together an action plan, and have it on my desk in three days,” she said.

I frowned, not particularly caring for her high-handed tone, addressing me like an employee.

“I’ll need a week. Maybe more, then I’ll let you know something.”

She looked me in the eye for a moment, not quite glaring, and I stared icily back. If she wanted me to do this for her, then I would do it my way, not hers. Tension hung between us as she weighed what to say next. Finally, she gave a slow nod and leaned forward to plant her elbows on the desk and rest her chin on her hands.

“One thing you haven’t asked me yet,” she said.

“What’s that?”

“What’s in this for you?”

I shook my head. “I don’t know what you think about me as a person, but I’m not doing this because I want anything from you. I can get by on my own, with or without this town. I want to help because there are good people living here, and they’re in danger. I’m not going to stand idly by and let the Legion rape and pillage this place. One way or another, we need to shut those sons of bitches down.”

The mayor sat back and arched one well-plucked eyebrow, breaking into a smile.

“Well. Aren’t you just full of surprises?”

*****

The rest of the day saw me running around town trying to track down the skilled trades I would need to begin working on the town’s defenses. Tom was, as always, glad to throw his toolbelt into the mix. He had traveled to Tennessee with us from Morganton and, in addition to being an all-around solid guy, he was one of the most talented craftsmen I had ever known.

I also enlisted the aid of a couple of stonemasons, a mechanic, a guy who ran a quasi-functional machine shop, and a few other guys for general labor. One thing you could always count on around here, if there was payment involved, be it food or trade items, there was no shortage of people looking for work.

Once all the necessary deals were hammered out, and all the necessary hands shaken, I stopped by Gabe's place to have a word with him. The mayor asked me to brief him on our conversation but had also warned me not to tell anyone else. For now, the plan had to remain in the dark.

Gabe made tea when I arrived, and we sat down at the little table in the kitchen. After recounting what happened at the mayor's office, I sat quietly for a moment to see how he would react. I could tell by the tightness in his shoulders that he was not happy.

"This is insane, Eric. It's a fucking suicide mission." His fingers tightened around the cup in his hand, and I began to fear for the little porcelain vessel.

"You have to admit," I said. "I'm a good candidate for the job. No one around here knows me."

The big man stood up, nearly tipping over his chair as he began to pace around the kitchen.

"This is complete bullshit, Eric. She didn't pick you because you're new in town. She picked you because she thinks you're fucking expendable."

"Listen, Gabe-"

"If she thinks I'm going to let her get away with this, she is fucking stupid. Tomorrow morning I'm going down to her office and-"

"I accepted the assignment."

He stopped. It was the second time I had ever seen him taken completely off-guard.

"You did what?"

"You heard me."

Gabe sat back down in his chair and carefully folded his hands on the table. He took a few deep breaths before speaking again.

"Why would you go and do a stupid thing like that?"

"Who else is going to do it?"

His calloused palm hit the table like a gunshot, rattling the silverware. "Anyone! Fucking anyone could do it. Or better yet, nobody. Did you even bother to ask her why we need a spy in the first place? There are other ways to find those bastards. Hell, if the Army can give us air support, they're as good as dead. It's just a matter of time."

"Gabe, would you calm down?"

"Fuck that. You need to start getting worked up."

"Why are you so upset about this?"

"Because you're the only goddamn family I got left and I don't want anything to happen to you!"

Gabe was standing up by the time he finished, the powerful resonance of his voice eliciting a high, ringing echo from the kitchen sink. We stared at each other quietly for a moment, all the years of shared hardship filling the space between us. Slowly, a tired smile crossed my face.

"Gabe, I think that's the nicest thing you've ever said to me. Maybe we should hug, or something."

Gabe glared for another moment, and then sank back down into his chair. The tide of his anger receded, washing back and fading into the slump of his shoulders. He ran a hand over his tattered face.

"How the hell did we get ourselves into this mess?"

"Wasn't the straightest of roads."

Gabe laughed bitterly. "Ain't that the goddamn truth."

I took a sip of my tea and thought about the mayor's offer. I thought about the wall around this town and how painfully fragile it looked from the landing of a guard tower. I thought about Allison, and the militia, and how far away Colorado now seemed, like a distant dream. I wondered how everything had gotten so complicated.

"My bottle of Knob Creek still in the cupboard?"

Gabe nodded. "Spare a little for me while you're at it."

I did as he asked, pouring a couple of fingers of amber liquid into a set of heavy glass tumblers before sitting back down at the table. We sipped our whiskey quietly for a few moments, enjoying the warm burn in the chilly room.

"I don't suppose they revealed to you the details of this great plan of theirs, did they?" Gabe asked.

"No. Said they'd give me the details after we finish training the militia."

"Which is to say, they don't trust you."

I shrugged. "Can't say I blame them. The stakes are pretty high in this game."

Gabe tossed back the rest of his whiskey and reached for the bottle. He didn't grimace.

"Let me tell you something about war, old friend." He filled his glass and picked it up, looking at me over the top of it.

"War is not a game."

*****

Allison's bicycle was chained to the porch railing when I got home. It was late, and I had stopped after two drinks so that I wouldn't be wasted when I walked through the door. The walk home from Gabe's place was only a quarter-mile, but with the sun tucked behind the horizon, it was plenty far enough for me to get chilled under my thin canvas jacket. I would have to break out the Gore-Tex pretty soon.

The smell of wood smoke drifted to me through the boughs of graceful old oak trees scattered throughout the yard. After such a long day, warming myself in front of the fireplace was high on my list of priorities. So was bathing. And making love to Allison. Not necessarily in that order.

I left my muddy boots on the porch and stepped through the front door. Allison squatted in front of the fireplace stirring a pot of stew. She was wearing a light gray sweater, tight black leggings that clung to her like a second skin, and she had tied her hair back in a single braid that ended just north of her lower back. I'd never seen a woman look so adorable.

"Hey, babe," she said as I walked into the living room.

"Hey, yourself. Smells good in here, whatcha cooking?"

"Beef stew and your favorite." She held up an iron skillet. "Flatbread."

"Mmm. Sounds good."

While I hung my jacket on a hook beside the door, Allison stood up and came to me with her arms outstretched. I picked her up and held her tight. It didn't take much effort; she hardly weighed anything. I breathed in her scent and nuzzled her neck, swaying back and forth with her.

"You smell good."

"You always say that." She leaned back, her face only a couple of inches from mine.

"It's always true."

Her smile flashed like a hundred-watt light. I drank it in and smiled back, feeling the warm, comfortable weight that had been growing in my chest since the day I first met her. Lips softer than a whisper brushed against mine, and I pulled her closer, my hand cupping gently around the back of her neck, knowing she liked it when I did that.

Allison responded by wrapping her legs around my hips and squeezing. She could feel that I was happy to see her and began moving her hips around in languid little circles, pulling herself tighter against me. I kissed her harder, and she kissed me back, soft moans escaping from deep in her throat. My heart beat faster in my chest, and my skin began to heat up. The grinding of her hips grew faster and more insistent. Her nails dug into the skin of my shoulders, carving shallow furrows that would leave marks for days. For just an instant, she leaned her head back, breaking the kiss.

"Kitchen table," she said, and went back to work.

That was all I needed to hear.

An hour later, after we cleaned ourselves up, pulled the table back to the center of the room, and picked up the chairs we had knocked over, we sat down in front of the fireplace with steaming bowls of stew and cold apple cider. Warm light from the fire danced around us on the hardwood floors and cast twisting shadows on the paneled walls.

"So what did you do today?" Allison asked.

I turned my head to look at her. Her dark brown eyes shined in the firelight, warm and happy. It made me ache to see her sitting there, so beautiful and trusting. As important as it was to keep my forthcoming mission a secret, I hated the idea of lying to her.

"Steve came by and got me this morning after work. You heard about the Army bringing supplies into town today, right?"

"Heard about it? That big-ass helicopter scared the bejesus out of me when it flew over the clinic. I thought we were about to get bombed or something. Was that Steve's doing?"

I nodded. "He negotiated for supplies and equipment for the recruits, and I think for some communications equipment. We'll find out tomorrow when we take everything to the camp."

"Well that's good, we need all the help we can get. I don't suppose they're going to be sending us any troops, are they?"

"Actually, two guys came in on the helicopter. Steve told me they're both Navy SEALs."

Her eyebrows shot up. "No shit? That's awesome. Did you get a chance to talk to them?"

"No, but they're supposed to come by the camp tomorrow to introduce themselves to everyone."

"That's cool. You'll have to tell me what they're like. Didn't some Army guys come in as well? Someone at the clinic was talking about that."

I nodded, swallowing a mouthful of stew. "Yeah, the freaking general in charge of Army Special Operations Command."

"That sounds important."

"It is."

"What's he here for? Is he going to be helping us out against the Legion?"

I shrugged. "I don't know. He's in town for at least a couple of days, so I imagine we'll find out soon."

Allison put her bowl down and stared into the fire. "You know, this is exciting stuff. The Legion has been making life hard for us for so long. Maybe soon we won't have to worry about them anymore."

I ran a hand up her back. "We'll deal with them, babe, one way or another. By this time next year, the Legion will be a memory."

"I hope you're right. This town has seen enough heartache. It would be nice to have some peace and quiet for a while."

There was a weight of pain in her voice that made me want to pull her into my lap and hold her. I let my hand move over her back.

"Oooohh, can you scratch?" she said.

I did as she asked, gently raking my nails over her shoulders in little circles.

"Lower, lower … a little to the right … ahh, right there."

I smiled, scratching at a spot just above her right hip. She gave me permission to stop after a few seconds, then scooted over to sit closer to me. Warm, slender arms wrapped around mine as she leaned her head on my shoulder. Between her and the fire, I was warmer than I had been all day.

"How's the new mommy?" I asked, shoving a poker at the bed of coals.

"Jenny's doing great. That woman is a machine. She'd be back in her vegetable garden by tomorrow if I let her. That baby of hers is just about the most adorable thing I've ever seen."

"You say that about all babies."

"Yes, and it's always true."

I chuckled, putting an arm around her shoulders and pulling her tighter against me. "I had a meeting with Mayor Stone today."

"Uh oh. What about?"

"Well … I can't really talk about it right now. She wants me to work on a few projects around town, and then there's a bigger assignment that I'll be helping out with after we finish training the militia."

Allison sat up and leaned away from me. I studiously avoided her intelligent, glittering stare, afraid that those eyes would cut into me.

"Does it concern the Legion, this 'assignment'?" She made little air quotes with her fingers.

I kept my face blank. Or tried to, anyway. "I can't say."

"So that's a yes. Next question: Is it dangerous?"

"Allison, please, let's not do this, okay? I only brought it up because it's going to pull me away from town for a while. I just want you to be prepared when the time comes for me to leave."

"Well that answers my second question. It is dangerous."

I sighed and rubbed a hand against my forehead. Life had been so much simpler when I was just a shallow womanizer.

"Allison, someone has to fight those assholes out there, okay? I signed up to do the job. At some point, things are going to get bloody and, when that happens, I'm going to be involved. If you're going to get like this every time the subject of me doing something risky comes up, then you're going to be spending a lot of time pissed off at me."

She glared a little longer, then looked down, her expression softening.

"Eric, I just don't want you to get hurt again. I love you too much to watch you-" She stopped, realizing what she had just said.

Her cheeks flushed as she looked up at me, her eyes a deep well of glistening vulnerability. There they were again, those three words. Not for the first time, I felt the course of my life hinging upon them. But this time, I wasn't afraid. This time, I was ready. I smiled and reached out to her. She slipped her soft, slender fingers around my thick calloused ones and held on with both hands.

"It's okay, Allison. I love you, too."

She smiled, and the happiness in her eyes pierced me like an arrow, punching through all my armor and making me grin like a schoolboy with his first crush. I would have said more, but Allison's arms shot around my neck and squeezed so hard that for a few moments, I couldn't breathe. For being so small, she was surprisingly strong.

After a moment, she let go, and just as I was drawing a breath to speak, she pushed me over onto my back and straddled me. Her lips met mine with frantic urgency while her hands tugged at my shirt. She leaned up for a moment to struggle out of her sweater, her firm breasts spilling out, and anything I was about to say suddenly didn't seem all that important anymore.

Chapter 4

The Journal of Gabriel Garrett:

Burdens

I was sitting at the kitchen table again, brooding. For some reason, this cramped little room had become my favorite place to do that. Maybe it was the window that overlooked the back yard, or the proximity to the warm stove, or maybe it was the smell of wood polish that had been worked into the floors for God knows how many years. Whatever the reason, it was a good place to think.

While I was sitting there, it occurred to me that there is a distinct difference between thinking and brooding. The kitchen was a place for thinking, being that it was indoors and protected from the worst of the elements. It was quiet, with a minimum of distractions. Brooding, however, is best done outside in the fresh air, where a man can see the sky and feel the smallness of his existence. Maybe there would be clouds. Clouds are conducive to brooding.

Eric left his bottle of whiskey sitting on the kitchen table, which I took as an invitation and carried it outside to the front porch. I sat down in a rocking chair like the old man I was slowly becoming and poured myself a tall one. Crickets chirped in the woods while marlins chased mosquitos under a bruised purple sky. It was a good environment for brooding, I decided. And also for self-medication. The bottle of Knob

Creek was probably the last of Eric's stash, but that was okay. I'd give him a bottle from mine if he made an issue of it.

The whiskey warmed me up as I stared out into the darkening night. My thoughts began to wander, as they often did, back across all the long years to the war, and everything after. The demons were getting restless again. Time and distance had made them weaker, but they were still there. Waiting. I tossed back another drink.

If I had to point out one decision, one single instant of time that had caused my life to go so horribly wrong, I would have to say it was when I decided to leave the military. That was when the trouble started.

After leaving the Marines, I swore to myself I'd live a life of peace. I'd get a job, settle down, start a family, and enjoy all the things I had risked my life to defend. I even met a nice girl and got married, maybe a bit too quickly in retrospect. I thought I could turn away from the war and do something good with my life, decide for myself what kind of person I wanted to be. But instead, my marriage fell apart in less than a year, my wife kicked me out of the house and, stupid bastard that I was, I fell right back into my old habits again.

I remember sitting in a shitty fleabag motel room, staring back and forth between a piece of paper with a few numbers scribbled on it and the telephone. I had just gotten laid off from my third shit-paying job in six months, and I only had enough cash in my pocket to keep a roof over my head for two more days. After that, I'd be out on my ass.

I didn't know where to turn, so I called my old friend Rocco. He and I had worked together as a sniper team in Fallujah. He was good. Ruthless, efficient, and utterly lethal. Just like me.

He had sent me an e-mail not long after I left the Corps telling me about the contract work he was doing for the intelligence community. He'd told me if I ever wanted to get back in the shit, and make some serious money doing it, then I should give him a call. I didn't relish the idea, but at the time it was either that or wind up homeless.

I thought about all those poor old bastards with greasy, scraggly beards who populated street corners with bottles of cheap booze in brown bags and grimy ball caps proclaiming them veterans. I thought about all the oblivious people that walked right by them every day without ever bothering to look down. I thought about how most of those people didn't possess the faintest concept of what those veterans had been through and what they had given up for their country. A country that treated them like trash. I thought about how short of a distance it was to that place, and how quickly my seemingly solid life had fallen apart.

A choice between destitution and getting back on my feet was no choice at all. I picked up the phone.

"You got skills, bro," Rocco told me, the crappy phone connection buzzing in my ear. There was laughter in his voice, like he'd known all along that I'd be calling sooner or later.

"A badass like you, you can write your own ticket, man. I can put in a good word and have an interview set up for you by the end of the week. Can you get down to D.C. by then?"

I told him I could. He gave me an address. I did a quick count of the precious few bills left in my wallet, and determined that I could indeed afford the bus fare. I packed up a bag, left my key on the front desk, and never looked back.

There were missions in Beirut, Tehran, Bali, and Bogota. A couple of surveillance jobs in London and Munich, and finally a six-week stay in a hospital after a botched rescue operation outside of Baghdad. That had been a bad one, the closest I had ever come to punching out. Shrapnel from an RPG cut a gash in my abdomen big enough for me to see my own guts. I still have nightmares about it.

Rocco came to visit me at Bethesda. He was pissed that the CIA had sent me into that snake pit on nothing more that the shit intel their man on the inside had provided.

“That fucker was probably a double agent, you realize that, right?” He bounced his leg rapidly as he spoke, his pupils narrow as pinpoints from the cocaine he’d just snorted in the bathroom. I remember looking at that big Italian nose and wondering how long it would be before his mucous membranes wore thin and he started getting chronic nosebleeds.

“You got to stop working for those goddamn spooks, man,” he went on. “You should let me put in a good word for you at this new outfit I signed up with a few months ago. They’re down in Atlanta, call themselves Aegis. You’d love it man. No more of that go-where-we-tell-you-to-and-don’t-ask-questions bullshit. With these guys, you get to pick your missions, they pay you up front, and if shit goes tits-up, you can always bail and give them their money back. It’s a fucking sweet deal man.”

After talking my ear off for another half-hour, he finally got up and left a card on the table beside my bed. I stared at it, and ignored the bad news on the television until it was time for my next dose of morphine.

A month later, I was healthy again, and a week after that I was on the payroll. Like most of the colossal fuck-ups I’ve made in my life, it seemed like the right thing to do at the time. My phone hadn’t rang in a while, and I had a nagging suspicion after what happened in Baghdad that it wasn’t going to. I had some cash saved up, but it wouldn’t last forever, and it’s not like there was a lot of demand in the private sector for professional murderers. Like a fool, I took the easy way out. And like a fool, I lived to regret it.

Not that it mattered anymore. The CIA, the NSA, Aegis, and maybe even Rocco were all gone, swept aside under the tide of undead that now dominated the world.

And here I was again, sitting out in the cold trying to drink the memories away. I looked up the hill toward Doc Laroux’s place. Eric was no doubt at home enjoying a quiet domestic evening with his new girlfriend. I was happy for him, but I also had to admit to being a bit jealous. They had a good thing going, those two. My love life, meanwhile, had taken a bit of a strange turn.

Whiskey number four had just gone down the hatch when I heard tires humming on pavement. I looked up and saw a bicycle slowing down to turn into my overgrown driveway. The figure riding it was too dark to make out in the gloom, but if I had to guess, I would say it was a woman. I set my empty tumbler on the table beside me and stepped down off the front porch.

The figure came to a halt just a few feet away from me. I took a few steps forward to see who it was.

"Hello, Gabriel. I hope I haven't come at a bad time."

I was about to say something exactly to that effect when she shook out her hair and hit me with that scalding smile of hers. The words died on my lips.

"Mind if I come in?" She brushed past me and ran a lingering hand over my arm. The graceful sway of her hips beckoned as she stepped through the front door.

"Liz, I have to be at the camp early tomorrow morning," I said, stepping in after her. "It's already late. I don't know if this is the best time."

She placed her helmet on the coffee table and sauntered across the room, that smile pinning me in place the whole way. She pressed herself against me, her hands sliding up my chest. Slender fingers curled around the back of my neck.

"You say that every time I come to see you, yet somehow you always manage to perform your duties the next day. It's a testament to your endurance."

Her voice was low and husky, her pupils wide as the moon. Those full lips were so close to mine, right there for the taking. I wanted them against my skin so bad I could taste it.

Elizabeth nibbled at my lower lip, and the last vestiges of my resolve crumbled. A whimper escaped her throat as I bruised her lips with a ferocious kiss, lifting her up and pressing her against me. Nails dug into the back of my neck and legs wrapped around me as I carried her toward the bedroom. My lips traced down to her tender, graceful neck and I sank my teeth in, biting hard. She moaned and clutched at me.

"Oh my God..."

I reached the bedroom and released her neck. She tried to kiss me again, but I threw her roughly onto the bed.

"Turn around." I growled. She complied, rolling over on her stomach and crossing her arms behind her back.

I ripped off my belt and kicked the bedroom door shut behind me.

*****

As always, when I woke up the next morning, she was gone. I rolled over onto my back and felt the sting of the bloody marks she'd cut into me with her long, sharp nails. It was always like this, both of us tender and bruised the next day. Elizabeth did a good job of covering it up, but rumors were beginning to fly nonetheless. No one had made the connection between me and the mayor's mystery lover yet, but it was only a matter of time. When I thought about it, I decided that it wasn't worth worrying about. It was her problem, not mine. Small-town gossip could kiss my ass. I had work to do.

It was still dark outside, and cold, when I set out for the camp. It was early, even by my standards. Training wasn't scheduled to begin for another hour, but I had nothing better to do.

The walk to the north gate helped me clear my head. On the way, it occurred to me that I had forgotten to ask Elizabeth about Eric, and her insane plan to use him as a spy to infiltrate the Legion. Maybe it was the whiskey, or maybe it was just my own mindless libido, but the subject had slipped my mind completely. I would have to remedy that, and soon.

The guards greeted me when I reached the gate. I had been leaving at about the same time every morning for weeks, and I had gotten to know most of the guys who worked the graveyard shift. Mike Stall, a guy who lives down the street from me and occasionally kicks my ass at poker, came down from his guard tower with a steaming cup of coffee in each hand. He was wearing his usual cowboy hat and snakeskin boots, with a big-bore revolver slung low on one hip. In the crook of his elbow, he carried a .357 Henry repeater that he'd won from Eric in a card game. Between that and the thick mustache, the tall, lean man looked like something out of a Zane Grey western.

"The hell you doin' here at this ungodly hour, Gabe?" he called out. "Your alarm clock broke?"

"I get here early every day."

"Yeah, but this is early even for you."

He stopped next to me at the guard shack and handed me a coffee. I sniffed at it. "This the instant stuff?"

"There any other kind these days?" He took a sip and grimaced. "Christ, this shit tastes like hot vinegar. I'd give a kidney for a cup of good old Folgers."

I blew steam from the top of mine to cool it down. "It ain't Starbucks, but it gets the job done. It's better than nothing."

Mike leaned against the wall while I signed out on the register and inclined his head in the direction of the camp. "You got something special planned this morning?

"Not really. Just figured I'd play a little cowboys and Indians. See if I can count coup against the perimeter guards."

He chuckled. "You still giving those kids live ammo for them toy rifles they got?"

Mike was old school. If a gun wasn't made of hardwood and steel, as far as he was concerned, it wasn't fit for use.

"They need something to protect themselves out there," I said. "Last I checked, the walkers aren't deterred by harsh language."

Mike nodded, slowly. "Yeah, I guess so. Well, you be careful, amigo. Don't spook them greenhorns too much. The last thing we need is to lose a good man to friendly fire." He clapped me on the shoulder and turned to walk back to the tower.

"We still on for poker next week?"

He stopped and looked over his shoulder. "Yep, same time as usual. Got a fresh batch of hooch out in the still just beggin' for somebody to drink it. Should be a good time. Oh, and invite your friend Eric again. Tell him I need some ammo for my new rifle." He bounced the Henry on his shoulder twice and grinned.

I laughed and pointed. "You know, it damn near broke his heart when you won that hand. I don't think he's forgiven you for it yet."

Mike started walking again. "He'll get over it. He can always try winning it back."

I chuckled, shook my head, and waved at the other guards. "See you fellas tomorrow morning."

A chorus of 'later Gabe' and 'we'll see ya' followed me out to the gravel path that led to the camp. The door shut behind me, and I heard the heavy thump of the steel reinforcement bar sliding home. A short time later, I reached the tree line and stepped off the path, melting into the woods.

*****

Due to being located outside the wall, the camp was under constant threat from Legion raiders and wandering infected. The town's security patrols did a good job of keeping threats to the camp mostly at bay, but every once in a while something managed to slip through. Usually the infected.

Fearless and fearsome, the creatures felt no pain and were undeterrable once they had detected prey. Always wandering in groups, they infested the countryside searching for food. Being as remote as it was, Hollow Rock didn't usually see the kinds of massive hordes that plagued other parts of the country, but we still had to deal with our share. As a result, the carbines that the recruits carried on watch were loaded with live ammunition, adding an element of danger to sneaking around camp in the middle of the night. Any recruit with an overactive imagination and an itchy trigger finger stood the potential to ruin my day. If it meant keeping my recruits safe, however, it was a risk that I was willing to take. Especially considering what happened to a guy named Joseph Harrigan a couple of weeks ago.

Harrigan was a regular on the sheriff's security detail. Everyone who knew him said he was a decent, responsible man. Which made it all the more inexplicable when one day he came back through the gate with a carefully hidden bite wound on his side. Rather than report it, he went home and acted as though nothing had happened.

The deputy in charge of the watch had reported hearing gunshots from where Harrigan was patrolling but dismissed it as nothing out of the ordinary; the guards put down at least a dozen infected every day. Most of the time they used axes or bludgeons to save ammo, but the sheriff had always admonished them never to hesitate to use their firearms if the situation required it. No one had any reason to question him when he reported back for shift change and said it was no big deal, just a couple of walkers that got too close for comfort.

He was hiding in his basement when he finally turned. He often stayed down there late at night working on small carpentry projects, so his family didn't think anything of it.

They went to bed at sundown just like they always did, not knowing they were sharing a house with a ticking time bomb.

How a man could so idiotically endanger the lives of his family, I'll never understand. Did he think he was somehow immune? That if he ignored the bite long enough it would go away? Stupid. Just plain stupid.

One of his neighbors heard the screaming and rushed over with a shotgun, but by the time he got there, it was too late. Harrigan had already slaughtered his wife and his twin girls. The neighbor did what needed to be done.

Three days later, after a little ceremony at which the mayor gave him a plaque to commemorate his quick thinking and bravery, the neighbor went into his bedroom, sat down on his bed, propped his shotgun under his chin, and painted the ceiling with his brain.

His name was Michael Crenshaw. He was twenty-six.

In the aftermath of the tragedy, Sheriff Elliott began requiring that all personnel returning from security patrol had to undergo a strip search before they returned to town. He pressed a couple of nurses and other townspeople with medical experience into service on a rotating basis to carry out the searches. It was not a popular rule, but the mayor backed it, and even the dumbest people in town could understand the necessity.

It was incidents like these that compelled me to punish breaches in security as harshly as I did. All it takes is one lapse, one person not doing their duty, one failure to follow protocol, and good people end up dead. One way or another, my recruits were going to learn to take that concept seriously.

I pushed the door to the barracks open slowly. It slid quietly on well-oiled hinges, not making a sound. The sentries outside hadn't spotted me yet, even though I had passed within a few yards of them. I got through the door and turned around, easing it closed.

"Don't move."

I froze. The voice was low, barely above a whisper, behind me and to my left.

"Keep your hands where I can see them. Move backward toward the sound of my voice."

I hesitated. Not because I was afraid, but because that was what a real intruder would have done.

The voice hissed, thickly accented, "There is a rifle pointed at your fucking head *cabrón*. You run, and you die. Now back up toward my voice, slowly. Do it now. I won't tell you again."

I could almost feel the laser sight bouncing around on the back of my head. I did as the sentry ordered, moving slowly backward with my hands up.

"Down on your knees, hands on top of your head."

Just as the sentry said that, the door opened and one of the perimeter guards leveled his M-4 at my face, blinding me with a tactical light. I smiled.

"Drill Instructor Garrett. Password is white balloon," I said.

The bright LEDs lowered, leaving me sightless in the dark room. My night vision was shot to hell.

"Sorry about that, sir," the recruit at the door said.

I waved off the apology. "Don't be sorry for doing your job, recruit."

The kid straightened a bit and looked almost proud of himself. A red-lens flashlight clicked on behind me, bathing the entrance in dark crimson. I turned around to see who had gotten the drop on me.

"Well I'll be damned, Sanchez. You're growing less useless by the day."

Sanchez grinned. "Thank you, sir."

I reached out for his flashlight. He handed it to me and I shined it on the other sentry. "Don't you have somewhere to be, recruit?"

"Yes, sir. On my way, sir." He closed the door. The sound of booted feet running over grass pounded away from the barracks as he sprinted back to his post.

I swung the flashlight over to Sanchez. "You're the watch commander tonight, correct?"

He nodded. "Yes, sir."

"Come with me." I turned and walked into the small office near the entrance set aside for instructors. It was small, consisting of a metal desk, file cabinet, a few chairs, and a cot barely large enough to sleep on. I motioned toward a chair.

"Shut the door and have a seat, recruit." He did as I told him.

Most of the time, when I pulled someone into my office, they were pants-shitting nervous. No one ever got invited there so that I could sing their praises. If someone was seated in front of my desk, it was because they had fucked up, and I was about to explain to them why they were stupid. That usually got people sweating. But in Sanchez's case he was calm, his expression unworried.

Whatever he had been through during the Outbreak, it made life here in the camp seem like a walk in the park by comparison. I had files on each of my recruits, having interviewed them all before training to assess their skills—military or otherwise—and his story was a tough one.

An up-and-comer on the professional boxing circuit, he was living and training in Nashville when the Outbreak hit. He had fled westward when Nashville was overrun and, according to Sheriff Elliott, he had shown up at the north gate with a couple of cans of food, a crowbar, and an old .38 revolver. His gun only had three bullets in it, and he was barefoot, his shoes having fallen apart on the long hike.

Most of the people fleeing Nashville had headed south to Jackson, which was also overrun a short time later. When asked why he'd chosen to go west instead of going along with the evacuation, he'd simply shrugged.

"The Army couldn't handle the *muertos* in Nashville, and they'd had more soldiers then," he had said. "Jackson wasn't going to be any different. I figured I would be better off on my own, maybe all those people going south would draw the hordes away."

I had nodded, agreeing with his simple pragmatism. His willingness to strike out on his own alluded to a toughness and independence that makes for good soldiers—something I knew a thing or two about. I decided right then that I wanted him in my militia and had been watching him closely since. He was one of the few recruits who never slowed down, never showed fatigue, and never complained, even during the most grueling parts of training. Whatever else anyone might say about him, the kid was tough.

"So explain to me what your strategy was," I said, leaning back in my chair. "You obviously gave some kind of signal to the perimeter guards to hold off and wait, and then close in when you caught me. How did you do it?"

He shook his head, not quite managing to keep a smirk off his face. "Actually, sir, it was the other way around. They saw you coming and signaled to me."

I raised an eyebrow. "Clever. And reassuring, I thought I'd gotten by them unseen. How did you pass the signals?"

He picked up his carbine and tapped the laser sights, flicking them on and off a few times. I watched the little green light appear and disappear on the ceiling.

"I told all the sentries to keep an eye on the door," he said. "If they saw you, they were supposed to light up the window over the front door three times and wait for you to close it before approaching."

I nodded. "Mmm hmm. So the sentries were watching the door. Who was keeping an eye on the perimeter?"

"They were doing that, too, sir," he said, defensively. "They took turns. One of them watched the door while the others covered his lane."

"And how long was it between when you saw the signal through the window, and when I came through the door?"

He shrugged. "I don't know. A few seconds."

Busted. I had hidden in the shadows, slowly creeping up on the door for at least ten minutes. If they had spotted me approaching, they would have given the signal long before I reached the entrance. I leaned forward in my chair and rested my arms on the table.

"Well, Sanchez, I'll give you credit for this much. You caught me. I can't deny that. But I do have a few issues with how you set this up."

I held up a finger. "One: you knew I was coming. It's easy to set up an ambush for someone you know is going to show up. You even knew which ingress point I'd be using, so what you did tonight wasn't anything special."

I held up another finger. "Two: I still managed to sneak by the guards. I thought maybe they caught me for a second there, but from what you're saying, they only saw me when I went through the door. And even that was probably a lucky break."

Sanchez narrowed his eyes, his cockiness beginning to wane. "And most importantly," I pressed on, leaning further across the desk, "there was only one of me. What if there had been more, waiting from a distance? Your sentry would be dead right now."

The kid shifted his gaze down to the floor. If he was half as smart as I gave him credit for, he was seeing the holes in his scheme. I went through this song and dance every night with whomever Grabovsky—one of my drill instructors—had put in charge of the watch. The watch commander was free to set up the perimeter and barracks security any way he or she wanted. Later on in training, I would be teaching them more effective tactics, but for phase one, I wanted to see what they could come up with on their own.

"Tell me what you're thinking, recruit."

He was silent for a long moment. "The problem is, you got too close before we spotted you. You didn't need to get inside to do damage. You could have set the place on fire, blocked the door, maybe planted a bomb or something."

"Anything else?"

He looked up, his black eyes angry. "If you're sneaky enough to get by the sentries, then you're probably sneaky enough to take one or two of them out without alerting the others."

"Bingo," I said, pointing a finger at him. I stood up from my chair and walked around to sit closer to him on the edge of the desk.

"There are two lessons I you want to take away from this tonight," I said. "The first is that there is a world of difference between setting up an ambush and establishing a secure perimeter. The former is a fuck-ton easier than the latter. A good perimeter requires layers, alert sentries, and proper planning. All you need for an ambush is the other guy's location, a place to hide, and the means to kill him."

Sanchez nodded slightly. I continued, "The second lesson here is that while you can never plan for every single thing that could possibly go wrong in any scenario, if you focus too much on one single threat you will ignore all the others. That's a good way to end up dead. Understood?"

"Yes, sir."

"Good." I gave him a light pat on the shoulder. "Don't worry, this is the last time you'll have to play watch commander. Starting next week, we move into phase two, and you'll learn how to do this shit the right way. No more pulling ideas out of your ass."

I went back around the desk and sat down again, waving a hand at the door. "You're dismissed, Sanchez. Get back on watch."

"Yes, sir."

He stood up to go. I waited for him to lay a hand on the doorknob before speaking again.

"One last thing."

He turned halfway around. "Sir?"

"Except for a chosen few, upon graduation, everyone in this militia will start out at the rank of private. When training is over with, me and the rest of the staff will choose a few people to be NCOs."

I let that hang for a moment. Sanchez watched me silently, his eyes intent. "Everyone in this militia will fight," I went on, "but a few of them will be charged with bearing the burden of leadership. We'll be looking for people who are willing to step up. People who aren't afraid to take on responsibility. Anyone who wants to get noticed should probably start thinking about ways he can help his fellow recruits succeed. Start doing things to build trust and confidence."

I fixed him with a level stare.

He said, "I'll keep that in mind, sir."

"Good. Now get your ass back on watch."

"Yes, sir. Thank you, sir."

He left, closing the door quietly behind him.

Chapter 5

Escalation

I woke up long before my wind-up Donald Duck alarm clock was set to start ringing, so just before dawn I reached over and turned it off. No sense in waking Allison up unnecessarily. She was lying on her side, facing away from me, wrapped in her blanket and snoring softly. I placed a gentle hand on her shoulder and kissed the side of her neck. She stirred in her sleep, lips curling into a faint smile.

I took my clothes into the living room to get dressed. It was still dark, and I had to light a couple of candles to see where I was going. After I had armored myself against the cold and tied on my sturdy hiking boots, I crunched across the frost in the back yard to my newly constructed outhouse.

My current toilet situation, located a prudent distance away from the back door, was the result of water restrictions that Mayor Stone had implemented in recent weeks. Hollow Rock was fortunate enough to have running water—gravity-fed by a water tower on a nearby hill—but rainfall had been sparse during the summer, and as a result, water reserves were low. So low, in fact, that wasting it on things like showers and toilets was no longer an option. Hence the outhouse.

It was a good outhouse, as far as things like that go. Made out of pine studs, plywood, and asphalt shingles on the roof. Nearly as big as a tool shed, it even had vinyl siding, insulation, and wood paneling on the inside. The seat was low enough to accommodate Allison's shorter legs, and it boasted a cushioned lid that I had scavenged from an abandoned home improvement store a few miles outside of town. Tom had helped me build it—as well as two others for him and Gabe—and for a place to do one's business, it was aces high. There was even a window I could open if things got a little too emotional.

Sitting there in the quiet, my dwindling supply of toilet tissue as my only company, my thoughts began to wander toward the recently signed treaty with Central Command, and how it was going to affect the fight against the Legion. The signatures hadn't even dried yet, and already we had Chinooks riding into town dropping off supplies, Navy SEALs, and one grizzled old Army veteran with a star on his collar. I had no doubt that the raiders skulking around in the woods had seen the chopper coming this way and had reported it back to whatever passed for leadership among them. If we were lucky, maybe those leaders would decide that Hollow Rock was too tough of a target and look for greener pastures elsewhere. But even that thought made me clench my fists in anger, someone else suffering in our place. The scars on my ribcage were all the reminder I needed of just how ruthless those marauding scum could be.

No, I decided. I hoped they took the Army's presence here as a challenge, and I hoped they did something stupid, like try to attack. If they did, we would be ready for them.

I finished my business and tried to banish the dark thoughts dwelling in my head. The last thing I needed was to be distracted while teaching the morning class … and then it occurred to me that it was Sunday. There wasn't going to be a morning class. Sunday was visitors' day, when the recruits' friends and family could come to the camp to see their loved ones and hear about their training. And considering that General Jacobs and the men who flew in with him would be at the camp to meet with Gabriel and the new militia, things were shaping up to be especially interesting.

Before I left for the day, I started a fire in the stove for Allison, put some chicken jerky and cold flatbread in a cast iron skillet to warm up, and refilled the big metal mixing bowl in the kitchen that we used as a washbasin. Little things like that were important her, and she had no qualms about showing me how much she appreciated it when I remembered them.

My rifle hung from its customary spot next to the door, along with my pistol and web gear; cleaned, oiled, and ready to go. I rarely went anywhere without them, even if only for a few minutes. The world had become a deadly place, and it was never a good idea to leave home unarmed, no matter how safe things might seem. I geared up, checked my weapons, and stepped out the front door.

My breath fogged in the chill morning air, and the sun was just beginning to crest over the eastern sky, bathing the gently rolling hills in amber and gold. Birds took wing in the distance, calling to one another through the dissipating haze. Closing my eyes, I turned my face to the sky and breathed in it, letting the warm sunrise wash over me. In that place, standing under the light of another day, for just a brief moment in time, I was a man at peace.

I like to imagine that the lines on my face smoothed, the creases in my brow relaxed, and I looked more like the man I had been before the Outbreak—young, confident, and carefree. Before I had watched the end of the world, and before the first time I had done murder. When I was a man who had known sorrow but was ignorant to the true meaning of hardship. A man who had never known the biting cold of a hungry winter or the aching desperation of love in a world gone mad.

If I had known how the rest of the morning was going to go, I would have stood there for a good while longer.

*****

Gabe wasn't alone on the Grinder when I emerged from the gravel path leading to the camp. Groggy recruits were unloading two wagons full of supplies under the watchful eye of Sergeant Raymond Grabovsky—one of the two soldiers under Steve's command who had traveled with him from North Carolina. The squat Green Beret walked in precise circles around hives of activity, constantly tapping his 'teaching aid', a slender length of cane, against the outside of his boot.

Although I stood nearly five inches taller than he did, he probably outweighed me by a good twenty pounds, and none of it on his waist. Nearly as wide through the shoulders as he was tall, Grabovsky was a dense, bulky, fireplug of a man.

"Took you long enough," Gabe said as I pulled the brakes on my bicycle and stopped next to him, standing on one leg.

"Hey, it's my day off. You should be kissing my ass for showing up at all. Where's Marc and Curtis?"

Marcus Cohen and Curtis Wilkins were the other two drill instructors. Marc was an ex-Marine and current sheriff's deputy, and Curtis was the second Green Beret under Steve's command.

"They're with the general's men at the old pawn shop doing inventory," Gabe said. "Got another supply drop coming in today at around noon."

"They send us any uniforms yet?"

He shook his head. "Not yet. Hopefully they'll come with today's drop. We did get some rifles, though, and a couple of crates of ammo."

"M-16s?"

"No, M-4s. Also a few grenade launchers, claymores, and a couple of M-240s."

"Good. Now you just have to teach these kids how to use that stuff without blowing themselves up."

Ahead of us, a recruit dropped a box of food he was carrying, and Grabovsky cracked him on the back of the leg with his cane. "Watch what you're doing, knucklehead. Those supplies are worth more than your life."

The offending recruit rubbed the back of his leg and glared at Grabovsky before picking up his box and carrying it to the mess hall.

“Do you think it’s a good idea, letting him do that?” I said, keeping my voice low. “Sooner or later, he’s going to hit the wrong person and things are gonna get ugly.”

“He knows what he’s doing,” Gabe replied. “That stick saves time and effort getting the point across. How many times have you seen someone make the same mistake twice around Grabovsky? And anyway, I’d put money on him against any one of these kids. He’d break ’em in half.”

He had a point. The Army veteran’s methods may have been harsh, but I couldn’t argue with the results. And if any of these recruits had delusions of grandeur and tried to step up to the G-man, well … it would be over quickly, at least.

I stepped off my bike and pushed it over to the instructor’s barracks. I didn’t bother locking it up; no recruit would be stupid enough to risk stealing it. Gabe would rain death and fire on their heads if they tried. The smell of hot butter and frying eggs wafted from the mess hall, making my stomach rumble in response. Breakfast would have to wait, however. I wanted to see what kinds of goodies Uncle Sam had brought us.

On the way to the supply building, the distant *thup-thup-thup-thup* of the Chinook carried to me faintly over the treetops. I stopped and looked westward, catching a speck of movement against the far horizon. Gabe walked over and stood next to me, looking in the same direction.

“Never thought I’d be happy to hear that sound again,” he said.

“Makes you want to reenlist, doesn’t it?”

He glanced at me and snorted. “Yeah, it’s on my to-do list. Right under gouging my own eyes out and cutting my balls off with a rusty nail.”

The helicopter became larger as it grew closer, a bulging cargo net swaying slowly beneath it.

"Come on man, it wasn't that bad, was it?"

"You remember that fight with the Legion a couple of months back, right?"

I grimaced, absently touching the scars on my side. "How could I forget?"

"Imagine doing shit like that day in, and day out, for fifteen months at a time, with only seven months of downtime between deployments. Then repeat it five times. Do that, and you'll have the beginning of an idea of what it was like over there."

I turned to look at him. "Jesus, five deployments?"

He nodded, his mouth set in a firm line.

"No wonder you're such a grumpy bastard. If I had to go that long without getting laid, that many times, I'd probably be an asshole, too."

He didn't quite manage to keep the grin off his face when he punched me in the arm. Hard.

"Hey, not in front of the kids," I said, pointing a thumb at the recruits behind us. "Nobody wants to see mom and dad fighting."

Gabe was still grinning when he opened his mouth to say something, but a low chattering sound in the distance brought him up short.

"The hell was that?" I asked.

Gabe had gone still, staring toward the chopper. "That's a fucking fifty-cal."

Just as he said it, the Chinook began to lose altitude and for a brief, heart-pounding moment, I thought it was going to crash into the forest and I would have to stand there watching, helpless to do anything about it. At the last second, the cargo net detached and dropped down into the trees, freeing up engine power for the massive helicopter to gain altitude and take evasive action.

"Grabovsky!" Gabe turned and yelled. "The chopper's under attack!"

The other soldier was already moving and barking out orders. "Squad leaders, round up your squads. Do it now! Sanchez, Flannigan, Vincenzo, get to the armory and start issuing weapons. Marone, Helms, Jeffreys, we need trauma kits and stretchers. Robinson, you're my runner. Get your skinny ass into town, find Doc Laroux, and tell her to get ready for wounded. MOVE IT!"

I yelled out that Allison was at home. Robinson took off as fast as his long legs could carry him. The other recruits erupted into a flurry of action. I slipped my rifle around to the front and gripped it, watching the Chinook climb higher and turn back in our direction.

"What now?" I asked, looking to Gabe.

He was still watching the chopper, fists clenched at his sides. "We need to secure that cargo before the Legion gets it. Tell Grabovsky to get these recruits ready to move out platoon strength, then grab two people and meet me at the west trail."

With that, he turned on his heel and sprinted for the instructor's barracks. I assumed he was going for his weapons, pried my hands loose from my rifle, slid it around to my back, and ran toward the armory.

"Grabovsky," I called out on the way. "We're gonna go find those supplies. Gabe wants you to get the recruits ready to move out and meet us out there."

He gave me a thumbs-up. "Will do. Watch your ass out there, Riordan, the place is probably crawling with Legion. I'll be there as soon as I can." He turned and began shouting orders at the recruits with renewed vigor, speeding them along with his cane.

When I reached the armory, I grabbed the two closest recruits and shoved them at the door. "You two hand out rifles. Sanchez, Flannigan, you're with me, let's go."

They both grabbed a carbine, a bandolier of ammo, and followed me as I ran toward the western edge of the field. Gabe caught up with us on the way. He had two long, green cylinders slung over his back, and he was carrying his big SCAR 17 battle rifle.

"Are those rockets?" I asked, pointing over his shoulder.

"Yep. I don't know where they got that fifty, but I want to make sure we have the firepower to take it out. Grabovsky can fucking bill me."

Flannigan spoke up from behind me, "Hey, you wanna tell us where we're going?"

"Hold up, Eric," Gabe said, slowing to a halt. I stopped.

"Listen, playtime is over." He turned to face the two recruits. "This is the real deal. That cargo you saw drop? That's shit we need, and we can't let the Legion get their hands on it. We have no idea how many of them there are, and the fuckers have a fifty-caliber machine gun. We have to get there, take out that fifty, set up a perimeter, and hold out until backup arrives. You two come with us, you might not come home. If you want to back out of this fight, now would be a good time to do it."

"Fuck that," Flannigan said. "This is what I joined up for."

Gabe's mouth flattened into a tight smile. "What about you Sanchez. You ready for this?"

The Mexican shrugged. "Probably not, but you gotta die of something, right?"

"Great. Awesome," I said. "Can we get a move on now?"

"Quick check." Gabe tapped his rifle. "Safeties off, round in the chamber. You two, secure those bandoliers around your waist, you want that ammo quick at hand."

We all checked out gear, and I was glad Gabe had said something. In all the excitement, I had forgotten to chamber a round.

"Everybody good?"

We were.

"All right, I'll take point. The rest of you fan out, five-yard intervals. You two watch our flanks. Eric, you keep an eye on our six. Stay low, stay quiet, keep your heads on a swivel, and when the shooting starts, stay in your lane. Let's move."

Gabe turned and jogged down the trail. The rest of us followed.

*****

One of the many lessons Gabe taught me about warfare is that going after an enemy head on, when said enemy knows what direction you're coming from, is never a good idea. Success in combat comes down to three things: sufficient firepower, knowledge of an enemy's location, and most importantly, the element of surprise. Contrary to popular belief, modern warfare, rather than being an outrageously bloody slugfest, is more of a prolonged series of sneak attacks, traps, and ambushes. In this arena, if a man wants to live to a ripe old age, then he had better damned well make sure that when the shooting starts, he is the ambusher, and not the ambushee.

It was with this lesson in mind that I found myself growing increasingly nervous as we drew closer to the area where the Chinook's cargo had taken a swan dive. We had not encountered any opposition, and had seen no sign of the Legion having been there, despite the fact that we were about to cross into their territory. The forest was quiet.

The ground under my feet had been sloping steadily upward for nearly half a mile, and I knew we had to be getting close to a ridgeline. Sure enough, up ahead Gabe held up a fist. He flattened his hand, lowered it slowly toward the ground, and then moved it forward. Turning around, he pointed two fingers at his eyes. In plain English, this meant stop, get down, belly crawl to my position, enemy sighted.

I was the first to reach Gabe, crawling next to him to see what he was looking at. The hill beneath me sloped abruptly downward, sparsely dotted with trees, and terminated at a steep berm above a section of crumbling two-lane blacktop. Ahead of us, we saw six men milling about, and more than a dozen heavy-duty plastic crates scattered across the empty highway. On the side of the road, an old Browning heavy machine gun lay next to a wheelbarrow, along with a tripod and two boxes of ammunition. Gabe and I exchanged a glance, then backed off down the hill to wait for Sanchez and Flannigan.

"Here's the plan," Gabe whispered when they arrived. "I'm going to stay here on the ridgeline. Flannigan, you go back down the hill about twenty yards and keep an eye on our flanks. Remember, check both sides, check our six, then do it again. Keep at it until I call for you. Clear?"

"Crystal." She nodded.

"Sanchez, you work your way nice and quiet about twenty-five paces that way from my position." He pointed to a spot on the ridgeline. "Stay low, and for God's sake, don't skyline yourself. Eric, you take the other side. I'm going to count to sixty, and then I'm going to fire a rocket at that machine gun. When it hits, you two use the distraction to start taking out those six raiders. If you can, wound a couple so we can take them prisoner. Any more show up, give them the same treatment. We have to hold this ridge until Grabovsky gets here with reinforcements. And don't forget, all this noise is going to draw the infected, so don't waste ammo. Make 'em count; we might have to shoot our way out of here. Everybody clear?"

We all gave an affirmative and moved into position.

I adjusted the magnification on my scope, attached a suppressor to the barrel, deployed the spring-loaded bipod from the foregrip, and settled down into a firing position. I was well hidden on a depression just beyond the edge of the ridgeline. From there, in just a few quick steps, I could move back down the embankment and out of sight in either direction. This would allow me to take cover and relocate if the raiders below tried to concentrate fire on me.

A strong breeze picked up from the north and whipped over the hills, carrying stinging swarms of autumn leaves across the low valley. The trees around me made a good windbreak, but the raiders down the hill had nothing to shield them from the blinding debris. As the wind picked up, they had to shout to hear one another. From the snippets of conversation I could make out, it sounded like they were excited.

"Fuck me, look at all this shit," one of them yelled. "We're gonna be drowning in pussy for a month."

I gritted my teeth at the implications of that, and took a deep breath to steady my aim.

Seconds that felt like hours ticked by while the raiders worked on a few crates, trying to pry them open. I forced myself to stay calm, slowed my breathing, and sighted in on one of the men below. He was tall, with broad shoulders, a bushy beard, and long hair. Kind of like Gabe before he shaved and got a haircut. Gauging the distance at about a hundred yards, I made another sight adjustment and waited.

Come on Gabe, any time now.

Just as I was beginning to wonder if Gabe had lost count and started over, the concussive blast of the rocket launcher shattered the air. The warhead, powerful enough to destroy a fully armored tank, slammed into the road in the blink of an eye, swallowing the fifty-caliber and the wheelbarrow in a cloud of white smoke. The force of the explosion thumped upward through the ground and into my chest, leaving me with an odd, hollow feeling in my gut. Concussion and shrapnel ripped into the raiders nearby, shredding one of them like a side of beef and knocking two others to the ground. One writhed in agony, bloody and screaming, while the other laid still, white bone protruding from a jagged hole in his thigh. Rocks and metal rained down around where the rocket had hit, and only a crater remained where the machine gun had been just a few seconds ago.

For a moment, all I could do was stare. I had seen rockets detonate before on television, but never like this—up close and personal. Looking down at that instant, rocket-propelled destruction, a fervent hope took root inside of me that I would never find myself on the receiving end of such a terrible thing.

The raider farthest from the explosion recovered first, snatched up his rifle, and started spraying bullets at the leftover smoke cloud where Gabe had fired. Knowing my friend, he had probably already dropped the canister and was moving to another position, but I wasn't about to gamble on that. I leaned down over my rifle, took aim, and triggered a three-round burst. All three bullets hit center of mass, dropping the raider to the ground. He let go of his rifle, clutching at his chest—wounded, but still alive. I hit him again, and finally, he went still.

The last two, shellshocked and terrified, turned and bolted for the other side of the road. I tried to take aim at one of them but couldn't get a good shot. A single muted *crack*, the familiar report of Gabriel's SCAR, sounded from my left. The shot took one of the would-be escapees high on the back, punched a hole straight through him, and erupted from his chest in an arterial spray. He pitched forward, screaming and trying to crawl toward the trees. Another crack sounded, and the top half of his head disintegrated in a red mist.

Powerful stuff, those .308 rounds.

The other one had already made it to cover, running in a serpentine pattern through the foliage. Sanchez's M-4 cracked a few times sending splinters flying around him, but nothing hit. The stands of trees were too thick, and soon, he disappeared over the edge of a hill, out of sight.

I cursed, got up on one knee, and began sweeping the far embankment for movement. It didn't look like we had any other company, so I fell back and made my way over to where I had last seen Gabriel. One of the rocket launchers lay on the ground among the leaves, smoke curling from the open ends, but no sign of him. I made a low whistle, hoping his ears weren't ringing so badly that he couldn't hear me. A few seconds went by. Nothing. I whistled again, louder. This time, I heard him whistle back, ahead of me and off to my left, closer to Sanchez's position.

Now that I knew where he was, I worked my way back down the hill toward Flannigan, approaching slowly and with caution, not wanting to spook her into doing something I would regret. As I got closer, I heard her voice hiss out through the trees.

"Bluebird."

It was one of the standard challenges that Grabovsky had drilled into them, a way to identify friend from foe.

"Actual." I hissed back, surprised at how quickly I remembered it. I suppose the G-man had done a good job teaching me as well.

Flannigan stood up from behind a thick maple trunk and came over to kneel beside me. "What happened back there?"

"Gabe took out the fifty, and five guys down the hill are having a very bad day."

"I thought there were six."

"There were. One got away."

She nodded, turning her head to scan the forest, pale blue eyes flitting back and forth.

"I'm gonna head back up the hill," I said. "Stay hidden, and if you see anything, give a holler. I'll come running."

"Won't I give away my position if I do that?"

"Yes, but we don't have radios, so it's the best we can do. Don't be a hero. If trouble shows up, call for help. Understood?"

She nodded. "Yes, sir."

I gave her a pat on the shoulder and made my way back up to my firing position. The wind had died down, and the road had gone still and quiet, save for the weakening cries of the lone surviving raider. He lay in a widening pool of blood, and even from this far away, I could see that his skin was ghostly pale. So much for taking a prisoner.

After what felt like half an hour had gone by, I looked at my watch and saw that it had only been five minutes. The raider down the hill had gone still, and when I looked at him through my scope, it didn't look like his chest was moving. Too bad for him. He should have thought twice before trying to steal from the United States Army.

Looking at the crater left behind by the LAW rocket, my brain finally revved into gear, and I started puzzling out the pieces of the morning's events. The presence of a heavy machine gun, combined with the fact that the Legion had known where to set it up, all begged some very pressing and disturbing questions.

Where they had gotten the hardware from wasn't all that difficult to guess. During the Outbreak, when it had become clear that there was no saving the Eastern Seaboard, the president had ordered a massive evacuation across the Mississippi River. The Army had hung back, trying to hold off the undead long enough for millions of refugees to escape to what they thought was safety. It was a valiant effort, but ultimately, it had proven futile. The dead found their way across the Mississippi, and the apocalypse had continued unabated.

During the fighting, countless military units were overrun, and their comrades, helpless to do anything about it, had been forced to leave them behind. As a result, there was an untold wealth of military hardware out in the wastelands just waiting from someone to come along and pick it up.

Hollow Rock wasn't far from the Mississippi River.

The Legion could move freely for nearly a hundred square miles.

It didn't take a genius to connect the dots.

As for how they had known where to set up their ambush, there were a couple of different ways that could have played out. The most frightening possibility was that someone from Hollow Rock had known what direction the Chinook would be coming from and had somehow fed that information back to the Legion. If Hollow Rock had a spy in its midst, then our problems had just gotten a hell of a lot more complicated. Which was ironic, considering that we were preparing to do the exact same thing to them.

Another possibility was that the Legion had found more than one machine gun, and had set up several firing positions around town on likely paths of approach for the helicopter. It would not have been difficult to do, considering how many abandoned buildings there were scattered throughout this portion of Carroll County. If that was the case, then the Legion's threat level had just jumped up the scale from annoying to fucking terrifying.

As if that weren't bad enough, the fact that the Legion had actually managed score a few hits on the Chinook meant that they had at least one person with military experience in their ranks who could not only operate a heavy weapon, but do so skillfully. Unlike what was once portrayed in the movies, hitting an aircraft on the wing with a ground-based weapon, even one as powerful as the ma deuce, is extremely difficult to pull off. It would have taken an experienced, well-trained gunner to do it. That did not bode well.

My thoughts were interrupted when I heard faint footsteps crunching through leaves on their way to my position. Through the trees, I saw Gabe approaching, moving slowly and scanning the woods behind us for threats. He must have wanted me to notice him coming. Otherwise, I never would have heard a thing until he was right next to me.

Gabe's ability to disappear into thin air is as uncanny as it is unnerving. Occasionally, he amuses himself by sneaking up on me and appearing from nowhere at my side (which is annoying as hell), but he never does it when he knows that I'm holding a weapon. Which is wise, on his part.

"See anything? Any movement?" he asked when he reached me.

"No, nothing. But I have been thinking about that fifty-cal."

Gabe nodded grimly. "Yeah, that occurred to me, too. I got a feeling things just got a lot worse for us in this fight."

"You didn't happen to bring a radio, did you?" I asked.

"No. Didn't have any charged up. I loaned the solar panels to Sheriff Elliott last week. Didn't figure we'd need 'em."

I snorted. "Well ain't that just great. I trust you'll be getting those back, assuming we get out of this alive?"

Gabe smiled ruefully. "Yeah, at least enough of them to charge our radios, anyway."

I looked back down the valley. "So what's the plan now? You want to go on recon, or stay here and wait for backup?"

He thought about it for a moment, staring down the hill. "No, we should stay here. If it were just you and me, I'd say let's see what we can find, but with the other two …"

"Understood," I said. "You should probably have Flannigan move closer to our position. If she gets flanked, she'll be isolated, and one of us will have to break off to help her."

"Good idea. Keep your eyes peeled."

With that, he moved off lower down the hill toward Flannigan.

Alone again, I started doing a deliberate, systematic scan of the opposite ridgeline and both approaches on the highway—a technique Gabe had taught me to ward off boredom and stay alert. I was only at it for maybe another five minutes before I caught movement. I had been worried that the raider who escaped might be coming back with friends, and it looked like my concerns were justified. At first there were only three, then four more appeared, and another couple of dozen behind them.

"Shit," I muttered. "Shit, shit, shit. This is not good."

They were staying low and advancing in a leapfrog fashion, taking turns moving up and providing cover. One of them left himself exposed as he kneeled down behind a tree, so I took careful aim, let out a breath, and squeezed off a single shot. The match grade bullet punched a hole in his forehead, just above the eye, and blew a spray of blood out the back of his skull. He went limp and slumped to the ground.

I had no doubt that Gabe and the others had heard the crack from the shot, but the suppressor did its job, and it didn't seem to have reached the men across the hill. They kept advancing, oblivious to the fact that one of their number lay dead just behind them. Figuring this wouldn't last long, I shifted my aim and bagged another one at the rear of their formation. Still no response.

Come on, just one more ...

Another gunman kneeled behind a narrow pine trunk that was too thin to cover him. The angle was awkward and, when I fired, my aim was slightly low and the shot took him through the throat. He dropped his rifle and fell down kicking and screaming, blood spurting from the wound in his neck.

The reaction from his comrades was immediate; they all stopped, shouted to each other, took cover, and began laying down suppressing fire. Behind them, more figures emerged over the hill and began moving up.

Bullets peppered the berm below me and slammed into the trees over my head sending splinters and rocks flying in staccato bursts. Nothing was hitting close enough to hurt me, but it was still damned unnerving. Getting shot at is never fun, no matter how far away the shots are landing. I briefly considered backing off, but my firing position was a good one, and they clearly hadn't seen me yet. If they had, they would have been concentrating fire at my section of the ridge.

Gritting my teeth, I hunkered down, peered through my scope, and kept shooting. Sharp reports from my left let me know that Gabe and Sanchez were also returning fire. If Flannigan was smart, she would do what she was trained to do—stay low and continue to watch our flanks. It might not be as exciting as getting into the heat of a gunfight, but it was no less important. Being as high up as we were, if we got flanked, we would be royally screwed. It was her job to make sure that didn't happen.

Since the raiders obviously had an idea of where we were, stealth was no longer an issue, and there was no point in trying to make headshots. Another point in my favor was that the advancing enemy, as far away as they were, couldn't see the muzzle flash from my barrel, which allowed me to take my time and fire with impunity. I picked a target, put my scope reticle center of mass, squeezed the trigger, and sent a three-round burst downrange.

In less than a minute, I had reduced their number by four, Gabe had accounted for at least twice that number, and the rapidly mounting casualties forced them to retreat to the other side of the hill. The volume of enemy fire died down to just a few rifles, and instead of the near-panicked fusillade that they had thrown at us before, they settled down into a more disciplined suppression pattern.

It doesn't take much to keep an enemy's head down—usually just a few shots at a time—and someone had obviously taught these men that lesson. Their shots weren't terribly accurate, which told me they were probably not military veterans, at least not all of them. But the tactics they used were fairly advanced, which meant that someone had been training them.

So if I were in their position, what would I do? They knew we weren't going anywhere, at least not without that cargo. And even if we did, we only had one line of retreat. It I were in charge, I would have had a few men lay down suppressing fire, pulled the rest of them back, and then spread them out in both directions in a flanking maneuver with instructions not to attack until they had closed the circle, effectively trapping us. That way, they could eventually overwhelm us by sheer force of numbers and superior firepower.

The part of the road I could see was at the elbow of a sharp curve that wound around the bottom of a hill. The raiders would not have to go far to get out of sight in the thick forest on either side of the road, which would make it that much easier for them to surround us. Not good.

Time to change tactics.

I fired a few more shots, not really caring if I hit anything, and backed off down the hill. I was out of the enemy's direct line of fire but was still in danger of catching a ricochet from any of the dozens of bullets careening overhead. Keeping my head down, I made my way to Gabe's position as fast as possible, and found him lying prone at the base of a hickory tree. His rifle coughed out military grade projectiles in a slow, steady cadence, no doubt taking their pound of flesh from the Legion assholes across the road.

I dropped down to one knee and shouted up the hill, "Hey Gabe, how much you wanna bet they're trying to flank us right now?"

He fired again and paused for a moment, still peering through his scope. "That did occur to me. Flannigan's not far behind you, and Sancho's watching our flank about ten yards to your left. Standard diamond formation. How about you take up position on the right?"

"Will do," I said. "You got anything fun on you besides than that other LAW?"

He fired a few more shots before answering. "I thought you were scared of those things."

"Not when I'm outnumbered and about to be surrounded."

Gabe rolled over onto one side, canting his rifle as he did so, still firing. "Four pockets just above my hip. Take three, and give one to the others. Show 'em how to use the things first. Last thing we need is for those two to blow themselves up."

I crawled to him, took three grenades—frags by the look of them—and crawled to Sanchez first, then Flannigan. The two recruits got a quick crash course in how to use the little green death-balls, and then I took position behind cover on Gabe's right flank.

The shooting from across the way had died down a good bit, but I had a feeling it was only the calm before the storm. If my quick visual count had been correct, then we had somewhere in the neighborhood of twenty-five to thirty well-armed, pissed off Legion marauders about to make a concerted effort to loose us from our mortal coils.

In the brief moment of relative quiet, with nothing else to occupy my mind, I began to think dark, worrisome thoughts. I thought about the recruits coming to back us up, and how green most of them were when it came to combat. I thought about the Legion, and the fact they seemed to be fighting with near-military efficiency. I thought about Allison, and all the things I wanted to say to her if I made it out of this one alive. Most of all, I thought about Grabovsky, and wondered what the fuck was taking him so long. If reinforcements didn't show up soon, they would be rescuing a pile of dead bodies.

Clearing my mind, I took a deep breath, leveled my rifle, and in a rare acknowledgement of my Catholic upbringing, I prayed.

Chapter 6

Battle Damage

... Holy Mary, Mother of God,

pray for us sinners,

now and at the hour of our death.

Amen.

It was the fourth time I had repeated the prayer, and I sincerely hoped that someone up there was listening.

Bringing my scope up, I carefully scanned the trees again. No visual yet, but I could hear them, crunching through the carpet of dead leaves, their footsteps carrying up the hill as they closed in on our position. It wouldn't be long now.

I almost said the Hail Mary again but decided that it smacked a bit too much of begging. If bared teeth and blazing rifles were to mark the end of my life, then for my last prayer, I wanted something that spoke of defiance. After thinking for a moment, I settled on an old favorite.

The Lord is my shepherd; I shall not want.

He maketh me to lie down in green pastures:

He leadeth me beside the still waters.

I wondered if there really were green pastures and still waters in the afterlife. That sounded better than constant warfare, swarms of flesh-eating monsters, and old age in a world that spared no pity for the infirm.

He restoreth my soul:

He leadeth me in the paths of righteousness for His name's sake.

Leaving Allison behind would be the hardest part. I had only told her once that I loved her, and I wished that I had said it more often. It seemed silly now, holding back because I was worried she wouldn't feel the same.

Yea, though I walk through the valley of the shadow of death,

I will fear no evil: For thou art with me.

I could see them now, thickly clothed figures making their way through the close stands of trees and underbrush as they climbed the hill. Before I could recite any more of my prayer, gunshots rang out to my right, probably from Flannigan. A scream of pain echoed from down the embankment, and I grinned.

Attagirl. Give 'em hell.

The raiders over on the far ridgeline opened fire again, forcing us to keep our heads down while their comrades moved in and tightened the noose. Suppression fire made its way up toward us, but nothing accurate. Just people spraying and praying. I settled in behind cover with as little of my body exposed as possible, and waited for someone to come within range. The only advantage we had was that we held the high ground, and I intended utilize that strength for all it was worth.

A brown and green shadow moved from one tree to another, and I managed to fire a burst at it before it disappeared behind cover. Luck smiled on me, and the figure went down with an agonized yelp. I hit it with three more shots just to make sure, and then started looking for another target.

Several more gunmen began to resolve from the brush, leapfrogging with short bursts of fire as they worked their way up higher to my left. I caught one of them in the leg and then put two in his chest when he fell, forcing the others to stop advancing and take cover. To their right, more raiders emerged to back them up.

While they were busy yelling back and forth to one another, I stayed low and moved to another spot a short distance farther up the hill. It wasn't as good a spot as the one I was leaving, but I didn't want to stay in one place for too long. If they concentrated fire on my position, I was done for.

Being careful to stay low, I put my cheek to the stock, my eye an inch or so from the scope, and settled the crosshairs on a knee jutting out from one side of a thick maple. Two quick trigger pulls turned that knee into a flapping, bleeding clump of meat. When the raider fell down, rather than finish him off, I waited for someone to go to his aid. Sure enough, some brave, dumb bastard broke cover firing an AK-47 at the place I had just vacated and ran to help. He got three rounds in the stomach for his effort. Now it was his turn to scream.

The men behind him halted, probably realizing that they were facing a sharpshooter, and not just some yahoo with a gun. Good. It would buy me some time. Behind me, I heard more rifle fire from Flannigan's and Sanchez's M-4s, and the heavier report of Gabriel's SCAR. Judging from the shouts coming from the Legion's direction, my friends were making their shots count.

A volley of bullets hit the trees below me and brought my attention back to the problem at hand. I could see five more of them in my lane, hunkered behind cover and peppering bullets at anything that looked like somewhere a man might take cover. Unfortunately for them, that was a lot of places, and none of them were anywhere near where I stood. I risked two more shots at a head poking out over a rifle obscured by a tree, missed him on the first try, and then dropped him like a sack of bricks with the second.

Hot damn, score one for the good guys.

Not wanting to push my luck, and well aware that if I tried to run now they would undoubtedly spot me, I decided to play my ace in the hole. The last four gunmen were trying to reach the two wounded who still lay where I had shot them, bleeding out and begging for help. Once they were sufficiently close together to suit my intentions, I took out my grenade, pulled the pin, counted to two, and then let it fly.

I played pitcher for my high school baseball team, and when I throw an object at something, it usually hits where I want it to. The grenade flew straight and true, right into the middle of the marauders' congregation, and detonated with an ear-splitting *WHOMP*. I broke cover and ran toward their position, staying low and moving fast. I got close, took cover, and after a moment, realized that no one was shooting at me. I risked a peek around the trunk I knelt behind.

The two men I had wounded looked like they had been dragged over a hill of glass shards, and three of their would-be rescuers lay motionless in similarly gruesome condition. One of them, however, was still moving. He didn't look like he was going to put up much of a fight, being that he was bleeding out of his eyes, spitting up blood, and gasping around a lungful of shrapnel, but I wasn't about to take any chances. I stood up, took aim at his head, and squeezed the trigger twice, putting him out of his misery. I did the same to the remaining bodies, and then moved on.

Not wanting to get caught out of ammo, I pulled the magazine out of my M6, stashed it in a pocket as a last resort, and smacked in a fresh one. A few tense moments went by as I waited to see if anyone else was going to show up. No movement caught my eye, and the only sounds I heard were gunshots to the south where the others were still engaging the Legion. It occurred to me that I might have just taken out the entire force that had been sent to this side of the ridge.

Yay, me.

Breaking cover again, I worked my way across the embankment and down, trying to put myself behind the gunmen advancing up the hill toward Flannigan. If I could draw their fire, maybe I could lead them away from the others and split their forces. It wasn't the best plan in the world, and it would leave me isolated and outnumbered, but for now, it was all I could think of.

Following the sound of gunfire, I didn't have to go far to get a visual on the enemy. They were about thirty yards down the hill from me, and it looked as though they had divided their forces into two groups: one going straight up the middle at Gabe and Flannigan, and the other flanking left to take out Sanchez. That meant the gunmen I had just dispatched on the farther end of the ridge had been sent with the intention of taking out yours truly.

Sorry, guys. Better luck next time.

The fact that my side of the hill was now unoccupied meant that if I could somehow get Gabe and the other's attention, they might be able to fight their way over and we could make a run for it. But I didn't have a radio, or any other way to get word to them, so that plan was out.

I'd like to say that the idea of just turning around and slipping quietly away didn't occur to me, but it did. And it was a damned tempting idea. I had enough food on me for three days if I rationed it, plenty of ammo, the means to make fresh water, and two well-maintained firearms. I could bug out, leave Hollow Rock behind, and head west. Live off the land, and forget I ever saw this place.

But that was just the old Eric talking. I could no more abandon Gabe and the others to their fate than I could stand the thought of never seeing Allison again. No, running away was not an option. That left only one course of action.

As I drew closer, being careful not to let the raiders see me, I noticed that quite a few of them wore balaclavas and scarves, probably to protect their faces from the cold. My hand went to the thick wool scarf around my neck, and I grinned as a plan took shape.

Moving quickly, I made my way down the hill and around behind the Legion's advancing line. This next part was going to be tricky—if they had left anyone behind to watch their backs, things could get dicey. I moved carefully and deliberately, using the forest to stay hidden.

When I finally drew close, I realized that I needn't have worried. The raiders were so focused on the firefight in front of them that they would not have noticed me if I had ran naked and screaming into their midst. Not a single one was paying attention to what was going on behind them.

Dumb move on their part.

I wrapped my scarf around my face, detached the suppressor from my rifle, and ran up the hill toward the closest knot of gunmen. They were working in three-man fire teams, spread out at five-yard intervals. Not much room to work with, but it would have to do.

"Hey!" I shouted as I drew near.

One of them turned to look at me. He was young, not even old enough to grow a beard, and he looked frightened halfway out of his mind.

"They got a sniper dug in up this way," I called out, pointing to the right, "He's shot six guys, but we got him pinned down. Come on, I need more help to take him out."

With that, I turned and began running back up the hill.

One of the many lessons I've learned in my life is that if you act like you know what you're doing, nine times out of ten people will buy it. After a few running steps I stole a glance over my shoulder and, sure enough, the three men had left their post and were following me up the embankment. I was a good thing I had covered my face, otherwise they might have seen me smiling as I tried not to laugh at them.

When we were halfway back to the scene of my original firefight, one of the raiders behind me snagged his foot on a root and pitched face-first into the dirt. One of his companions, the oldest of the three, stopped and turned around.

"Goddammit, Grayson, watch where the fuck you're going," he said, reaching down.

They were his last words.

The report of my rifle startled the man next to him, who had been looking backward when I put a bullet through his friend's head. He had half a second to register shock before two more bullets ventilated his brain and sent him to his final reward.

I looked down at the last of them, fully ready to pull the trigger again if he moved. His rifle had gone flying from his hands when he tripped, and lay on the ground several feet way, out of reach.

"Please," he said. "Please, don't kill me. I didn't want to do this, you have to believe me."

Tears began to drip down his ruddy cheeks, and even though I firmly believed that he would have killed me if the tables had been turned, something made me hesitate. Maybe it was the sincerity in his voice, or the fear in his eyes, or maybe it was just the fact that he was so damned young, I don't know. But I didn't shoot.

"What's your name, boy?" I said, pointing my rifle between his eyes.

"G-Grayson. Grayson Morrow."

"Tell you what, Grayson Morrow, I'll make you a deal. If you want to live to see another day, you will do exactly as I tell you to. Make one false move, or even twitch in a way that displeases me, and I will paint the ground with your fucking brains. Do I make myself clear?"

"Y-yes s-sir."

He was shaking now, eyes wide with fear. Good.

"I want you to put your face down on the ground, look away from me, and put your arms out with your palms up to the sky. Do it now."

He did as I said, his back twitching with quiet sobs.

"Cross your feet."

He did.

I took one hand off my rifle, drew my pistol, and then slid the M-6 around to my back. Keeping my gun trained on him, I grabbed one of his upturned palms, bent his arm at the elbow, and planted a knee into the back of his neck. With his arm trapped on his back, and his face planted in the dirt, he had nowhere to go. I holstered my pistol so that I could grab a few zip-ties from a pouch on my belt.

"Give me your other hand."

He struggled awkwardly, but finally managed to flop his arm onto his back. I seized his wrist and pulled his hands together, then switched my grip to his fingers and applied pressure. The boy hissed in pain but didn't try to move.

"I'm going to put zip-ties around your wrists. I will need both hands to do this. If you try anything, I will kill you. Understood?"

He nodded as best he could. "Yes, sir, I'm not gonna try anything."

It took me a few seconds to secure his hands, but he was as good as his word. He didn't move.

"I'm going to bind your legs now. Again, if you try anything, you will die."

I moved down to his feet, tied his knees and ankles together, and then rolled him over onto his back. I needed a gag but didn't have anything to make one out of except my newly trussed-up prisoner's clothing (I sure as hell wasn't using mine), so I pulled my fighting knife from its sheath. Upon seeing the blade, the boy started bucking and thrashing to get away from me.

"NOOO! Please, don't-"

I cut him off by putting a knee in his chest, a hand over his mouth, and my knife against his throat.

"I'm not going to kill you," I hissed, leaning close. "I'm going to cut off strips of your shirt, and then I'm going to put a gag in your mouth. But if you make one more goddamn sound, I will open you up from neck to nuts and leave you for the infected. Do I make myself clear?"

He nodded, his eyes bulging.

Another nervous minute went by as I sliced up his shirt, stuffed a wad of material into his mouth, and then tied it off with strips from his heavy jacket. All the while, I kept an eye on the woods around me, half expecting a dozen raiders to step out from behind trees with guns blazing. Thankfully, that didn't happen.

With my captive secured, I dragged him under the low hanging boughs of a nearby cedar, used a length of para-cord to tie a slipknot around his neck, and then anchored the other end tightly around the trunk of the tree.

"You should be well hidden if you stay still," I said, leaning in to whisper to him. "If you try to get away, that cord around your neck will tighten. I'm sure I don't have to explain to you what will happen next."

The boy nodded and tried to talk. I couldn't make out what he said, and leaned closer.

"What was that?"

"Hu-ahout eee enhehud?"

I patted him on the cheek and smiled my nastiest smile. "If the infected show up, then I strongly encourage you to strain against that cord as hard as you can, and pray it chokes you to death before they get to you. From what I hear, getting eaten alive is a shitty way to go."

I left him there, and just as I was about to start moving back toward the sound of the fighting, a bright red flare lit up the sky about a quarter-mile away.

Well it's about goddamn time, Grabovsky.

Another flare went up, this one near the top of the ridgeline, signaling the cargo's position to our reinforcements.

I set out at a dead sprint, trying to get back to where I could hear Gabe and the others still fighting for their lives. No more than ten steps had flown under me before I heard the cataclysmic *crack-BANG* of the other LAW rocket, followed by the shattering *THUMP-THUMP* of two grenades, which was then followed by the *rat-tat-tat* of automatic fire. Unless I missed my guess, my friends had just blown a hole in the marauders' line and were shooting their way out.

My theory proved correct when, after nearly a full minute of running toward where I last heard them, Sanchez came around the upturned root of a fallen oak and damn near ran head-on into me.

We both skidded to a halt, stopping close enough to reach out and steady each other before we fell over.

"Holy shit, you okay man?" I said, looking over his shoulder for the others. "Where's Gabe and Flannigan?"

"Right behind me," he said, breathless. "Come on, we gotta keep moving, the Legion isn't far behind."

He let go of me and kept running down the hill. I waited until I saw Flannigan winding her way through the trees, and the larger shape of Gabe bringing up the rear. Every fifteen steps or so he turned, cracked off a few shots, and then continued sprinting down the hill. Flannigan saw me and opened her mouth to yell.

I cut her off. "Just keep going. Catch up with Sanchez, and get your asses to the bottom of the hill. Reinforcements will be here any minute."

I waited for Gabe, taking cover behind the fallen tree. He sprinted down the hill and stopped just behind me.

“Come on, let’s keep moving,” he said. “There’s too many of them, we need to fall back and meet up with the reinforcements.”

“Okay, go on,” I replied. “You go first, I’ll cover you.”

A couple of figures were visible up the hill, winding their way down through the trees. Gabe sprinted for cover farther down, while I stayed where I was and waited for a clear shot to present itself. I didn’t have to wait long.

Gabe’s pursuers didn’t see me, which made it easy to stitch the nearest one with three rounds straight up the middle of his torso. His partner saw him go down, and tried to skid into cover behind a tree, but I already had a bead on him. Two shots to the legs dropped him, and two more to the head finished the job.

Not seeing anyone else, I turned and ran to get behind Gabe’s position, staying low and making sure I didn’t cross into his line of fire. When I was halfway to him, he started firing at something up the hill behind me. I heard a scream, a few voices shouting, and then I was past Gabe. I counted twenty steps, then stopped and took cover behind a tree trunk.

“Move!” I called out.

Gabe fired two more shots, then stood up and retreated. “Four more,” he shouted on the way by. “High up on your right.”

I peered through my scope where he had indicated, and saw more raiders hunkered down taking potshots at us. While I was taking aim at one of them, I noticed that the weapons they all carried were either military issue M-16s or AK-47s. Curiouser and curiouser.

My first shot took the gunman through the throat, so I followed up with two more center of mass. He was still moving and, even from a distance, I could hear him screaming. But he wasn’t going anywhere. Good enough. The other three resumed shooting at me in earnest, evidently having spotted me, and started concentrating fire on my position. Not good. I triggered a short full auto burst over their heads to get a break in the fire, then backed off and ran in the same direction as Gabe.

We went on that way for what felt like forever, taking turns retreating and laying down cover fire. All the running was beginning to take its toll. My lungs burned, and my legs were starting to get shaky. It seemed that for every one marauder we took out, two more appeared to take their place. But their pursuit had slowed, no doubt because of the high volume of casualties they were taking. I guess there is something to be said for good marksmanship and high-quality optical sights. That, and the psychological effect of watching someone's heart get blown out through their spine didn't hurt either.

As we were crossing a dry streambed near the base of the hill, Gabe looked up and saw movement through the trees behind us. He tapped my arm with the back of his hand and motioned ahead.

"Can you see who that is? And please, for the love of God, tell me it's backup."

I raised my scope and peered through it. "It's Grabovsky. He's with a squad of about twenty, fanned out and on approach. You got another flare?"

"Yeah, I do. Come on, let's take cover. We'll hold the line until they get here."

We jumped down into the streambed and laid our rifles on the bank, taking aim at the enemy advancing in the distance. Checking my vest, I found that I was down to my last two magazines, not counting the half-empty one in my pocket. Good thing the G-man was close; things might have gone badly for me otherwise.

I deployed my bipod and began looking for someone to shoot while Gabe took another flare from his vest and popped it. Grabovsky could now see where we were, but on the downside, so could the raiders. In their place, seeing my quarry sending up a signal would have given me pause. Why would we want to be seen if we were outnumbered and on the run? Seemed like a logical enough question. I looked up the hill to see if our pursuers were wondering the same thing.

Nope. Apparently not.

Not only were they still coming, they had actually sped up and were baying back and forth to one another like a pack of wild, excited dogs. I had to shake my head at that. Never underestimate the power of stupidity.

My first target was a tall guy with an AK. I put a three-round burst into his stomach, watched him fall, and waited to see if anyone wanted to be a hero. Another man a few steps behind stopped and tried to drag him behind a tree. I shifted my aim and triggered another burst through the side of his chest, killing him before he hit the ground.

While looking around for someone else to shoot, it occurred to me that I was getting entirely too comfortable with using the old wound-and-wait trick. It was effective, but damn if it wasn't brutal.

No one else tried to be a hero. The others spread out, split up into two-man fire teams, and started advancing down the hill in a skirmish line. I dropped from sight below the edge of the bank and ran to another spot a few feet to my right. Gabe opened up with his SCAR, fired three rounds, and got three screams of pain for his efforts. He dropped down and moved in my direction while I popped up and started laying down short bursts of suppression fire.

Come on, G-man, hurry the hell up.

From behind me, just as I was getting ready to cease fire and run for cover somewhere else, I heard the distinctive, hollow *phump* of someone triggering a grenade launcher.

"Shit, get down!" I yelled, but Gabe was already taking cover.

The grenade flew over our heads and detonated into the hillside about thirty yards up from us. I wasn't sure if it hit any of the marauders, but it sure as hell got their attention.

Two more grenades came flying through the air, followed by the staccato burst of someone opening up with a squad automatic weapon (or just SAW, for short). It was, quite possibly, the sweetest sound I had ever heard in my life.

"Come on," Gabe shouted to me. "Let's get the hell out of here."

I followed him around the edge of the streambed, practically crawling to stay below the edge of the berm, and kept moving until we were out of the Legion's range and somewhere behind our own forces. Feeling a little safer, we climbed up the steep bank, drank some water, and took a moment to figure out which way we needed to go.

"Sounds like they're up that way," I said, pointing northward.

"I think you're right," Gabe replied. "Come on, let's get moving."

A few minutes later, Gabe stopped and knelt down behind a thick oak trunk, motioning for me to do the same.

"What is it?" I asked. Gabe flapped his hand at me to stay quiet.

"Blacksmith," he called out.

A moment went by in silence, then from ahead of us I heard, "Eagle."

I would have recognized that accent anywhere. We got up and stepped around the tree.

"Where's Flannigan?" Gabe asked as Sanchez emerged from cover.

"Over here," she said, standing up from behind a fallen log.

Sancho grinned. "What took you so long?"

“Got held up at that dry creek bed,” Gabe replied. “Come on, let’s find the others.”

I bummed a couple of magazines from Sanchez, reloaded, and followed them toward the sound of the fighting.

*****

It was mostly over with by the time we reached them.

Using exactly the same tactic the Legion had employed against us, Grabovsky had split his forces into three assault teams and deployed them in a pincer formation, spreading them out and surrounding the raiders at the top of the ridge. He led the main assault force straight up the middle, but occasionally slowed down and let the Legion hold its ground for a while. This used up a lot of ammo, but it gave the two squads moving up the flanks time to get into position.

The marauders, backed up against the top of the ridge with nowhere else to go, had tried to make a break for it by running down the steep hillside leading to the highway. Grabovsky waited for them to reach the bottom—where they were out in the open with no place to take cover—before signaling to the squads lying in wait to open fire.

It was a slaughter.

Two SAWs and about twenty M-4s opened up on them all at once, hitting them in a twin vector that pointed like an arrowhead toward the far side of the highway, and the escape that they would never reach. The raiders positioned on the other ridge and, while still trying to lay down covering fire, decided that discretion was the better part of valor and melted back into the hills. The G-man sent a few fire teams to find them, but they had disappeared.

Once the dust settled, it was clear that the militia had scored a solid victory against the Legion, but it did not come without a price. Four recruits were wounded, two of them seriously. Not wanting to waste time waiting for wagons to arrive, Grabovsky ordered the wounded carried back to town on litters. Half the platoon volunteered to help, which allowed them to set a running pace by rotating carriers every few hundred yards. I watched them hustle away and hoped that they would get to Allison in time.

Just as they passed from view, the first distant moans of the undead slithered to my ears from the surrounding forest. I hustled back to where Gabe and Grabovsky were ordering recruits to round up the fallen cargo and stage it for retrieval.

"Hey G-man, I don't suppose the helicopter is coming back this way is it?" I asked.

The muscles of his thick neck writhed under his skin as he shook his head. " 'Fraid not. Fucking bullet clipped a hydraulic line. She's grounded until we can get repair parts flown in."

One of the recruits standing near us stood up straight. "Hey, do you hear that?"

Gabe looked in the direction the sound was coming from. "Yep. Sounds like the infected found us."

He placed his hands around his mouth and shouted, "All right ladies and gentlemen, we have incoming. The walkers are on their way. We need to get this cargo squared away and take up defensive positions. LET'S MOVE."

Hearing the moans made me remember my prisoner, and I slapped a hand to my forehead.

"Fuck me running," I hissed.

Grabovsky looked at me. "Sorry, you're not my type."

"No, shit, dude, I totally forgot."

"Forgot what?"

"I captured one of them."

"One of them who? The Legion?"

“Yes.”

He faced me. “Are you fucking kidding me?”

“No.”

“Well, where the hell is he?”

“I left him tied to a tree.”

He stared incredulously for a moment, and then threw up his hands. “Well go fucking get him before the goddamn walkers do.” He turned and grabbed a couple of recruits. “You two, go with him. Prisoner retrieval, move your asses.”

I had a feeling that if Grabovsky’s cane had been in his hand, I would have felt the business end of it urging me on as I sprinted up the embankment on the far side of the road. Honestly, he would have been justified.

Chapter 7

Price of Freedom

When I pulled back the cedar branches I had hidden my prisoner beneath, I half expected to find him dead of strangulation. As it was, he was lying on his side and shaking with silent sobs, tears dripping from between tightly squeezed eyelids. It was a good thing I reached him when I did. If the walkers had gotten any closer, he might have done something rash.

I grabbed his foot and shook him. “Rise and shine, buttercup. Time to get you out of here.” He opened his eyes, glanced around in consternation, and then nodded vigorously. I cut the cord binding his legs, and the one at his throat, then pulled the gag out of his mouth and helped him stand up.

“Think you can run?”

He looked at me and nodded again.

“Good. Now let’s get one thing straight.” I touched the barrel of my pistol to his temple. “Try anything, and you’re a dead man. Clear?”

He swallowed a couple of times, and gave a single bob of his head. “Okay.”

“Come on, let’s get moving.”

The two recruits Grabovsky had sent with me watched our six as we trudged back down the hill as quickly as we could manage. I kept a firm grip on the prisoner’s arm and marched him ahead of me, occasionally having to catch him to keep him from falling. The moans of the infected grew louder and louder as we made our way down and, as we emerged from the treeline, Grabovsky saw us coming and shouted at the recruits standing with him to hold their fire.

Three dozen gun-toting, hostile faces glared coldly at Grayson Morrow as I marched him through the perimeter and over to where Gabe and Grabovsky waited for us. The sight of the two grim, stone-faced warriors was enough to make his steps falter.

"Keep moving," I growled, shoving the barrel of my pistol into his kidney.

I stopped him in front of Gabe, who looked the kid up and down briefly before turning his attention to me. "I want you to take him on the first wagon headed back to town. Get this kid to the police station and lock him up. Stay with him and let the sheriff know that this man is in federal custody."

"You sure you don't want someone else to take him?" I asked. "There's a lot of infected coming this way. You're gonna need all the help you can get."

Gabe opened his mouth to speak, but Grabovsky interrupted him. "He's got a point, Garrett," he said. "Riordan can shoot the nuts off a hummingbird. We need him here."

The hardness in Gabe's eyes said that he didn't like it, but he couldn't argue with the G-man's logic.

"Fine," he said, after a moment. "Have Sanchez and Vincenzo take him, but make sure they know to keep him safe. This prisoner is too valuable to lose to a lynch mob."

I didn't think it was possible for my prisoner to get any paler, but he proved me wrong. His arm trembled under my hand as I walked him to the far edge of the perimeter and passed him off to Sanchez.

"You're off the hook, Sancho," I said. "Find Vincenzo and head back to town with this guy as soon as the wagons get here."

The scrappy Mexican glared at Morrow with open hostility and stabbed a finger into his chest. "The only reason you're still alive, *cabrón*, is because I'm under orders not to kill you. If it were up to me, I'd chain you to a tree and leave you for the fucking *muertos*. So don't give me an excuse. *Comprende*?"

Morrow kept his eyes down and nodded quickly, not daring to speak. I didn't blame him.

With the prisoner in Sancho's capable hands, I jogged back to the center of the perimeter where Gabe awaited. He stood atop an olive drab crate, peering northward with a pair of binoculars. I climbed onto the crate next to him and brought up my scope.

"You seeing what I'm seeing?" he asked without looking at me.

I took a moment to sweep both sides of the road as it wound around a curve in the distance, and let out a tired breath. "Couple hundred of them, at least."

Gabe lowered his binos and reached over to pat my shoulder. "Don't sweat it, amigo. We've handled worse than this by ourselves. This time we got help."

I looked around at the recruits. "Yeah. Yeah we do."

They had arranged the heavy crates in a circle and taken position behind them. Flannigan and a couple of others had scrounged up a few entrenching tools and were busy filling sandbags to use as bench rests. That was good thinking on their part. Having something to prop their rifles on would help everyone shoot more accurately, and save ammo. I just hoped the factory zero on their ACOG sights was as good as the manufacturer used to advertise.

Not wanting to use up his limited supply of .308 ammo, Gabe swapped his SCAR battle rifle for Sanchez's smaller and lighter M-4. The kid grinned as he handled the high-tech weapon, eliciting a stern warning from Gabe that if anything happened to his beloved rifle, he would visit a thousand flaming dooms upon Sancho's head. The grin disappeared.

I walked to the northernmost edge of the perimeter and found a crate that came up to the middle of my chest, set my rifle on its bipod, and dialed down the magnification on my scope. After conferring briefly with the two shooters on either side of me to designate lanes of fire, I settled down over my rifle, took a deep breath, and waited. Ahead of me, a host of shambling, ragged figures began to appear from between the trees, filtering down the hillsides and onto the highway.

The landscape around us provided both an advantage, and a disadvantage. The natural steepness of the hills would direct the walkers down to the road—the dead tend to follow the path of least resistance—but it also meant that the troops positioned to the north and south would have to bear the heaviest volume of fire. As the dead grew closer, Gabe noticed the same thing and began barking out orders.

Five people took up position on each of the two flanks facing the sides of the road, while the rest formed ranks along the blacktop facing north and south where the bulk of the infected would hit us. The idea was that each shooter would use up a full magazine, retreat to the back, reload, and wait for another turn on the firing line.

Looking out, I saw that they were coming at us from all directions now, shuffling and moaning toward the sound of food. The walkers began to bottleneck as they converged, the faster and more recently dead ones pushing their way past their slower, less mobile counterparts. None of them moved faster than a brisk walk, but then again, they didn't need to. Their strength was their numbers, and the fact that they would never, ever, get tired. I did a few breathing exercises to calm my nerves and heard Gabe's voice booming over the cacophony of moans.

"Remember, take your time and line up your shots," he shouted. "Use the sandbags to steady your aim. Make every shot count. If your weapon jams, raise a hand and fall back.

Either me or Sergeant Grabovsky will help you clear it. Keep your rifles pointed downrange at all times while on the firing line. If I catch you away from the firing line with your safety off, I will cram my boot so far up your ass you'll taste my shoe polish."

He was smiling when he said that last part, drawing a few smiles and nervous chuckles.

"Remember kids," he went on, "this is just like we drilled. Stay calm, keep your head screwed on straight, and we'll all get out of this just fine. Shooters on the front ranks, take up position and get ready to fire. Everybody else, check the person next to you and make sure your weapons and ammo are squared away before you step up to the line."

The recruits did as he said, looking each other's rifles over and loosening straps on mag carriers. The tension in the air lessened under the sound of hands patting shoulders, and voices reassuring one another that they were good to go. It was a simple ritual that banished nervousness and made the recruits stand a little straighter, taking confidence in the man or woman next to them. In that moment, under the glare of the midday sun, I understood something about the military that had, until then, escaped my attention.

There was a camaraderie there on that stretch of empty road that transcended any boundaries that might have otherwise separated us. We were alone, surrounded by monsters, and we had no one to depend on but each other. If I wanted to live to see another day, I had to count on the man standing next to me, and he had to count on me. It didn't matter who he was, what he had done in his life, or what beliefs he held. We were on the same side, we would fight to the death to protect other, and that was all that mattered. It was us against them, plain and simple.

"Shooters in the front, thumbs up if you're ready," Gabe shouted.

I held up an arm, but not a thumb, using an altogether different digit. It took the big man a few seconds to catch it.

"Go fuck yourself, Riordan."

I could hear the smile in his voice as heads swiveled in my direction to see what he was talking about. Laughs and chuckles followed, further breaking down the pervading atmosphere of nervous tension.

"Anybody else does that, and I'll break your fingers."

"All fucking around aside," Grabovsky broke in, playing the part of bad-cop, "tighten your shit up. This is the real deal, ladies. Let's do it right."

Smiles disappeared, eyes narrowed, and mouths set into hard lines as the recruits took deep breaths, shook off the levity of the moment, and settled down over their weapons.

I peered through my scope and sighted in on the closest walker in my lane, centering the reticle just above its forehead. It was impossible tell what it had looked like in life, what its race had been, or even if it was a man or a woman. Its clothes were long gone, and its skin, what was left of it, looked like bleached saddle leather stretched tight over blackening cords of muscle tissue. A gaping hole spilled out from what had once been its abdomen, and its left arm was missing from the elbow down.

As I looked at the walker's face, with its yawning teeth and milk-white eyes, I felt all the old conflicted feelings bubble to the surface again. Revulsion tugged at the gag reflex in the back of my throat, pity twisted in my chest, and an icy, razor-edged ball of fear roiled in my gut, threatening to give me the shakes.

I shoved it all down, took a deep breath, and tapped my fingertips against the cold metal of the trigger guard.

Concentrate.

"Enemy in range," Grabovsky called out. From the corner of my eye, I saw him looking through a handheld rangefinder.

"Roger that," Gabe called back. "Soldiers on the firing line, mark range one hundred yards. Standby."

I slipped my finger over the trigger, breathing steadily. A few more seconds ticked by, and the ghouls shuffled ever closer, their moans drowning out everything but the hammering of my own heartbeat.

"Eighty yards," Grabovsky shouted.

"Roger, standby."

The walker in my crosshairs grew larger, its eyes locked in my direction. I could swear it was looking at me. I willed my pulse to slow down.

"Sixty yards."

"All right, this is it," Gabe bellowed, his voice ringing out over the low valley. "Ladies and gentlemen, this is what we trained for. You've fought well today, but the day ain't over yet. You all know what to do, now let's see you do it. FIRE AT WILL."

A dozen rifles fired in rapid succession, the reports drowning out the wailing cry of the undead. I added my own rifle to the fray, dropping the walker I had been watching with my first shot. The walker behind it didn't flinch or slow down, not even when brain and bone shards splattered into its face. I shifted my aim and sent another round downrange, hitting the mark and sending it to join its friend.

The tightness in my shoulders loosened and I felt myself begin to relax, settling into a steady rhythm and pulling the trigger with metronome cadence. Not for the first time, a zenlike state descended upon me. The world narrowed down to the lens of my scope, the stock against my shoulder, and the cool roughness of the trigger under my finger.

Aim, *crack*, down goes a walker.

Aim, *crack*, down goes a walker.

In thirty seconds, I fired thirty shots, and put down thirty infected. I almost reached for another mag, but I remembered that I was supposed to fall back and let another shooter take my spot while I reloaded.

The man behind me settled down on the crate I had just vacated and began racking up a score of his own. I dropped my mag, stuffed it into a pouch, and popped in a fresh one. The two people in front of me were shuffling with impatience, anxious to get in on the fight.

I smiled at their backs, thinking about how far these survivors of the Outbreak had come. When they were living their old lives, back before the world went insane, did they ever think they would be standing in formation behind a barricade of U.S. Army cargo crates, fighting off wave after wave of flesh-eating monsters? I shook my head.

Of course they didn't, no one did.

But here we were.

A cloud blew past in the sky overhead, revealing the sun and letting yellow light diffuse down to the world below. The rays that broke through were pale and weak, as though ashamed to waste their brightness on such a gruesome scene. If I had been a ray of light that morning, looking down upon the carnage on that lonely stretch of road in western Tennessee, my shine might have faded a bit as well.

*****

I wondered if before the Outbreak, had the Army been as well prepared to fight the undead as these militia recruits, how might things have gone differently? Could the National Guard have stopped the Phage in Atlanta, and prevented it from wiping out nearly the entire world?

I guess we'll never know.

As it was, I only got three turns on the firing line before Gabe called a ceasefire to conserve ammunition. Thirty-seven rifles, mine included, had whittled the horde's numbers down to just over a dozen. Gabe rounded up half that number of recruits, ordered them gather up an assortment of blunt instruments, drew his Falcata, and set out to split a few skulls. Where most people shied away from fighting the undead hand to hand, for Gabe, it was therapeutic. I watched his hulking form stalk toward the last walkers, naked steel in hand, and couldn't help but chuckle.

While dealing with the horde, not everyone had displayed the same level of marksmanship as I had (the average kill ratio was only about one ghoul for every two shots), but it was enough. Considering that they only had six weeks of formal training under their belts, the fledgling militia had performed amazingly well. Both against the infected, and against the Legion.

My thoughts turned to the four recruits being carried back to town for medical attention, and I felt my stomach sink into my shoes. I knew what it was like to be in that position. Wounded, hurting, and wondering if tree branches cutting through sunlight would be the last thing my eyes would ever see. I offered up a quick prayer for them to whoever might be listening, and then got to work helping to clear the mass of dead bodies from the highway. As I was helping to toss the withered husk of one of the last corpses into a ditch, the crack of a whip and the urging call of a teamster at the reins echoed from the south.

About damn time.

Grabovsky had Sanchez and Vincenzo turn the first wagon around and take the prisoner back to town straightaway while the rest of the recruits started loading up crates. Gabe and I, along with a few others, patrolled the perimeter and put down any walkers that straggled out of the forest. There weren't many of them, but it was enough to keep us busy, and enough to chip away at my dwindling supply of 5.56 NATO ammunition. When I got down to my last three magazines, I slid my M-6 around to my back and switched to my pistol. It wouldn't do at all to be out of ammo for my rifle if the Legion decided to show up again.

The sun was low in the sky, and the eastern horizon was just fading into the dark blue of night, when the last box was finally loaded. There wasn't enough room for everyone to ride back to town, so Grabovsky had the recruits form into ranks and follow behind on foot as the wagons trundled down the road. We were all tired, hungry, and a little dehydrated, and all any of us wanted was to find a quiet spot to lie down and rest for a while.

Gabe and I stayed on patrol around the edges of the convoy, occasionally gunning down anything dead and hungry that strayed into our path, and generally struggling against exhaustion to keep up with the nervous pace the horses set on the way back to town. I was worried that the horses might break and run at the sight of the undead, but oddly enough, they were more spooked by our rifles than they were by the infected. Sad world that we live in when even animals aren't impressed by the walkers anymore.

Occasionally, as we walked, I looked at the faces of the recruits with their hollow, glassy eyes and vacant expressions, and it was clear that the day's fighting was beginning to take its toll. Not that these men and women had never seen violence or hardship—they certainly had, as had anyone who had survived the Outbreak—but being in a firefight and seeing one's friends wounded and bleeding and crying out in agony was enough to soften the resolve of even the hardest of fighters. Victory and glory are all well and good until the blood on your hands belongs to you or someone that you care about. When that happens, you realize just how dangerous of a game you're playing when you take up arms against a determined enemy.

I wondered if any of the recruits realized that, as tough as the day had been, this was only the beginning. We had drawn blood against the Legion, and had done so in spades. The Legion was bound to retaliate, and when they did, there would be no holding back, and no quarter.

From here on out, the bloodshed was only going to get worse.

*****

It was after nightfall by the time I got home.

Allison was still at the clinic and would likely be spending the next several days there tending to the surviving wounded. Two of the recruits who were brought in were still in recovery after getting patched up, and were expected to make a full recovery. But the other two, however, were not so lucky.

One of them, a young man named Theodore Russell, had suffered a gunshot wound that nicked his femoral artery and, in spite of the militia's frantic efforts to get help in time, he had bled out on the way to the clinic. Allison checked his vitals, pronounced him on the spot, and moved on. The other person who didn't make it was Jennifer Blankenship, age twenty-three, recently engaged to one Brett Nolan.

Brett did not take it well.

The rest of the recruits, along with General Jacobs and his retinue, the sheriff, Mayor Stone, and the families of the wounded, packed into the church across the street, filling up the chapel and the fellowship hall to wait for news. When it came, the palpable air of fear and anxiety broke down into grief and anger.

Shocked, red-eyed people sat in clusters, clinging to one another and, in many cases, weeping quietly. I sat alone in a corner pew near the bathroom, put my head in my hands, closed my eyes, and tried desperately not to think, not to feel. There was too much growing and swelling inside of me, and if I didn't get it under control, it was going to rip me apart at the seams.

The bodies of the fallen were taken to a nearby funeral home, and their families left to go see them one last time. They would have to be buried the next day due to the lack of a functioning morgue to keep them in, so Allison asked that anyone who wished to pay their respects do so before morning. After delivering the news, she excused herself quietly and began making her way back to the clinic. I slipped out a back door and hurried to catch up.

"Hey, Allison, wait up."

She turned to look at me, and even in the darkening gloom, I could see the shadows circling under her eyes. When I caught up to her, she slipped her arms around my waist and buried her head in my chest, clinging tightly. We stayed that way for a few minutes, just holding on and taking comfort in each other's warmth.

"Are you okay?" she asked, finally.

"Not really. But I'm uninjured, if that's what you mean. What about you?"

She leaned back and gave me a wan smile. "I've had better days. That's for sure."

I reached up to brush a lock of hair from her face. "If there's anything I can do to help, let me know, okay? I hate seeing you like this."

She took my face in her hands and stood on her toes to kiss me. "I'm a big girl." She looked me in the eyes. "I'll be fine."

I nodded and tried to think of something to say, but I couldn't think of anything. Allison let me off the hook by asking me to get a few things from the house and bring them to her at the clinic. I promised I would, and hugged her one last time before letting her get back to her patients.

Back at the church, Gabe had politely asked everyone not in the militia to give him a few minutes alone to say a few words to his people, and then waited as they filed out into the fellowship hall, leaving him alone with his troops. I stood at the back and watched, while Grabovsky moved next to Gabe at the pulpit to address the recruits seated in the pews.

"Right now, I'm not talking to you as your drill instructor." Gabe began, a deep huskiness pulling at his voice. "Right now, I'm just a man trying to offer what comfort he can to a group of fine, brave young men and women who have fought hard and gone through hell today."

A few people absently nodded their heads, eyes staring off into space. Gabe heaved a deep sigh before continuing, his tone gruff and to the point.

"You don't need me to tell you about Russell and Blankenship, about what kind of people they were. You all knew them better than I did. They were good soldiers, and they died protecting the place they called home. If there is a more honorable thing for someone to give their life for, I don't know what it is. The best thing we can do for them now is to remember them for their courage, and honor their sacrifice by making sure that they did not die in vain."

The recruits focused on him now, paying attention. I saw Sanchez and Flannigan seated next to each other, hard expressions sharpening their youthful faces. I couldn't tell for sure, but by the angle of their arms, it looked like they might have been holding hands.

"As much as I know we're all hurting right now," Gabe continued, "and as much as I know you don't want to hear this, it needs to be said: The Legion is still out there. We dealt them a blow today, but they're not done yet. Not by a long shot."

There was a pause while he let that sink in.

"I want you to remember this day," he went on. "I want you to remember the way you feel right now, and I want you to remember the sacrifice that those two made to defend the people they swore to protect. I want you to remember that it was the Free Legion who brought this on us with their stupidity, and their belligerence. I want you to remember that this fight isn't over yet, and that this town, these people here who have worked so hard to make Hollow Rock a good place to live, still need you. I still need you."

Gabe looked out over the faces staring back at him, and met their eyes. More than a few of them raised hands to brush at their cheeks, while others simply sat still, stiff with suppressed rage.

"We're all going to need a little time to get ourselves together," Gabe said. "I'm giving all of you three days' leave. Go see your families, visit your friends, do whatever you need to do. If any of you don't want to report for training on Thursday, I won't think any less of you for it. And if you need to talk to someone about what happened today, a shoulder to lean on, or just somebody to listen, I encourage you to do so. You all know where I live, and my door is always open. Don't hesitate to walk through it."

With that, he stepped down and walked out the front door. The militia followed him, and dispersed toward their respective homes in silence. I thought about following Gabe, but decided against it. He needed some time to himself, and for that matter, so did I.

*****

A bottle of Mike Stall's homemade hooch sat on the table in front of me, the cork still wedged firmly into the neck. There was a corkscrew under my palm. The metal was cold against my skin, and I was seriously considering putting it to hard use. It had been weeks since the last time I had gotten drunk, and if there was ever a good time to break the streak, today was it.

I thought about Grayson Morrow's terrified face, and the tremor in his voice as he begged me not to kill him. I thought about the LAW rocket that had laid waste to three lives in less time than it takes to blink, and the odd giddiness I felt when the explosion hit me in the gut. I thought about the screams of all the Legion troops I had wounded, and the way the trigger felt beneath my finger when I shot the men who tried to rescue them. Their faces, and the faces of many others, hyper-magnified through the lens of a scope, stared at me every time I closed my eyes, agonized and accusing.

Before I realized what I was doing, the cork was out of the bottle and a splash of clear liquor spilled into the glass in my hand. It went down hot and angry, and blazed into a pool of fire in my gut that slowly, ever so slowly, eroded my waking thoughts until, with barely an inch of liquid left standing from the bottom, I stumbled out of my boots and into bed.

I didn't dream that night, but dreams are patient things. They are always there, silent, waiting, and unswayable in their determination to tear at our minds with their claws. And dreams, much like hangovers, don't create themselves, but are a function of consequence, created by our own folly, hubris, and cowardice in the face of our darker natures. As strong as I sometimes fool myself into thinking that I am, and as much as I wish I could be, I am no more immune to these things than anyone else.

Part II

Know your enemy; know his sword.

-Miyamoto Musashi
The Book of Five Rings

Chapter 8

The Journal of Gabriel Garrett:

Need to Know

As I walked home, I thought about Sadr City. The memories of that place, like all my memories, stood out as stark and clear as the day they happened.

The insurgents there had numbers, but they were outgunned, out-skilled, and facing the most advanced military force on the planet. We had weapons at our disposal against which they had no defenses. We had virtually unlimited resources of firepower, communications, aircraft, artillery, and armored cavalry. We occupied the streets of their cities, we lived in the battle zone, and we hunted them down and killed them where they lived.

Muqtada al-Sadr—that fat piece of shit—sent wave after wave of his Mahdi street rats after us and, time after time, we burned the bastards down. It was only after we had wiped out nearly his entire homegrown army that he finally decided to sit down at the bargaining table with Coalition leadership and put an end to that chapter of the war in Iraq.

No one left to die for him, his political allies running for the door, facing the prospect of being on the wrong end of a drone strike, and the fucker finally capitulates.

Imagine that.

I had a feeling things weren't going to be any better with the Legion.

The steps of the front porch groaned under my weight when I stepped on them, as though sensing how I was feeling at the moment. When I went into the cold, empty living room, there was no light inside. I followed the silver luminescence of moonlight until I found the kitchen, lit a single candle, poured myself a strong drink, and sat down in the silence. Alone.

My ears were still ringing from the LAWs I had fired, the right side of my face was stinging from shrapnel that had blasted into it at some point, and my shoulder was sore from the repeated recoil of my SCAR. I rubbed the bruised skin on that side, and reminded myself to chase down Sanchez tomorrow and get my rifle back. If anything happened to it, I was going to hand him his ass on a plate.

Right after I asked Grabovsky to put him in for a Bronze Star, that is.

Flannigan, too.

Out the window, the last cobalt bands of the daytime sky were darkening into black, and the crescent sliver of the moon shone bright against a cloudless sky. It was cold enough in my little house to see my breath in the air. Not wanting to wake up freezing my ass off, I stepped out the back door to gather up a bundle of firewood, brought it inside, and got to work starting a fire. Not for the first time, I wished my kitchen was big enough to push my bed into so that I could sleep closer to the heat of the stove.

Squatting there, hands in front of the flames trying to work some feeling back into my fingers, I heard footsteps crunching up the gravel drive. By the tread, and the cadence of the steps, I had a pretty good idea who it was. When the knock at the door came, I didn't move.

Go away, woman.

The knock came again, more insistent this time.

"I know you're in there, Gabe. Please, I just want to talk."

I pinched the bridge of my nose between my fingers and squinted, feeling the beginnings of a migraine coming on. Taking my time, I popped a prescription-strength Motrin big enough to choke an elephant, washed it down with a shot of booze, and opened the door.

"Can I come in?"

I stepped back and held out an arm toward the couch. She stepped inside, shut the door, and stood close in front of me, looking up at my face. Her hands reached out and curled around mine, drawing me closer.

"I'm so sorry," she said, her eyes shining in the dim light. "I would have sent help, but everything happened too fast. There wasn't time …"

"There was nothing you could have done."

"I know, but … I just feel terrible."

Where normally she looked poised and collected, at that moment, she just looked miserable. As much as I wanted to be angry, standing there in that quiet room with that handsome, frightened woman, my irritation bled out of me and left me feeling empty. I sighed through my nose and shook my head.

"This isn't your fault, Liz," I said. "None of it."

My fingers cupped her chin, and I kissed her gently. "You're doing the best you can, same as everybody else. It's the Legion that did this to us. Not you, not me, not anyone else in this town—the Legion. Don't forget that."

Her arms went around my waist and she squeezed, her head buried in my chest. I tried to tell myself that I didn't want her there, didn't need her, that I just wanted to be alone. But my arms—traitors that they are—encircled her shoulders and squeezed back. I smelled the homemade soap she washed her hair with, and leaned my cheek against the top of her head, closing my eyes to breathe it in.

She could have had her pick of any man in town, single, married or otherwise. Hell, there were even a few women she could have chosen from. Instead, she had chosen me. A tattered, war-weary man in his early forties who was old enough to know better than to get mixed up with her, but still young enough to find it exciting. Added to that, I was not one of her citizens, not one of her voters, not one of the people she was responsible for governing. I was an outsider, and when my business here was finished, I would quite literally be packing my bags and moving on. Any problems our liaison created for her would be wiped away the moment my shadow darkened the north gate for the last time.

Up until that point, I had thought that the mayor only wanted two things from me: the destruction of the Legion, and a warm body to hop in bed with. Now, I was beginning to wonder.

We stood there holding each other for a while, rocking gently, until my aching knees reminded me that not only was I getting older, but that I had put my body through a lot that day and I needed to rest.

"Come on," I said, taking Liz's hand and leading her into the kitchen. "My everything hurts. I need to sit down."

She smiled, and followed me.

We sat by the stove in silence, enjoying the warmth and taking comfort in having each other close by. I made tea for her, poured another whiskey for myself, and watched her as my eyes adjusted to the dark, the heat from the stove slowly radiating throughout the room. She sat a little too still, her shoulders a little too tense, and in her eyes, I caught a trace of hidden unease.

"Something on your mind?" I asked.

She sipped her tea and looked away before responding. "You're going to be debriefing with General Jacobs tomorrow, right?"

I nodded.

"I know it's probably a bad time, but I was hoping you could tell me what happened out there."

She saw my eyes narrow, and quickly reached out a hand to cover mine. "Look, Gabe, I'm sorry about what happened today, but I need information. I'm the mayor of this town, and if I'm going to do my job, then I need to know what this fight cost us today, and how badly we hurt the Legion. You're the first person in forever to fight them up close."

I sighed, and felt the headache get a little worse. "What do you want to know?"

"Anything you can tell me," she said, her dark eyes growing serious. "How many of them were there? What were they armed with? Did they have vehicles or horses? Were they all men, or were there women, too? Did you overhear them saying anything to each other?"

I got the picture and held up a hand. "Okay, okay. You need something to write with?"

She nodded. I got her a notepad and a pencil, poured another shot, and sat back down at the table.

"Okay, anything you remember. No detail is too minute, tell me all of it."

So I told her.

All of it.

From the chatter of the fifty-cal that was the harbinger of my shitty day, to standing rear guard and gunning down infected as the last few wagons passed through the gate. When I had finished, several pieces of paper lay on the desk, written on front and back, and Liz was massaging the muscles of her palm.

"I haven't heard a story like that since David got back from the war," she said.

"David was your husband?"

She nodded. "He was in Nashville on a golf weekend with some of his old Army buddies when the Outbreak hit. The last I heard from him, the infected had cut him off from coming home, and he was leading a small group of people north into Kentucky."

"Nothing since?"

She shook her head and looked down at her hands. I reached out and gave her shoulder a gentle squeeze. "I'm sorry."

"We've all lost people," she said. "I know it's kind of strange, but I find comfort in that. In knowing that other people feel the same as I do."

"That's not strange, Liz. It's human nature. It doesn't make you a bad person."

As if I'm one to talk.

She turned her eyes up to me and smiled. "Thank you, Gabriel."

After leaning forward to give me a quick kiss, she began gathering up her papers and stuffing them into her messenger bag. I noticed that the bag was a Louis Vuitton, and felt one side of my face turn up in a wry smile. Even at the end of the world, ladies want nice things.

"I have to get back to the funeral home," she said. "Can you come see me at town hall tomorrow after you meet with the General?"

"Can do."

I stood up and hugged her again, then shut the door behind her after she left. Back in the kitchen, I sat down and pondered pouring another drink, but decided against it. I was already feeling a little buzzed, and considering the day I had ahead of me tomorrow, waking up with a hangover would be an extraordinarily bad idea.

I took off my boots, stripped off my torn and filthy clothes, ate a quick meal of cold bread and dried meat, and climbed in bed. I didn’t quite manage to get all the way under the blanket before I fell asleep.

Chapter 9

The Cold Logic of Necessity

I was still in bed at noon the next day when a loud knock from the foyer sent peals of agony tearing through my skull. Cursing the offending party, I lurched to my feet and stumbled blearily into the living room to see who it was, praying that it wasn't Allison. Bright sunlight lanced through my eyes, sending me back a step when I opened the door.

"Jesus, Riordan. What the hell happened to you?"

I was still blind, one hand held over my face to ward off the pain, but I recognized the voice.

"What does it look like? I got drunk."

Steve stepped inside and shut the door behind him. "All things considered, I'd say you were entitled to it."

"Yeah, well, I'm regretting it now."

I walked over to the couch and collapsed onto it face first. A rustling sounded from across the room as Steve sank down into a chair and regarded me in silence. A couple of minutes passed while I breathed in the stale odor of upholstery and listened to the house creak around us.

"Grayson Morrow is quite an interesting young man."

I shifted enough to peer at him with one eye. "How so?"

"He told us a hell of a story this morning."

"And?"

Steve smiled. "Maybe you should take a few minutes to get yourself together. You'll want to have a clear head when you hear all of this."

I sighed and sat up, wincing at the increased pounding in my head. "All right. Give me ten minutes."

"Take your time."

Standing up took far longer than it should have, and on the way outside to the outhouse, I had to pause a few times to allow the dry heaves to run their course.

Thoroughly emptied of everything in my stomach and bowels, and after expelling putrid liquid from every orifice in my body capable of doing so, I stripped down, poured a bucket of cold water over my head, and swallowed a couple of prescription pain killers. After drinking enough water to nearly turn my stomach again, and shamelessly violating the ten-minute restriction I had placed on myself, I reconnoitered back to the living room in marginally better condition than when I had left it.

"Not bad," Steve said, nodding in approval. "You are now well on your way to merely looking like shit."

"That's what I like about you, Steve," I said as I collapsed back down onto the couch. "Always quick with a kind word and a smile."

He ignored me. "You up for a little walk this morning?"

"Probably not, but I have a feeling I'm gonna do it anyway."

"Good." He stood up and walked to the front door, stopping to look at me. "You coming?"

I groaned, sat up, and got my feet underneath me. The day was going to suck no matter what I did, whether I went with Steve, or stayed home. So I figured I might as well get off my ass and do something useful.

*****

Morrow looked small in the wide confines of his cell.

The bars on the door were haze gray, like the color of a warship, and the surrounding walls were cold and unyielding, made of chipped white cinderblock with all manner of obscenities carved into the paint. It was designed to hold several inmates at once, but rarely saw use other than the occasional drunken brawl or domestic dispute. Today, Morrow had it all to himself.

"Got someone here to see you," Sheriff Elliott said, unlocking the door.

I passed under the Sheriff's disapproving glare and sat down on a bench opposite the prisoner.

"I appreciate you meeting us here, Walter," Steve said. "I know you have a lot to do. If it's all right with you, we'd like a few minutes alone with Mr. Morrow."

Elliott shifted his stern gaze from Steve, to me, to Morrow, and then back to Steve. "Suit yourself. Cohen will be here to lock up when you're done."

Steve nodded, and the Sheriff turned and left, shutting the door to the cell behind him. I faced Morrow and leaned back against the wall. Steve took a seat on the other side.

"Good to see you still breathing." I didn't quite manage to keep the venom out of my voice. Steve glanced in my direction, gave a slight shake of his head, and mouthed, "Not yet."

Morrow missed the exchange, being too busy staring at the floor and avoiding eye contact.

"I know you've been through a lot since yesterday," Steve said. "But I need you to go over everything again with Mr. Riordan here." He waved a hand at me.

The boy asked, "What do you want to know?"

"All of it. Everything you've told me since last night."

Morrow sat up and eyed me from across the cell. His eyes were red and sunken, and the bones of his face stood out in gaunt relief, casting shadows on his hollow cheeks.

"It's a long story."

I crossed my arms and stretched my feet out in front of me. "I got nothing to do today."

He sighed, and looked desolately at Steve before launching into it. He spoke slowly at first, then faster and faster until the words tumbled out of him almost too quickly for me to keep up.

By the time he was done, I didn't know quite what to think of him. If everything he said was true—and I wasn't quite ready to bite on that just yet—then this kid was as much a victim of the Legion as he was an accomplice to their crimes. It was enough to make me feel sorry for him.

Finished with his story, and leaking silent tears down onto the floor between his feet, the kid looked imploringly back and forth between us. "What's gonna happen to me? Whatever it is, just tell me. Anything's better than sitting here not knowing."

Steve gave him a flat, reptilian stare, allowing a small smile to creep up the corners of his lips. I had seen that smile set hardened men to shaking in their boots, and the effect was not lost on Morrow.

"That's entirely up to you, Grayson. The information you have is invaluable, assuming it turns out to be true. If you help us bring down the Legion, I can arrange to have you taken back to Colorado, and you'll have a chance to start a new life. But if it doesn't …" He shrugged. "Your fate will be at the discretion of Sheriff Elliott. I think you already know how that will end."

"Look, whatever you want to know, I'll tell you," Morrow said. "There's nobody in this room that hates those fuckers more than I do. You can burn every goddamn one of them alive for all I care."

Steve's smile broadened, but it was devoid of humor. "Get some rest." He stood up and patted the kid on the shoulder. "I'll send someone around to bring you some food and some hot water for a bath. The guards should be able to scrounge up some clean clothes for you. Get yourself together, and I'll be back tomorrow. We'll talk more then."

*****

"I don't feel quite so bad now about not finding their base of operations," Steve said.

I nodded, staring mutely at my hands. We sat on a bench in front of the Sheriff's station trying to glean some warmth from the clear, cloudless sunshine. It was the kind of day that was warm on your skin as long as you stayed out of the shade.

"We're going to have to move up our timeframe for that thing we talked about." He leaned forward and kicked at a piece of gravel with the toe of his boot.

I turned my head to look at him. "You still expect me to do that? After everything he just told us?"

"You got any better ideas? Morrow only knows about the one tunnel entrance. He can't tell us how big their network is, or how far it extends. The fastest and best way to find that out is to infiltrate them."

I thought about it for a moment, and finally shook my head. The only other option was to send Morrow back, and that, quite simply, was not going to happen. Not after everything the Legion had put him through.

"You can do this, Eric. You're smart enough, you're tough enough, and no one on their side knows who you are. You can help put an end to this fight."

I stood up and walked across the parking lot to the street, stopping next to a willow tree. The bark was rough against my hand as I leaned against it and gazed at the houses lining Seminary Road. Just looking at them, quiet and scenic under the late September sky, you would never have known that the Outbreak had ever occurred. That the world had ended, and that none of the houses on this street had electricity. I reached out to a willow branch, broke off a slender twig, and threaded the soft, vinelike wood between my fingers.

"You know, pharmaceutical companies used to get salicylic acid from this stuff," I said, half turning to Steve and holding up the twig. "Used it to make acne medicine."

He continued to stare at me, his yellow eyes waiting for an answer. I dropped the stick and looked back out at the road.

"I have a few conditions."

Steve left the bench, walked over, and stopped a few feet to my right. "Okay."

"First, if there really are innocent people involved, we need to do everything we can to save them."

The Green Beret nodded. "My thinking exactly."

"And the Legion is fucking done. No taking prisoners, no options for reform, no reparations, and no fucking apologies. We wipe the bastards out. Root and branch."

Steve frowned and made an impatient gesture with one hand. "When do you get to the part where you tell me something I wasn't already going to suggest to General Jacobs?"

"If anything happens to me …" I clenched my teeth for the space of a second, then turned to Steve and put a hand on his shoulder, leaning close. "Allison will need someone to look after her. You keep her safe, you hear me?"

His eyes were steady, hiding nothing. "I can do that."

I watched him for a moment, gauging his sincerity. He didn't budge. Satisfied, I stepped away.

"And help Gabe get to Colorado, for Christ's sake. If you can get a Chinook and all those guns and shit all the way out here, then you can get one man to Colorado Springs."

"That shouldn't be a problem."

"Good." I walked back to the bench and sat down again. Steve followed and sat next to me.

"So how are we going to do this?"

Steve laid out a plan. It took him the better part of an hour to do it, and I had to stop him about halfway through because I had to take a piss. My watch—a windup piece that had survived the end of the world with me—told me that it was just after two in the afternoon when he finished. My stomach came back to life and told me that I needed to find something to put in it, pronto.

"Do you think you have a handle on all of this?" Steve asked, getting up from the bench.

I nodded. "For the most part, yeah. We'll have to go over it all again before I leave."

"You'll have time."

"Okay."

Steve looked at his watch. "I'm going to go find the general and see what resources we can scrounge up, and get on the radio back to Central Command. We're going to need their help with this."

I nodded silently, staring at the space between my knees and trying to stem the growing tsunami of anxiety that threatened to clench my bowels in its grip.

"I'll come by and see you this afternoon, or maybe tomorrow, depending on how things go. Try to be at home as much as you can, okay?"

I nodded again. Steve watched me wordlessly for another moment, then turned and strode away, leaving me alone on the bench. When he was out of sight, I stood up, shoved my hands in my pockets, and started walking down the road toward home.

Chapter 10

The Journal of Gabriel Garrett:

Job Prospects

General Jacobs was in a grim mood.

He had requisitioned the administrative office in the VFW hall, and sat behind the desk in a comfortable looking leather chair, the kind with little brass studs running along the outer seam. A cup of instant coffee sat on the desk in front of him, half-empty and forgotten. He pressed a button to turn off his hand-held voice recorder, leaned back in his chair, and stared at me.

"Mr. Garrett, I don't suppose you have any interest in coming back onboard with the military, do you?"

I hesitated, surprised by the question. "It hadn't really occurred to me, General."

"Call me Phil."

"Okay, Phil."

His face lightened into a brief, tight smile before he picked up his coffee, sipped at it, and grimaced. He put it back town.

"I can't offer much in the way of pay, things being what they are. But I can offer you a field commission as a captain. We need someone to help coordinate reclamation efforts in this part of the country, and I think you'd be perfect for the job."

I stayed deliberately quiet for a few moments, holding his gaze and weighing carefully what I should say next. It was no accident that Jacobs had sprung the question on me out of nowhere—he wanted to catch me off balance. Probably thought he could fast-talk me into agreeing to his offer. Put it on the table, and make it sound like he was doing me a favor. It was a smart strategy, and it had probably worked for him with other people. But this was not my first rodeo.

"Phil, before I first came to this town, do you know what I was doing?"

His granite-colored eyes stayed steady as he shook his head.

"I was leading a small group of survivors westward, bound for Colorado. We weren't going that way to join up with the military and fight the infected, or marauders, or anything else. We were trying to find a safe place to put down our guns and live in peace. That's what we wanted."

Jacobs tilted his head at an inquisitive angle and leaned forward, crossing his arms on the desk.

"I keep hearing you say 'we' this, and 'we' that. Is that really what *you* wanted? What were you going to do, be a farmer? Raise chickens and grow potatoes? Maybe sign on with a public works crew and dig ditches? You really think any of that would be the best use of your talents?"

I smiled, and shook my head. Bum-rushing me didn't work, so now he was attempting good old-fashioned manipulation. I had to give the man credit. He was persistent.

"Aren't we getting off topic, Phil? I thought I was here to talk about the skirmish yesterday."

The old soldier picked up the voice recorder. "I have your statement right here. I'll hand it over to Captain McCray when he gets here and let him decide what to do with it."

He saw me arch an eyebrow, and understood my question.

"I'm not here to lead the fight against the thugs plaguing this town." He explained. "That's McCray's job, and I trust him to handle it. What I'm here to do is gather information, make an assessment of what this town needs, and make sure that the beancounters back in the Springs get off their asses and send it. My presence here is as much diplomatic as anything else. Command figured that showing up in person, bringing in supplies, and waving my star around would show the people here that we're serious about helping them. Hell, I got two more communities to visit before the end of the month."

"And the men you brought with you?" I asked, "What are they here for?"

He frowned, knowing I was trying to change the subject, but went on anyway. "They'll be staying behind to help you train your militia, and to help cripple the insurgency."

"Insurgency? Is that what we're calling the Legion now?"

Jacobs shrugged. "It's a term with a very specific resonance. Lets people know where the federal government stands on the issue."

"And what about those communities that don't want anything to do with the federal government? Are they insurgents now, too?"

His gaze turned to flint, and his scowl deepened. "What we're trying to do, Mr. Garrett, is prevent this country from descending any further into chaos and bloodshed. Right now, there is a gigantic power vacuum out there, and a lot of forces are vying against each other to fill it up. I don't know about you, but I'd hate to see this nation reduced to a bunch of scattered outposts constantly warring with one another over resources and territory. I would rather see the people of this nation come together to rebuild, and bring it back to something like the place it was before the Outbreak. I believe we can do it. If I didn't, I wouldn't be here. But we're going to need the right kind of leadership to make it happen. Quite frankly, Mr. Garrett, what we need is people like you."

I shook my head, and gave him a tired smile. "That was a nice speech, Phil, but you didn't answer my question. What about those communities in the Midwest and California that have told the government to stay out of their business? What's the president's plan for them?"

Jacobs was quiet for a long moment. The hardness in his stare diminished, and the lines of his face seemed to deepen.

"Diplomatic efforts are ongoing," he said. "Ambassadors have been sent to begin negotiations."

I snorted. "You know, Phil, when people start talking to me in the passive voice, and regurgitating hackneyed political buzzwords, my bullshit detector starts beeping."

His jaw twitched a few times, and he turned his eyes down from mine, suddenly finding the surface of his desk interesting. He didn't say anything.

"It's bad, isn't it?"

The general nodded. "They've held elections."

"Which ones?"

"The two biggest ones," Jacobs said. "There's a network of small, fortified city-states that stretches from Ohio to Illinois that call themselves the Midwest Alliance. They're the biggest threat, and the most hostile. Then there's the Republic of California. We don't know much about them yet."

I absorbed that for a moment, and said, "You think it's going to come down to a fight?"

"Maybe, maybe not. They haven't tried anything yet. If they do, we'll be ready, but everyone back in the Springs is hoping that it doesn't come to that."

"You think they could win if it does?"

He shook his head. "Doubtful. We have pretty significant resources ourselves, and we're actively working to get access to more. Unlike the other groups, we know where all of the doomsday stockpiles are. It's just a question of reaching them.

And both groups know that even if they do manage to win, they would take such heavy losses that it wouldn't be worth it for them to try. Not yet, at least."

"Meaning?"

"Meaning we're working against the clock. It's probably only a matter of time before they officially declare themselves as independent nations, and we need to be ready when they do."

"Which is why you're here in Hollow Rock. To garner support. Help people form militias, arm them, get them on your side. And you're doing the same kind of thing elsewhere?"

He nodded. "It's not just about territory, it's about numbers. The Midwest Alliance, all combined, is at least the equal of the loyalists in Colorado. We don't know for sure what the numbers are out in California, but we know it's a lot, and we know that they're … expanding."

"Expanding?"

"Taking over new territory. A few refugees have fled as far east as our outposts in Nevada and their reports are worrisome, to say the least."

I was about to ask him to elaborate on that when a knock sounded from the door behind me. A look of irritation swept over the general's face.

"Yes, what is it?"

The door opened a fraction, and one of Jacobs's personal guards stuck his head in the door. He was a tall man, broad-shouldered, crew-cut, and had eyes like a winter morning—blue, merciless, and cold.

"Captain McCray is here to see you, sir," he said.

"Ah, outstanding. Tell him to wait outside and I'll be with him in a minute. Thank you, Sergeant."

The soldier nodded once, and then closed the door quietly.

“Do you need anything else from me, General? I have two wounded recruits expecting me to pay them a visit today.”

He put a hand under his chin and studied me again. Someone had put a new battery in the clock on the wall, and I heard a faint ticking as it counted down the seconds. Other than my own breathing, it was the only sound in the room as I waited for him to speak.

“You never did give me an answer, Mr. Garrett.”

“Actually, I thought I made myself pretty clear.”

He frowned. “So the answer is no?”

“Correct.”

“You don’t have any interest in being an officer in the most powerful military force in the country?”

“No, I don’t.”

“You don’t care about all the good you could do, all the lives you could save, all the people you could help? You just want to be selfish, and waste your abilities scraping in the dirt, or scavenging for a living? Is that it?”

My teeth clenched and my face began to heat up. “Don’t put words in my mouth, General. I did my time, I served my country, and I gave a hell of a lot more than I ever got back. You think you know me? You think you know anything about me? What I’ve been through, and what I’ve given up?”

I leaned forward and pointed a finger in his face. “You don’t know shit. You’re just like every other dumbfuck officer I’ve ever seen. You think you have all the answers because you sit behind your desk, and fly around in your helicopter, and send men to their deaths. You think you know what’s going on out there because you read after-action reports from men whose boots were on the ground doing your fighting for you. You never stop to question the decisions you make that cost them their lives. And none of it matters to you as long as you accomplish your mission. Let me ask you something, General, when was the last time you had your ass in the grass, huh? When was the last time you fired a fucking shot in anger? When was the last time you had to pick up a rifle and fight for your life because some West Point piece of shit with delusions of grandeur told you to? When was the last time you did anything except sit on your ass and ask better men than yourself to die for you? When General? Fucking when?"

My voice rose steadily as I spoke, and by the time I finished, I was nearly yelling in his face. The door opened behind me, and the same soldier from before stepped inside.

"Is everything all right in here, sir?"

Jacobs sat perfectly still for a few heartbeats before holding up a hand. "Everything's fine, Sergeant. Please close the door."

"Yes, sir."

The door closed, and Jacobs let out a sigh as he reclined in his seat. He passed a hand over his jawline with a rasp of beard stubble. His eyes stared into a dark middle distance for a few seconds, and his façade of authority faded, leaving him looking old, tired, and rundown.

"Please don't mistake my intentions here, Mr. Garrett," he said, weariness grating in his voice. "I'm not evil, I'm not heartless, and I'm not a monster. I'm just desperate. We're stretched thin. I've got too few people trying to do too many things over too big a territory, and I need all the help I can get. I need people who can lead, and individuals with your … unique skill set are a rare thing to find. I won't press you anymore on it today, but if you reconsider—and I sincerely hope you do—come find me or Captain McCray, and we'll get things moving for you. Fair enough?"

My temper has always been a quick thing, to the point where it is almost an understatement to call me short-fused. But I have lots of fuses, and the anger I had felt a moment ago, intense as it was, left me in a rush. Jacobs should have been angry that I had insulted him, but he had taken it in stride. Probably nothing that he hadn't heard a hundred times from any number of pissed off survivors still holding a grudge. Insults didn't bother him, but my refusal to sign on and help him did. That said a lot about the man.

"Listen, I appreciate the offer, Phil. I really do. And I'm not unsympathetic to your predicament. I'm just tired. Tired of fighting, tired of killing, and tired of people looking to me for answers. I know what I am, I know what I'm capable of, and I can see why people want me working for them. The problem is, no one ever bothers to take a second to consider what *I* might want."

Jacobs nodded silently at that, stood up, and reached out a hand. "I appreciate your time, Mr. Garrett, and I want to thank you for what you did yesterday. If you were still in the service, I'd put you in for a Silver Star. That was damn fine work."

I held his stare for a few seconds, thinking about those two kids' families as they sat huddled and weeping in the funeral home. I released his hand, turned around, and walked out the door without another word.

As I left, I saw Captain McCray sitting at a small table in the main hall talking with one of the soldiers on General Jacobs's security detail. He was back to wearing nondescript fatigues, brown combat boots, and the only weapon he had on him—at first glance at least—was a military-issue Beretta M9. It was odd seeing him without his ever-present tactical vest and tricked out M-14 rifle. He looked up and nodded to me as I walked by. I acknowledged him, and left through the front door.

I paused for a moment outside the hall, blinking to allow my eyes to adjust to the light, and without being too obvious about it, looking around for witnesses. Seeing no one, I put my hands in my pockets and began walking along the sidewalk to where it led around to the service entrance in the back.

The VFW hall was a squat cinderblock structure with a large banquet room in the front, a kitchen behind that, a bar along one wall, a storeroom, and two small offices tucked into the corner. If my estimation was correct, Jacobs's office was two windows down from the edge of the building to the far right. As I rounded the corner, I saw that the ground at the rear of the hall sloped sharply downward, and that the window in question was several feet off the ground. Perfect.

A glance to my right showed me a broad, overgrown field of chest-high grass stretching off for maybe three hundred yards before terminating at a narrow road. A cluster of trees and small houses stood on the other side. I could only see their roofs, which meant that from that distance, unless they had a telescope and a ladder, there was no way they could see me.

I squatted down, kept my head below the sill of the first window, and walked along the edges of my feet until I was standing beneath the window directly behind Jacobs's chair. A conversation was already in progress, and by pressing my head close to the wall just below the bottom edge, I could make out what they were saying.

"… Riordan's on board, sir. I'll need a couple of weeks to get him ready, but we should still be able to stick to the new timetable."

A sigh. "That's the first good news I've had all day. Assuming he really is up to the task."

A short pause. I could almost see Steve nodding in his patient way. "If anyone in this town is, sir, it's him."

"Fine. You've done a good job so far, Captain. I trust you'll continue to do so. Have you taken Riordan's statement about the incident yesterday?"

Incident? Christ's sake, is that all they think of it?

"Not yet. I'm going to pay him another visit this afternoon. I was hoping you would come along and hear it for yourself."

The general's tone was impatient when he answered. "Captain, we already have several viable candidates for the program, and they all have exemplary service records. I fail to see what a civilian with no formal training would have to offer that they can't."

"You see, sir, that's the problem," Steve said. "They're all military and law-enforcement types. They stick to the strictures of their training. The situations that these new operators are going be facing are highly unconventional, and adhere not in the least to the rules and tactics that were effective for these kinds of things before the Outbreak. Riordan doesn't suffer from that handicap. As much as I hate to use this phrase, in this case it applies—he thinks outside the box. He's quick-minded, resourceful, personable, and highly adaptive to his environment. Rather than solely counting on his training, he uses whatever is around him, be it people or materials, to find clever solutions to difficult problems. Beyond that, he has a sense of presence that tends to inspire trust, and in terms of combat skills, he's on the scale of an Army Ranger with combat experience and high-level marksmanship. He might not have formal training, but his abilities are nonetheless quite remarkable."

Jacobs was quiet for a long moment. I heard a creak that told me he was leaning back in his chair. "Captain McCray, you know I lean heavily on your advice, but on this one, I must admit I have my doubts."

"Which is why I want you to be there when I speak with him," Steve said quickly. "From what the others who were there yesterday have told me, his performance under fire was impressive. And having seen him in action myself, I don't doubt the validity of their statements."

"All right, fine. I'll go with you and hear the man out. But I'm not making any promises, understood?"

"Perfectly."

There were a few seconds of silence, then a scrape of plastic on wood. "Here's Garrett's statement," Jacobs said. "Go ahead and get reports from Grabovsky and anyone else you think might know anything, and compile a report to send back to Command. Great Hawk and Marshall are working on getting generators up and running, so you should have a 3G connection available before the end of the day."

McCray said, “Secure connection?”

“As best we can manage, yes. It’ll have to do.”

“Understood, sir.” In a lower voice, he asked, “Speaking of electricity, is Command still going to be sending us a facilitator?”

“As of now, yes, but not until we deal with the insurgency here. Facilitators are too valuable to risk sending into hot zones. The sooner you take care of this so-called Free Legion, the sooner you can help these people get the lights back on.”

A few seconds pause. Again, I could almost see McCray nodding, his yellow eyes narrowed in thought.

“Sir, there’s something else you should know about. Something Grabovsky found yesterday after the skirmish.”

Jacobs said, “And what’s that?”

“The weapons that the Legion were using, the AK-47s. They all matched the descriptions of the weapons recovered in Nevada. Same manufacturer, same ammo. Near as we can tell, anyway.”

Jacobs was silent for a few seconds. “How many did you recover?”

“A lot, I don’t have an exact number yet. Grabovsky is out there with a work crew today gathering them up and collecting the corpses. Great Hawk is going out there later to see what he can find out.”

“If anybody can make some sense out of this, it’ll be the tracker,” Jacobs replied.

“Do you think this has anything to do with the ROC?” Steve said.

“Could be,” Jacobs replied. “The flotilla pulls into Humboldt Bay, secures the waterfront, offloads their ships, and a couple of months later, the ROC is suddenly a major player. Can’t be a coincidence.”

"But if they're making arms shipments to the Legion, who else are they supplying?" Steve asked.

"That's the million-dollar question, Captain. I think we both know the answer to that."

There was a creak and a rustle as one of them stood up. It was faint, so I figured it was Steve.

"One last thing, sir."

"Hmm?"

"How did things go with Garrett? I thought I heard raised voices."

Jacobs chuckled, but it was mirthless. "Once again, you get to say I told you so."

"He refused?"

"I think at one point he actually called me a dumbfuck. I'm not sure, I was too busy being scared shitless the big fucker was gonna jump over the desk and snap me like a twig before Sergeant Krymeier could do anything about it."

There was a smile in McCray's voice. "Yes, he has that effect on people."

I smirked. Nice to know I still had the old magic.

"There anything else you need, Captain? Anything you want me to have sent out to you?"

"Not right now, no. I should have everything I need for the time being."

"All right then. I'll be in meetings until about sixteen-hundred. Come by and get me after that, and we'll go see about this Riordan character."

"Will do, sir."

The door opened and shut again. I crept to the end of the building and listened as McCray's footsteps marched off toward the north side of town, growing fainter and fainter until they were out of earshot. Risking a quick peek around the corner, I saw that no one else was around, and set off toward town hall as quickly as I could without running.

Liz was going to be very interested to hear about this.

Chapter 11

Breach of Confidence

By the time Steve returned with General Jacobs that afternoon, my hangover had mostly faded.

Not all the way, but enough that I could eat without throwing up, and I could move my head without a hammer pounding away at the interior of my skull. Mike's hooch was quality stuff, but it would be a long time before I let myself drink that much of it again.

Feeling less shaky, I spent the latter part of the day cleaning and working on small projects around the house until, at about a quarter after four, a pair of footsteps stopped at the front door. I opened it before Steve had a chance to knock, and he stood startled for a moment with his knuckles poised in the air.

"Come on in, gentlemen." I made a gesture with my arm, waited as they stepped by, and shut the door behind them.

"Have a seat," I said. "I'll be right with you."

While the two soldiers made themselves comfortable on the couch, I put a kettle on the stove and popped two more painkillers. It wouldn't do to spend the conversation with teeth my gritted and wincing every time I turned my head. I had an idea where this meeting was about to go, and it would behoove me to stay sharp.

"Here you go fellas." I placed a large silver try on the coffee table.

"Is that real sugar?" Steve asked.

"Yep." I smirked. "Scavenging is risky business, but for the brave, the rewards are many."

I poured a cup for each of the men, one for myself, and sat back in my chair. Steve was hesitant as he spooned a small amount of sugar into his cup, as though not quite sure how much propriety allowed him to take.

"Take all you want," I said, gesturing to the small bowl. "I've got plenty."

Steve glanced at me. "You know how much this stuff is worth, right?"

I nodded.

"Well, hell," Jacobs chimed in. "If you're offering, I'm not too proud to take it. I can't remember the last time I had sugar."

They dug in again, more generously this time, and practically moaned as they sipped the hot tea.

"My God," Steve said. "You know, you go so long without having this stuff, you forget how good it is. Can't believe I ever took it for granted."

Jacobs chuckled. "I find myself feeling that way about a great many things these days."

"Amen to that," I said.

We were quiet for a while after that, to the point where it began to grow awkward. Finally, Steve cleared his throat and set his cup down on the table.

"I appreciate the hospitality, but we do have some business to take care of this afternoon." He reached into a pocket, took out a digital recorder and pressed a button on it. "Test, test." He clicked another button, played his voice back, then cleared it and handed it to me.

"We need to get a statement from you about what happened yesterday. I'm putting together a report to send back to Central Command, and hopefully if we can show them how bad things are getting out here, we can convince them to send us more troops."

"That would be nice," I said.

"Anything you can remember will help us, Eric, anything at all. Just start from the beginning, and tell us as much as you can remember."

I tapped my fingers on the recorder, hesitating. "You know, everything happened really fast, it's kind of a blur. I'm not sure if I can remember all of it."

"Don't worry about it. Just do the best you can. I'll ask questions along the way to help jog your memory."

I took a deep breath and turned on the recorder. It took me the better part of an hour to tell all of it, and when I was done, a few things stood out, and one minor mystery was solved.

When I expressed concern over the fact that the Legion had known what direction the Chinook was coming from, Steve provided a simple explanation: The chopper had come in on the exact same vector the crew had used the day before. Anybody with a pair of eyes and a sense of direction could have found that path and set a trap on it. I was a little embarrassed that I hadn't thought of that myself, but it was a lesson learned. General Jacobs said he would make sure the aircrews didn't repeat that mistake.

Another point of significance was the weapons the Legion used during the firefight. The M-16s could have been scavenged from any number of places, but the AK-47s were a mystery. Civilian versions were cheap and fairly abundant before the Outbreak, but the ones the Legion used had fully automatic capability—not something that would have been available in large numbers. I watched the general while I talked about it, and he grew strangely pensive.

"Something on your mind, Phil?" I asked.

He opened his mouth, hesitated, closed it, and then drummed his fingers on his knee for a few seconds while deciding what to say. "I don't want to go spreading ridiculous rumors, but I've read a few reports from our outposts out west that have me thinking …"

Steve and I watched him while he ruminated, and finally he said, "There's a large group of separatists out in California and Oregon who, according to what our scouts tell us, all seem to be armed with an inordinately large number of AK-47s, most likely of Chinese manufacture. I can't help but wonder if the two things might not be related."

Steve and I exchanged a glance and were both still while we pondered that.

"Well, either way," Steve said, "it doesn't change what we have to do. We know what they're armed with now, and we can plan accordingly. That's the important thing. I'll talk to Grayson Morrow tonight and see if he knows anything about it."

Jacobs conceded the point with a nod and turned his attention back my way. "Is there anything else you can think of that might be important? Anything at all?"

I thought hard for a moment, but other than what I had already gone over, I couldn't come up with anything. "No, I'm afraid not. If I think of anything, I'll write it down and let you know."

Jacobs's gunmetal eyes stared at me appraisingly, and I could almost hear the gears turning over in his head. I felt uneasiness bloom in the pit of my stomach, perhaps something akin to what a prized heifer might feel like on the block at a cattle auction. As he watched me, I noticed a scar above one of his eyes and suddenly remembered where I recognized him from.

Back during the Outbreak, I had watched news footage of an Army unit retreating from Dalton, Georgia. They had crossed paths with a convoy from the Tennessee National Guard en route to reinforce them. General Jacobs had been a colonel then, and he'd ordered the officer of the Guard troops to turn around and head for another fallback position. Dalton had been overrun, and there was no saving it. At the time, Jacobs had worn a bandage over one eye. Whatever caused the injury, it had left the scar I was looking at.

Before I could say anything, Jacobs began speaking again. "Let me take a second here and make sure I have all of this straight." He began counting off on his fingers. "You have no background in law enforcement, no military experience, and no formal training. Yet somehow you managed to survive a firefight where you were woefully outnumbered, you succeeded in eliminating no less than twenty-five enemy combatants, made shots that a veteran sniper would have had trouble with, and helped Mr. Garrett cover your retreat under heavy fire. Afterward, you engaged and destroyed no less than a hundred infected and helped make sure that the supplies we nearly lost to the insurgents were recovered with minimal damage. Does that about cover it?"

I blinked a couple of times and shrugged. "Um … yeah. I guess it does."

Jacobs smiled. "More specifically, when the insurgent leaders sent several fire teams to your position to take you out, you single-handedly punched every one of the sons-of-bitches' tickets, and did so with verve and assurance."

Well, when you put it that way …

"That's true, except for the verve and assurance part. If memory serves me, I was scared shitless."

Jacobs laughed. "And where, might I ask, did you learn how to fight like that?"

"Gabriel," I replied simply. "The guy taught me everything I know."

"The same Gabriel, as in Gabriel Garrett, that is currently training the volunteer militia?"

I nodded.

“Hmm.” He nodded slowly. “Well, if your performance in the heat of combat is any indication, I’d say those recruits are in good hands.”

“I agree with you on that, with one caveat: I’ve known Gabe for a long time.”

The pleased expression on the general’s face began to fade around the edges. “Meaning?”

“Meaning I had personalized instruction from the man on a daily basis for over two years, and sporadically for over five years before that. That’s a long time, General. The militia is coming along well, but Gabe only has three more months to work with them, and they aren’t going to get the same one-on-one attention that I did. You shouldn’t expect them to do the same things I can do when they graduate. They might get there eventually, but it’s going to take time.”

Jacobs’s expression sobered, and he nodded. “That’s a good point. Important. I’ll be sure to remember that.”

The way he said it seemed odd to me, and I studied him for a moment trying to figure out why. It was as though he wasn’t agreeing with me, but rather with some internal dialogue. If I had to put money on it, I would have said he looked like he had been debating something for a while and had finally come to a decision.

“Well,” he said, standing up. “I appreciate your time, Eric. And I can’t tell you how grateful I am for everything you did yesterday. I told your friend Gabriel earlier today that if he were still in the service, I’d put him in for a Silver Star. All things considered, I believe I’d have to add your name to the request as well.”

I had no idea what a Silver Star was, but it sounded important. “Uh, thanks, General. That’s … very nice of you.”

He chuckled and shook his head at me, then turned to Steve. “Captain McCray, do you have everything you need?”

“Yes, sir, I’m all set.”

I stood up and shook both of their hands, starting with the general. "Well, thanks for stopping by, guys. If you need anything else from me, let me know. I'll be around."

"I'll probably be by tomorrow," Steve said, his mood growing more casual. "You gonna be around at say, ten-thirty, eleven-ish?"

"Yeah, I'll be around then."

"Great. I'll see you tomorrow."

I waved to them as they left and then shut the door behind them. Through the living room window, I watched them walk back toward the VFW hall, talking back and forth as they went.

I thought again about General Jacobs's odd behavior, his strangely distant demeanor at the end of our conversation, and wondered what it might portend for the mission that lay ahead of me. I thought about Steve's plan to have me infiltrate the Legion and wondered how much Jacobs would be involved when the mission was a go, when I was finally knee-deep in the proverbial shit. I thought about Allison and how she would react when I told her I would be leaving, and that I wasn't sure how long it would be before I came back. If at all.

Finally, I thought about Grayson Morrow, and how important he was going to be to all of this, assuming the information he gave us was correct. For both of our sakes, I hoped that it was.

The two soldiers soon wandered out of sight, and as I stood there thinking, the powder blue of the afternoon sky began to darken to charcoal in the east and burnished orange in the west. A familiar silhouette emerged as it turned the corner onto my street and began walking up the gentle hill, striding forward with purpose and swinging big, meaty hands at his sides. I grabbed my coat and set out on an intercept course.

*****

“So what did the mayor have to say about all that?” I asked.

Gabe set a mug of Earl Grey on the kitchen table in front of me and settled back into his chair. “Damnedest thing.” He brought up his cup and blew a puff of steam from the top. “She already knew.”

My eyebrows went up. “She told you that?”

“Not in so many words, but her body language gave it away.”

I blinked a few times and looked down, feeling heat begin to rise in my face. If General Jacobs wanted to keep secrets from me, then in his case, I could understand that. He bore a great deal of responsibility and had access to a tremendous amount of information. For the sake of the men under his command, he had a responsibility to be careful with that knowledge, to keep it guarded.

But for Steve to hide things from me, especially plans that involved me directly, that was a different matter entirely. We had been through some serious shit, the two of us, and I had thought I could trust him. In light of what Gabe had just told me, I was beginning to have my doubts about that. Worse, I couldn’t mention anything about it because if I did, they would know Gabe had spied on them. This was going to put a strain on our future dealings.

“Jacobs mentioned something about separatists out west when we were talking earlier,” I said. “He must have been referring to the Republic of California. He didn’t say anything about those other groups though. The Midwest Alliance, or the flotilla. You think that factors into their plans for me somehow?”

“Could be.” Gabe shrugged. “No way to know for sure.”

I leaned back and sighed. “I guess it really doesn’t change anything. The Legion is still out there, and before we worry about anything else, we have to take care of that problem first."

Gabe nodded and said, "What concerns me right now is them using you to infiltrate the Legion. Which, by the way." He pointed a large finger at me. "I still think is a fucking stupid idea. If you're determined to go through with that foolishness, I'll do what I can to help, but Eric, believe me when I tell you this: Don't trust McCray any farther that you can throw him. I know you think he's your friend, but you need to remember that his first loyalty is to the Army. Period. Anything, and *anyone* else, is expendable."

I mock glared at him and said, "You know Gabe, I'm sure glad I have you around. No way would I have ever figured that out on my own. Gosh, you're such a genius."

Gabe shot me a scowl that said, *smartass*, then took another sip of his tea.

"What about that other thing they mentioned, the facilitator?" I asked. "You have any idea what that might be?"

Gabe stared into the distance for a few seconds, thinking, and said, "I'm not sure. But what they said about getting the lights back on is definitely interesting. I'd ask them more about it, but …" He shrugged.

"Then they would know you were spying on them." I sighed and ran a hand through my hair as I leaned forward on the table. "Did you happen to ask the mayor about that special project Steve wants to recruit me for? I'm assuming it's something beyond his plans to destroy the Legion."

Gabe shook his head. "She said she didn't know anything about it, but I don't think she was telling the whole truth. I've spent enough time with her lately that I can tell when she's not being honest with me."

I narrowed my eyes at him, confused. "Spent enough time with her? I thought you two only spoke once or twice a week?"

He went still. His cup stopped halfway to his mouth, and his eyes grew wide at the edges as though realizing he'd said too much. Dark red color began to creep up into his cheeks, and he looked down quickly to cover it up.

My jaw didn't quite hit the floor, but it was a near thing.

"You have got to be kidding me," I said.

Gabe remained silent.

"You and the mayor? No fucking way."

More silence.

It took maybe a full minute for the shock to wear off, and then I felt a broad grin spread across my face. "Gabe, that's … that's great, man."

He glanced up, brow furrowed. "Really?"

"Yes, really. Are you kidding me? Way to go man, nicely done." I reached across the table and slapped him on the shoulder hard enough to rock him over to one side.

"You don't think it's a bad idea?"

I laughed, incredulous. "A bad idea? Shit, dude, this might just be the best idea you've ever had. I'm fucking thrilled for you. How long has it been, like three, four years or something like that?"

He frowned at me, but it was swimming upstream against a grin. "It hasn't been that long."

I held up my hands. "Whatever, man, I'm just glad you're finally getting some action. God knows it took you long enough. Now that you're getting laid on the regular, will you stop acting so damn grouchy all the time?"

His punch was quick, but I was already scooting back when he threw it at my shoulder, and I leaned back just out of range.

"I assume I can trust you to keep this between us?" he said, not quite hiding his smile.

"Why? What are you hiding it for? You should be proud, shacking up with a hottie like Mayor Stone. Hell, I would be."

"It's not that," he said, his humor fading. "If people around town find out, it … could make things difficult for Elizabeth."

I raised my chin in understanding. "Ahhh. Got it. I can see how that might be perceived as a conflict of interest."

"Just keep your mouth shut about it, okay? I've got enough problems."

"Yeah, except for being lonely. Looks like you've got that one *nailed*."

He threw a spoon at my head, and I just barely managed to duck it. Judging by the whistling sound it made as it passed, I'm pretty sure it would have hurt like a bastard if it had hit me. Figuring that I should get well out of arm's reach before pushing my luck any further, I stood up and began to make my way toward the front door.

"Look man, we'll talk more about this later. I have to get some food over to the clinic for Allison. You need anything from the general store while I'm there?"

He shook his head. "No, I just need you out of here, you annoying bastard."

"Come on man, don't be like that," I said, as I slipped on my coat. "I told you, I'm happy for you."

"Thanks." He didn't look up.

I got halfway out the door before turning around and leaning my head back inside.

"Hey, Gabe?"

"What?'

"I've got a meeting with the mayor tomorrow to discuss allocating resources for improvements to the outer perimeter. It would help me out a lot if you could make sure she's in a good mood. You know, put in a little extra special performance for me."

I'm not sure what Gabe threw at me—I ducked out too fast to see it—but it hit the door hard enough to rattle it on its hinges. I jumped off the porch, giggled like an idiot, and ran off for home.

Chapter 12

The Journal of Gabriel Garrett:

Citizen Soldiers

On the morning that the militia's furlough was set to expire, I took my time getting ready for work.

Maybe it was worry over the events transpiring in the wider world. Maybe I was reading the writing on the wall, and seeing all the ways I could get sucked into the trouble brewing on the horizon. Maybe I was fighting my growing feelings for Liz, and trying to reconcile that against the remnants of my infatuation with Sarah. Maybe I was just scared. Could have been a lot of things. But the bottom line? I did not want to report for duty that morning. Not one bit.

Truth be told, I was afraid I would show up to an empty parade ground. I sincerely doubted that any of the recruits would want to continue with training after getting their first taste of combat. And I couldn't make them, no one could. It was a volunteer militia. The town wasn't paying them, or even granting them any special privileges. They could quit anytime they wanted.

So I took my time. I got up early, long before the sun was up—not that I had gotten any sleep the night before. I made some shitty instant coffee, warmed an iron on the stove, and used it to press my fatigues. Polished my boots. Ate breakfast. Sharpened the Bowie knife my dad left me after he died. Not that it needed it; I could have shaved with the thing if I'd wanted to. But there was something comforting about it, the smooth stag-horn handle, and the rasp of steel over stone. It reminded me of my father's voice. Rough, but steady. When I sharpened that big knife, I felt like he was there with me. Solid rock of a man that he had been.

I often wondered what he would have thought of me, of how I had turned out. Would he be proud? Disappointed? Ashamed? How would he feel about the things I'd done, the people I had killed? I would never know. Not in this life, at least.

Mom had been proud of me, once. That much I knew. She had cried the day I left for basic training. I was seventeen then, having graduated high school a year early. I had to get her permission to enlist.

Mom had cried, and held me, and told me to be careful and stay out of trouble. I held her back, careful not to squeeze too hard, and told her I would. Told her I'd write to her, and call her as soon as I had the chance. We hadn't known it then, but that was the last time I would see her alive. The cancer had already gotten ahold of her. She was riddled with it but didn't know. Her symptoms had been mild. Flulike. No big deal, nothing worth paying a doctor for.

Until one day, she collapsed at work. She had her diagnosis within a week. Pancreatic cancer. Terminal. Nothing they could do.

I put in for emergency leave, and the Corps granted it, but not soon enough. She was dead before my plane landed in Louisville. As soon as I stepped out of the gate and saw my uncle's face, I knew. He had broken down on the spot. He kept saying how sorry he was, and I kept telling him it wasn't his fault. It wasn't anybody's fault. Still, he had cried and cried. A tired, broken-down old man, holding on to the last person he had left in the world.

Uncle Aaron died himself a few years later. The doctors said it was a heart attack. It took him down quick. He probably didn't know what hit him.

I never believed that.

He'd seen too much pain in his life. First he lost his wife, then his brother, then his sister-in-law who had lived with him for ten years, whose son he had helped to raise. I think it was just too much for the old man. I think death is a greedy, hungry thing, and when people lose their will to live, it comes swiftly. Life held only pain for Uncle Aaron, and I think he was ready to be done with it.

As I thought of these things, I realized that the sun was creeping over the horizon, and that my hands had gone still. The knife and the whetstone lay forgotten in my lap. I put them away, tugged on my boots, and walked down the road to face the music.

*****

I kept my head down on the walk to the camp. Watched the ground pass between my feet. Dirt, and gravel, and mud from the morning dew. I thought about those two soldiers I had lost, and the desolation on their families' faces when Allison delivered the bad news. As I walked, the mud crept up the sides of my boots and ruined the polish I had put on them that morning.

I was fifty yards into the clearing before I looked up. I'd expected to be greeted with the sight of an empty field. Not the Grinder anymore, just a field. It was only the Grinder if there were people there to grind on it. Instead, when I looked up, what I saw stopped me in my tracks.

The first thing I noticed was the platform. Grabovsky was standing on it, as well as the other drill instructors, Cohen and Wilkins. The two navy SEALs that had flown in with General Jacobs were there as well. Great Hawk and Marshall. In their black fatigues, they were a marked contrast to the other three men. In front of them, standing in neatly ordered ranks, was the militia.

I did a quick head count, length times width. They were all there, all the surviving members, less the two whose injuries prevented them from returning. For a moment, all I could do was stand and stare. I had seen things before that had hit me in a profound way, that made me step back and reassess my lack of faith in the human race. But never had anything struck so sharp of a chord. Never had any other sight made my throat tighten, and my chest burn, and my legs go shaky. There, standing in that field at parade rest, was my sense of purpose. My contribution to society. Something I was working to build, something of lasting importance. Something that the world, or at least a small part of it, could remember me by. Something good, and decent, and right, in a lifetime of mistakes.

I took a deep breath, got ahold of myself, and marched up to the platform. I was glad the recruits were required to be silent while in ranks. If any of them had spoken to me, offered any small words of encouragement, I might not have held it together. God, would that have been embarrassing.

I walked up the three wooden steps and stopped in front of Grabovsky. He saluted, even though I wasn't technically an officer, and I saluted back.

"All present and accounted for?" I asked, even though I already knew the answer.

"All present and accounted for."

I nodded, and Grabovsky moved back with the other instructors. Stepping to the edge of the small stage, I addressed the recruits.

"I know it must have been difficult for all of you to return to training. I know how tough it is, losing friends. It's a danger we face every day as warriors. But as proud as I am to see you here today, and as much of an honor as it is to serve with you, I still have a job to do. Your training is not complete. You've all seen combat now, and you all fought bravely, but you still have a long way to go. Now is not the time for me to take it easy on you. Now is not the time to slack off. If anything, we have to train harder. Push ourselves. Do whatever it takes to get ready for the fight ahead of us. That's what I'm here to do. I think you all understand that now. Am I right?"

They responded in unison. A single, strident voice, "YES, SIR!"

I had to grit my teeth to keep from tearing up. "Very well."

I turned back to Grabovsky. "Have the squad leaders form their squads and report to the mess hall. Do a quick briefing and then lay out the plan of the day. We'll introduce the new instructors shortly. They're all yours, Sergeant."

Grabovsky took my place and began cracking off orders. The recruits fell out, organized into squads, and set off for the mess hall. The other four men, Cohen, Wilkins, and the two SEALs, stayed behind. Judging by the looks on their faces, we had much to discuss.

*****

Marcus Cohen and Curtis Wilkins are my workhorses.

They're steady, dependable, efficient, and I wouldn't trade them for all the thoroughbreds in the world. Grabovsky and I handled the lion's share of the recruits' combat training, but there was a great deal more that went into running the militia. That's where Cohen and Wilkins came in—the administrative stuff. They made sure that the recruits got their meals, their equipment, and their medical evaluations. They kept track of the militia's personnel records, our ammunition inventory, made sure all the weapons were accounted for after firing exercises, and about a hundred other dull, monotonous jobs that Grabovsky and I simply did not have time for. And they did it all without complaint.

As the last recruits disappeared inside the mess hall, Cohen held out a hand to me and smiled. He was a tall, rangy kid with dark hair, a square jaw, straight teeth and hazel eyes. The kind of good looks that had half the single women in Hollow

Rock setting their sights on making an honest man out of him. Lucky bastard.

He had been an infantryman in the Marines before the Outbreak. Did a tour in Afghanistan, saw action there, and had the scars to prove it. He had been home on leave when the Outbreak struck, and like many members of the armed services when the call had come down to report for duty, he had ignored it. He'd stayed in Hollow Rock to look after his family. Considering how things had turned out, I didn't blame him, and I had made sure he knew as much.

Now, even though he still wore his MARPATs and carried an M-4, he only helped out with the militia part-time. (If you can call thirty to forty hours a week part-time.) He was also a full-time sheriff's deputy, and one of the few people entrusted with maintaining law and order in Hollow Rock.

"Good to see you again, Gabe," he said. "Glad to have you back."

"Back?" I said. "What do you mean, back? The militia's been on furlough since Sunday."

"Yeah, but we haven't," Wilkins chimed in.

"Huh?" was my eloquent response.

He smiled, his white teeth contrasting with his skin, so black it was almost blue. He was tall like Cohen, but with a heavier build. Neither man was quite as tall as me. But then again, few people are.

Wilkins had come to Hollow Rock by way of Fort Bragg. When Steve got his captain's bars, both he and Grabovsky had been placed under his command. The three Green Berets later traveled to Tennessee to investigate reports of a large community of survivors, and although they were still technically under the authority of Central Command, they had pretty much gone native.

"We've been doing inventory on everything the Chinook brought in," he said. "Stocking up on supplies, getting everything ready for training to pick back up, that kinda thing. Got a lot of nice stuff, man. Rifles, SAWs, grenade launchers, mortars, LAWs, even a few Carl Gustavs. Not to mention uniforms, ammo, boots, radios, portable solar panels, all kinds of shit."

He handed me a three-ring binder with a report inside. "S'all in there, man. Everything we got."

I flipped through it, reading the columns and rows detailing every molecule of equipment the militia had at its disposal. They must have been at it for the last two days, at least. I never would have been able to get all this done on my own, and having this list at hand would make my life a lot easier.

"We also updated all the personnel records," Cohen added. "Notated their unit citations and individual awards. Took the liberty of issuing uniforms and other gear. Figured it would save everybody time if we went ahead and knocked it out."

I closed the binder and smiled at the two men.

Workhorses.

"Damn fine work, fellas. Don't know what I'd do without you."

Cohen snorted. "Fall the fuck apart, that's what you'd do."

I let that one go, and turned to the two black-clad SEALs.

"Gabriel Garrett, nice to meet you." I held out a hand. The shorter of the two men shook it.

"Gunner's Mate First Class Wayne Marshall," he said, the lack of R's in his pronunciation practically screaming Massachusetts. "The big guy back there is Boatswain's Mate First Class Lincoln Great Hawk. But his friends just call him the Mad Apache."

The tall, dark-skinned man swiveled his obsidian eyes to Marshall disapprovingly for a moment, and then went back to staring blankly at me. His face looked like it was carved out of mahogany, stark and striking, with a heavy brow, high, flat cheekbones, and a large, blade-shaped nose. I figured him for about six-foot-three and maybe a solid two-thirty.

"I am *Mashgalénde*," he said. "The Spanish called us *Mescaleros*. You ignorant whites call many nations the Apache, as if we are all the same. We are not."

Marshall nodded, and hooked a thumb toward Great Hawk. "You'll get used to the noble savage here. He grows on you. Kind of like nail fungus."

I decided to get the conversation moving. "Is there anything we need to discuss before we introduce you to the militia?"

"The only one of us you need to introduce is me," Marshall said. "Great Hawk doesn't do training. He's just here to kill people and blow things up. I'll be the one helping out with the militia."

I looked at Great Hawk and studied him for a moment. He stared back, his face an impassive mask. We needed to have a talk, the two of us. But I let it go for the moment, turning back to Marshall.

"So you're not here to help us fight the Legion?"

"Officially, no. But my orders have this wonderful way of changing every five minutes, and the next thing I know I'm ass-deep in fucking alligators. So I wouldn't rule it out."

"But for right now, you're here in a support capacity. Is that right?"

"For right now, yeah."

"How much training experience do you have?" The last thing I needed was this guy undoing all my hard work.

"I trained two other militias in the past eight months. One out in Nevada, and another up north of here in Kentucky. Just finished with that last one about three weeks ago, then got orders down here."

I nodded. "Fair enough. Anything else before you get started? You have lodging, food, everything you need?"

“Already took care of it,” Cohen said from behind me.

Marshall nodded in agreement. “Yeah, your guys here have been great. We’re good to go.”

“All right then.” I turned to my two instructors. “I’ll leave the introductions in your capable hands.”

Marshall left with Cohen and Wilkins, headed toward the mess hall. Great Hawk stayed behind, still staring at me.

“Is there something you need?” I asked once the other three were out of earshot.

“I need you to brief me on the situation here in Hollow Rock,” he replied.

“Nobody filled you in on the way out here?”

He shook his head. “Only in general terms. You have fought the enemy. You have looked into his face. I need to know what you have seen.”

There was a steadiness to him as he spoke, but also a kind of dangerous energy. Like a mountain lion perched on a rock, warming itself in the sun. His claws might be sheathed, but they were still there. Still deadly.

I motioned toward the instructors’ barracks. “Let’s step inside. I’ll tell you whatever you want to know.”

He gave a single nod and turned to step down from the podium. On his lower back, he carried a knife in a simple, hand-tooled rawhide sheath. The weapon had a leather grip, a brass finger-guard, and a turquoise ring set near the pommel. It looked old, the opening of the sheath frayed from frequent use. I remembered hearing somewhere that the Apache were renowned for their skill with knives. Supposedly, the ancient tribe had produced some of the best knife-fighters in the world.

It occurred to me that I might want to tread carefully around Lincoln Great Hawk.

*****

I filled him in on everything I knew, starting with the firefight against Ronnie Kilpatrick and his band of traitors, and ending with the previous week's skirmish against the larger Legion force. He stayed mostly silent while I spoke, asking few questions. His only reaction was to tilt his head back an inch or two when I mentioned that many of the raiders had been armed with AK-47s. Other than that, he was as still as a statue.

I leaned back in my chair when I had finished, and crossed my arms over my chest, waiting for him to respond. He kept me waiting a long time, long enough that I started to wonder if he was going to speak at all. I got the feeling that Apache patience operated on a scale of geological proportions—far in excess of what most white men could manage.

Finally, he said, "These men who call themselves the Free Legion; they are better trained and better armed than most of the thieves and murderers I have fought. Most of those were slow and weak. Stupid, like sheep. These may actually test me before I kill them."

He said it like it was the sunrise, or the tides. I felt a chill go down my back.

"Well, our first order of business is to find them. You and Grabovsky have any luck searching the battlefield?"

"Tracks. Many of them, leading in all directions. Too many to follow. Then there is the matter of their weapons. I have seen rifles like the ones the Legion used before. They are Chinese-made. Everywhere I go, where there are people fighting the government, I find these rifles. The symbols are all the same. They were all made at the same factory."

"You can read Chinese?"

The sides of his mouth titled slightly upward, and his shoulders hitched in what might have been a laugh. "No. But there are people in Colorado Springs who can."

I nodded. "Right. Well, what do you make of it? Where do you think these rifles are coming from?"

"China, most likely."

I frowned at him. "What I mean, is how did the Legion get their hands on them?"

"Either someone gave the rifles to them, or they traded for them."

This was starting to get on my nerves. "I realize that, thank you. I'm talking about what it means in the bigger picture. What does it have to do with the forces aligning against the federal government?"

The Apache shifted in his seat, just barely. "This is what I think: There are people who have these guns, and they are giving them to the enemy of their enemy. Who these people are, I do not know. Perhaps General Jacobs knows. If he does, he has not shared that knowledge with me. Regardless, it does not change the fate of the Free Legion. It just means that they may put up a fight before I send them to their ancestors."

I met his eyes for a long instant, and I could see that he meant every word of it. It wasn't bravado, or even confidence. That would imply the possibility of failure, of an outcome other than what he expected it to be. What I saw staring at me from across my desk was certainty. Absolute, immovable certainty. Lincoln Great Hawk was not a man who bragged about what he was going to do. He simply stated the facts.

"On that account," I said, "you and I are in agreement."

We were both silent after that, thinking our own thoughts. I stood up to leave, and Great Hawk stood up with me.

"I have heard what the militia says about you, Gabriel Garrett."

I raised an eyebrow at him. "Really? What did they say?"

"They said you are like a ghost. Like a nightmare that kills from out of nowhere. That you never miss. I thought they were all liars until Grabovsky told me the same thing. I know him to be a man of truth. He would not have lied to me."

"I don't know about that. Soldiers have a tendency to embellish."

"Not Grabovsky," he said flatly. "He speaks the truth, and there is no bragging in him. That is why I listen to him, and ignore others."

"How do you know Grabovsky, exactly?"

"We worked together on a mission in Iraq. Long ago, before the Outbreak. I was happy to find out that he was still alive and serving here in Tennessee."

I stared at him for a few seconds and thought about how small of a world we lived in. He stared back with glacial patience, giving me time to gather my thoughts.

"Why are you telling me this?"

"Because I may ask you for your help. Because you fight like one of us."

"One of us who?"

"The *Mashgalénde*. The people who are close to the mountains."

"You mean the Apache?"

He smiled then, showing his white teeth, and a pair of longer-than-normal incisors. It was … eerie. "Whatever suits you."

The smile slowly disappeared, the sharp teeth hidden again behind the wooden mask of his face. I blinked a few times to clear the image and opened the door.

"If you need me, you know where to look," I said.

He nodded and walked out the door without another word, turning southward back toward town. I watched him go for a while, then shut the door and sat back down at my desk. The room seemed lighter without the big Apache in it. Like a shroud had been lifted, and the air was easier to breath.

"Well, that was strange," I muttered to myself.

Shaking off the uneasy tension, I got up and made my way toward the mess hall. If Great Hawk needed my help, I would give it. But for the time being, I had to focus on training my recruits. There was plenty of grief on the road ahead of me, and I didn't feel like borrowing any from tomorrow. As my mother used to quote me, sufficient unto the day is the evil thereof.

Chapter 13

The Subtle Art of Conveyance

Allison Laroux, M.D. is, for the most part, a gentle woman.

At least until you piss her off.

When that happens, her temper comes boiling to the surface, and when it does, it is a hell of a thing.

A few days after I talked to Gabe, Allison and I went for a stroll along the walkway that connects all the guard towers. The evening started out amiably enough. We held hands and talked about little things, like how cold the weather was getting, how encouraging it was that there were so many pregnant women in town, what was going on with all the single folks, who was sleeping with whom, that kind of thing. We had fallen into a comfortable silence, both of us smiling and watching the sunset, when I had to go and ruin things by bringing up my mission against the Legion, and when I would be leaving.

I had practiced this conversation and, at least from my perspective, it boiled down to a series of salient points:

Where am I going?

To infiltrate the Legion and spy on them.

How long will I be gone?

I don't know. As long as it takes.

How am I going to accomplish this without getting myself killed?

I can't talk about that.

Am I out of my goddamned mind?

It is a possibility.

I should have prepared better, and maybe solicited a little advice from my friends because, to put it mildly, things did not go well. In fact, I'm fairly certain that if she had been strong enough, my petite girlfriend would have lifted me bodily, hurled me over the wall into a ditch full of sharpened stakes, and saved the Legion the trouble of wasting ammunition on me.

And that was *before* she started yelling at me.

Long story short, she kicked me out of the house and refused to talk to me for a week.

You might have thought, with Gabe being my oldest and best friend, that when I asked if I could crash in my old room for a few days, he might have offered a little sympathy. You know, cut an old buddy some slack.

You would be wrong.

Instead, I endured jibes, barbs, thinly veiled sarcasm, and Gabe snapping his hand forward in a whipping motion and making an annoying *wha-pssshhh, wha-pssshhh* sound every time he asked if Allison had agreed to talk to me yet. All I could muster in response was an irate glare and the extension of my middle finger.

He was not deterred.

As bad as that was, waking up alone in my bed every morning without Allison there was even worse. I missed being able to reach out and touch her hair, or wrap an arm around her and pull her close. I missed her warmth, her smell, and the softness of her skin. I missed talking to her, laughing with her, and seeing her smile at my stupid jokes. And yes, I missed making love to her, but that wasn't the most pressing thing on my mind.

What bothered me most was that I didn't know for sure if she would ever get over it. Time was growing short, plans were moving forward, and the current of events was sweeping me inexorably along. What would happen if I had to leave before we had a chance to patch things up? I couldn't stand the thought that if something went wrong, I would leave this world knowing that Allison, the only woman I had ever loved, thought badly of me.

It didn't take Gabe long to recognize that my mental state was deteriorating rapidly. I wasn't eating. I hardly slept. My frame grew gaunt, the hollows under my eyes deepened, and no amount of levity on his part could get a rise out of me. Finally, he agreed to have Liz talk to Allison for me to see what she could do to help. (Mayor Stone and I got to know each other during that time, and she insisted on first-name status.)

As it turned out, Allison wasn't doing so well herself. Liz gave me very specific instructions, reminded me that Allison was a good friend of hers, and laid out the consequences for failure to comply. Not wanting to add any more names to the list of formidable people pissed off at me, I swallowed my pride, screwed up my courage, and did as I was told.

I went on a short expedition to the greenhouses on the south side of town and, after paying an exorbitant sum of tea and sugar in exchange for a dozen roses, I left a bouquet on Allison's front porch along with a handwritten note:

Allison,

I get it.

I understand why you're mad at me, I really do.

I walk into your life, I let you care about me, and the next thing you know, I'm about to leave on some dangerous, stupid assignment that is as likely to get me killed as it is to succeed.

I'm not asking you to forgive me, all I'm asking is that you try and understand why I am doing this. It's not just for the Army, or for the people of this town, or even for retribution against the Legion for everything that they have done to us.

I'm doing this for you. Because I love you, and I want you to have a safe place to live. Giving you that is worth fighting for, and if it comes down to it, worth giving my life for.

Even if I don't get to spend it with you, I want to make sure that you have a future.

I miss you.

I'm sorry.

E.

The next morning, when I got up to leave for training, Allison was waiting for me on the front-porch swing. When I froze in place, she looked up at me with her soft brown eyes—eyes that looked nearly as red, haggard, and exhausted as mine—and patted the seat next to her. I sat down slowly, not daring to make a sound for fear that I might scare her off.

"You're an asshole, you know that, right?" she said, softly.

The sun rising over her shoulder shone through her eyes, her pupils isolated tiny and clear in the golden light. The tightness in my chest became sharp, like fabric stretching around the tip of a knife. I looked down at her hands, and saw that her skin was dry and cracked. Probably from all the hand washing she had to do at the clinic. I wanted to reach out to her, but the timing didn't quite feel right.

"I have been told that, once or twice," I said.

Her lips turned upward, ever so slightly. "You know, it occurred to me this morning that I hardly know anything about you."

"What do you want to know?"

"It also occurred to me," she said, as if I hadn't spoken, "that you don't know much about me."

I shook my head. "I know everything I need to know about you, Allison."

She turned her shoulders to look at me fully. "Like what?"

"You're kind. And strong, and caring, and you deal with situations that would send most people running for the hills like they're no big deal. You have courage, and grace, and you're about ten times smarter than I could ever hope to be. I don't know what you've done in your life, or what kind of person you were before the Outbreak and, to be bluntly honest, Allison, I don't care. You're here now, you're the best woman I've ever known, and all I want is for you to love me half as much as I love you. Without that, not a whole lot else matters to me anymore."

Allison's hand came up to my chin, and when she lifted my face with one delicate finger, I saw that her cheeks were gaunt, her hair was a mess, and the cold, dry air had carved a thousand miniscule fractures deep into the pale flesh of her lips. She wore no makeup, her clothes were rumpled and threadbare, and she looked painfully thin under her oversize jacket. But when she smiled at me, it was the most beautiful thing I had ever seen.

"Okay. That's good enough. You can come home now."

*****

During my brief exile from Allison's good graces, Steve began the process of training me to infiltrate the Legion.

To say that he grew frustrated with me during that first distracted, listless week would be to understate the issue by a significant degree. Most of those days ended with him being fed up and disgusted with me, and questioning, quite loudly, my commitment to not getting myself killed. He even threatened to call off the mission if I didn't pull my head out of my ass and get serious. At the time, I had just shrugged. The whole thing was becoming less and less important to me as each day passed and Allison refused to see me.

The day after we patched things up, and I showed up for training with some of the old spring back in my step, Steve was relieved and we got down to the business of preparing me for what lay ahead.

His first order of business was to coach me on establishing my cover. We kept the story simple so as to make it difficult to screw up, and we spent long hours in conversations where he tried to get me to trip up and say something that would give me away. As it turned out, I was surprisingly good at lying. The trick, I learned, was to get into character and tell myself that everything I was saying was actually true. Really believe it, to the point of feeling raw emotion when I talked about my fake past, and my not-so-fake dead family. Within a couple of weeks, Steve was satisfied that I could hold my own, and he is not an easy man to convince.

I have a talent for acting. Who knew?

While this was going on, the militia members returned from their short leave to resume training. Gabe had been worried that not many of them would want to continue on after their first taste of real combat, but on the appointed day, much to his surprise, every one of them showed up. I had to hand it to those kids, they had grit.

Their first phase of training had consisted of—in addition to a brutal conditioning regimen—basic marksmanship, unarmed combat, an introduction to squad tactics, land navigation, camouflage, cover and concealment, and low-crawling.

(Why so much time and attention was devoted to a skill as simple as low-crawling, I have no idea. But apparently, it was important.)

Phase two was set to include advanced weapons training, combat marksmanship, tactical formations, advanced land navigation, countering booby traps and explosive devices, defending positions, and patrolling.

Urban combat had originally been scheduled for the end of phase two, but at Steve's request, Gabe moved it up to the beginning. The militia relocated to an abandoned portion of town just outside the wall that had been refurbished for just this purpose.

Much of the training I received with the militia in those two weeks I had already learned thanks to Gabe's diligent instruction, but it was a good opportunity to practice that knowledge in a team setting with experienced trainers. I got to know the new instructor during that time, Marshall, the Navy SEAL, and found him to be patient, knowledgeable, and highly effective. He had trained other militias in the past, and his experience shined through. I walked away from those weeks a much-improved gunfighter.

The other SEAL, Great Hawk, remained aloof. I tried to engage the big Apache in conversation a few times, but only managed to get a few grunts and single word answers out of him. According to Marshall, this was quite remarkable. Most people he simply treated as if they weren't there.

While all of this was going on, Steve and I continued to map out the details of how I would carry out my mission. We spent a lot of time with Grayson Morrow, and if everything he told me to expect from the Legion was true, then I was going to have my work cut out for me. Assuming they didn't just kill me outright, the initiation process was going to be prolonged, and possibly quite brutal.

And lest anyone think that I didn't have enough to do, I also kept up with Tom and his efforts to improve the town's defenses against the infected. I had hoped to head that project up personally and oversee most of the work, but my other commitments simply took up too much of my time. Instead, I met with Tom every morning before he left for work, discussed what progress was being made, and offered suggestions. Other than that, it was his baby.

Time went by quickly during all this, and before I knew it, all the pieces were in place. As I looked at the date on my clock one morning, I realized with a jolt that I was set to move out in less than seventy-two hours. I spent half of that morning panicking that I had so little time to get ready, but as it turned out, Steve had already taken care of everything. For my part, I only had one last order of business to attend.

It involved Allison, some local anesthetic, a small incision, and an electronic device about the size of a nickel. I would rather not mention into which portion of my anatomy the device was inserted, but suffice it to say, it would stand up to all but the most vigorously thorough searches.

After that, I had the next two days to say my goodbyes, get my affairs in order, and get ready to go for a ride on a stealth helicopter. I devoted most of my time to Allison, but I also informed the Glover family and the guys at my poker game that I was going out of town for a while. They were curious, but understanding enough not to push when I told them I couldn't talk about it, other than to say it was for the Army. When they wished me luck, I had smiled, thanked them, and thought to myself that I was certainly going to need it.

*****

We set out under cover of darkness, a couple of hours before dawn.

The stealth helicopter looked like something out of a science fiction movie, all smooth lines and sleek angles, and I could only imagine how expensive it was to build back before the Outbreak. Steve told me that it was really just a heavily modified Black Hawk.

I told him I wanted one for Christmas.

“Not likely,” Steve replied. “Do you have any idea how many strings I had to pull to get Command to send us this thing? If General Jacobs wasn’t back in the Springs lobbying for us, it probably never would have happened. I’d have to teach you how to parachute and drop you out of a Chinook at fifteen-thousand feet.”

I thought about that and couldn’t quite suppress a shudder. Fast-roping—one of my newly acquired skills—was scary enough. Jumping out of a perfectly good helicopter, with only a thin balloon of fabric separating me from certain death, was enough to give me the dry heaves.

“Well, let the old man know I’m grateful for the help,” I said.

Steve nodded and turned to face me. The helicopter’s blades were winding up, and a faint whining sound was beginning to thrum from the engine. A man in unmarked black fatigues and night vision goggles made a signal that they were ready for me to board. My heart began to beat a little faster.

“Good luck, Eric,” Steve said, holding out a hand. “Watch your ass out there.”

I shook his hand and felt my face tighten into a strained smile. “I always do.”

I grabbed my small pack, took a deep breath, and boarded the chopper.

*****

The flight to the drop-off area was mercilessly uneventful. I sat with my back to the wall—or bulkhead, as the aircrew called it—and concentrated on controlling my breathing. I had never ridden in a helicopter before, and I can’t say that I am in a hurry to do it again. Air travel and I have never exactly been on the best of terms, and the bumpy ride in the high-tech Black Hawk did nothing to sway my opinion on the subject.

Thankfully, however, the ride was short. They were only carrying me a little over thirty miles, and the helicopter covered that distance in just under fifteen minutes. The pilot maintained altitude at over eight thousand feet for most of the flight, and only brought the chopper low when it came time to disembark. A crewman, whose name I didn't even bother to ask, helped me connect my harness and kept a hand on my shoulder until it was time to go. When the pilot brought us down to hover at thirty feet, the crewman slapped me on the shoulder and motioned for me to get moving.

I slid down the rope as fast as I dared, heat building in my gloves from friction, and hit the ground just a bit harder than I meant to. Recovering quickly, I dropped my harness, signaled that I was clear, and watched for a few moments as the helicopter gained altitude, turned back the way it had come, and drifted silently off into the night sky.

Gotta love technology.

As cool as watching the chopper was, Steve's axiom about surviving insertion in hostile territory rang loudly in my ears: *When your boots hit the ground, get your ass away from that LZ. You never know who might be watching.*

I scanned the landscape around me, and while I'm sure that during the daytime it looked exactly as it did in all the satellite photos, at night, it just looked like a big-ass empty field. Thankfully, the grass was low because of wandering goat herds that were once domesticated but now ran wild around the county. I strained my ears to listen, but didn't hear any of them.

Good.

Goats would only draw the infected, and that was exactly what I wanted to avoid. At least until I ran out of food. Then I might have to find out what goat steak tasted like.

Behind me, and circling to my right across dozens of acres of field, was a large swath of uncut forest dotted infrequently with houses. It may as well have been the border to hell itself.

I had no intention of going that way. Not only did my goal not lie in that direction, the woods were probably infested with walkers.

To my left, the field terminated at a road with no visible structures on either side of it as far as I could see. Flat, level ground marched away into the darkness, only dimly illuminated by pale moonlight. According to the maps I had studied, there were three places less than a mile away where I could take shelter for the night.

I took a few moments to check my weapons and equipment, what little I had, and set out due south. The cold, spongy ground ate up the sound of my boots as I jogged along, constantly scanning my surroundings for movement. Every hundred yards or so I stopped, checked my compass to make sure I was still on track, and then took off again.

After twenty minutes of setting an easy pace, the blurry outline of my destination revealed itself against the unrelenting blackness of the night. Where the field terminated at a natural depression lined thickly with trees, shrubs, and tangled vines, there was an old cinder-block utility shack surrounded by a rusty, half-collapsed chain-link fence, and piles of long-forgotten electrical equipment. Vines and creepers twisted up the walls like skeletal fingers, nearly obscuring the lone steel door that permitted entrance to the building. I cleared them away and then tried the door handle.

Locked. But that was okay. I had a trick up my sleeve for just such an occasion.

From a pocket on my web gear, I produced a small can of rust-breaking compound, and a lock-picking device that Gabe had graciously loaned me. It looked like a tiny gun with a big trigger, and a needle in the place of a barrel. The needle was the part that did the picking, and it had several different attachments I could swap out for different kinds of locks. I sprayed a little of the compound into the lock, waited a few minutes for it to soak in, and then tried the pick. It took some jiggling and twisting back and forth, but eventually I managed to work the compound into the rusted internal components and threw the bolt back with a satisfying click.

Rather than open the door, I stood outside with my ear pressed against it and listened. Nothing happened. I knocked softly a couple of times, just loud enough to be heard inside and waited again. Nothing. No moans, no scrapes, nothing being knocked over, no sound at all. I let out a breath and swung the door open.

The darkness inside was a palpable thing, impervious to the dim light of the half-moon overhead. I grabbed a flashlight from my belt and shined it around. The small building was empty except for dusty racks of wiring, sheathing, and various electrical components, and a bank of long-dead meters against the far wall. The dust that covered everything inside was thick, and cobwebs hung from between walls, corners of the ceiling, and shelves. If I was going to sleep here tonight, and not get eaten alive by spiders and God knows what else, I was going to have to do a little cleaning.

I found a narrow length of aluminum pipe in the piles of junk surrounding the building and crafted a makeshift broom out of cedar boughs and creeper vines. Bed, Bath and Beyond never would have sold it, but for what I needed, it would work just fine.

After knocking down the cobwebs, brushing away the worst of the dust, and sweeping the collective detritus out the door, I spent a few minutes sneezing quietly before laying out my small bedroll. It had been less than an hour since I'd roped down from the helicopter, but it felt like much longer and the tension was beginning to wear on my nerves. When I shut the door and threw the deadbolt, I blew out a sigh of relief. The walls around me were thick and solid, and as long as I didn't make too much noise, it was unlikely the infected would find me here. Good enough for the moment.

Out of habit, I clicked on my flashlight, removed the red lens cover, and took a more careful look around. There were a few things here—spools of copper wire, tools, climbing pegs the size of railroad spikes, etc.—that might have been worth scavenging if I were anywhere near civilization. But out here alone, they were worthless.

With nothing else to do, I rummaged in my pack until I found a palm-size lantern that, rather than being battery-powered, could be charged by rotating a small hand crank for a couple of minutes. It worked well, but turning the crank was surprisingly hard work. My arm was burning by the time I was done.

After charging it, I used a section of copper wire to hang it from a metal strut in the ceiling, and laid all my weapons and equipment out on my bedroll for a quick inspection.

When determining what to bring along for this mission, I had applied a couple of litmus tests to each item before deciding on it:

First: Is it the kind of thing that a survivor, who stays alive by staying mobile, would be willing to carry? Mobility meant traveling light. Ounces, pounds, pain, and so on.

Second: If it is light enough to carry over long distances, what purpose does it serve? Will it help me obtain food, water, shelter, or protection? Could it provide more than one of these things?

From there, I had to prioritize. An Outbreak survivor's first priority is, above all else, weapons. The infected are everywhere, but they are only half as dangerous as living people who might take exception to one's continued existence. Not to mention packs of wild dogs, increasingly aggressive wolves and coyotes, predators escaped from zoos that now flourished in the prey-rich vastness of North America, and a host of other dangers. Anyone traveling alone through the wastelands was going to have to defend himself on a daily basis. If said individual did not have a weapon on hand when the walkers (or whatever) showed up, he was dead. End of story.

Next to that, dehydration and starvation were distant runners-up.

The most important thing to consider when choosing my weapons was authenticity. I was playing the part of the nomad. To avoid suspicion, my gear needed to fit that persona. Drawing on my own considerable experience as a scavenger, I knew well what kinds of hardware a wandering survivor might expect to scavenge, and I had planned accordingly.

Before the Outbreak, .22 long rifle was the most inexpensive and abundantly available caliber of ammunition in the United States. Millions of households had some kind of firearm chambered for it and, in most cases, plenty of ammunition as well. The cartridges typically came in boxes of between one-hundred to five-hundred rounds and, due to their small size and relatively low weight, one could carry literally thousands of rounds in a backpack without taking on an unbearable amount of strain. At ranges out to fifty yards, a good .22 rifle can kill a walker with only one or two shots and, if one exercises proper marksmanship, they can be equally as deadly to game animals and even living people.

All of that being said, any survivor who had engaged in a firefight and lived to tell the story would also understand the undeniable value of good old-fashioned firepower. A .22 can kill a man, but it won't stop him in his tracks like many of the larger calibers, which means that a wounded enemy could still shoot back before succumbing to his wounds. Because of this fact, any survivor worth his salt is going to want to have something with a little more *oomph* in his arsenal. Additionally, said survivor would also want a backup weapon, and some kind of hand-held bludgeon or heavy blade.

For a primary weapon, I chose one of the most common rifles in existence—the Ruger 10-22. It is simple, lightweight, reliable and, most importantly, ubiquitous. Go to any town in America, search enough houses and, sooner or later, you'll find one of these things.

The one laying on my bedroll had a scuffed and scratched black polymer stock, a low power scope, and a quartet of 25-round magazines, all loaded and ready to go. The rifle, like all the rest of my equipment, had been acquired courtesy of Steve and his access to the U.S. Army's vast trade network. It's amazing what a little instant coffee and toilet paper will buy these days.

Although it would have been great to bring along my M-6, the technologically advanced rifle was rare even before the Outbreak, and it would have been a dead giveaway once I made contact with the Legion. What I needed was something more common, and easier to explain how I came to possess it. I could have picked from a variety of different weapons, but for the last few years I had relied heavily on the AR-15 assault rifle platform and, to be plainly honest, I'd grown used to it. It is reliable, accurate, easy to shoot, and standard .223 ammo isn't terribly heavy. I didn't see any point in fixing something that wasn't broken.

Luckily, even during a period in pre-Outbreak history when firearms sales were declining nationwide, the AR-15 was one of the most popular rifles on the market. Gun dealers sold millions of them and, much like the 10-22, if one searched long and hard enough, he could find an AR-15 just about anywhere in the country. Furthermore, because the ammo used by AR-15s was fairly expensive, gun owners tended to buy it in bulk to save money. Which means that if you find an AR, you'll probably also find plenty of ammo to go along with it. All of this made it easy to explain why I would have a civilian semi-automatic version of the M-4 carbine in my kit.

Manufactured by Smith & Wesson, it was inexpensive, widely popular, and a number of law enforcement agencies had even used it as a patrol rifle. The weapon was bare bones, boasting only iron sights and an adjustable stock. But it was in good operating condition, and I had three full magazines for it and a hundred spare rounds. It gave me a lot of firepower, but without a suppressor to reduce the loud report, I would have to save it for emergencies only. For all their other useful qualities, unsuppressed ARs are really freaking loud.

For secondary weapons, I had two pistols; one chambered for .22, and the other in nine-millimeter. The .22 was my old Sig Sauer Mosquito (sans suppressor), and the nine-mil was a venerable CZ-75. And just in case I ran out of ammo, I also carried a short handled woodcutting ax and a two-foot crowbar with athletic tape wrapped around the shaft for a better grip. In addition to being fine melee weapons against the undead, axes and crowbars had a multitude of other uses that made them indispensable to any survivor's toolkit.

The rest of my gear consisted of a small pack with a built-in water bladder, a couple of canteens, zip-ties, batteries, para-cord, fishing line, Ziplock bags, over-the-counter painkillers, a hunting knife, a multi-tool, and several different fire-starting kits. What little food I carried consisted mainly of smoked meat, a few small bundles of wild edibles native to the region, and a container of vegetable shortening. Exactly the kinds of things one would expect a longtime survivor to have.

My clothes looked like something I might have scavenged from an abandoned sporting goods store, and my web gear could have been pilfered from any number of dead soldiers whose corpses lay strewn about the Eastern Seaboard—a reminder of the brave but ultimately futile struggle that claimed their lives.

After looking everything over for the umpteenth time, I stowed all my gear back where it belonged, made sure all my guns were loaded, placed the CZ close at hand, and settled down into my bedroll. There were a hundred worries racing around in my head threatening to keep me up all night, so I sorted them out, put them in little stacks, and filed them away for future reference. That's the key to keeping your cool in bad situations. Compartmentalize. Prioritize. Make a list of tasks, and carry them out one at a time.

My first task was to get some sleep. After that, move toward my next destination, and try not to get myself killed.

Lather, rinse, repeat. It was what came after that had my guts twisted in a knot.

I shoved that thought back into its box, shut my eyes, and slept.

Chapter 14

Hatchet Man

Waking up in pitch-black darkness is never fun.

At first, you're confused. Then there is a second of panic as you bat feebly at the imaginary monsters lurking in the black just in front of your face. Finally, the pistons of memory begin to fire, and you remember what the heck you're doing wrapped up in a sleeping bag on a cold cement floor. My hand fumbled around the edge of the bedroll until the cold metal of my flashlight touched my palm. I flicked it on.

The interior of the utility shed was exactly as it had been the day before, albeit a bit warmer. Surmising that the sun was already up, I glanced at my watch and saw that it was just after nine in the morning—much later than I had hoped to get started.

Dammit. As Wil Anderson would have put it, I was burnin' daylight.

I rolled up my bed, ate a quick breakfast of venison jerky and crushed cattail root, chewed a little chicory to get my blood flowing, and got myself ready to move out. The M-4 went strapped to my back, but still within reach if I needed it. The CZ went into a cross-draw holster on my chest, and the Sig rode on the back of my right hip. The 10-22 I carried in my hands. My other weapons dangled from my belt.

With everything ready to go, I moved to the door and put an ear against it. Nearly a full minute passed. Nothing. I turned the handle on the deadbolt, sliding it back slowly until it stopped. I eased the door open to peek outside, ready to slam it shut again if I spotted any walkers. The brightness of the morning sky made my eyes water after being in the gloomy shed for so long. I grabbed the pair of polarized ski goggles hanging from my neck and slipped them on to dial down the glare. Peering out again, I scanned the field as I gradually pulled the door back but didn't see anything.

I almost stepped outside, but then hesitated, realizing that from where I stood I couldn't see very much. What if I had been spotted when I roped down from the chopper? What if someone was out there lying in wait? Anxiety quickened my pulse. I stood in the doorway for a long minute debating what to do.

Enough of this foolishness. An old, familiar voice in my head whispered. *You can't account for every possibility under the sun. Keep your head on a swivel, your gun at the ready, and get yourself moving. Time's a wastin'.*

Steeling myself with a deep breath, I stepped outside and diligently scanned around the shed, walking close to the walls and cutting the pie on each corner before stepping around it. Nothing but a few trees, a burned out building or two, and farm equipment that looked like it had been abandoned since long before the Outbreak. Pale brown grass stretched into the distance under a clear sky.

Turning my attention from sight to hearing, I closed my eyes and listened. Birds chirped. Leaves rustled. Small rodents skittered through the grass looking for seeds. Nothing out of the ordinary.

My confidence began to return, filling my chest up like water on a dry sponge. I chuckled at my own paranoia. "Hell. I'm probably the most dangerous thing out here," I muttered.

It was a dumb thing to do, putting a sentence like that out there into the universe. I should have known it would come back to bite me in the ass.

*****

The first few miles went under my feet without incident. I set an easy pace, kept my eyes moving, and stopped frequently to make sure I wasn't being followed. Every once in a while I spotted movement in the trees—a swaying limb where there was no wind, a rustle of foliage, a shadow passing between trunks—but whatever it was, it was staying out of sight. It was too stealthy and moved too fast to be a person, but beyond that, I had no clue what it was.

And I sure as hell wasn't going in after it.

I would have to keep an eye out, but with a hundred yards of open ground separating me from the forest, I wasn't worried about being taken by surprise. I kept moving.

Consulting my compass, I felt confident that I was on course. My destination was an abandoned industrial park that Grayson Morrow had identified as a Legion base of operations. He knew it well, as it was the place where he had been captured and held prisoner.

The terrain around me was mostly flat, which made for easy travel; by the time I stopped for lunch, the first waypoint on my journey was within sight. It was too small to warrant a stoplight, or even a name for that matter. But I guess you could have called it a town. There was a small collection of houses and a trailer park across a set of railroad tracks from a rundown strip mall, a farm-equipment repair facility, and a rusting grain hopper. Although everything looked like it had been abandoned since the Outbreak, I still had a feeling that there were a few infected kicking around somewhere. In places like this, there always were.

Ordinarily, I would have avoided this place entirely unless I was in desperate need of supplies. And even then, I would not have come alone. Taking on a town full of infected without help is just next door to suicide, but I had to do it. There was something here that I needed.

During his time with the Legion, Grayson Morrow had secretly drawn a map of the encampment where he had been imprisoned that detailed the disposition of troops, supplies, and nearby equipment. Not long after drawing it, he had actually managed to escape and had fled north toward his home state of Indiana.

He didn't make it very far.

Hunting down escapees is one of the Legion's favorite pastimes. They tracked Morrow to the little community ahead of me, where they eventually captured him. Morrow had known he was caught, and what his punishment was going to be, and he didn't want the raiders to find the map on him. If they had, they would have killed him after they had their fun with him. As for what they did to him, well … it's probably best left unmentioned.

I shook my head to clear it of dark thoughts and darker anger, peered through the Ruger's scope, and started looking for the best way to approach the strip mall.

I spotted an old irrigation ditch that ran along a gradual slope in the landscape that would hide me while I snuck in from the west. It was probably an unnecessary precaution—it didn't really stand to reason that there would be anyone still living here—but I hadn't stayed alive this long by being stupid.

Staying low, I followed the crease in the terrain and approached at an angle that would make it tough for anyone looking out a window or from a rooftop to see me. As I got closer, I heard birds flitting and chirping through broken panes of shattered windows, and the intermittent moans of infected.

The walkers hunger for birds the same as they do any other animal, but even with their rot-addled brains, they still manage to figure out that they can't catch the swift little creatures. Or maybe it's just that there are always other birds around to catch their attention. Either way, when walkers see birds, they moan at them. But not much else.

Oddly, as soon as the sun goes down, this behavior stops. During this time, the infected only make noise when they are near larger, ground-based prey. No one knows why. It's just another one of the many mysteries surrounding the walking dead.

I soon reached the small cluster of buildings near the railroad tracks that were once businesses but were now just broken shells. There was a trailer park ahead of me and, farther down the road, an assemblage of small brick-walled houses. The trailers looked like something out of a low-budget horror movie, with crumbling porches, broken windows, and stained aluminum siding. Their insulation had been ripped out by wind, rain, and water damage, and lay strewn around the overgrown yards like orange and yellow confetti. The houses beyond didn't look to be in much better shape.

Reaching the strip mall, I poked my head around the corner and did a quick scan. The trailer park was directly across from me, and in front of it was a single crumbling road running parallel to the railroad tracks. The moaning I heard was coming from the storefronts to my left, where the community's former residents wandered aimlessly, groaning and bumping into one another. They all gazed upward, staring disconsolately at a contingent of barn swallows that had taken up residence in the nearby rooftops.

On any other day, I might have found the situation sad, and vaguely humorous in a fucked-up kind of way. But not this time. The infected were right in front of the building where Morrow had stashed his map and, in order to get it, I had to get past them. If Gabe had been with me, it wouldn't have been a problem. But alone, it was a gigantic pain in my ass. I ducked back around the corner and weighed my options.

I could get their attention and lead them away, but doing so would burn up time and energy I could ill afford to lose. Another option was to climb onto a rooftop and just shoot them, but the noise would attract every walker within a square mile. If I did that, I would have to set a hard pace southward and hope I could reach my next stop before they found me.

Considering the distance involved, that didn't seem likely. That left me with only one option.

Gently and quietly, I took off my pack and laid my rifles down against the wall. The CZ and its holster were just going to get in the way, so I left them behind as well, but I kept the Sig. Shooting my way out of here was a bad idea, but I still wanted the option available, just in case.

Now I had to decide which implement of destruction to use—ax or crowbar. Unlike Gabe, I'm not strong enough to brandish a weapon in each hand and cut through hordes of infected like a pissed-off scythe. Staring back and forth between the two weapons, I began to sorely miss my small sword. Or pig-sticker as Gabe liked to call it. (Sometimes he mixed things up and called it the ghoul-ka-bob.) Despite my friend's snarky comments, it was a great tool for dispatching the undead. My technique was to find a Y-shaped tree limb, trim it down, and use it to hold a ghoul in place by jamming it under the creature's neck and lifting up. Holding the stick like a lance gave me leverage against my target, and left my other arm free to deliver the killing strike—a stab straight through the eye-socket.

It wasn't the most crowd-pleasing way to kill a walker, but it was fast, effective, and it kept them out of arm's reach. The absolute last thing you want to happen is to let a walker to get a grip on you. They're not any stronger in death than they were in life, but due to the fact that they never get tired, and they can use one-hundred percent of their strength at all times, they feel super-humanly strong when they grab you.

Sadly, my small sword was at Allison's house back in Hollow Rock, so I would have to make do with the tools at hand. The crowbar was great for crushing skulls, but it was slow. It usually took me two or three good whacks to put a ghoul down for the count. For that reason, in my case at least, crowbars are only useful against one or two ghouls at a time. Any more than that and I run the risk of being overwhelmed.

The ax, on the other hand, was good for more than just brain busting. I could sever a walker's head, or use the broad blade to disable their legs and reduce their mobility, making them easier to kill. Considering that I had quite a bit of work ahead of me, I decided that the ax was the best tool for the job. I cinched my scarf over my mouth, tightened the strap on my goggles, and retied my headscarf. Hefting the ax in my hands, I stepped around the corner.

A ghoul spotted me immediately and let out a hiss that sounded like a porcupine raping a rattlesnake. I lifted the ax over my head and chopped into his forehead, cleaving his skull like splitting wood.

"Shut up, you."

I wrenched the ax free as it fell, then took a few running steps to the next-closest ghoul. She was in reasonably good shape for a corpse. Most of her skin was still in place, not all of her hair had fallen out, and she was still recognizable as human. Might have even been pretty, once. Her only visible wound was a mouth-shaped gouge on her forearm. A small one. Like from a child.

"Poor thing. I hope it wasn't your kid that did that."

I swung the ax again, this time burying the blade through her temple. She dropped, and it took me a couple of precious seconds to pry the blade loose.

Meanwhile, the other walkers had spotted me and began growling and keening, their faces twisted and their hands grasping as they lurched toward me. I backed off a few steps, took a quick look around, and jogged back around the corner of the building. A rutted old gravel path started at the end of the cracked pavement, ran through a field of patchy grass, and terminated at the grain hopper next to the railroad tracks. My best bet was to lure the walkers into the open, run circles around them, and pick them off one by one. It was going to take a while, and it was going to be hard work.

"Nothing for it, Riordan. This is why you stay in shape."

I turned and waved an arm at the walkers who were lunging forward as a single mass.

"Come on then, you fuckers. Let's do this."

I quickened my pace out to the middle of the field and began to sidestep in a wide circle around to my left. The first two walkers that came within range were nearly on top of each other, shuffling shoulder to shoulder. A front kick to the chest sent the smaller of the two tumbling backward and gave me the space I needed to behead his companion with a two-handed backswing. The one I had kicked landed at the feet of two others who promptly tripped over him and landed in a heap of struggling, moaning limbs. I dashed into the opening and used two quick swipes to cut the knees of ghouls on either side of me, then retreated and circled around to the other side.

So far, so good. I spotted another infected walking in front of two larger ones close enough to trip them. Taking two running steps, I executed a textbook jumping sidekick and planted my size twelve into his sternum. The bone crunched under my boot, and the little ghoul's arms flapped comically as it bowled into the walkers behind him. I had enough time to chop two of their heads open as they struggled to get back up, and then the other ones began to close in, forcing me to back off.

To my left, a massively obese man reached toward me with one arm, and one ragged stump that ended just above the elbow. I ran around to his unprotected side, took half a step behind him, and brought the ax down at an angle into his knee. The blade cleaved through flesh and bone, and the big ghoul toppled over sideways. A quick follow up swing divided his skull into two equal halves before I backed off yet again, and circled the horde.

The dance continued for at least five minutes, and round and round we went. Five minutes may not sound like very long, but when you are running, throwing kicks as hard as you can, and swinging a heavy ax, it feels like an eternity. I managed to whittle their number down to just ten ghouls before my strength started to flag. With my arms trembling, and my lungs burning, I jogged away about a hundred yards and put the ax head on the ground, bending over it and leaning on the handle while I gasped for breath.

"Fuck me."

I straightened up, dug a canteen off my web belt, and took a long, grateful drink.

"What I wouldn't give for a silencer right now."

The temptation to simply pull my pistol and get this thing over with was strong, but doing so would only lead to having more walkers to contend with, so I left the Sig in its holster. Besides, I had handled this many. What was ten more?

Backing off, I let the walkers follow me closer to the tree line. I would need plenty of space give ground once I circled them and started busting heads again. As I watched, one of them tripped on a depression in the ground and face-planted into the grass. I couldn't get to him—he was in the middle of the pack—but it felt good to laugh.

When I was down to twenty feet of breathing room, I broke into a jog and ran around their left side. Finding a good vector, I turned, ran in at a sprint, and channeled my momentum into a spinning swing that sent the top half of a walker's head flipping through the air. Another step brought me in range of what had once been a skinny, tattoo-covered young man who couldn't have been a day over twenty when he died. I batted his arms aside, sheared off the front of his knee, and backed off as he went down. Rather than deliver a killing stroke, I retreated. He wasn't much of a threat anymore, and the other walkers were getting too close for comfort.

"Okay. Two down, eight to go. Let's get this done."

I blew out a couple of deep breaths, and ignored the trembling in my arms. The ax was getting damned heavy.

The horde got close again, and this time I managed to take out four more of them before backing off. Two of them marched close to one another, just over arm's length apart, and it was a simple thing to dart between them, hack their ankles like brittle saplings, and then kill each one with a downward stroke to the back of the head. Another ghoul behind them tripped over their bodies, and I wasted no time stepping up and dispatching him. The fourth was alone, and a simple baseball swing to the throat sent her head spinning one way and her body the other.

As I stood waiting for the remaining walkers to come within range again, a rustling of branches and the sound of something running over dead leaves caught my attention. Looking behind the walkers, I caught a brief flash of color, and the fleeting impression of a massive body running at incredible speed before it disappeared into the shadows of the forest.

That brief flash of color, a burnt orange glimpse of sleek fur stretched tight over rippling muscle, told me exactly what had been tracking me all day. My blood ran cold, and I wanted to kick myself for not bringing my rifle, not that I was entirely sure it would have done me any good. Facing a thousand walkers—something I had actually done before—would have been far preferable to taking on the thing dogging my trail.

"Okay, Riordan, you know animals hate the dead. It won't get close while these things are around. Focus on what's in front of you. One threat at a time."

I steadied my breathing, clutched my ax, and waited.

They shuffled onward, ever onward, and I met the first of them with an overhead chop. He was a good bit taller than I was, and the angle was awkward, so I didn't kill him on the first try. Another swing, harder this time, and he ate dirt. The rest were close behind, so I circled left to make the tall ghoul's body perpendicular to their path. The next closest one tripped over him, making it easy to end its unnaturally prolonged life. I stayed close to the body to get a shot at one of the last three.

What happened next, I can only ascribe to bad luck and fatigue. My breath was coming in short gasps, my arms trembled, and the ax felt like it weighed about a hundred pounds. A couple of blisters had sprung up on my fingers, and I was beginning to feel weak from having eaten so little that day. It wouldn't have happened a year earlier when I was raw-boned and full of whipcord muscle, toughened by the struggle to survive in the harsh, unforgiving Appalachians. But several months of plentiful food and soft living had sanded away my hardest edges, and made me a shade less sharp than I used to be.

I know. Excuses, excuses.

The last three ghouls were in a cluster, their arms brushing one another's shoulders as they reached for me. I swung for the first one, but my weary arms didn't quite raise the ax high enough, and the blow clipped the walker low on the face, the blade lodging in his jaw. If I had been less tired I could have pulled it free, but I wasn't.

When I pulled on the ax, the ghoul came with it, dangerously close. It reached out, grabbed the lapel of my heavy jacket, and without hesitation, it hauled on me with more strength than any human body, dead or alive, should be able to muster. I wrenched the ax sideways and pushed it with both hands across the creature's jaw, lodging the handle in its teeth and neutralizing it for the moment. I had enough strength left to keep it at bay, but I couldn't hold it forever, and the other two were just feet away.

One of the many lessons Gabriel taught me about fighting the undead is that it is never a good idea to throw them. Unlike living people, they don't care if you fling them ass-over-head. Nothing hurts them. And nearly every throwing technique imaginable, from a shoulder toss to a rolling hip-lock, brings them within biting distance—something you never, ever want to happen. A trip, a sweep, or a knockdown blow from a well-aimed boot is always a better option.

But in this case, I didn't have much of a choice. The other two walkers were closing in, and the one in front of me wouldn't be denied his feast for much longer. So I opted for the only option I had available. I backed off a step, pulled the ghoul's head against me to trap the ax handle between my chest and its jaw, and rolled into what was quite possibly the sloppiest hip-toss I've ever thrown.

It worked, sort of. The creature flipped over and slammed onto its back. I managed to keep my feet beneath me, and landed with a knee on its chest, pinning it to the ground. Unfortunately, my back was to the other two, and I could practically feel their rotten hands growing inexorably closer. Meanwhile, the ghoul I was sitting on had maintained its grip on my jacket, and was pulling with everything it had to bring my face closer to its mouth. I didn't have time to rip the jacket off, so I seized the arm holding me, trapped its wrist beneath my armpit with its elbow on my knee, and leaned down.

The limp snapped like a twig, and while the bastard's grip didn't loosen, the downward pressure finally let up. It kept trying to pull, but with the bones between its upper and lower arms disconnected, the muscles had no leverage. Gripping the ghoul's wrist with one hand, I stood halfway up and pivoted on my knee to face the last two walkers.

They were closer than I thought.

The one in front—squat, fat, and obviously long dead—reached out and was only a foot away from gripping my shoulders. I couldn't shrug out of the jacket in time, and if it got its hands on me, I was done for. My mind scrambled desperately for an idea, some way to escape. And then I remembered that I still had my fighting knife on my belt. Reaching down, I drew it, gripped it hard, and waited. The walker's hands were just brushing the fabric of my coat when I struck with as much force as I could muster, driving the blade upward through walker's soft palate and into its brain. As it stiffened, I gave the knife a hard twist that sent syrupy black ichor running down my glove, and the ghoul went limp. As it fell, I pushed it away from me. The knife, however, was stuck fast in its skull, forcing me to let it go.

One more down, but my problems weren't over yet. The last ghoul followed close behind and lunged for me. I snatched the ax up from where it lay on the corpse beneath me, and lacking enough room to swing it, I shoved it against my attacker's throat. The viselike squeeze of its hands gripped my shoulders, iron fingers gouging painfully into my skin. I let out a hoarse shout of pain and fear, and shoved it back as hard as I could, a desperate surge of adrenaline lending strength to my arms. It wouldn't last long, and I knew I didn't have much time to come up with something.

Rocking my weight to the left, I lifted up my right leg, planted my foot in the ghoul's waist, and rolled backward, letting my arms go slack as I did. The combined push-pull effect from the walker's arms and my outstretched leg sent the creature flipping over my head to land with a solid thump. For a couple of precious seconds, it lay immobile—probably trying to figure out what the hell just happened—and gave me the chance I needed to unzip my jacket and shrug my arms free.

Rolling to one side, I got up and sprinted about twenty yards away. When I turned back around, the two ghouls were also standing again and, as they always do, they were coming for me. The broken arm of the first one I had fought dangled uselessly from the elbow, the skin holding it together stretched and twisted. I stood up straight and filled my lungs with deep breaths: once, twice, three times. The adrenaline began to subside, leaving me weakened and shaky.

I needed a rest. I needed water. I needed something to eat, and I needed to wash the damned stinking gore-splatter off my clothes. But none of that was going to happen until I finished the job in front of me. The urge to pull the Sig returned more strongly than before, but again, I fought it down. There was no need, all I had to do was let these two meat sacks chase me a little ways, then run around them and retrieve my ax. I could see it lying on the ground next to the walker with a black Krylon knife-handle protruding from its lower jaw.

I pulled on my elbows to stretch my arms and back, touched my toes to ward off a cramp that was threatening my left hamstring, and walked quickly around behind the last two ghouls. With my weapon back in my hand, I felt the panic that had gripped me just a few short moments ago fade away, and in its place, a hot, burning anger began to take hold.

I had been dealing with this shit for more than two years. Two years of nightmares, and fear, and wondering if each day was going to be my last. All because these motherfuckers were *hungry*. Because they were mindless, and stupid, and cared for nothing but the endless, driving need that gnawed away at their rotten guts. It had consumed the world, that ravenousness, and all the pain and hardship I had endured as a result was *their fucking fault.* Even worse than that was the knowledge that after everything I had been through, everything I had survived, I almost got my ticket punched in some nameless, shithole backwater in middle-of-nowhere Tennessee because I got cocky, and complacent, and bit off a little more than I could chew.

It was a gut-check moment. No more fucking around.

I walked up to the one with the broken arm and cleaved its head in half, swinging so hard that the blade went through cranium, sinus cavity, and jaw, and lodged in the creature's spine. It fell, and I let the ax go with it.

One left.

I let it get close enough to almost grab me, then seized its wrist, placed a palm against its elbow, and with a quick twisting, pulling step I slammed it down onto its face. Raising my boot, I stomped down hard onto the back of its neck, stomp after stomp, until I felt a crunch. Two more stomps for good measure, and I stepped away.

Behind me, I heard another moan.

"You gotta be fucking kidding me."

Turning around, I saw the tattooed kid whose knee I had sheared nearly in two. He was still pursuing me, pushing himself across the ground with his good leg while pulling with his arms. I laughed, grabbed the handle of my ax, and after a little wrenching back and forth, pulled it free.

"I'll give you this much, you're a persistent fucker."

Stopping a few feet away from him, I stood watching, the ax held loosely at my waist.

"What was your name, huh?"

It responded by leaning up, fixing its milky white eyes on me, and croaking. I lowered my voice into my best Samuel L. Jackson.

"That don't sound like no name I ever heard of."

It gripped the ground and pulled itself closer, its face contorting in hunger. It slid a few feet, then fell down as its grip faltered in the loose dirt.

"I'm sorry, did I break yo' concentration?"

It moaned, kicked with renewed vigor at the sound of my voice, then went silent as it reached forward and dug its fingers into the ground again.

"Oh, you were finished? Well, allow me to retort."

The ax swung down, and the walker went still.

I walked back over to my pack, grabbed a bottle of rubbing alcohol, and wiped down the blade, going over the handle as well just to be safe. When I finished, I held it up and looked at my grainy, distorted reflection in its surface.

"When you absolutely, positively got to kill every motherfucker in the room, accept no substitutes."

The ax was no AK-47. And yes, I was switching movies. But hey, you take your laughs where you can get them.

Chapter 15

Dominion of Beasts

Goode Brothers Feed and Supply had seen better days.

One of six units in a bland, slowly collapsing strip mall that looked like it had been built in the late-seventies, the store had been looted down to everything but the shelves. And even a few of those looked to have been ripped out. The sign over the door was broken and filthy, with several of the letters tipped on their sides, or hanging upside down. Glass littered the pavement out front where the windows had been shattered, and a single Ford pickup with flat, rotten tires stood lonely vigil in the parking lot.

My habitual urge to search the truck, the buildings in front of me, and all of the residences nearby itched like a mosquito bite, and tugged at the avaricious, lizard part of my brain that got a kick out of scavenging in places like this. There were probably guns, food, clothing, tools, ammunition, toilet paper, and who knew what else just waiting for some enterprising soul to come along and collect them. But with the schedule I had to keep, I would have to settle for simply remembering this place for another time. Assuming I lived long enough to come back for it.

Crunching over the glass, I walked into the shredded store and went toward the back where Grayson Morrow had instructed me to look for the manager's office. It was around a corner behind the checkout counter, and to reach it, I had to step over a busted cash register that lay next to a white skeleton with a huge chunk of its skull missing. If the bullet casings nearby were any sign, it looked like whoever this person was, he had died defending the store. By the condition of the clothes, and the lack of stench, I guessed that the poor fellow had been sitting there since the early days of the Outbreak.

"Tough break, pal," I said, giving the bony shoulder a sympathetic pat. "Should have just let them have this shit. Maybe you'd still be alive."

I looked over my shoulder through what was left of the front windows, took in the bare branches clawing at the sky in the distance, the creak of rotting wood, and the fetid odor of corpses blowing along in the icy breeze. I felt a wry chuckle shake itself out of me.

"Or maybe not. You're not missing much."

The door to the office opened with a push, and the desk I had come here to search stood near the back wall. I opened the top drawer and found a single piece of white cloth folded into a neat square a little bigger than my palm. Taking it out, I unfolded it and studied it in the light through the window. It was a little larger than a square foot, and drawn with careful attention to detail. A legend on the bottom explained what the various symbols meant, and there was even a rough estimate of the distances involved. On the back, Morrow had scribbled a few notes about the people who worked in different areas of the Legion's compound, the leadership structure, and guards he thought he could bribe into helping him escape. Even though it had ended badly for him, I had to give the kid credit. It was a well thought-out plan.

I folded the map, sealed it in a plastic sandwich bag, and stashed it in my pack. Studying it would have to wait until I had found a place to rest for the evening. Back at the front of the store, I stepped over the cash register and the skeleton again, and paused on my way out.

"Do me a favor, will you?" I said, looking down at the broken skull. "If you happen to run into a guy named Michael Riordan, or his wife Julia, tell them Eric sends his love, okay?"

The skull stared back in silence.

“All right, then. You take it easy, partner. If I come back around this way, I’ll see about giving you a proper burial.”

I tipped an imaginary hat to the pile of bones, adjusted my pack, and left the town with no name behind.

*****

Four miles and a little over an hour later, I saw something that I hadn’t seen in well over a year.

A dog.

I had reached the halfway point of where I planned to travel for the day, and the wide, grassy fields I had been traversing had given way to sparse woodland and abandoned clusters of houses. Where I stood, I was knee-deep in grass that had once been someone’s back yard. The plan had been to cut across the yard to a gravel road that would provide smoother walking for the next few miles. When I was halfway across, the dog stepped out from behind a toolshed, spotted me, and froze in his tracks.

I think he was just as surprised to see me as I was to see him.

The canine population in North America, and probably the rest of the world, had been all but annihilated during the Outbreak. Most dogs, lacking the ability to hunt, and dependent upon their human masters to provide for them, had either starved to death or fallen prey to the infected during the first brutal months of the Outbreak. Additionally, dogs tend to bark like crazy when the infected are nearby, which does nothing to improve their chances of survival. Because of this, most humans drive them off if they come near. Assuming, of course, that they don’t simply kill them for their meat. As a consequence, only the toughest, smartest dogs survived, and they had no love for humans, alive or dead.

And they had learned to be quiet. Damned quiet.

The dog staring at me from across a narrow expanse of field had the chest and head of a mastiff, but the long legs of a Great Dane. It probably weighed every bit of two-hundred pounds, and I was reasonably certain it could fit my entire head in its mouth if it really tried.

We watched each other for a minute or two, neither of us willing to make the first move. His head was high in the air, and his tail—a long one, not the short, clipped variety—waved slowly at half-mast. The big creature made no sign of aggression, but he didn't seem interested in backing down either. There was a steadiness in his posture that spoke of eagerness, almost like a puppy poised to run after a stick the instant before it's thrown. Looking closely, I could see that his hide was crisscrossed with scars around the neck and snout, and hard, striated muscle rippled along his flanks. This dog had seen his share of fights, and he was definitely not starving.

That meant two things: He wasn't afraid of a good scrap, and he wasn't alone. Dogs hunt in packs or they go hungry. This monstrosity didn't look like he'd missed too many meals.

"Well, we can't just stand here all day."

The dog lowered its head when I spoke. Although I'm no expert on doggie facial expressions, I could swear he was glaring belligerently. Testing the waters, I took a single step forward, and switched the Ruger to my left hand, leaving my right free to draw the pistol on my chest. For a beast like this, a .22 wasn't going to do much more than piss him off. The nine-mil was the better option.

"Listen, partner, I don't know what your game is, but I don't have time for it." I slipped the CZ into my hand, flicked the safety to the off position, and fell into a one-handed shooting stance. "Either make a move or be on your way."

The massive head came down even further, and this time the black-furred lips curled away from white, glistening fangs. A growl that sounded like an idling diesel engine rumbled from his chest, and he let out a low chuffing sound. I heard scrambling noises behind him, and three more dogs came around from behind the shed.

"Fuck me."

Two of them were unidentifiable mutts, albeit large ones. The last one had the distinctive dark coat, broad chest, and bullet-shaped head of a Rottweiler. They fanned out around the large mastiff and began trying to encircle me.

"Oh, hell no."

Figuring that he must be the pack leader, I raised the pistol and put a round into the dirt directly in front of the big mastiff's feet. The report startled them, and they all backed off a few steps, ears back and tails down. I stepped forward into the breach, puffing myself up and raising my voice.

"I don't want to kill you, but I will if you make me."

We all stopped and stood still for a few seconds, each side waiting for the other to make a move. Sensing hesitation on their part, I shouted like a gunshot, "GET OUTTA HERE!"

Whether I broke their nerve, or if they were just smart enough to realize how much danger all the noise had put them in, I don't know. But they turned and took off for the trees at the edge of the yard, and that was good enough for me. I waited until they were well out of sight and the sound of their running had faded into the distance before relaxing. I holstered the CZ, lashed the Ruger to my pack, and switched to the M-4. Between wild dogs, and the big critter that had stalked me earlier in the day, I wasn't trusting my life to a little .22 any longer.

Soldiers like firepower for a reason.

*****

As I got nearer to my destination, I began to see signs of the large predator following me again.

The fields I had crossed earlier in the morning gave way to a dense, crowded forest that blocked out what little warmth the sun had to offer. Summer's green had long ago dried up, turned brown, and fallen to the forest floor, which meant that the beast following me had little in the way of cover. Occasionally, I saw movement in the stillness, and heard the crunch of something heavy as it walked over crisp, crackling leaves. My heart beat faster, and I quickened my pace.

Finally, as the sun was sinking low and the horizon simmered down to an angry magenta, I spotted the small cluster of buildings that would be my stopping point for the night. Halting in the middle of the road, I cast a glance behind me and listened carefully. The trees were still, with nary a breeze to sway their skeletal arms, and the birds chirped away unabated.

"If it's a fight you want, you'd better come on out now," I called into the woods. "I plan on being behind a closed door by nightfall, so if you're looking for trouble, now's the time to do something about it."

The forest had no comment.

I covered the last few miles at a runner's pace, and arrived just as the last red-streaked clouds darkened into a somber blue. Ahead of me, the sign that welcomed visitors to town shared the roadside with a pair of opposing gas stations, one on either side of the highway. I stopped between them and surveyed the leavings of a long-ago carnage.

As Grayson had described, dead bodies littered the pavement for hundreds of yards in all directions. A man could barely take two steps without tripping over one. They had mostly rotted away, but there was still enough tissue left on their bones to raise an outrageous stink. It hung wet and sticky in the air, a nauseating, unrelenting miasma. I adjusted my scarf over my nose and mouth, and began picking my way toward one of the few businesses that had not been burned down or looted—a furniture store.

All of the corpses around me were the handiwork of the Free Legion, which several months ago had decided to use this town as a fallback point, clearing out the infected population. Ironically, I was to be the beneficiary of their hard work.

The front door to the furniture store was closed, but not locked. Grayson had taken the bell off the door the last time he was here, so there was no ringing jingle to announce my entrance. After a quick pause to check behind me, I closed the door, locked the deadbolt, and then pushed a large chest of drawers in front of it. It wasn't much of a barrier, but anything breaking through it would have to make a hell of a racket, which would give me at least a few moments' warning. In dangerous situations, you always take whatever advantages you can get, even the small ones.

I moved quickly through rows of sofas and love seats, turned a corner around a king-size bed, and went through a door leading to the upstairs portion of the building. The stairway had been hacked away—just as Grayson had said it would be—all the way up to the first landing where the stairs switched directions. Legion workers had nailed a couple of crossbeam supports just below the landing, and covered them with a sturdy, rough-hewn two-by-six. It was a crude but effective way to make the upper levels of a building walker-proof.

I tossed my pack and my weapons up, then turned my back to the wall so that the two-by-six was above and in front of me. Reaching up, I did a half pull-up while raising my feet and kicking over my head as I pulled. My torso hit the landing just below the chest, forcing me to shimmy backward to keep from falling over the edge.

As I stood up, an acute, visceral tension drained out of me, and I was able to stand a little straighter. I felt this way every time I had closed the gate behind me at my old cabin, and every time I stepped through the heavily guarded entrance to Hollow Rock.

Like most people, I felt the danger posed by the infected as a constant, unyielding pressure. A fear like a low-banked fire, ready to flare up at any moment. This fear was good for survival, but if felt for too long it could begin to wear away at a person's sanity. A place like this, a refuge from the legions of undead, was like a back massage for the mind. For just a little while, I could stop worrying about at least one threat.

I climbed the remaining stairs and went through the door to what used to be the store's administrative office. It was a large room, nearly as big as the showroom downstairs. The largest portion boasted a fine teak desk, a leather chair, expensive carpets, cherry-stained bookshelves, and a few large file cabinets in the corner. Prints of English horsemen on foxhunts and lounging ladies in Victorian-era dress adorned the walls, along with a few pieces of the more modern, mass-produced artwork that would have been available downstairs. All in all, not a bad place to catch a few winks. I had certainly slept in worse places.

Although well-appointed, the office was dusty as hell. I climbed back down into the showroom to strip a set of sheets from one of the larger beds so that I would have a relatively clean place to bed down for the night. The sheets went over a thick Persian carpet, over which I laid out my bedroll. That done, I pushed the leather chair over to one of the large windows and stared out at the street that ran through the middle of town.

After the day's exertions, sitting down in a comfortable chair was just next door to heaven. Muscles that I had not realized were tense suddenly relaxed, and I was tempted to simply lean back and go to sleep right where I was. Resisting that urge, I fished the map I had recovered earlier in the day from my pack, spun the chair around so that my back was to the window, and clicked on my flashlight.

Half an hour went by as I studied it. The sullen blue haze outside the window darkened into the fullness of night, and as exhaustion sank its claws into me, the lines on the map grew blurry. I refolded it, and was about to stash it, when I caught the last four words on one of the notes Morrow had left. It was the name of the town I was in, followed by "Morrison Family Restaurant." Beside it was the symbol that Morrow used for a weapons cache. A small W with a circle around it.

"No way," I muttered. "Too fucking easy."

My weariness forgotten, I took an LED headlamp out of my backpack, fitted it over my headscarf, grabbed the M-4 and the CZ, and left the furniture store at a fast walk. The lamp lit the way down the grisly street as I went two blocks down, barely restraining the urge to run. At the restaurant, there was a chain and a padlock on the door, but the lock pick Gabe had given me took care of that problem in short order.

Inside, the restaurant was stripped and empty. No chairs, no tables, even the condiments and salt and pepper shakers had been taken. A counter ran along the back of the restaurant, and I spied a swinging double-door that led to the kitchen. I took a few steps inside and did a quick search to check for booby traps. Sure enough, just in front of the entrance to the kitchen, I spotted a tripwire connected to some kind of homemade pipe bomb with a shotgun-shell trigger. I slipped a finger over the triggering mechanism, snipped the wire, and then pried the shotgun shell out of the tube. Inside the pipe was a large amount of what looked like Pyrodex powder, and enough ball bearings to shred a grizzly bear.

"Well, at least they locked the door."

I took the bomb outside and poured the powder and bearings out onto the grass. Back inside, I eased my way into the kitchen, wary of more traps. The kitchen had also been stripped bare, except for a large stainless steel table in the center of the room. There was another padlock on the door to the refrigerator.

Like before, I checked for traps and found another of the crude bombs wired to the top of the door beneath a ventilation hood where it was difficult to see. I disarmed it, picked the lock, and slowly opened the stainless steel door.

Inside, the shelving was still in place, but rather than holding boxes of frozen french fries and hamburger patties, there were wooden crates with Chinese symbols printed on them. Stepping inside, I shined my light around and saw a number of cardboard boxes stacked near the back. One of them was open, and I saw the brassy reflection of a Mason jar lid.

The wooden crates were nailed shut, so I left long enough to retrieve my crowbar from the furniture store, and then pried one of them open. Inside the crate, lying in neat, staggered rows, were a dozen AK-47 assault rifles. I took one of them out and looked it over. It looked like every other AK I had ever seen, made of wood and heavy steel, with simple iron sights and a long, banana-shaped magazine. The writing on the receiver was easily recognizable as Chinese characters. Some of the writing on the box, however, was different.

I shined the light on a piece of paper stapled to the front. It looked like some kind of shipping label, and unlike Chinese glyphs, the writing on it was blockish rather than spidery. It definitely was not Japanese—I'd traveled to Japan a couple of times when I was younger, and I would have recognized Kanji, Hiragana, or Katakana—so maybe Korean? Having never been to Korea I couldn't be sure, but it seemed like a logical assumption.

Not having any use for the weapon, I put it back in the crate and continued searching. There were ten more crates full of rifles, and an equal number filled with twenty-round boxes of ammunition. The writing on the ammunition crates was Cyrillic, meaning they were clearly of Russian origin.

"So, we got Chinese rifles, Korean shipping manifests, and Russian-made ammo." I reasoned aloud, shining my light on the crates. "Where the hell did you Legion guys get this stuff?"

That was the million-dollar question.

The rest of the cache yielded first-aid supplies, vacuum-sealed bags of some kind of jerked meat, and cardboard boxes full of vegetables canned in Mason jars. I didn't quite trust the jerky, but the seals on the jars were intact, so I grabbed a couple filled with cubed potatoes and carrots and set them aside. Behind a stack of boxes in the back, I found two small propane grills, and a canister of fuel for each one.

"Sweet Mary, please tell me you're full." I picked one of the canisters up and hefted it a few times. Yep. Definitely full.

Behind the grills, three large, black cases leaned against the wall. My headlamp reflected off the checkered plastic, and I passed a hand over the surface.

"Well, what do we have here?"

I picked one of them up and carried it to the table in the kitchen. When I opened it, I found myself staring down at a Stryker hunting crossbow, complete with a ten-bolt quiver and a low-power scope. I let out an excited laugh and picked the crossbow up to look it over.

I didn't know much about crossbows, but this one seemed to be of good quality, and the scope was a Leupold that I knew for a fact was expensive—I had an identical one in my own collection. The other two plastic cases contained the same equipment, but I only took the bolts, giving me a total of thirty. It would be extra weight for me to carry, but the ability to hunt game in silence was well worth it.

After emptying one of the crates full of rifles, I threw in my new weapon, the bolts, canned food, and one of the camping grills, and carried it all outside. To make my presence less obvious, I put the chain and padlock back on the front door on the way out. Not that it would have stopped anyone from getting in if they were really determined, but there was no sense making it easy on them. And if any Legion troops happened along, leaving the lock off the door would tip them off immediately that someone else was here. Better safe than sorry.

When I got back to the furniture store, I set up the grill, poured some potatoes and dried venison in a small pot, and left them to simmer for a while. As they cooked, I kept thinking about the writing on those crates, and the weapons inside. I thought about General Jacobs, and the reports he'd read about the Republic of California, and their weaponry. I thought about Grayson Morrow, and how he'd heard some of the Legion leadership talking about weapons shipments, but never who was bringing them, or where they came from. Finally, I thought about the map in my pocket, and how I could best make use of it.

I turned off the heat and set the stew aside to cool, along with thoughts of the Free Legion. If all went according to plan, I would be their guest at some point in the next two days, and if I played my cards wisely, maybe I could find answers to some of these questions. I ate my stew, curled up in my bedroll, and slept.

Chapter 16

Fearful Symmetry

I awoke to the sound of clattering on the pavement.

After loading the crossbow, I crept slowly to the window, crouched down beneath the sill, and peeked outside. On the street below, an eight-point buck stepped gingerly through the collection of scattered corpses, limping heavily on one of its hind legs. Through the crossbow's scope, I could see a large gash on the injured leg, and above it, what appeared to be a huge bite wound.

"Wasn't a walker that did that," I whispered. "What got ahold of you?"

The deer's path was going to take it directly in front of the furniture store. I aimed the crossbow through one of the broken windowpanes and waited.

Come on. Just a little closer.

I held still, controlling my breathing and not moving a muscle. The wind picked up and whistled through the broken glass. The deer, with its finely honed instincts, knew danger was near and stopped every couple of steps to look around.

Clip-clop. Clip-clop.

Scan left, scan right.

Clip-clop. Clip-clop.

Scan left, scan right.

I ignored the heat in my bladder, the stiffness in my back, and applied careful pressure to the trigger. I hadn't practiced with the crossbow, so I just had to trust that the scope was zeroed, and that the trigger pull wasn't too heavy. The deer took a few more steps, stopped, and raised its nose to test the air.

Perfect.

The crack of the string was surprisingly loud. The buck started, and then took off at a broken sprint for about forty yards before it faltered and pitched face first into the blacktop. I left the crossbow in the furniture store, grabbed my hunting knife and the M-4, and set off after it.

The buck was dead by the time I reached it. The bolt's razor-sharp broadhead had punched through his heart, shredded it, and kept right on trucking. I was amazed he had run so far, considering the damage. A pool of thickening blood spread out from beneath the buck's chest and began to widen, staining the pavement crimson. In its smooth surface, I saw my reflection looking down, darkened and featureless. The hair on my arms stood up, and I wondered what it would be like if the tables were turned. If the last thing I ever saw was my killer gazing down at me, blade in hand.

I put my hunting knife back in its sheath for the moment, and inspected the damage to the buck's hind leg. As I had suspected, it looked like a large dog bite. I'd seen plenty of deer branded with them over the last few years, victims of wild dogs, wolves, and other predators.

Worried that the dead buck's attackers might still be in pursuit, I stood up and scanned the periphery of the street. For a few seconds, all was quiet. Then I heard a rapid clicking, several in number, and moving closer. Like the sound of hard nails running over pavement, gripping for purchase.

The clicking increased in volume until, from behind a building up the street, a familiar black-furred shape came running around the corner, spotted me, and skidded to a halt. It glared hatefully at me, its tongue lolling from the corner of its mouth, flecks of foam caked around its snout, flanks heaving with labored breath. I leveled my M-4 and took a few steps toward it.

"You've been chasing this thing a long time. Haven't you, boy?"

The mastiff lowered his scarred head and growled, not quietly like before, but viciously, and with murderous intent. I strained my ears for more clicks, looking around, left, right, and behind, waiting for the other three who were no doubt closing in.

"Tell you what," I said, stopping. "I don't need much. Let me cut off a leg, maybe a tenderloin, and you guys can have the rest. How about it?"

The big dog took a few steps forward, testing my resolve. I raised the rifle and fired a round into the pavement in front of him, spraying his legs, chest, and snout with shrapnel. He yelped, and began backing off. As he did so, two more of his pack rounded the corner and stopped to survey the scene. I shifted my aim and triggered a few rounds close to them as well, peppering them with bits of pavement. It had the same effect as with their pack leader, startling them and taking them out of hunter/killer mode. They began to ease back, tails down, watching me with thinly veiled malice.

The Rottweiler was last to arrive. His shorter legs didn't allow him to run quite as fast as his companions. As soon as he saw me, he switched directions and barreled for me at top speed, mouth open and trailing streamers of saliva. He was probably forty yards away, but as fast as he was coming, he would cover that distance in a few seconds.

With no time to think, I raised the rifle, put the front sight on his chest, and fired four times. The massive dog yelped, stumbled, and hit the ground, rolling to a stop just a few feet in front of me. The other three dogs stayed where they were.

The last report echoed away into the distance, leaving the feral pack and me in silence. The dogs stared nervously at their fallen pack mate, as unmoving as statues. I knelt down beside the Rottweiler and touched his side. He did not stir beneath my hand.

His skin was warm, almost hot to the touch from chasing the deer. Blood poured from two wounds on his chest, and another on the back of his neck. One of the shots I fired must have gone into his mouth and penetrated straight through his head. The dog's eyes were still open, but there was no light in them. His mouth hung open, his big tongue limp and lifeless. Gone was the fearsomeness, the sharp fangs, and the murderous eyes. The immense power of his muscles lay flat, like a discarded weapon. The silence pressed in on me, gathering pressure between my ears until it became a ringing, rising and falling with the pounding of my heart. A slow heat began to spread in my face, and through my chest. My boots grated on the pavement as I stood up, a bleak noise in the gore-strewn square.

"Are you happy now?"

My voice was barely a whisper, struggling to escape the tightness in my throat as I walked toward the three wild dogs.

"You know what this is, don't you?" I shook the rifle at them, and they flinched. "You know what it can do, right? What the hell were you thinking?"

My words grew in volume until I was shouting. I ran at the dogs, intent on kicking them, but they trotted away, keeping their distance. Finally, I stopped and lowered my voice.

"When you see a human with a gun, you stay the fuck away. Haven't you learned that yet? How the fuck are you still alive?"

I shook my head and stared at them. Their ears were flat, tails down. One of the mutts let out a barely audible whine. The pressure in my head receded, taking the ringing in my ears with it, draining out of me and leaving a cold hollowness behind. My legs became shaky, and I swayed a bit on my feet.

“Get out of here. I’ll take what I need from the carcass, and you can have what’s left. Come back for it later, when I feel a little less like killing all of you.”

They stood still, understanding my posture, but not my words.

“GO ON!” I shouted. “GIT! FUCK OFF!”

That got them moving. They set off at a trot to the edge of town and disappeared around one of the gas stations. I walked back to the deer, set the M-4 on the ground, and drew my hunting knife.

*****

Later, I sat alone in the furniture store eating a plate of grilled deer steak and boiled potatoes, and waited.

While I had been butchering the buck, my thoughts kept turning to the creature that had followed me here, the one I had first glimpsed back at that nameless town. I didn’t doubt that he was still out there somewhere, maybe waiting for me to move on again.

Here, I had the advantage. If it came into town, I had places to go where I could reach it, but it couldn’t reach me. If it caught me out in the open, well … I didn’t like to think about that.

Time to get creative.

Using my hunting knife, I carved off one of the buck’s legs, tied it off to a length of para-cord, and threw it over the arm of a streetlight, paying out the cord until the dripping meat was just a few feet off the ground. The streetlight was just across the way from the furniture store, giving me a perfect vantage point from which to watch. I left the deer’s guts on the pavement and dragged the remainder of the carcass with me to my hiding spot. I still planned to let the dogs have it after I was finished but, for now, I had to deal with more pressing matters.

The bait set, it was just a matter of who would show up first: the feral dogs, the beast, or the infected. I didn't have to wait long to find out.

The first moan carried to me from the eastern side of town. Another answered it, followed by a few more, and in short order, a horde began to gather in the streets. Thankfully, the Legion had been diligent in their efforts to clear the countryside of walkers, and there were only a two dozen of them. I let them have the deer guts and the dead Rottweiler for their last meal, and then watched as they followed the scent left behind from when I had dragged the buck's carcass away. It led them to the furniture store, and as expected, they noticed the leg hanging from the streetlight.

It was the work of a minute or two eliminating the first batch, the .22 rifle sending hot lead into their craniums from less than twenty yards away. Others straggled in over the next hour or so in ones and twos. I dealt with them, and eventually, things went quiet.

I had expected more ghouls to show up, drawn by the crack of the Ruger, but it didn't happen. When Scar (as I'd come to think of him) and the two mutts showed back up, I figured I was in the clear. They nosed around where the infected had eaten the deer guts, then approached the haunch hanging in the street. A single shot from the Ruger and a couple of shouted threats dissuaded them, and they bolted away.

The seconds slipped by in silence while I waited, the emptiness around me punctuated only by the occasional birdcall, a breeze, or the creak of wood shifting in the walls around me. The relative warmth of the last couple of days had been nice—it had actually stayed in the forties when the sun was up—but the good weather had moved on for greener pastures. My breath made frost-white spouts in the frigid air.

I stayed that way for hours, hardly moving, only getting up to answer the call of nature or munch a few handfuls of jerky and potatoes. Impatience began to nag at me, reminding me that I was already a day behind, and that I couldn't afford any more delays. The sun crept farther to the west, shifting the shadows of the buildings as I watched the street. Nothing happened. The beast didn't show up.

"Well, Eric. Failure is a part of life," I said to the empty room. "You gotta know when to cut your losses and move on."

Grabbing the buck by his antlers, I dragged him back down to the first floor and out into the street. His coarse fur rasped on the sidewalk, then the pavement, and then I dropped him just beneath the streetlight where his leg was hanging.

"You know, I'm really sorry about all this." I said to the carcass as I cut the para-cord hanging from the post and carried the leg back to its former owner. "You got the shit end of this deal, my friend. But at least you died quickly. You weren't going to last much longer anyway, with that torn-up leg."

One of the deer's empty eyes stared up at me, unseeing. A fly buzzed around it, landed on it, and crawled over its glazed surface. I tossed the leg down and turned to go back to the furniture store. Just as I was opening the door, I heard a sound behind me. Like someone running a hand over a piece of coarse cloth, faint and rasping.

I moved unhurriedly, my hand inching for the M-4 hanging from my back. I gathered it and brought it to my shoulder, careful not to make any sudden movements. Slowly, I turned and faced the street. Not twenty feet away from me, standing over the dead buck and sniffing at the incision where I had gutted him, was the most terrible, magnificent thing I had ever seen.

A full-grown Bengal tiger.

All six hundred pounds of him.

His paws were the size of dinner plates, his tail was as thick as my forearm, and I had seen boulders that were smaller than his head. The tips of his shoulders came up almost to my chest, and all along his frame, powerful muscles rippled like steel cables under a glossy coat of black-striped, reddish-orange fur.

My knuckles went white on the rifle's grip. I stood rooted to the spot, listening to my hammering pulse and the quickening rasp of my breathing. Coldness settled in my stomach and began spreading upward into my face, down my arms, and into my hands. Somewhere in the dark recesses of my mind, in a place that still remembered fleeing from sharp teeth on some distant, long-ago savanna, a voice began to cry out. It was a voice that knew why people feared the dark, why we find safety in numbers, and why we scream when we're in danger. The voice began pounding at me, growing insistent, drumming against the rational surface of my mind with a single, urgent command: RUN!

But I didn't listen. Running would have just provoked the creature, and there was no way I was going to get away from it if it decided to give chase. Not from this distance, anyway. So I did the only thing I could do. I stood perfectly, absolutely still.

The tiger took a half step to his right, pushed his blunted snout under the flap of the buck's flank, and began licking at the muscles along its ribcage. After a few seconds of this, he began to gnaw at the meat, his massive fangs easily tearing through tendons and sinew. A few bites seemed to excite him, and he began chewing away at the carcass with gusto.

In a rush of thought, as I stood there watching one of the largest apex predators in the world snacking on a deer as big as a full-grown man, several things occurred to me at once. First, if the tiger had wanted to kill me, he could have done so. Easily.

Second, it didn't take me twenty seconds to walk from the deer's carcass to the furniture store. But that was enough time for the beast to emerge from his hiding spot, trot across an unknown expanse of street while dancing over a slew of rotting corpses, and approach with such stealth that if he had not stopped to sniff at the deer's carcass, I never would have known he was there.

Third, I had a decision to make. Stand here and hope he goes away, or take a chance and ease my way into the store. Maybe the fresh meat in front of him would keep his attention and allow me to slip away. Maybe not.

My plan had been to kill the tiger from my perch in the furniture store with the M-4, but standing there looking at him, I realized how foolish that idea had been. The .223 rounds in the M-4 were simply not designed to tackle a big critter like a Bengal tiger. Hell, they were only marginally effective against people. Unless I caught the big cat behind the ear, or managed to split the difference between a couple of ribs and take out his heart, shooting him would have done nothing more than piss him off. And an injured, pain-maddened tiger on my trail was the last thing I needed.

So.

What to do.

I began to ease my weight backward, preparing to shift my feet and reach for the door. My boot made a noise on the ground, and the tiger lifted his head to look at me. I froze.

Bright golden eyes regarded me for a few heart-stopping moments. He licked blood from his chops, lazily and slow, making loud smacking noises. There was a languidness to his movements, a confident ease. His posture was relaxed, and his expression seemed … placid. Calm. Like there wasn't a thing in the world for him to worry about. There was no distrust, or warning, or hostility in that alien gaze. He was just looking at me like he would look at a tree, or a rock, or some other inconsequential thing. His muscles did not tense, and I sensed no imminent attack coming from him.

"Hi there," I said.

The tiger tilted his head to the side, an oddly doglike gesture. I kept still, not wanting to startle him.

"You're a big one, aren't you? Must be why you're so hungry."

The tiger gazed a few seconds longer, then lowered his face and went back to eating. My pulse began to slow down, the coldness that gripped me receded, and I loosened my grip on the rifle. The frantic, panicked voice urging me to flee went silent, and the locked synapses in my brain began to fire again, allowing me to think.

What the hell was an animal native to Southern Asia doing in Western Tennessee? He must have escaped from a zoo, or maybe he was once some wealthy eccentric's pet.

I remembered a newscast I saw during the Outbreak in which police had gone into a zoo to stop the zookeepers from letting the animals out. It had become clear that the walking dead were too much for the military, and the people responsible for the animals wanted to give them a fighting chance. It started with one zoo, and soon spread to hundreds of others. Maybe this guy's presence was the result.

When I thought about it, it made sense. It would explain why this tiger had followed me, and why he didn't seem to think I was a danger to him. If he was a zoo animal, then he would be accustomed to the presence of humans. Maybe he'd even been born in a zoo and raised by people, fed his meals by them. Could be that's what he thought this was, me dragging out the buck. Feeding time.

I took a few tentative steps forward, making sure the tiger could hear me, and keeping my rifle at the ready. The big cat ignored me.

A few more steps. He kept eating.

My feet seemed to take on a mind of their own, and I got closer, and closer, until I was just a few inches outside of arms reach. I leaned over, muttering nonsense words to avoid startling him, and reached out a hand toward his rear flank, my pulse quickening, amazed at my own audacity.

The tiger's fur was thick, and surprisingly soft. He stopped eating for just a moment to look back at me, licked his face a few times, and then went back to his meal. I ran a hand along his back and felt the iron-hard muscles beneath his thick skin. The vitality within him was electric, a high-voltage, humming radiance that made my breathing shallow and caused a sweat to break out on my forehead.

The voice in the back of my head started sending out warnings, but I ignored it. Beneath my hand was one of the most highly evolved killing machines that nature had ever created, and I was scratching his back like he was a house kitty.

A few minutes went by, me moving my hand along his flank while he munched on dead deer, until finally he swung his tail and swatted me on the leg. I looked over to see him watching me. He made a chuffing noise and shifted his backside into my hip. It was just a slight motion for him, but it nearly knocked me on my ass. The message was clear.

Stop bothering me.

I'm eating.

*****

I watched the tiger finish his meal from the window above the furniture store. He ate a hell of a lot of meat. Must have been ravenous.

As I watched, I sat in the leather chair and pondered the conundrum I had on my hands. I no longer wanted to kill the creature—not after getting up close and petting him—but I didn't want him following me around either. He wasn't interested in killing me right now, which was good, but he was still a wild animal. I did not want to spend my last seconds screaming in the jaws of yon massive beast.

So what was I going to do about it?

I took a piece of jerky from my pack and chewed on it, thinking. The tiger stopped gnawing away at the deer, wandered over to a patch of sunshine between the shadows of two buildings, and stretched out on the concrete. He spent a few minutes preening before he laid his massive head down and heaved a deep, satisfied sigh. He napped for a while, then got up and wandered off. Probably thirsty, going out in search of water.

That made me thirsty, so I took a sip from my canteen, and turned my mind to the business of reasoning this problem out.

There was no way I could shake the tiger from my trail without resorting to violence. I did not want to do that, so the only option I had left was to just accept the situation. He could follow me if he wanted to and, if he attacked, I would defend myself. But I wasn't going to kill him for no reason.

I spent the rest of the afternoon wandering around and searching through the few buildings that didn't look like they were about to collapse. I found some interesting things, but nothing that I could carry with me. If I survived the destruction of the Legion, assuming of course that it actually happened and I wasn't just throwing my life away, I would definitely be coming back to this place.

There were things here that the Legion might not have had much use for—furniture, nice clothes, jewelry, art, scrap metal, dishes, cookware, etc.—but I knew plenty of other people who did. This place was worth a fortune in salvage, even without the weapons cache.

As the sun was disappearing again, I sat on a bench in front of what had once been a police station and thought about what the future might hold for me. Was this to be my next career, places like this? Was this what I would do for a living when I got to Colorado, run a salvage operation? I could just imagine it, written on a big hand-painted sign over a chain-link fence—Eric Riordan: Junkman.

The theme to "Sanford and Son" played through my head, and I laughed until my ribs hurt. Until I almost fell off the bench. Maybe Gabe could go into business with me, and I could exclusively refer to him as You Big Dummy.

I laughed harder.

A crow seated on an awning across from me tilted his head quizzically, decided that being close to an armed man with a few screws loose was not conducive to a long life, and flew away.

*****

Scar and his pack showed up at some point during the night.

I awoke to the sound of them growling and ripping into what was left of the deer carcass. It was cold, so I didn't bother getting up to go to the window. Even if I had, I doubted I would have been able to see them; it was too dark outside.

From where I lay, I could see the silver light of the moon obscured through a thick bank of clouds that must have rolled in at some point during the night. The space between the furniture store and the building across the street was pitch black. The kind of darkness where you can't see your hand in front of your face.

I lay still, moderately warm in my layers of clothes and blankets and the sleeping bag. I listened to dogs grunt, and tear, and eat. It was strangely comforting.

I went back to sleep.

*****

It was time to move out.

I had woken up with the dawn, and outside the wind had picked up. It howled over the tops of buildings, blew detritus around on the street, and whistled an eerie refrain through broken windows. It was going to be a cold, blistering day, but there was nothing for it. I had already lost enough time. I had to get moving.

I packed my gear, checked my weapons, and climbed down from the loft for the last time. I left the grill behind, as well as the crossbow. It would have been nice to bring them with me, but when the Legion eventually captured me I didn't want them to know that I had found their cache. That probably wouldn't go over too well.

The tiger was back. He sniffed at the remaining scraps of deer meat left on cracked bones and walked away. He sat down on the sidewalk with a disappointed sigh.

"Didn't leave you much did they, big fella?"

He looked at me blankly, then went back to staring at the remains. Giving him a wide berth—he was hungry, after all—I ducked between two buildings and headed due south. I had gone maybe a hundred yards from town, and just entered the edge of the surrounding woodland, when gunshots rang out behind me.

I stopped and whipped around, rifle at the ready. More gunshots sounded, and with the gunshots, came a scream.

The tiger. Had to be. Nothing else could have made a sound like that. It wasn't quite a roar, or a growl, but higher in pitch, keening and agonized. Almost like the moans of the infected, but a hundred times more powerful. It tore at me, raking around the inside of my skull and stabbing into my ears. I had to resist the urge to clap my hands to the sides of my head to block it out.

More gunshots. Lots of them, from automatic weapons, and with a distinctive sound. There is only one rifle in the world that sounds like that.

AK-47.

And there was shouting. A lot of shouting. At least three voices, maybe more. I ducked behind a tree, dropped my pack and the Ruger, and waited.

A few more shots. Semi-automatic, more focused, directed. The screaming stopped, and I went cold. The startled panic in me subsided, washed over by the icy current spreading outward from my chest. Before I knew what I was doing, I was moving.

AK-47s meant the Legion. The fact that they started shooting so soon after I left meant that we had missed crossing paths by a narrow margin. They must have approached from the highway, or from the other side of town. If I had hung around just a minute or two longer, they might have seen me and gotten the drop on me. But they didn't, which meant that for the moment, I had the advantage. An advantage that would last until they discovered their ransacked weapons cache, and the still-warm grill that I had cooked my breakfast on. Then they would know that I had been there, and would start searching for me.

I couldn't let them capture me, not here. They would find Grayson Morrow's map that I was still carrying, and they would put two and two together. I wouldn't live long enough to regret it.

I unbuckled the belt on my web gear, took off everything but the CZ and the spare ammo, put the belt back on, and moved westward. My shoulder hit a wall two blocks down and a couple of blocks over from where the gunshots had come from. From what I could tell, all the shots had sounded from the same place. It started with one rifle, then others had joined in. Probably one or two guys spotted the tiger, panicked, fired upon it, and alerted the others who added their guns to the fray.

Sons of bitches.

I pied on the corner, saw nothing, and moved up. There was a narrow street connecting the buildings around me with the buildings going through the central part of town. I looked one way. Nobody. I looked the other way. Nothing. I darted across the street and took cover behind a large green dumpster, eased around it, and worked my way forward until I reached the corner. I looked east, away from the sound of the gunshots. No one there.

Again, I pied my way out, moving in tight little increments, exposing as little of my head and shoulders as possible, keeping my gun trained in the same direction as my eyes. There, at the intersection in front of the furniture store, standing over the twitching, convulsing body of the tiger.

Five of them.

Five dead men.

I slipped back, went to the end of the building, and used the side street to get close. First one block, then another. I leaned into a corner and listened. I could just make out what they were saying.

"… scared the shit out of me." A nervous laugh. "Big motherfucker, never seen anything like it."

A different voice. "Think that's why we found them goats the way we did? Maybe this thing did it?"

A third voice. "Could be. Didn't look like nothin' no dog could do."

"It don't fucking matter." Fourth voice. Older, deep, rough. "We're here for ammo. Mark, go get the pull-cart out of the post office. Dave, take Aaron and start staging the crates in the restaurant. Don't forget about them goddamn booby traps, I don't want to be scraping your asses up with a squeegee. Me and Red are gonna go up on lookout. Keep your eyes open, and watch out for the dead. They might'a wandered in while we was away. Go on, get movin'."

This guy had the voice of authority. Like someone who was used to giving orders and having them followed. He would die last. He had things to tell me. But I had to move quickly. As soon as they stepped around the corner, they would see the infected I had killed. Fresh corpses among the bones of the long dead would put them on alert. I couldn't let that happen.

While they were talking, I eased my way out. I could see four of them, including the leader, all standing in a cluster around the dead tiger. Stepping out, I crouched down on one knee, steadied my aim, and let off the first shot.

I didn't have any optics, but I had spent plenty of time practicing with iron sights, and my aim was good. The shot took the first one in the side of the head and penetrated straight through. The man beside him was shorter, so the bullet missed him, but the side of his face went red from the splash of blood that erupted from his friend's head. He had a half-second to register shock before my second and third shots hit him center of mass, right in the chest. He doubled over, choked out a scream, and took a few running steps away. I shifted my aim and nailed a third one with another two-round burst, one in the chest, and one through the throat. He coughed out a spray of blood and fell down.

"Fuck!" The leader spotted me and raised his AK, but I was already moving.

Unlike what you see in the movies, when an assault rifle as powerful as an AK-47 opens up on a brick wall, the bricks disintegrate. You don't want to be standing behind them when that happens, especially at close range. I ran to the other side of the building, checked the corner, then turned it and sprinted toward the street.

When I reached the edge, the leader had stopped firing and was shouting at his last man, pulling on his arm. The other man's face was blank with shock. He stood still, his attention fixed on his choking, dying comrades.

"Dammit, Red, come on!"

Red was facing me while the leader stood to one side, out of my line of fire. I pictured a white line running from the base of Red's throat, all the way down to his belt buckle. Centerline of the body—a bad place to get shot. Lots of vital organs and big arteries there, and behind them, the all-important spinal cord. Put enough rounds through the centerline, and they're dead before they hit the ground. So sayeth Gabriel, world without end, amen.

I stitched four rounds up Red's middle, starting down just below his belt, and ending at the hollow of his throat. He didn't even scream, just toppled over like a felled tree. The leader turned to me, and tried to lift his rifle again. I let out half a breath, shifted the front sight, and fired a single shot at his right arm. The bullet slammed into his deltoid, probably breaking the bones beneath, and he dropped the rifle.

I stepped out of cover and approached. The leader was screaming, high pitched and pleading, like a child with his finger caught in a door.

"Shut up!" I yelled at him.

He fumbled for the pistol at his belt. I raised my rifle again.

"Don't."

He did anyway. I stopped, took aim, and put a bullet in his other shoulder. He cried out all over again, louder this time. *How do you like it, you fuck*?

I shifted my aim downward and pulled the trigger again, this time putting a round in his leg. I kept my aim outside, making sure it didn't hit the femoral artery. I didn't want him to bleed out. Not yet.

He fell, screaming nearly as loudly as the tiger had. I stood over him for a moment, staring down.

"How many others?"

His eyes were wide, bulging, panicked. Face pale, going into shock. "What?"

"How. Many. Others. Was it just you five?"

“Fuck you.” He spat the words out at me, a flare of defiance in his eyes. I smiled at him, and whatever he saw there dimmed his fire.

“I still have plenty of bullets, friend. You don’t want to know where the next one is going. Now, I’ll ask you one more time. How many others?”

“What … who … who the hell are you?”

I shook my head. “You’re not listening.” Slowly, I began moving the barrel up his leg, toward his torso. Smoke curled from the flash hider as it inched upward.

“How many others? I won’t ask you again.”

The barrel stopped just over his groin. If he could have jumped out of his skin, he would have. I’d already killed all of his men and shot him three times. There could be no doubt in his mind that I was more than willing to carry out the implied threat, but he wasn’t acknowledging it. Didn’t want to believe it. He was in denial. This couldn’t be happening. Just a minute ago, less than a minute ago, everything was fine. He was on a mission. He was in charge. He was in control. And now, he was lying on the ground, probably bleeding to death with a loaded M-4 pointed at his balls. Must have been a hell of a shock. The poor guy couldn’t get his head around it.

“It’s just us,” he said, breathing rapidly. “There’s just the five of us.”

“There *were* five of you.” I corrected. “What’s your name?”

“What?”

“Your name, asshole. What is it?”

“Carson. Mitchell Carson.”

I reached down and began searching him for weapons. With two blown out shoulders and a badly wounded leg, he wasn’t in much of a position to do anything about it.

“Okay, Carson-Mitchell-Carson. You and I are going to have a chat. “

I found a knife and a small .380 pistol. I tossed them away and made a pile of his weapons, well out of arm’s reach. Slinging the rifle around my back, I knelt down by Carson’s legs and drew my hunting knife. I held it up where he could see it, twisting the flat of the blade to catch the light. His eyes locked to it like a magnet, as if it had its own gravitational pull. A singularity of dense, unrelenting force, drawing him further and further into panic.

“I have a pretty good bullshit detector, and let me tell you Carson-Mitchell-Carson, I don’t like being bullshitted. Am I clear?”

He nodded quickly, eyes still locked on the hunting knife.

“Good. That will save me time, and you a lot of pain. Just to let you know, if I don’t like what you have to say, we’re going to start with your Achilles’ tendon. Then we’ll work our way up from there. Savvy?”

The quick nod again. Still with the wide, fearful gaze.

“Good.” I smiled. “Let’s get started.”

*****

We spoke for a long time, the two of us.

He told me a great many things, some of them useful, some not. He was a low-level leader in the Legion, middle management really. But he knew things that Grayson Morrow didn’t, and he gave me a fairly good idea of where the Legion was getting its weapons. As the questions became more focused and direct, he began to grow reluctant with his answers. Stuttering. Long hesitations between sentences. It finally got to the point where I felt that he wasn’t being honest with me.

That was the part where I severed his Achilles' tendon.

Left leg. It was a tough piece of tissue, and I had to saw at it a bit before it parted.

I had seen Steve do the same thing to a guy back in North Carolina, and it had worked remarkably well. I'd been pretty squeamish about it at the time, but the years since then had not been kind to me. I had seen too many people suffer horribly at the hands of those with no regard for human life, and I had lost all patience with would-be conquerors. This guy had thrown his lot in with the bad guys, the ones who murdered, and raped, and stole from others. The ones who had nearly killed me, and who had shot two of my closest friends. One of them just a little boy.

No. It didn't bother me to do it. Carson-Mitchell-Carson had made his choice, and the consequences were his to suffer.

Things went smoothly after that. I didn't glean enough information to change my mission, but I did learn enough to give me an edge. Finished with the interrogation, I stood up and thanked Carson-Mitchell-Carson for his cooperation.

And then I shot him in the head.

Chapter 17

Between Brave and Stupid

I reached the outskirts of the Legion encampment just after nightfall.

The bridge I was hiding under was part of a highway overpass situated atop a steep, man-made hill. Ahead, less than half a mile away, a sprawling warehouse squatted next to a stretch of empty four-lane blacktop. The featureless concrete structure looked like a white slab of dead flesh in the descending gloom. I was a few hundred feet above it and could see the entire complex from one end to the other.

From the outside, the place looked utterly abandoned. No sound, no stirring of voices, no flicker of campfires, no movement, nothing. The Legion had gone to great pains to make sure that the place looked unoccupied.

But I knew better.

The trek here, after leaving Carson-Mitchell-Carson lying in a puddle of his own blood, had been remarkably uneventful. I didn't encounter a single infected, a testament to the Legion's efficiency. It made me wonder, not for the first time, what vendetta the Legion held against the people of Hollow Rock. It wasn't as if the town had anything that the Legion couldn't provide for its own. These rogue militants had food, shelter, weapons, everything they needed. They had proven that they could protect themselves from the undead, and their fearsome reputation had kept other, smaller groups of marauders at bay.

Adding to the mystery was the question of how the Legion had evolved from a few loosely affiliated squads of raiders into an organized, well-supplied para-military force. Carson-Mitchell-Carson had conveniently given me one piece of that puzzle—the weapons.

The AK-47s were being transferred in via seven overland routes, all of them originating from different points along the Mississippi River. They came from all over, accompanied by troops from another, larger group that was aiding the Legion.

The Midwest Alliance. Had to be.

But that didn't explain the Chinese manufacturing stamps, or the Korean shipping manifests, or the Russian ammo. I had a piece of the puzzle, but not all of it. To learn the rest, I would have walk down the hill, get across the highway, and allow the Legion to capture me.

I sat there for a while, staring and thinking about the difference between planning a thing, and actually going through with it. It's all fun and games until you come face to face with the part of your mission that might get you killed.

"Well, I made it this far," I muttered, standing up. "Might as well see it through."

While checking my gear for the last time, I decided that there was no point in letting the Legion have all of it. After searching around for a while, I found an old culvert that ran beneath a raised stretch of road near the bottom of the hill. One side of the culvert had caved in, and thick debris clogged the other side, effectively preventing any water from flowing through it. I wrapped the M-4 and the CZ in a trash bag to keep them dry, along with the lock-pick, the multi-tool, and a bottle of water, and cached them in the culvert. The Sig, the hunting knife, and the Ruger I kept with me, as well as the ax and the crowbar. It would look strange if I showed up completely unarmed.

Finally, I cast a glance across the field at the warehouse, and set off toward it. My heart began to beat faster as I approached, and it took an effort of will to stay calm. I looked across the field, checking around and behind me just like any survivor would, but kept my movements casual, trying not to give away the apprehension that was building to a fever pitch.

I reached the road that ran alongside the structure and discovered the ditch beside the road was deeper than it had looked from up the hill. If I stood on the bottom, the edge of the pavement would be a little above my head. The ditch on the other side looked just as deep. I could climb it, but it would be a pain in the ass. Casting a glance around for a better place to cross, I saw a gravel road that intersected with the highway a quarter-mile to the north, near the edge of the surrounding woodlands.

Looks like a nice place to set up an ambush, I thought. Plenty of cover, deep depressions on both sides of the road. They could probably hide three or four people over there.

Holding the Ruger loosely in my hands, I headed toward it. As I got close, I saw movement in the tree line and heard metal scraping on dirt from down inside the ditch. If I were approaching with bad intentions, this would be a good time to open up on them. Take the initiative, and rock them back on their heels, maybe try to escape. If Gabe were here with me, we could leapfrog backwards, laying down covering fire as we went.

But Gabe wasn't with me, and my purpose was not to escape. So I kept walking.

I made it almost to the rise in the side of the road where the gravel path met the pavement before they sprung the trap. As I had suspected, there were four of them, all armed with the familiar Chinese assault rifles. Two of them emerged from cover in the woods where I had already spotted them, and the other two climbed a set of steps carved into the ditch on the opposite side of the highway.

"Stop right there!" one of them shouted. "Drop the gun and get your hands up!"

For just the briefest of moments, I hesitated. It would have been easy to sprint to my right, spraying bullets as I went. I was certain I could hit two of them on my way to the tree line before taking off through the woods. They would have a hard time getting a clean shot at me in the thick stands of pines and cedars. But then I reminded myself what I was doing this for, and remembered Grayson Morrow's instructions:

Don't try to fight them when they find you, just do as they tell you. If you try to fight, they won't hesitate. They'll kill you. Surrender quietly, and they'll take you to the tunnels. It's where they take everybody they capture.

Doing my best to look surprised, I let the Ruger fall to the ground, and raised my hands.

"Mike, get his weapons," the one in charge said. He was standing to my right, one of the two who had emerged from the trees.

"What the hell?" I said, stepping back.

"Don't you fucking move!" the leader shouted again. "Take one more step and you're dead!"

I stopped, and stared around in what I hoped was an expression of stunned disbelief. They must have bought it, because they didn't shoot.

The one identified as Mike strode forward. He was shorter than me, skinny, with a narrow, ratlike face. He grinned as he picked up the Ruger.

"Thanks," he said, holding up the rifle. "I've been wanting one of these."

"Mike, stop fucking around," the leader said, and motioned at me with the barrel of his AK. "You, drop the pack and the web gear. Try anything stupid, and I'll turn you into hamburger."

My hands shook a little as I took off the pack, and unbuckled the load-bearing harness. Rat-face Mike stepped forward with a swagger in his step and whistled as he looked over my equipment.

"Ooohh, Sig Mosquito. These are popular. I'll get a good price for it." He pulled the gun from its holster and stuck it in his belt. "What else you got for me?"

He smiled up at me, brimming with confidence, and I almost laughed at him. The little rat-fuck had no idea how close he was to dying. A quick strike to the throat would distract him, followed by a thrust from my hunting knife to finish the job. A twist of the blade on the way out, and he would be standing in a pile of his own guts. It would take seconds to do it, quick and easy.

I'm going to catch you alone sometime, Rat-Face, I thought. *We'll see how cocky you are when I open you up and strangle you with your own intestines.*

Stripped of my weapons and equipment, I stood still while Mike and one of the others searched me. It was not a gentle search, and I had to give them credit for being thorough. If there had been a weapon hidden on me, they would have found it.

"He's clean, Tommy," Rat-Face Mike said, stepping back and training his rifle on me. Tommy, the leader, stepped closer.

"What's your name, shitbird?"

He was taller than I was, and heavyset, with broad shoulders and thick, ham-sized hands. A grizzled beard coated his face all the way down to the collar of his shirt, and he reeked of body odor and old booze.

"Logan," I said, without hesitation. "Logan Morrison."

I saw the backhanded blow coming, but rather than try to get out of its way, I simply rolled with it. My head snapped to the side, and stars exploded in my vision. I managed to keep my feet until another blow crashed into my gut, slamming all of the air out of my lungs. That one put me on my knees.

"Wrong answer," he said. "Your name is maggot. And from here on out you are the property of the Free Legion."

I suppose I should start begging now.

"Listen, please, just take—"

The next blow was a kick aimed at my head. The leader, Tommy, stepped into it and brought it forward from about three counties back. If I had been stupid enough to sit still for it, it might have snapped my neck. Thankfully, I'm not stupid. I let it clip the side of my head and threw myself backward to make it look as if the kick had leveled me. Even though I dodged the worst of it, the force of the blow was still enough to rattle me, and I didn't have to fake the dazed expression on my face as a pair of hands lifted my roughly back to my knees.

"You will do as you are told." He punctuated the sentence with a vicious backhand. My right eye began to swell immediately.

"You will eat when we feed you, which won't be fucking much." Another strike. Harder this time.

"You will speak when you are spoken to." He reared back and slammed a fist into my face. I rolled with it as best I could, but it still hurt like a bastard. Warmth poured from my nose, and my next breath blew out a spray of blood from my upper lip.

"And if you even think about trying to escape, we'll string you up by your balls and skin you alive before we kill you." He finished with a final backhand.

It would have been easy to rear back and kick Tommy in the balls. I could have overhooked the arm of the raider to my left and dislocated his shoulder. After that, I could have thrown the one on my right at the rat-bastard covering me with a rifle. They were both smaller guys, and the impact would have knocked them over. I might have been able to grab a weapon, spray them all with lead, and escape.

Instead, I let myself go limp, head lolling down to my chest.

Satisfied that he had sufficiently beaten the shit out of me, Tommy stepped back and motioned to his men. “Zip this fucker up and take him to the pit. Looks like we all get booze and bitches when Lucian gets here.”

The two men holding me whooped and hollered as they planted me on my face and bound my hands behind my back with zip-ties. They pulled hard on the plastic restraints, tightening them until the hard edges bit deep into my skin. Once secured, they lifted me to my feet and began half-dragging me toward the back of the warehouse. On the way, I had to keep my head down to conceal a smile.

I survived, I thought. *I’m still alive.*

I raised my head enough to see the back entrance to the building, and the pitch-black interior beyond.

“Let’s go, sweetheart,” Rat-Face Mike said, and thrust me ahead of him.

I lost my footing, and fell forward into the darkness.

Part III

Under the sword lifted high, there is hell making you tremble.

-Miyamoto Musashi
The Book of Five Rings

Chapter 18

Gathering Dark

The first thing I noticed was that Grayson Morrow's description of the warehouse's layout was spot-on.

The second thing I noticed was the smell.

It was dark, earthy, and close, like a rag over my face. The smell of dirt, mold, and decaying leaves, all tied together by the fecal odor of decay. It reminded me of the mulch pile my father had kept in our back yard, only a thousand times more powerful.

Around me, the concrete floor stretched away into darkness except for a small, well-lit section near the far wall. There, someone had put up crude wooden partitions that reminded me of another warehouse I'd been in back in North Carolina. On that side were propane grills, candles, a few Coleman lanterns, couches, and boxes upon boxes of hard liquor. A few stooped figures hustled about sweeping the floor, tidying, and placing neatly folded clothes on beds. Only a small number of off-duty Legion troops occupied the area, all seated around tables and talking over plates of food.

On the far wall ahead of me, about two dozen rubber hospital mattresses lay on the ground, arranged neatly in rows. They had no sheets or pillows on them, only thin, rumpled blankets. Beside each palette, a heavy iron ring protruded from the concrete floor. Connected to each ring was a set of leg irons like the ones used by prisons. Most of the mattresses were empty, but on a few of them, figures sat huddled and shivering under their blankets. Chains extended from restraints on their ankles to the anchors driven into the floor. I was pretty sure they were all women.

Rat-Face Mike, and the asshole on my right, dragged me by my arms and dumped me on one of the thin green palettes. They clamped the leg irons to my ankles, and then, to my surprise, they cut the zip-ties on my wrists. My relief was short lived, however, as Rat-Face pulled a set of standard police handcuffs from his belt and clamped them over one wrist. His friend placed the barrel of his AK against my head.

"Give me your other hand," Rat-Face ordered.

I did as he said and held out my arm. He cuffed my other wrist, and then stood up and took a few steps away. At least now my hands were in front of me.

"We need to lay out a few ground rules." Rat-Face drew an expandable baton from behind his back and whipped it to the side, extending it to its full length.

"First: You don't speak unless spoken to. I don't want to hear any begging, or bribing, or bargaining, or any of that shit. Don't wanna hear it. It's annoying, and it won't do you any good anyway. If I want something from you, I'll take it, and there ain't a fucking thing you can do about it."

He pointed at me with the baton. "Second: You will do as you're told. I don't care what it is we tell you to do, you fucking do it. If someone tells you to lick his boots, you do it. If someone tells you to wash his clothes, you do it. If someone tells you to get down on your knees and suck his cock, you do it."

To punctuate, he stomped his filthy hiking boot on the ground in front of me. "There, your first opportunity to learn. Lick it."

This was the part I had been dreading.

In my long conversations with Grayson Morrow, he had told me about the methods by which the Legion recruited from the ranks of those they captured. Oddly enough, they weren't looking for people who were weak and pliable. They didn't want the meek, or the frightened, or the easily manipulated. They looked for people who were strong, tough, and defiant. They looked for the people who would rather swallow their blood than their pride.

These people they worked on, broke them down with beatings and hard labor. They kept at it until they had pushed them to the point of extreme mental and physical exhaustion, and then they started building them back up. But they didn't do this with all of their captives, only the ones that had the fortitude and the strength of will to endure it. The people who had the raw, stubborn spirit that the Legion could warp, and twist, and defile into something despicable. What Rat-Face was doing right now, the whole boot-licking thing, was the first step in the process. Their first indication as to what I was made of.

At least I could stop pretending to be scared.

"No way. Fuck that," I said.

Rat-Face smiled. "Y'know, I was hoping you'd say that." He took a couple of running steps, and his arm blurred toward me, swinging the baton.

There is a right way, and a wrong way, to block a strike from a bludgeon. You never want to cross your arms over your face in the classic defensive posture. This will only result in a broken ulna, in most cases. The proper way is to extend your arm straight outward, and let the offending object skirt down the outside of your arm until it deflects off the muscle of your shoulder. It's best to do this with one arm, while guiding the object away from you and moving forward to immobilize your opponent. Fortunately for Rat-Face, the cuffs on my wrists limited my mobility; otherwise, I would have taken that baton from him and rammed it down his scrawny throat.

Instead, I settled for stretching both arms forward, palms together as if in prayer, and circling them into the arc of the swing to disperse as much kinetic energy as possible. It still hurt like hell, but not bad enough to paralyze my left arm. More importantly, nothing broke.

The maneuver left Rat-Face off balance, so I stepped in and bumped him with my hip. I outweighed him by a good thirty pounds, and the impact sent him sprawling over onto his side. The other thug, the one still pointing his gun at me, laughed loudly.

"You are being pathetic," he said, in a heavily accented voice. Eastern European, maybe Russian. "Even he is being chained, and he beat you."

Rat-Face got to his feet. When he turned to face me, his skin had turned a dark shade of red and his knuckles were white around the grip of his baton. His thin lips stretched into a greasy smile. "You're gonna pay for that, sweetheart."

Next, he tried staying at the edge of where I could walk, bound as I was by the leg irons. He circled back and forth, trying to make me trip over my own feet, while sweeping the baton in short, flicking strikes. I countered by keeping my base planted and moving around from the waist to dodge the little ball of iron at the baton's tip. His arms weren't very long, and after seven or eight misses, he stepped back out of reach to ponder what to do next. All the while, the Russian laughed.

"He is being fast, this one," he said. "How do you say … *lusaf*?"

"I think you mean 'elusive,' you inbred Cossack fuck."

The Russian nodded, ignoring the insult. "*Da*, that is it. He is being elusive."

"Fine, here you go." Rat-Face flipped the baton around and offered the handle to the Russian. "Why don't you give it a try?"

The Russian shrugged, handed his rifle to Rat-Face, and took the baton. As he approached, I could tell just by the way he moved that he knew how to handle himself, unlike his uncoordinated friend.

His first swipe was a lateral, aimed at my waist. I bent forward and thrust my hips backward to avoid it. The Russian reversed the baton and brought it around toward my head in a deft, backhanded swing. I had to duck to get out of the way, which was exactly what my tormentor wanted. He let his momentum spin him around, and then sent a hammer-fist crashing into the back of my neck. My vision swam, my legs turned to rubber, and I fell forward onto my knees.

Yep. This one knew his business. That was exactly what I would have done.

The Russian chuckled, and from the corner of my eye, I saw him toss the baton in the air, let it spin a few times, and catch it. He held the handle toward Rat-Face.

"That is how you are to be doing it."

While I was still too dazed to move, Rat-Face took the baton and swung it with everything he had. It hit me on the small of my back, directly over the sensitive kidney area. The kidneys are a bad place to get hit; the two organs are not only filled with blood and big arteries, they are also filled with thousands upon thousands of nerve endings. A hard strike to the kidney hurts so bad that you literally cannot scream. Your muscles lock up, you can't breathe, and you suffer temporary paralysis of the torso and limbs. I was off balance when Rat-Face hit me, and the blow sent me toppling over onto my side.

I saw him making ready to strike again, and managed to go flat so that the only target he had available was my back. The baton bounced off my shoulder blade hard enough to make me wonder if it was broken. There was a whistling sound, and then the baton struck me again in the thick muscle at the middle of my back. Just as I was anticipating a fourth strike, I heard a single, fleshy clap.

"Not in the head, you fool. How are we to be having women and drink if we are having no slave?" the Russian said.

"LET GO OF MY HAND, YOU PINKO FUCK!"

I turned my head and saw the blurry outline of the Russian holding Rat-Face by the wrist, with the smaller man struggling to pull his hand away. Casually, with the same unworried ease as if he were swatting a fly, the Russian planted a knee in Rat-Face's gut. The little bastard gasped as his breath left him, eyes bulging, and went down to his knees. The Russian twisted the baton out his grasp like taking a lollipop from a petulant toddler, and shoved the other man over onto his back.

"Maybe you are not caring about pussy," he said, planting a boot on Rat-Face's chest, "but I am. We get nothing if this man is dead, *da*?"

He took a step back, tapped the baton against the sole of his boot to loosen the segments, collapsed it, and tossed it onto Rat-Face's chest.

"Get up," he said. "We are to be going back on duty now. I will to be coming back later and taking him to the mines."

He strolled casually back toward the entrance while Rat-Face struggled to his feet. He shot me a hateful glare as he got up, his eyes promising murder. He shoved the baton back into its holster, stared angrily for another moment, and then turned to follow the Russian out the door. When he had shut the door behind him, I rolled over onto my side, groaning.

"You shouldn't have done that." I heard a voice say from behind me. It was soft and whispering. Definitely feminine. I sat up slowly and craned my head to look.

"What?"

"You shouldn't have fought them like that. They'll come back, and there will be more of them. They'll make a game of it."

My vision cleared enough to see the person talking to me. She was young, maybe early twenties. She had long, blond hair that hung in filthy clumps down her dirt-encrusted face. Tear streaks marred the mud on her cheeks, leaving twin clean spots in their wake. She had a blanket wrapped around her but still shivered in the cold. I could see enough of her skin to know that she wasn't wearing any clothes, and that if she were cleaned up and fed, she would be quite pretty.

"Why are they doing this?" I asked. Of course, I already knew why, but I wanted to maintain my cover.

"They need workers," she said. "People to dig their tunnels."

Her eyes darted around, and she craned her head to see if anyone was listening. Then she leaned forward and whispered, "You're strong, and you can fight. If you stay alive, they'll try to recruit you. Try to make you one of them. But you have to keep fighting. Don't let them break you, no matter what. If you get through it, they'll let you live."

"What's your name?" I asked her.

"Miranda," she replied. "But don't tell anybody that. If they ask you for your name, say 'maggot'. Otherwise, they'll beat you again."

"Hey, shut the fuck up over there!" A voice called out from the table where the off-duty raiders were eating. We both sat quietly until the shouter went back to his meal.

"There'll be trouble for you now," the girl said. "You've caused a stir."

I chuckled, and lay back on my mattress. "Story of my life, Miranda. Story of my life."

*****

A few hours later, the Legion proved Grayson Morrow, as well as Miranda, wrong. They skipped the part where they sent a bunch of burly men to drag me off somewhere and beat the hell out of me. Maybe they figured they had done enough of that already. Instead, they went straight to phase two—isolation.

Not that I knew this right away. When I saw three raiders coming for me, one of them the big Russian, I thought my day was about to get a lot worse. I was right on that note, just not in the way that I thought I would be. They cuffed my hands behind my back, disconnected me from the iron ring in the floor, and fettered my ankles with another set of leg irons.

As they escorted me across the warehouse floor, the dank, earthy smell that pervaded the place grew stronger. Eventually, a lantern that one of the raiders carried illuminated the edges of a pile of dirt to our left. Craning my neck, I tried to see the top of it, but it disappeared into the murky black beyond the lantern's light. We passed more piles of dirt along the way, until finally we came to a stop.

Looking down, I saw a square had been cut into the thick concrete under my feet. The edges were fairly straight, and from the look of it, it had not been done recently. My guess was that whoever cut this hole had done so with heavy equipment, back when gasoline was still available. Which meant it could have been there for as long as two years.

There was a wooden platform built over the hole, with a smaller, square hatch in the middle of it. One of the raiders produced a key, opened a padlock on the hatch, and then disappeared down the ladder beneath. The Russian nudged me in my sore kidney with the barrel of his AK.

"Go on, maggot. Down the ladder."

I did as he said, and followed the fading light of the lantern down into the darkness. The ladder ended abruptly after only about twenty feet, and my feet hit bare dirt as I stepped away.

"Don't move," a voice said from the other side of the lantern. I squinted and turned my head away from it. "Stay right where you are. Try anything, and I'll kill you where you stand."

I waited, blinking and standing in place. The other two men climbed down behind me, grabbed me by the arms, and urged me forward.

“Let’s go,” one of them said.

I followed them down the tunnel and tried to glean as much information as I could along the way. So far, what Morrow had told me was holding up. Just as he had said, the tunnels were low and narrow, barely wide enough for two men to walk abreast while standing up straight. If I had been a few inches taller, I would have had to duck my head to avoid hitting the arched roof.

Every few feet along the walls, wooden supports ran from floor to ceiling and connected to thick, reinforced joists overhead. I’m no architect, but it looked to me that whoever had designed this tunnel system knew what the hell he or she was doing. It didn’t look like one of those crumbling death traps that drug smugglers had used along the U.S.-Mexico border back during the drug wars. This tunnel smacked of careful planning, and the expertise of a structural engineer.

After walking for what felt like miles, but was probably only a couple of hundred yards, the tunnel branched off in three directions. The lantern-bearer turned right, and the other two dragged me after him. The tunnel widened into a chamber that was maybe a hundred feet long, with six doors lining the walls on either side of a central walkway. The door frames were made of bricks and mortar that had been anchored into the surrounding hard-packed dirt, and the doors themselves had been fabricated from rebar and sections of angle-iron. Each one connected to its frame on heavy-duty steel hinges and had a large padlock holding it shut. The man with the lantern produced another key and unlocked one of the doors.

“In you go,” he said, grabbing me by the arm and shoving me through the door. I tripped over my leg irons and fell headlong onto the floor, just managing to turn sideways on the way down to avoid smacking my face into the dirt. The impact jarred my shoulder, and set my kidney to aching all over again.

“Enjoy your stay, maggot,” Lantern-Man said, laughing as he shut the door and locked it. The light faded with the sound of footsteps walking away, leaving me in complete darkness.

When I was sure that they were gone, I stood up and began walking the perimeter of the cell. It was square, and I measured it by walking heel to toe along all four sides. The walls were ten feet long, giving me a total of a hundred square feet of floor space. Not exactly the Waldorf-Astoria.

The floor was bare dirt, but it was hard-packed and dry. In one corner, I stumbled upon a five-gallon plastic bucket and wondered if my captors really wanted me to use it, or if it was some kind of psychological ploy. It wasn’t as if I could unbutton my pants with my hands cuffed behind my back.

“Speaking of …” I muttered, and sat down against the wall.

I had been hoping against hope that they would leave my hands bound in front of me, but evidently, my little display with Rat-Face and the Russian had made them cautious. If I wanted to avoid pissing my pants or shitting myself, I would have to get my handcuffs past my hips.

Leaning my back against the wall, I began experimenting. At first, it seemed impossible. My arms just weren’t long enough. But then I realized that I was holding my back too straight, and began working on relaxing it. After about an hour of stretching, pushing myself a little further each time, I managed to get my wrists halfway down my buttocks. Finally, by stepping away from the wall, blowing out all the air from my lungs, and hunching over as quickly as I could while keeping my elbows bowed outward, I finally got the cuffs over my hips and down to my thighs. From there, it was a simple matter of lying down on my side and working my feet through. Now that I could use my hands again, I relieved myself in the bucket, and then sat down in a corner to ponder my next move.

My options were pretty limited. Without my lock-pick, there was no way I was getting out of my cell, not that it would have done me any good. There was still the tunnel entrance to deal with, and even if I did somehow manage to sneak my way through, the Legion would be all over me before I made it halfway to the warehouse exit.

No, my best option for the moment was to simply play along. Grayson Morrow had told me what to expect from this part of the recruiting process, and although I wasn't looking forward to it, knowing what lay ahead of me made it easier to deal with. It was going to suck, there was no doubt about that, but the Legion needed troops. If I could stay strong and gut it out, I could soon find myself in a position to deal some serious damage to these assholes.

"All right then, motherfuckers," I whispered into the darkness. "Do your worst."

Chapter 19

Sun Doesn't Rise

The first couple of days went by quietly. At least I think it was two days, my only way of gauging the passage of time was to fall asleep and wake up again.

When I was awake, I stretched, did some light exercises, and practiced shifting my cuffs under my feet, back to front. Moving them back was easy enough, but getting them in front of me was still a pain. I kept practicing and got a little better at it each time, slowly building up flexibility. Other than that, pacing my cell and singing to myself were my only distractions.

No one brought me any food or water during that time. The hunger didn't bother me too much; I had gone hungry plenty of times. The thirst, however, quickly became a problem. My throat went dry, my lips felt like sandpaper, and the simple acts of blinking and swallowing became painful endeavors. By the end of the second day, I had stopped exercising and my throat was too parched to talk, much less sing. A throbbing started in the back of my head, low and faint at first, then growing and spreading until it felt like someone had opened up my skull and was pounding directly on my brain with a ball-peen hammer.

Occasionally, I heard voices drifting to me through the darkness and the pain, but I couldn't make out what they were saying. Some of them had the brash, arrogant tone of Legion troops, while others were more subdued, whispering, and hesitant, as though afraid someone would hear them. I could hear their chains clinking as they were marched back and forth, and the frequent clap of something striking bare flesh. I tried to count how many of them there were, but the rattling of chains and stir of voices was too indistinct.

Finally, right about the time I was beginning to think my captors had forgotten about me, I heard footsteps approaching in the corridor. I shifted my handcuffs to my back, and waited. A lantern shone through the bars to my cell, revealing the shapes of three men standing beyond, one of them rattling a key in the lock.

"Rise and shine, maggot," the one with the lantern said. I recognized him; he was one of the men who had dragged me down here in the first place.

I worked what little moisture into my mouth that I could manage, and tried to talk. On the first attempt, it came out as a croak.

The Russian stepped in behind him and leaned over, a hand poised behind his ear. "Sorry, what you are saying?"

The two troops behind him laughed. Whether at his comment, or his broken English, I wasn't sure. Dimly, I noticed that all three men were carrying something. The objects were long and slender, kind of like Grabovsky's. …

Shit. Not good.

"Don't suppose any of you fellas could spare some water, could you?" I said, my voice as rough as broken glass.

"Sure, here you go." The Russian pulled a bottle from his pocket, and tossed it down in front of me. "Go ahead, drink up."

More laughter. Evidently, they didn't know that I could move my cuffs around to the front. Just as I thought that, one of them pointed at the waste bucket in the corner.

"Hey, guys, look at that."

The Russian stepped over and looked at it. His smile vanished, and he turned a scowl at me. In the tepid light, I noticed that he had pale gray eyes, and his nose looked to have been broken at least twice. "How is it that you are to be doing this?"

"Wanna see?" I asked, and stood up. The three of them eased back a step.

It had occurred to me that they might question how I could use the bucket with my hands bound behind my back, so in preparation, I had loosened my belt a notch so that I could shimmy my pants down by tugging at the waistband. I stepped into the circle of light and demonstrated. The Russian chuckled.

"You are not being so stupid as most maggots. At least you are knowing better than to shit yourself," he said, as I pulled my pants up.

Lantern-Man placed the aforementioned device in a corner and stepped forward, brandishing his cane. "Can we get this show on the road? I have to be on watch in ten minutes."

"Fine, fine," the Russian said. He pointed his cane at me. "You see, we are having to punish you. You pushed my friend Mike to the ground. He is being stupid little shit, but is loyal, too. This is being a crime that we must not be letting pass."

"Listen, all I did was-"

I was interrupted by a cane, wielded by the third man, cracking against the side of my face. Burning pain shot through my skull, nearly dropping me to my knees.

"You are not to be speaking without permission," the Russian explained, his voice chiding, as though I were an unruly child.

It was in that moment that I knew, not thought, or felt, but knew, deep down in my bones, that I was going to kill that son of a bitch. Somehow, some way, I was going to get the Russian alone, and I was going to gut him like a fish. When I could open my eyes again, the three of them had surrounded me. The Russian looked at the other two men, smiled, and made an open-handed gesture in my direction.

They went to work.

I didn't try to fight them, it wouldn't have done me any good. I would only have earned myself an even worse beating.

The first few blows fell on my back and shoulders, and I let myself collapse. They kept at it, the canes lashing into my flesh like fiery rain, seeming to hit from everywhere at once. They tore into my arms, and my legs, and my back. A few blows caught me in the head, but only a few. They didn't punch or kick me but, to be honest, I might have preferred that. The pain from each welt continued long after the blow had landed. Finally, when it felt like my whole body was engulfed in flames, and I was just about to give in to the urge to scream, the Russian's voice cut through the haze.

"That is being enough." His tone was uninterested, almost bored.

Rough hands sat me up, and unlocked my handcuffs. They wrenched my arms back in front of me and locked them again.

"There. Now you can to be pissing like a man again." The Russian chuckled. "The water is being yours. You should drink it slowly."

He tilted my face up by placing his cane under my chin. "So. Is there anything you would be liking to say? I am giving you my permission."

"Just one question," I croaked.

"*Da*?"

"What's your name?"

He tilted his head quizzically. "Why are you to be wanting this?"

So I know what to call you when I tear your spine out through your mouth.

"So I can think of you as something other than 'The Russian.' "

He stared for a moment longer, then threw his head back and laughed. The other two men chuckled nervously.

"I am to be liking you," he said. "Perhaps you will not to be dying so quickly."

He leaned down at the waist and lowered his voice. "Vasily. Vasily Kasikov. I am being wolf among dogs, maggot. If you want to live, you are not to be forgetting this. *Da*?"

With that, he turned on his heel and left, motioning for the other two men to follow. The door clanged shut, and the lock clattered into place. I slumped over onto my side and stayed that way for a long time.

*****

They brought me more water, two bottles a day I think. But it was another four days before they fed me. In the meantime, I got no less than two beatings a day. Sometimes three or four.

I got to know a few of the Legion troops that way. There were six of them, rotating in and out. Rat-Face was never one of them. Maybe Kasikov was afraid of what he might do if left alone with me. Or maybe it was the other way around, maybe he was afraid of what I might do to Rat-Face. If that was the case, then he was right to be worried.

The beatings became a routine. First would come the footsteps, then the light filtering through the door, and finally the jangling of the keys. The people carrying out the beatings did so with far less ceremony than the first group had. Two men would come in, order me to stand up, and then proceed to cane the living shit out of me. Once done, they would exit the cell and lock it behind them, usually without saying a word. Sometimes they would replace my waste bucket. Very considerate of them.

If I didn't know what was going on, my sanity might very likely have fractured. The only thing keeping me stable was the knowledge that this wouldn't go on forever. That sooner or later, they would drag me off somewhere to dig tunnels for them. What they were doing now, the isolation, the starvation, and the beatings, it was just a way to break down my resolve. To frighten me, and cow me into obedience. It certainly seemed to have worked on other people.

My first Legion-provided meal came at the end of my seventh day of captivity. It was some kind of stringy, roasted meat with boiled potatoes and a big bottle of water. I wolfed it down like it was filet mignon. There wasn't much of it, but after going on an empty stomach for a full week, I was in heaven.

I didn't realize until I had some food in my belly, and plenty of water to drink, just how foggy my mind had been for the last few days. After eating, the haze began to lift, and I could think clearly again.

From what Morrow had told me, I should expect another test sometime in the near future. Probably when they took me down into what the Legion called "the mines." Not that they were actually digging up precious minerals, or anything like that. It was just what everyone called them. A phrase someone had coined.

Sitting there, alone in the darkness, I thought of Allison. I wondered what she was doing, and how she was holding up. I had no doubt that she must be worried about me. A tightness began to take hold in my chest, and I felt tears sting my eyes.

No, I thought. *Don't go there. Stay focused.*

Shoving thoughts of Allison aside, I pondered the methods that the Legion were using to break me down. The first thing that struck me as odd was the waste bucket. Morrow hadn't mentioned that part. Maybe it had just slipped his mind.

If the Legion really wanted to fuck with my head, why didn't they make me wallow in my own piss and shit? Why go to that minimal effort at sanitation? The only answer I could think of was that they didn't want me to get sick. Human waste is a breeding ground for all kinds of nasty bacteria, and getting just a little bit of it into a cut could cause a potentially lethal infection. The more I thought about that, the more the logic became clear.

They didn't want to kill me. Didn't want to kill anyone they captured. They wanted to keep me alive. Not that they would hesitate to kill me if I became a problem—they most certainly would. But they didn't want a corpse on their hands if they could help it. What they wanted was someone they could mold into a marauder or, failing that, keep around for slave labor. It made sense in an awful kind of way.

I shivered, huddled further into my corner, and tried to steel myself for what lay ahead.

*****

They left me in my cell for another three days, but the beatings stopped, and they brought me two meals a day. The meals were small, never quite enough to sate the hunger gnawing at my gut, and the amount of water they gave me was barely enough to keep me functioning. More head games. Keep me thirsty, keep me hungry, keep me distracted.

The waiting ended when Kasikov showed up with Rat-Face and Tommy. I sat cross-legged in the corner as they came in, staying silent.

Rat-Face smirked. "Looks like you finally learned to keep your mouth shut."

I ignored him, staring blankly into the distance and doing my best to look defeated. Kasikov stepped forward and shined the lantern on me.

"You are looking better, maggot. You are not being dead, or screaming like madman. That is good. Most maggots becoming like beasts, beating walls and crawling in dirt. There is being strength in you."

"On your feet," Tommy said. "Kas, cuff his hands behind his back."

I stood up and stayed quiet while they adjusted my restraints. Rat-Face looked on with a smile on his ugly mug, practically beaming with perverse delight.

"You are smelling like shit," Kasikov muttered. He gripped my arm and pulled me toward the door.

I followed them out into the corridor, and then left at the intersection with the other three tunnels. They were taking me back to the warehouse. Along the way, I again studied the way the tunnel had been constructed.

The air in my cell had been thick, but breathable, which coincided with what Morrow had said about the Legion's crude ventilation system. Most of the tunnels they dug were only a few feet underground, which made it a simple matter to connect pipes to the surface and hide them under the abundant foliage. I also knew that the tunnels immediately around the warehouse were much larger and better maintained than most of their other tunnels. From what Morrow had told me, compared to the mines, this place was like the Hilton.

The passageway terminated at the ladder to the warehouse, where Kasikov gripped my arm and ordered me to wait while Tommy and Rat-Face climbed to the surface. Once they had turned and trained their rifles down the ladder, the Russian unlocked my cuffs and motioned for me to climb up. At the top, they cuffed me again, and marched me toward the Legion's living area.

As the light grew brighter, I saw a man seated at a table with two others, all dressed in combat fatigues. I didn't recognize any of them. A bottle of whiskey sat in the middle of the table, and all three men had full glasses in front of them. Miranda sat upon one of the men's knees, stripped completely naked. The dirt was gone from her skin, and her long blond hair hung clean and untangled down her shoulders. She kept her face blank and stayed still as the man she sat on casually fondled her breasts.

"Is this the new meat, Tommy?" he called out. The other two turned to look.

"Yes sir. Caught him snoopin' around here 'bout a week ago. Got him broke down nice and docile."

Keep telling yourself that, you fat piece of shit.

Tommy dragged me into the light. The man at the table looked me up and down and nodded. "He'll do. He give you any trouble?"

"Nothing we couldn't handle," Tommy replied.

The man nodded again, and turned his attention back to the girl on his lap. Now that I was up close, I could make out his features. He was older, maybe late forties or early fifties. His hair was straight and black, with the exception of a smattering of gray at the temples, and cut close to his scalp. He was taller than I am, and powerfully built. The hands he used to grope Miranda were large and strong, and square, chiseled features defined his face. After spending so much time around military types, I had learned to spot them from a mile away. This guy was definitely military.

"What do you think, Aiken?" he said, looking at the man seated across the table from him. The two of them bore a strong resemblance. Brothers, maybe?

"Pickings are getting slim around here, Lucian. We have to take what we can get."

Yep. Definitely brothers. Even their voices sounded the same. The only way to tell them apart was that Aiken had a short, neatly trimmed beard.

Lucian flipped a hand at Tommy. "Fine, fine. The three of you can have my private stock for the week, and a couple of cases of booze. Be gentle with my property, though. I expect them to be returned in serviceable condition."

“Thank you, sir. Very generous.” Tommy had a smile on his face when he turned and shoved me toward Kasikov. “Take this piece of shit to the mines.” He jerked a thumb toward a shack behind him. “Hurry back, though. We gonna have us a party.”

As Kasikov began leading me away, I peered over my shoulder through the dim light to see what Tommy was talking about. Inside the shack, I saw several women huddled together, all of them young, healthy, and attractive. Shackles hung from their wrists and ankles, and their faces were uniformly dull and expressionless. No light shined in their blank, staring eyes.

“Come on,” the big Russian said irritably. “You are being keeping me from my reward.”

As he dragged me toward the ladder, I heard Tommy and Rat-Face laughing lasciviously, and the soft whimpers of the women in the shack.

Bastards. Sick fucking bastards.

*****

Back in the tunnels, Kasikov led me past the corridor to the isolation cells and then left at the intersection. The tunnel was new to me, and was much narrower than the one that connected to the warehouse. The Russian had to turn his broad shoulders sideways a few times to avoid striking the support beams.

“Soon you will to be missing your cell, I am thinking,” he said, grinning. “The mines are not being so nice place.”

I kept my mouth shut and focused on not falling down. Kasikov was setting a fast pace and, with the leg irons limiting my stride, I had to run in short little steps to keep up.

As he dragged me through the darkness, the lantern in his hand only chased the inky black away for a few feet. The ground became wetter as we walked, the hard-pack of the main tunnels giving way to slick mud that threatened to send my feet flying out from under me with every step. Even Kasikov had to slow down to keep his footing. Eventually we reached a T-intersection with a crudely drawn sign hanging on the wall in front of us. Two spray-painted arrows pointed in either direction, one of them labeled “CNCTR LP,” and the other “HR AXS.”

We turned in the direction labeled “CNCTR LP,” where the tunnel became even smaller, and we both had to duck our heads to avoid hitting the support struts in the ceiling. Along the way, I thought about the writing on the sign, and what the labels meant. It reminded me of something I had seen in an Anthropology class in college.

The class had been one of those easy A’s that padded the elective requirements of countless legions of lazy college students. The instructor, being one of those professors who believed that his fieldwork was far more important than a task as menial as teaching, deferred most of the classroom time to a show called “The Naked Archeologist.” I guess the producers thought that including “Naked” in the title would make it more interesting. I don’t think it worked.

On one episode, the host—a pretentious, annoying type who, thankfully, was fully clothed—explored the history of written language. One of the most significant advancements in written language was the invention of vowels, but according to the host, this was a bad thing. He felt that written language had far more style and nuance when it consisted only of consonants. Personally, I thought the guy was full of shit. But the examples of consonant-only writing that he displayed were very much like the sign back at the intersection.

“CNCTR LP,” if said aloud, would sound remarkably close to Connector Loop. But what about “HR AXS’? “Her Axis” didn’t make any sense. Maybe it was initials? Ignoring the HR for the moment, I focused on AXS. The only word other than “axis” that fit was “access.” HR access …

Shit. HR Access. Hollow Rock Access? The town was nearly fifteen miles away. That would be a huge undertaking and, from what I had seen so far, I wasn't sure that the Legion had that kind of manpower. At least not at this site.

By counting to sixty over and over again in my head, I estimated that it took us nearly two hours of hard walking to get where we were going. At the pace we were setting, that could have been anywhere from seven to nine miles, again confirming what Grayson Morrow had told me.

Finally, we came around a corner and I saw light up ahead of us. As we got closer, I saw that the source of the light was a set of lanterns, much like the one carried by Kasikov, all of them hanging from the ceiling. There were three men standing at the edge of the light brandishing AKs, and passing a bottle back and forth. The bottle disappeared as we came within shouting distance.

"*Zdravstvujtye*, shitworms," the Russian shouted jovially. "I am to be having new meat for you." He thrust me at the three men hard enough to make me lose my footing. I landed on my side in the mud at the nearest man's feet. "You are to be chaining him and making him to work. You," he pointed at the man who had tucked the bottle away, "be giving me that booze."

Reluctantly, the guard handed it to him. "You are not to be drinking this shit on duty," Kasikov said. "Are you to be forgetting that those maggots will cut your throat if you let them?"

He made a gesture to the far end of the corridor, and I craned my neck to look. Ahead of me, barely visible in the distance, were the struggling forms of at least a dozen men, all wearing chains and toiling away.

"Hey, we got this covered Kas," one of them said.

The big Russian's friendly demeanor vanished in an instant. His eyes went hard, and his lips curled back from his teeth as he got in the man's face.

“Do not be telling me what you are fucking covering,” he hissed, and grabbed the man by the front of his shirt, nearly lifting him off the ground. “You will to be doing what you are told, or I will to be breaking your goddamn neck.”

“Okay, okay. Shit, Kas, what the fuck?” the man said, holding his hands up in surrender.

Slowly, the Russian let him go. He looked around to each man in turn, favoring them with a wintry scowl. “You are to be taking this shit seriously. No fucking up, *da*?”

They all nodded, not risking speech for fear of angering the big man. A few tense moments passed before Kasikov turned on his heel and marched off back the way he came, leaving me on the ground with the three Legion troops.

One of them reached down the hauled me to my feet. “Let’s go, maggot,” he said. “You got work to do.”

I followed along down the corridor toward the clinking of chains. The light of the lanterns faded behind me, and soon, I had my first introduction to life in the mines.

Chapter 20

Maggots

I had to give the Legion credit; they had quite the operation going.

The crew I worked with consisted of fourteen men: two to dig new sections of tunnel, four to install the support beams and ventilation pipes, and the rest to haul away dirt. Most of the jobs rotated out from day to day, but for the first five days, all I did was carry buckets.

It was tedious work that first week, to say the least. Bucket after endless bucket. The dirt we dug out of the ground was stored in the warehouse, where another crew, working only under cover of night, would haul it away and dump it in a nearby lake. The pace of dirt coming out of the ground was always faster than the pace at which it could be hauled away, which explained the huge piles accumulating on the warehouse floor. Not that it mattered, really. The warehouse was massive, and the piles only took up a third of the floor space.

On the rare occasions when it was my turn to carry buckets up the ladder, I noticed that there was a huge stockpile of ventilation pipes, wooden beams, and other materials on the opposite end of the floor. Where the Legion had gotten all of it from I had no clue, but it looked like enough for at least a hundred miles of tunnel.

The other captives and I worked, ate our one meal a day, drank our inadequate supply of water, and slept on wooden pallets down in the tunnels, all under the watchful eyes of

Legion guards. There were only three of them, rotating out every four hours, but they were heavily armed and under orders to execute anyone who so much as thought about starting trouble. As long as we stayed quiet, kept our heads down, and did as we were told, the guards left us alone. I think they found the duty to be only marginally less miserable than those of us doing the actual work.

In those first few days, I noticed that there was very little talking among the captives. They only spoke to one another in the course of work, and even then only in whispers. And only when absolutely necessary. I tried starting up conversations with a few of them, but they just gave me a horrified look and scuttled away. On one occasion, one of the guards saw me doing it, and rewarded my efforts with a rifle stock to the kidney.

"Don't you know the rules, maggot?" He laughed as I dropped my bucket and fell to the ground. "No talking. Period. Let me catch you doing that again, and I'll beat you to fucking death."

Lacking anything else to do, other than backbreaking slave labor, I devoted my time to studying each Legion soldier and assigning them a name. Some of them I learned from overheard conversations, and others I simply made up based on some quirk or physical attribute. I didn't name them because I cared who they were, or because I felt the need to humanize them. It was simply a means of coming up with an accurate count.

From what I gathered, there were sixty men stationed here at the warehouse, and another fifty that patrolled between underground bases along the perimeter of Legion territory. This location seemed to be one of the least popular ones among the soldiers, and I always heard them complaining about how long it would be before they rotated out to a place they called Haven. It struck me as a remarkably innocuous name for a den of thieves, rapists, and murderers.

Sometimes, as I listened in on conversations, I had to resist the urge to grin. The information they were giving me was invaluable. Much of it I had already learned from Grayson Morrow, but I also gleaned new data that would be immensely useful once the offensive against the Legion began in earnest.

At the end of the fifth night, as I was sitting on my pallet and finishing off a meager bowl of beans and mutton, a familiar voiced boomed out through the darkness calling to the guards.

"Where is being the maggot I bring?" Kasikov asked. "I am wanting to be speaking to him."

One of the guards gestured with his rifle, and the big Russian made his way over.

"You are being alive. That is good," he said. "Are you knowing what tomorrow is?"

I kept my eyes down and shook my head.

"It is being Sunday." He squatted down in front of me, hands dangling between his knees. "We are to be having sport on Sundays. There is being prizefight." He held up his fists and punched the air a few times. "There is being great reward for winner."

He leaned in close and placed a hand under my jaw, almost gently. I raised my face to look at him. His gray eyes were only a few inches from mine, and I could see the cruelty that lay behind them. Cold and empty as the winter sky.

"I am thinking you are to be winning," he said. "You will to be competing, or I will to be coming back here."

He smiled, devoid of mirth. Just a movement of facial muscles, bereft of feeling. I couldn't help but wonder how many Vasily Kasikovs there were in the world. Empty, hollow creatures with a black pit where their heart should be.

"If I am coming back here, I am not being so nice next time. *Da*?" His hand tightened on my jaw, strong as a steel vise, until it became painful. I nodded my understanding, and the pressure stopped.

"That is being good," he said quietly, and stood up. "So, how are you liking it here in the mines, eh?"

I shrugged, and looked back down.

"It is okay, you are having permission to speak."

I looked up. "Honest answer?"

The Russian nodded.

"This place sucks my sweaty asshole."

It took him a moment to translate that, and when he finally did, he burst into a fit of laughter.

"That is being funny," he said, bent over with his hands on his knees, still chuckling. " 'Sucks my sweaty asshole.' I am to be remembering that."

He reached down and clapped me on the shoulder. "Be sleeping well tonight, maggot. Tomorrow, you make good fight."

With that, he turned and strode back down the corridor out of sight. I watched him go, and felt laughter struggling to burst out of me. I allowed myself a quiet smile as I lay down on my pallet.

You're right on that account, Kasikov, I thought. *I do love a good fight.*

*****

The next morning, they awoke us all at the same time, lined us up, and chained us together.

"All right, maggots. Get moving."

The guards kept their guns trained on us as we marched single file through the tunnels. When we reached the ladder to the warehouse, they unchained us from each other, but left our manacles and leg irons in place. When it was my turn, I climbed up and joined the others in a cluster near the hatch. Five armed guards were already in position waiting on us. Kasikov was one of them, and when I walked past him, he gave me a little wink.

One of the guards said, “Okay, over to the circle. You know the drill.”

The other prisoners started shuffling to a corner of the warehouse near where the women were kept. I followed, the chains on my legs hobbling my steps. The guards stopped us at a yellow circle, roughly thirty feet across, that looked to have been painted on the floor by hand. The patrols from the nearby satellite bases must have been called in, because nearly a hundred Legion soldiers surrounded the circle. From the way they were loitering on blankets and lawn chairs, it looked as though they were waiting for a party to begin.

A few feet away, Lucian and his retinue lounged on patio furniture drinking from bottles of whiskey and groping slave girls. I saw the blankness of the girls’ stares, the tear streaks on their faces, and had to fight down the urge to rush Lucian and his gaggle of psychopaths.

“Sit down, maggots,” a guard said. We all complied.

Lucian dumped the girl off his lap, took a pull from his bottle, then set it down and walked into the middle of the circle. He smiled, stood up straight, and held out his hands as if he were speaking at a business conference, and not addressing a group of starving, dehydrated slaves.

“It’s that time again, little maggots. Time for you to show us what you’re made of. Time to shake off the chains that have bound you your whole miserable lives, and learn how to live like men.”

The troops around us went silent as he spoke. Lucian’s grin would have been right at home on a shark.

"Are you tired of working in the mines?" he went on. "Tired of digging in the dirt all day? Tired of being hungry and thirsty and exhausted all the time? Well, here's your chance to do something about it."

He waved a hand at the Legion troops around us, and over at his entourage. "You see, most of these men were once like you. People who wandered into our territory uninvited. People who violated our borders and had to be punished. People who paid for their trespasses by putting in hard labor and contributing to our little society."

Stepping closer to the edge of the circle, he smiled down at us. "This is a new kind of nation you're living in, my friends. A nation where the strong thrive and the weak are subjugated. A nation where a man can exist as he was meant to. Not beholden to the erratic whims of women, or laws that were passed without his consent, or some arbitrary code of morals laid down by a god that doesn't exist. This new nation is governed by the simple, undeniable laws of nature. There are no suits and ties. No credit card debts, or mortgages, or student loans, or taxes, or any of that shit that used to ruin men's lives. No nagging wives, no PTA meetings, no homeowners associations, no politicians telling you what to think. No preachers, no cops, no judges, or lawyers, or Jehovah's-fucking-Witnesses knocking on your door. All that shit is gone. It's not coming back, and I for one, say good fucking riddance."

Every Legion troop in the warehouse applauded loudly at this, whooping and hollering. Lucian put his hands on his hips and grinned.

"Now, you've all been through the crucible. My men have beaten you, and worked you, and broken you down. Right now, you probably hate me for it, and if I'm honest, I don't blame you. In your place, I'd hate me, too. But mark my words, gentlemen, if you survive this, if you prove yourself, if you're strong enough to join my Legion, then one day, one bright fucking day, you will thank me. You will thank me with a song in your heart, and tears in your eyes. Because I'm going to show you what it means to truly live. I'll show you what it means to shake off the fear, and the doubt, and the sentiment that's been shoved down your throats since the day you were born. I'm going to show you how to be strong. To rise above the false gods, and false morals, and false beliefs that have crippled you since you were old enough to think. I will teach you to be the men you were meant to be. You will learn to strike fear in the hearts of lesser creatures. I will teach you to be warriors of the FREE LEGION!"

The troops cheered even louder this time, enough to make my ears ring. They clapped, and howled, and stomped their feet. Meanwhile, the slaves sat quiet and still. Most of them kept their heads bowed, staring at the ground in resignation. But a few looked up. A few stared at Lucian with a strange light in their eyes, as though he were a beacon in the darkness. The same look was on the Legion troops' faces as they cheered for their leader.

So this is how he does it, I thought. *Starve them, beat them, break their spirit. Put them in a miserable, hopeless place. Then offer them a hand up. Offer to let them join the club. Bring the deepest, blackest part of their soul to the surface, and feed that animal exactly what it's always hungered for.*

Most people who survived the Outbreak stayed alive by either joining a community, or by staying on the move. The people chained up next to me were all probably the latter. They had spent the last two years on the run, constantly in danger, never able to truly relax, or feel safe, or have any peace of mind. Theirs had been a life of hardship and fear. A life of hunger, and exhaustion, and constant, unyielding pressure. A life that held no joy, no comfort, and after all that they had suffered through, their only promise for the future was a lonely, painful death. In light of that, what Lucian was offering didn't seem all that bad. In fact, it sounded downright exciting. I would be lying if I said I wasn't tempted.

But then I thought of Allison, and the way the morning sunlight turned her eyes honey brown. I thought of Gabriel, and the strength I had drawn from him, and how he had helped me transform into something greater than the sum of my parts. I thought of Brian, and Tom, and Sarah, and all the friends I had made in Hollow Rock. I thought about the scars on my side, and the looks on the faces of those two militia troops' families as we laid them to rest. I thought of Ethan, and Andrea, and Stacy, and the people from that abandoned warehouse in Alexis. I thought of all this, and felt resolve harden in my chest, burning away the last tendrils of doubt.

Lucian walked back to his chair and sat down. At a gesture, the girl he'd shoved to the ground climbed back into his lap. "Tommy, get us started."

The fat man waddled over to where we sat and looked us over. "Any volunteers? Any of you pussies got a pair of balls on you?"

One of the prisoners a few feet away from me raised his hands. Tommy looked at him and grinned. "All right, we got one. Anybody else feel like bein' a man today?"

A few other hands went up, mine among them. Tommy rubbed his palms together. "Looks like we got some fights. All right, maggots. On your feet."

Those of us who had volunteered stood up. A quick count told me there were six of us, a nice even number. A guard went around and unlocked our restraints while the others kept weapons trained on us.

"Lose the shirts and the shoes. You can keep your pants on."

The six of us took off our filthy, mud-crusted shirts and tossed them in a pile with our boots. Tommy set up a few chairs on opposing ends of the circle, separated us into two groups, and ordered us to take seats. Another guard came around with a can of bright orange spray paint and painted numbers on our chests. Mine was three.

Tommy wrote our numbers on a piece of paper, tore it up, crumpled the pieces into little balls, and rolled them around in his hat. He dipped his thick fingers in, drew out one, and then another.

"One and six. In the circle, let's go."

One was a black guy, broad-shouldered, about my height. Maybe mid-thirties. Strong-looking. Six was shorter, older, and had the loose skin of someone who had undergone rapid, drastic weight loss. In spite of being outsized, his eyes shone with a fierce intensity, ready to fight. He shuffled back and forth on his feet, clenching and unclenching his fists. The two men stood barefoot on the concrete, the paint of their numbers running down their torsos, and stared each other down.

"There are no rules, ladies." Tommy stepped out of the circle and took a seat. "Anything goes. Fight's not over until one of you is unconscious. Go ahead whenever you're ready."

The Legion troops began cheering and chanting. "*Fight, fight, fight, fight …*"

I thought, *This isn't an army. It's fucking junior high.*

I almost laughed.

The two men circled each other, hands up in loose boxing stances. Neither one looked like he knew what he was doing. One, being the taller and stronger of the two, decided to take the initiative. He darted in and threw a flurry of punches at Six's head. Six blocked clumsily, and stumbled away. A bad move, backing straight up like that. One pursued him, trying to punch around his arms, and finally settled on slamming two hard uppercuts into his opponent's stomach. The smaller man's breath left him in a rush, and he sagged to the ground. One grabbed him by the hair, reared back for a knee strike, and brought his leg forward once, twice, three times. Six slumped backward, his nose shattered, and his front teeth missing. Tommy stepped forward and kicked him in the ribs. He didn't move.

"We got a winner!"

He held up One's hand and walked him around the circle. The Legion troops' applause thundered throughout the warehouse. Over the ruckus, I heard the voices of a few men walking through the crowd with notebooks, shouting for people to begin placing bets.

"Who wants to pick One for the win? One for the win. Place your bets …"

Men in the crowd began gathering around the bookies and shouting wagers at them, betting bottles of booze, weapons, food, and time with their slaves. I shook my head in disgust.

Tommy rooted around in his hat again and drew two more numbers. "Two and four, get in the circle."

The next two men looked evenly matched. They were about the same age, same height and build. Tommy gave the order to commence, and they tore into each other. Their fight went longer than the first one, neither man able to gain an advantage over the other. Finally, Two threw a sloppy punch that missed its mark, his feet slipped in a puddle of sweat, and he went down on his face. Four jumped on his back and applied a chokehold. Seconds later, Two was out.

The crowd cheered again, and the betting increased in volume and intensity. The warehouse began to have a carnival feeling, all of the troops drinking, and getting rowdy. As Two's unconscious form was dragged out of the circle, Tommy motioned to me and Five. We stood up, strode into the circle, and squared off.

Five was tall, maybe six-two or six-three. Even half-starved, he outweighed me by at least twenty pounds. From the corner of my eye, I noticed that Kasikov had pushed his way to the front of the crowd and was watching me with a smug grin on his face. I looked at him, and he nodded to me, shaking his fists.

"Aaaannnd FIGHT!" Tommy shouted, red-faced with excitement.

Five advanced cautiously, hands up, feet shoulder width apart. He didn't move like the others, clumsy and unsure. His steps were even, he didn't cross his feet, and he kept his elbows tucked in tight. This one had some training. From the way he stood, I was guessing some kind of kickboxing. I brought my hands up and began circling.

He was right-handed, so I circled left and switched my stance to southpaw. Keeping my hands just below eye level, I moved in and feinted a jab. He took the bait and sidestepped to slip it. I pursued and fired a left-right combination at his floating ribs. He had expected the punches to go high, and had his forearms up over his face, which worked out great for me. I turned my hips into the punches and was rewarded with a pained grunt from my opponent. He tried to counterpunch with a right hook, but I ducked it and circled away.

Five was angry now; those punches had stung him. He switched his stance to protect his bruised ribs, stepped in with a jab-cross that bounced off my forearms, and then tried to tie my head up in a Muay Thai clinch.

Yep. Definitely a kickboxer.

I slipped out of it, narrowly avoiding a knee aimed at my forehead. The momentum of the knee strike left him slightly off balance, and I took the opportunity to snap off two quick punches that rocked his head back, and step in for a takedown.

My arms wrapped around his lower back, pinning one of his arms in place. My right foot came down behind his ankle and I pushed my forehead into his chest, pulling hard against his back. He tried to balance by stepping backward, but only succeeded in tripping over the foot I had planted behind him. Right then, I knew I had the fight won. If Five had possessed an ounce of grappling skill, he would have been able to step out of that takedown. It was a simple technique—Day One stuff for any grappler. This guy wasn't a grappler.

I landed on top, still pinning one of his arms. Shifting my weight, I came up on one knee, posted my head against Five's shoulder, and brought my other knee up into his groin. He shouted in agony and curled up, pushing at my leg with his free hand to keep me from kneeing him again. I used the distraction to climb up into the full mount, centered my weight on his chest, and started throwing punches at his face.

Just as I had hoped, Five crossed his arms over his face and rolled over beneath me, giving up his back. I wasn't hitting him very hard—I didn't want to hurt him any worse than I already had—but it was enough to make him instinctively turn away. Just as I'd done in so many sparring matches on the Grinder, I hooked his legs, flattened him out, and slipped a forearm over his throat. With the choke locked in, I counted slowly backwards from ten. By the time I was done, Five had gone limp.

I released the choke, stood up, and faced Lucian. He met my gaze and stared back, a smile curling up one side of his mouth. It didn't touch his eyes. Slowly, he began to clap.

"Another winner!" Tommy shouted.

The noise was deafening at that point. The troops crowded around the circle and heaved at one another to get closer to the action. Kasikov and a few other senior troops had to shove the mob back at gunpoint to keep them from spilling over into the circle. Once they had restored some semblance of order, Lucian stood and held up his hands, shouting for everyone's attention.

"We've got three candidates left. Tommy, what do you think we should do?"

The fat man took a swig of whiskey and wiped his mouth. "Fuck it. Battle Royale!"

I didn't like the sound of that.

Tommy motioned for the other two remaining fighters to step into the circle. We all realized what was coming at the same time and searched each other's eyes.

I could tell the other two were afraid of me. Five had been a more competent fighter than either one of them, and I had beaten him in less than a minute. They looked at each other and exchanged a slight nod.

Fuck.

Honestly, I didn't blame them. It's what I would have done; deal with the worst threat first, then settle things between the two of them.

"Three men enter, one man leaves. Get it on!" Tommy stepped out of the circle, and the crowd went wild.

The other two fighters split up, coming at me from either direction. I needed to take one of them out quickly, and then handle the other one at my leisure. Four hadn't looked as strong as One in his fight, so I decided to deal with him first.

When confronted with multiple opponents, if you have nowhere to run, the best strategy is to simply go at the fuckers head-on and beat them with sheer aggression. Four was being tentative, waiting for One to make the first move.

I charged.

It took me two steps the cover the distance. I leapt at him with a flying knee that I knew wasn't going to land. Just as I had expected him to, he leapt to the right to get out of the way. As soon as my feet touched the ground, I hopped sideways, turned, and launched a spinning hook kick at the side of his neck. My heel made contact with a meaty thud, and Four toppled over like a felled tree. His head bounced off the concrete with a sickening crack. He didn't move.

A collective "OHHHH!!!" resounded through the warehouse as Four hit the ground. I spun to face One, and found him charging. He dropped his weight and rammed a shoulder into my waist, driving me to the ground. I went with the takedown and pulled him into my full-guard.

The guard is a tricky position. To the uninformed, it looks like the fighter on top has the advantage. But in truth, the fighter on bottom is the one in control, assuming he knows what he's doing.

One clearly had no experience fighting from this position, and began throwing wild punches at my head. I caught an arm, opened up my guard, and transitioned into a textbook triangle choke. One of my legs cut off the blood supply to his brain on one side of his neck, while pressure from his own shoulder did the job on the other side. I reached up and pulled down on his head to increase the force of the choke. Again, I counted slowly backwards from ten, and again, by the time I was done, he was out.

I released him and let him slump to the ground. The gathered troops were stomping and howling like madmen. Even Lucian was on his feet, pumping his fists in the air.

"Number three! Number three is the winner!" Tommy shouted, as if it weren't obvious.

Most of the troops were elated by the spectacle, but a few looked dejected. They must have bet against me.

Not a good idea, that.

Kasikov was standing at the edge of the circle with a satisfied smile on his face. The bookie in front of him ripped a piece of paper from his notepad and handed it to the big Russian. He looked at it and nodded, then started shouting taunts at the grim-faced men he had wagered against.

Lucian got up from his chair and shouted for silence. "All right, men. Playtime is over for today. Tommy, make sure everyone settles up their bets. Crew leaders, get your men back on duty. If you're off duty, I don't give a fuck what you do as long as you stay the hell out of my way. Kasikov, grab some bodies and get these maggots back to work. You," he pointed a finger at me, "you stay here."

I walked to the edge of the circle and waited. The Legion troops slowly dispersed as Kasikov led the remaining prisoners back to the tunnel entrance. Number Four, the slave I had knocked unconscious, still lay on the floor with a pool of blood expanding under his head. A cold feeling began to grow in my stomach.

"Hey, maggot. Wake the fuck up." One of Kasikov's men kicked the downed slave. He didn't move. I walked over and knelt down beside him.

"What the fuck do you think you're doing?" the guard demanded.

"Checking his vitals." I pulled up on one of his shoulders and put a couple of fingers against his throat. There was a pulse, but it was unsteady, erratic. Not good. I pulled one eyelid open and checked his pupils in the dim light.

"How's he doing? He fuckin' dead, or what?"

"He's still alive, but he's in bad shape. He needs a doctor."

The guard turned around. "Hey Kas, whadya want me to do with this guy?"

"What is wrong with him?" the Russian said, walking over.

Calling to mind everything I had learned from Allison about brain injuries, I felt the area where his skull had struck the concrete. A large hematoma had formed, and he was bleeding from a laceration as long as my thumb. I pressed on the skull around the hematoma and felt it give a little.

"He's hurt bad," I said. "Skull fracture, cerebral contusion, hemorrhaging, and probably cranial herniation. If he doesn't see a doctor soon, he's going to die."

The guard looked at me, then at Kasikov. "You know what the fuck he's talking about?"

Kas ignored him, and rose up on his toes to see over the crowd. "Klauberg! Where is being Klauberg?"

"Over here," a voice shouted to my right. "What do you want?"

I turned and saw a short, portly man with a balding head, a graying beard, and a pair of close-set, pig-like eyes emerge from the chaos. He wandered over and looked down at the unconscious slave.

“Oh, right.” He knelt down, pushed me out of the way, and performed the same checks I had just done.

“Nope. Sorry. He’s fucked.” The little man stood up to walk away.

“Wait,” I said. He turned to look at me, his brow furrowed over his cruel little eyes. I said, “Are you a doctor?”

“Yes.”

“Can’t you do something for him?”

He squared off with me and put his pudgy hands on his hips. “What am I gonna do, maggot? I’d need an emergency room, a neurologist, and a trained medical staff to save this piece of shit. Do you see anything around here like that? No? Didn’t fucking think so.” With that, he turned and walked away.

“Jenkins, Wilson. Get rid of this corpse,” Kasikov said, gesturing to two of his men. “Be making sure to dump his body far away. I am not wanting to smell it the next time I am on watch.”

The two men elbowed me out of their way as the grabbed the slave by his ankles and began dragging him away. I stared on helplessly, feeling the coldness in my stomach spread up to my face. My throat constricted, my eyes stung, and for a few moments, it was hard to breathe.

“Do not be worrying about him.” Kasikov clapped me on the shoulder. “You have done well, my friend. Soon, I am thinking you will be one of us.”

I looked at him, but he had already turned away. As he and his men led the prisoners back to the tunnels, the ones I had beaten cast hateful, envious glances at me. The two I had choked out didn’t look the worse for wear, but Six was in obvious agony with his broken nose, and shattered teeth. He sobbed quietly as he was led away, blood dripping down his face.

“Kasikov.” I called out. He stopped and turned to look at me.

“What about their clothes?”

He glanced at them. “*Da*. You are being right. Go on, maggots. Get your clothes.”

Some of the venom left their gazes as they picked up their belongings. I looked each of them in the eye and made a silent promise.

Somehow, some way, I’m going to get you out of here.

Chapter 21

Of Monsters and Men

A tunnel connected the warehouse to a smaller building nearby that had once been the distribution company's administrative offices.

Several of Lucian's men led me there after putting me back in irons. Lucian himself stayed behind to hold a meeting with his senior staff, and sent his brother to see to my interrogation. We emerged from the tunnel into a basement filled with rusting, long-disused machinery. Elevator equipment, a few banks of servers, HVAC units, water pumps—all useless now.

The guards led me up a flight of stairs to the main floor where long ranks of empty cubicles sat dusty and forgotten. I tried to imagine the place as it must have been before the Outbreak. People sitting in those cubicles, staring at computer screens, occasionally gazing out the windows and wishing they were at home, or at the beach, or out with their families, or doing pretty much anything except sitting there under fluorescent lights with a bunch of other people just as miserable as they were. I wasn't sure which was more depressing, the past or the present.

We walked through the building until we came to a large corner office farthest from the main entrance. The computers and other devices had been taken out and lay in a pile a few feet from the doorway. In their place was a large wooden desk, a few chairs, and several boxes of files and office supplies. Pens, printer paper, file folders, clips, staples. All neatly organized.

The guards had me sit down in one of the chairs. Aiken took a seat behind the desk and ordered the guards to wait outside. When they had closed the door, he picked up a manila folder and a pen.

"What's your name?" he asked.

"Logan Morrison."

He wrote the name on the folder, and then glanced up at me. "From here on out you will address me as 'sir.' Understood?"

"Yes, sir."

He picked up a piece of paper and set it on the desk in front of him. "Where are you from, Morrison?"

"Tyler, Texas, sir."

He scribbled it down in flowing, easily legible handwriting. "Date of birth?"

I told him.

"Did you graduate from high school?"

"Yes, sir."

"College?"

"Yes, sir."

"Where did you study?"

"Texas A&M, sir."

"What did you major in?"

"Business and English, sir."

"Where did you learn to fight like that?"

"A place called First Strike Martial Arts, sir. My dad was a huge MMA fan. He had me start training there when I was eleven. I kept at it until I left for college."

"What was your father's name?"

"Roland, sir."

"His full name."

"Roland Albert Morrison, sir."

"Mother's name?"

The questions kept coming, one after another. A droning, mind-numbing litany. Morrow had warned me about this. Warned me about what he was going to do. Grayson had been selected to join the Legion the same way I had—by fighting and beating other slaves. Afterward, he had been dragged away and questioned for more than two hours by the very man sitting across from me. Aiken looked exactly as Morrow had described. Tall, strongly built, squarish features. Salt-and-pepper hair, neatly trimmed beard, and cold, lifeless eyes.

The purpose of the questions was not so that he could get to know me—he didn't give a rat's ass about me. As far as he was concerned, I was just another expendable piece of meat to be used and disposed of at his discretion. The purpose of the questions, rather, was to try to trip me up. To get me to reveal dishonesty. To root out any deception.

To make sure I was who I said I was.

The first round of questions took about half an hour. Then he started in again, same questions, different order. Then he wanted to know more about my family. My favorite subjects in school. Pets that I had owned. What cars I had driven, girls I had dated, movies I liked.

Where had I traveled to? What was my favorite flavor of ice cream? Had I ever been in a car wreck? Had I ever been injured? Had major surgery? Ever been in trouble with the law? Ever got a speeding ticket? Endlessly, the questions came.

It was good that I had drilled for this with Steve. This Aiken guy was thorough. If I had come here unprepared, he would have gotten me. As it was, I had to give the conversation my full focus to remember everything I was supposed to say. If I screwed up, if I left a single thread dangling, Aiken would seize it, pull it, and my whole story would come unraveled.

After more than two hours, I was mentally exhausted. Aiken, however, seemed to have enjoyed the exercise. When it came to mental endurance, I was a sprinter, and this guy was a triathlete. Satisfied that I wasn't bullshitting him, he called the guards back in and ordered them to escort me outside. They had me sit down on the floor while one of them kept a rifle trained on my head.

Aiken took his time before leaving his office. I imagined he was looking over his notes, trying to find any discrepancies in my story. If he found anything, I was going to be tortured without mercy until I told them the truth. I did a few silent breathing exercises to calm my nerves, emptied my mind of fearful thoughts, and resolved that I would not let them put me to the question. If it came to it, I would fight like a madman until they killed me, and make damned sure I took a few of them along for the ride. Death was far preferable to giving up information that could get my loved ones killed.

Finally, after what felt like forever, Aiken emerged and ordered his men to escort me back to the warehouse. Once there, they had me sit on the floor and wait while Aiken went over to talk to his brother. I kept my head down and feigned disinterest.

"You're out of here next week, right?" one of the guards said, keeping his voice low.

The man beside him whispered, "Yeah, man. Back to Haven. I can't wait; I haven't seen my son in a month."

I almost snapped my head up, but managed to stop myself. I felt like someone had just dumped a bucket of ice water on my head.

"I'm fuckin' jealous, man. I got another two weeks before I rotate back. You mind checking in on Marcy and the girls for me? Make sure they're doin' okay?"

"No problem."

Lucian stood up from his desk and began walking in our direction. The guards went abruptly silent. Their leader snagged a chair, spun it around, and sat down facing me with his arms draped across the back.

"I have good news, and I have bad news. Which do you want first? You have my permission to speak."

Stay calm. Breathe. "It's been a while since I had any good news, sir."

He grinned. "You passed the first test. Aiken thinks you're on the level. Which is good, because if he didn't, I'd have my men string you up with fishhooks. As for the bad news, I'm afraid we can't accept your application at this time."

He saw my confusion and held up a hand. "Not that I don't think you would make a good soldier. You obviously know how to fight. It's just that right now, I need workers more than I need soldiers. I've got big things planned in the next few weeks, but before that happens, those tunnels need to be finished. The more hands I have digging, the sooner things can happen. So for the time being, I need you in the mines. Don't worry though, I'll make sure they double your rations and tell the guards to take it easy on you. But don't forget," he pointed a finger at me, "the rules still apply. You do what you're told, when you're told, and you don't talk to the other prisoners. We don't want them getting any crazy ideas. It'd be bad for their health."

He stood up and motioned to the guards. "Take him back down and pass along my orders. Make sure he's treated right. As for you, Morrison, once the tunnels are complete, we'll see about getting you on a salvage crew. How's that sound?"

"That sounds like the best idea I've heard in years, sir."

He laughed, and reached down to clap me on the shoulder. "Don't worry, son. You're almost done paying your dues. Keep your nose clean, do your job, and we'll have you out of the mines in no time."

He walked away, and the guards helped me to my feet. Gently this time. As they led me away, the guards' words kept echoing in my head.

Haven. My son. Marcy and the girls. Did these guys have families? What the hell was Haven?

And what did it mean for the coming fight?

*****

Over the next few weeks, life was easier.

Word spread among the troops that Lucian had authorized me to join the Legion. The guards no longer hit me at the slightest provocation, I didn't have to wear chains anymore, and they fed me twice a day instead of just once. The portions were actually enough to live on.

This did nothing to endear me to the other prisoners, especially the ones I had beaten. They divided their time between staring longingly at my food, and glaring daggers at me whenever the guards turned their backs. Whether it was because I had beaten them, or because they were jealous of my forthcoming ascension, I wasn't sure. Probably, it was both.

It bothered me that they hated me so much. If I could have shared my food, I would have. If I could have split my water ration with them, I would have done it. But I couldn't. The guards were always there, and I had come too far to risk blowing my cover over something so small. But with every day that passed, my resolve to rescue these men became stronger.

Work continued on the tunnels at a furious pace. Lucian was relentlessly pushing the engineer in charge of the project to get it finished. I saw the engineer a few times, dressed in clean clothes and wearing sturdy rubber boots, as he come down to inspect our work. From his chatter, I gathered that the connector loop was nearing completion.

Early one morning, nearly five weeks after I had been captured, the two men working at the edge of the tunnel shouted for the guards. The one in charge walked over.

"What is it?"

"We broke through, sir."

"No shit …" The guard held up a lantern and stepped forward. A hole the size of a basketball emerged from the gloom, with dim yellow light glowing from the other side.

A voice called out, "That you, Central?"

The guard smiled. "Who the hell do you think it is?"

"Goddamn, I'm glad to hear your voice. Come on, you fucking maggots. Finish this shit up."

The guard stepped back and motioned to the diggers. "Go on, get this wall down."

While the slaves worked, he ordered one of the other guards to go back and notify Lucian. He showed up a few hours later with the engineer in tow, offering smiles and handshakes to the troops who emerged from the other side.

"Well, it's about damn time," he said jovially. "Now we can start staging supplies and equipment for the offensive. Fenton, how long do you think it'll take to lay down the planks?"

The engineer—a thin, balding man with thick glasses—tapped a finger on his chin as he thought about it. "If we get twenty more people from each site, I'd say about another week. Maybe less."

Lucian turned to the senior guard. "Go topside and find Kas. Tell him to get a crew together. We need twenty men. Ask for volunteers first, but if nobody wants to do it, then volun-tell the motherfuckers. Got it?"

"Yes, sir." He turned and left.

As the leaders stood around talking for a little while longer, I sidled closer and listened, absorbing as much as I could.

There were still more questions than answers, but I was starting to build a picture of just how big the Legion's operations really were. When they had finished, Lucian stopped to speak to me on his way by.

"Morrison, I think you've been down here long enough. It's time to see about getting you on a crew. Follow me."

He strode down the corridor, and I followed.

Finally, I thought. *Time to set things in motion.*

*****

Lucian turned me over to one of the men in his personal guard. "Take him through orientation," he said with a wave. "Explain the facts of life, get him outfitted and, for fuck's sake, get him cleaned up. He smells like shit."

He walked off to where his senior lieutenants had gathered around a large table, poring over a set of maps. The guard looked me over and wrinkled his nose. Hygiene didn't seem to be much of a priority with most of the Legion troops, but even by their lax standards, I must have looked a mess. I hadn't bathed in nearly six weeks, my beard had grown out, my hair was tangled and matted, and every square inch of me was covered in a crusty layer of dark brown dirt.

"First thing we need to do is get you cleaned up and get you some new clothes. That shit you're wearing looks like it's about to fall apart. Come on."

He set off toward the far end of the warehouse, motioning for me to follow. We reached the same door that Rat-Face Mike had thrown me through more than a month ago, back when this nightmare first started. When he opened it, I had to swallow a few times at the lump in my throat.

It's hard to describe what it's like to go for weeks on end without seeing the sun. Humans are diurnal animals, and access to sunlight is as important physically as it is psychologically. Without sunlight, our circadian rhythms are thrown off, our moods destabilize, and it becomes difficult to sleep. Combine that with sixteen hours a day of backbreaking labor, not enough food, and constant dehydration, and you have a recipe for insanity.

When that door opened and I stepped out into the sunshine for the first time in five weeks, even though it stung my eyes like a firebrand, it was like being reborn. I stopped outside the door, smiled, and turned my face up to the sun, soaking it in.

“It’s nice, isn’t it?”

I held a hand over my face and looked at my escort, trying to blink away the glare. “What’s that?”

He pointed upward. “The sun. I spent about two months down in the tunnels before I finally fought my way out. The first time I went outside, I cried like a fucking baby. The guys in my crew still give me shit about it."

It took me a minute to force my eyes to focus, but finally they adjusted and I could see the man standing in front of me. He was a little shorter than me, late twenties, dark hair, long beard, strong Southern accent.

“It was a couple of months before I stopped hating the tunnels,” he went on. “But now it doesn’t bother me anymore.”

“You were a slave, too?”

He nodded. “Yep. Just like you.” He pointed at the office building next door. “Let’s head over that way. Quartermaster is on the second floor.”

We set off toward the building. On the way I said, “The last time I went over there, Aiken’s men took me through a tunnel.”

“Yeah, he doesn’t like coming outside during the daytime. Not sure why.” He stepped closer and lowered his voice. “A word of friendly advice: Stay the fuck away from Aiken.”

“Why’s that?”

"Guy's a fucking psycho. He's into torture and shit. Anytime somebody needs to be punished, he's the one that does it. He also likes to buy women from slave traders and take them down into the tunnels. I'm not sure what he does with them, but sometimes, if you stand near the hatch, you can hear them screaming. He brings them back in fucking trash bags, man. I'm telling you, stay away from that guy."

"Thanks for the heads up."

"No problem. My name's Paul, by the way. Paul Harris."

"Logan Morrison." I shook his hand.

"You from around here?"

"No, I'm from down south. Texas."

My eyes had fully adjusted to the sunlight and as we crossed the parking lot to the admin building, I took a moment to look around. The place looked just as abandoned as the first time I had seen it, but now that I was on this side of the highway, I could see dugouts in the side of the road where lookouts were stationed. Anybody who passed by on the road would run right into their line of fire. Along the treeline, I saw evidence of other watch stations positioned well apart, but all within sight of each other. It wasn't the strongest perimeter, but it didn't have to be. Between the warehouse and the tunnels, the Legion troops stationed here had plenty of protection. I wondered how I could use that against them.

"Listen man, there's a few things you need to know," Paul said. "Rules of the road."

"Okay."

"First, don't go thinking that the leaders trust you. They're not stupid; they know you're probably pissed at them for all the shit they put you through. They'll watch you close, and if they don't think you're serious about joining up, they'll send you right back down to the mines. I've seen it happen plenty of times. Couple of guys even got themselves killed."

"Good to know. Anything else?"

"Yeah. Don't try to run away. The last guy that did that was this kid named Morrow. He was a smart fucker; he almost made it, but one of our trackers caught up with him in a little town not far from here. They worked him over pretty bad, and then stuck him back in the mines for a month."

Morrow, you poor bastard. Everything you told me was true. "What happened to him after that?"

"He straightened up and got on board with things. Fought his way out, and got assigned to a crew. Kid had bad luck, though. About two weeks later, he got killed in a firefight down near Hollow Rock, along with a bunch of other guys. Fuckers set a trap for us."

A trap? Is that what the leadership around here was selling? I guess they had to cover up getting their asses kicked somehow.

It occurred to me that if this guy was one of Lucian's personal guards, then he'd probably overheard a lot of information that I might find useful. We were still a good two hundred yards from the admin building, and setting a leisurely pace. I decided to go fishing.

"What's Hollow Rock?"

"Little town southeast of here. You should see it, man. They got this big-ass wall that goes around the whole town. The place is surrounded by farms, and they got more food than they know what to do with."

"Why would they attack the Free Legion?"

" 'Cause they're still operating under the old rules," he said contemptuously. "They don't want to trade with us because we allow slavery. The fuckers just don't get it; the old ways are dead. It's all about survival of the fittest now. But that's all right, they're gonna learn. They think because they got the Army on their side they're protected from us." He snorted, a grin creasing his face. "They don't know shit. Lucian's gonna make them pay for what they did."

"Is he going after them?"

"Shit yeah. What do you think the tunnels are for?"

My heartbeat went sluggish, and I remembered the sign at the main intersection in the tunnels. HR AXS. Hollow Rock Access. Lucian talking about an offensive.

The pieces fit.

We arrived at the office building and stepped inside. Just beyond the threshold, a pair of watchmen challenged us and Paul told them we were headed up to the quartermaster's office.

"Meet the newest member of the Legion." He gestured to me.

"Congratulations," one of them said, offering me a handshake.

"Thanks."

"Welcome aboard, man." The other guard clapped me on the shoulder, smiling.

Why the hell was everyone being so nice? These guys were supposed to be hardened criminals. What was with all the smiles and handshakes? It was making me nervous.

Paul led me around the corner and up the stairs. When I walked out of a vestibule and through to the work area, I stopped and stared at what was in front of me. When Paul had said that the quartermaster's office was on the second floor, I thought he had meant just a small part of it, an office or something. But that description hadn't been accurate. The quartermaster's office wasn't just *on* the second floor, it *was* the second floor.

Everything had been stripped out. The cubicles, file cabinets, desks, and computer equipment were nowhere to be found. In their place stood row after row of shelves all the way to the ceiling. A few men meandered through the stacks filling out inventory sheets and stacking boxes on pallet trucks. A desk had been built near the stairwell door, and seated behind it was a plump, surly looking man flanked by two armed guards.

"Mr. Harris. What can I do for you?" Upon recognizing one of Lucian's assistants, the man's mood brightened immediately.

"We got a new recruit." Paul slapped me on the arm, sending out a plume of dust. "Need to get him cleaned up and outfitted."

"Sure, sure," the man said, all smiles. "Come on back, young man. Let's have a look at you."

He motioned me forward, and I stepped through a low, swinging door to his desk.

"Christ's sake, you must have just come from the mines. Well, let's get you sorted out then. Tyrone, would you mind helping our young friend here get what he needs?"

Tyrone, a tall black man with biceps the size of my head, grunted and led me to a bathroom at the far end of the building. Much like the main floor, the bathroom had been stripped out. The room's only features were a mirror to my right, broken pipes jutting out from the walls, and a single pipe protruding from the ceiling that branched out into four shower heads. The opening the pipe came through was rough, as though cut by hand.

"Holy shit," I said. "You have a working shower."

"Mmm-hmm," Tyrone replied. "There's a water tank up on the third floor. Helped build it myself. We cut holes in the ceiling and ran a couple of pipes down. It ain't the Hilton, but it ain't bad."

He stepped outside for a moment and came back with a bar of soap and a towel. "Here you go. I'll go find you some clothes. What sizes you wear?"

I told him, factoring in how much weight I had lost. He left, and shut the door behind him.

Stripping out of my clothes, I tossed them into a pile in the corner, kicked my boots on top of them, and turned the valve to let the water run. It was cold, but not freezing. I spent a half-hour scrubbing myself down over and over again, trying to clean off all the dirt that had accumulated in every crack and crevice in my skin. My hair and beard were the worst parts, tangled and matted as they were.

Once done, I looked at myself in the mirror. My ribs stood out in stark contrast under pale skin, and I could see the striations and bulging veins in my muscles. The hard work I had done in the mines had made me stronger, and even though I had lost weight, I was denser now. Compact. Stringy.

A knock sounded from the door. "You done in there?"

"Yeah."

The door opened. Tyrone thrust his arm inside, holding a small white trash bag. "Here's your clothes."

I took it from him and he withdrew his arm, shutting the door. Inside the bag was a set of thermal underwear, an unopened packet of boxer briefs, a few plain T-shirts, socks, two pairs of sturdy Carhartt pants, two Army surplus bush jackets, and a thick Gore-Tex winter coat. Further down, I found a knit cap, gloves, belt, and a pair of Browning combat boots. Not bad. Not bad at all. I got dressed and stepped outside, carrying the bag. Tyrone was waiting for me.

"You look a damn sight better. How you feelin'?"

I managed a smile. "Much better now. Thanks."

"Come on with me." He turned and walked back toward the front desk. When we arrived, Paul was there chatting with the pudgy man behind the counter.

"Look at you, Morrison. You look like a human being again."

I forced a laugh. "I feel like one, too."

"Grab a backpack and a sleeping bag from that shelf over there. George has a few presents for you."

I went where he pointed and picked out a few items that looked adequate. Taking my new clothes out of the trash bag, I stowed them in a rucksack and went back over to the desk. Paul motioned to the man behind the counter, who produced a small cardboard box. "This is yours," he said.

I pulled it across the table and picked through it. There was a Faraday flashlight—the kind you shake up to charge—a wind-up lantern, paracord, zip-ties, a mess kit, two emergency ponchos, a multi-tool, and a Swedish fire steel. I nodded in approval and stuffed them in my pack.

"Thanks, man. This is good stuff. What about weapons?"

The fat man chuckled. "Not while you're still a prospect. You can have an ax or something to protect yourself from the infected, but no guns. Not till you've proven yourself."

He dismissed me with a wave. "Good luck, kid. You're gonna need everything in that box before it's over with."

"Let's head downstairs and go through all the orientation stuff," Paul said. "Then we'll see about getting you assigned to a crew."

I nodded and followed him down the stairs. Back on the first floor, he led me to a corner on the opposite side of the building from Aiken's office. The room was empty except for a folding table and a couple of office chairs. On the table were a few binders and a box of file folders. Paul rooted around in the files until he found one with my name on it and pulled it out. He motioned for me to sit down, and then took a seat at the table across from me.

Over the next fifteen minutes, he laid out the rules of serving in the Free Legion. There weren't many of them, but they required explanation. The first and most important rule was loyalty. Loyalty to the Legion, and loyalty to my crew. That meant following the orders of my crew leader, the senior staff—which they called the Carls—and the Warlord, Lucian. I asked if Warlord was Lucian's actual title, and Paul confirmed that it was. I almost laughed, but seeing the serious expression on Paul's face, I held it in.

(Seriously, though. Warlord? Shouldn't the guy be wearing assless chaps and a spiked codpiece, and drive around in a dune buggy or something?)

My crew leader was responsible for my training, which would begin sometime in the next week or two. They had a strict curriculum, and everyone in my crew would help. The training would consist of basic marksmanship, land navigation, urban combat, patrolling, setting up perimeters, land warfare, traps, unit tactics, and an introduction to explosives. Gabriel had taught me all that stuff years ago, but Paul didn't need to know that.

Next, we discussed salvage. Even as the low man on the totem pole, I was entitled to a share of anything I found. If the quartermaster didn't want it, it was all mine. Any male slaves I took belonged to Lucian and the Carls, but they would compensate me for them. As for women, the first one I captured belonged to the Legion, but any others were mine to keep. When I asked what happened to the women who were given to the Legion, I got about the answer I expected. I didn't reach across the table and rip Paul's heart out through his mouth, but it was a near thing.

Last, we talked about ascension through the ranks. My current rank was that of prospect. If I proved myself, I could become a regular, like Paul. If I demonstrated intelligence, motivation, leadership, and resourcefulness, I might be considered for promotion to crew leader. Promotion to Carl, however, was a dim possibility. Unless the Legion got big enough to warrant commissioning more of them, or if one of them died, it was unlikely that I would achieve that rank anytime soon. I nodded understanding at that, all the while thinking to myself that the Legion's growth prospects were about to become extraordinarily grim.

Once finished, Paul had me sign a document confirming that I understood the terms conditions of membership in the Free Legion, and that I consented to abide by them.

As if I had a fucking choice.

We then went back across the parking lot to the warehouse and tracked down Kasikov. He was down in the tunnels supervising the grumbling Legion troops that Lucian had ordered to begin work on a walkway of wooden planks. The planks would provide an even surface for the luggage carts they would use to move supplies and equipment back and forth between sites. I tried to sneak a peek down the Hollow Rock access tunnel, but all I saw was darkness.

"There are not being openings on any of the crews except one," the big Russian said with a grin.

Paul raised an eyebrow. "Which one is that?"

Kasikov's grin swiveled in my direction. "Mine."

Paul seemed pleased. "Well, that was easy. Logan, say hi to your crew leader."

"I thought Tommy was your crew leader," I said.

"He was," Kasikov replied. "He is being reassigned. An entire crew was slaughtered near one of our supply depots."

"What?" Paul said, eyes widening. "Which one?"

"Carson and his men. A patrol found them yesterday and sent runner to tell Lucian. They have been dead many weeks."

"Son of a bitch." Paul looked stricken. "What were Lucian's orders?"

"He is sending Tommy and some others to track down the people who are being responsible."

People. Plural. I wondered what they would think if I told them it wasn't an army, or a team of Special Forces operators that slaughtered their men. Just little old me.

"So what's next?" I asked, shuffling and trying to look unsure of myself. "I mean, what do I do now."

"For now, you are to be going topside and finding Mike. You remember Mike, *da*? Skinny little man, face like a rat."

"Yeah, I remember him."

"Tell him you are being on our crew. He will be setting you up."

"I can do that. Then what?"

The Russian smiled and grabbed me by the shoulders. "Then you have drink! And woman! We celebrate tonight, *da*? Go now, my friend. I have work to do."

I forced a smile, but my heart was sinking. Slowly, I made my way back to the exit hatch.

*****

Rat-Face wasn't thrilled that I was on his crew, but he seemed to take it in stride.

"There's your bunk," he said, pointing. It sat beside three others in a shabbily constructed plywood shack. Heaps of weapons and equipment cluttered the bunks around it. "Just so you know, the penalty for stealing is twenty lashes, administered by Aiken himself. Believe me when I tell you, you don't want that."

"I'll take your word for it." I made my way over to the bunk and began unloading my few belongings.

"Don't get too comfortable," Rat-Face said, sitting down in front of a Coleman stove. "We're heading out the day after tomorrow."

I walked over and sat down in a chair across from him. The smell of grilled mutton wafted from the stove. The only light in our corner of the warehouse was a single propane lantern that did little to chase away the gloom.

"Where to?"

"Fucking McKenzie." He said it like it hurt. "Place is a goddamn horror show. Infected everywhere."

"Then why are we going there?"

He pointed at the stove. "Goats."

I blinked. "Goats?"

"Goats. Place is lousy with them."

I had learned about the large herds of wild goats that roamed Western Tennessee months ago. But Logan Morrison wasn't from Tennessee, and hadn't been in this part of the state for very long. He was just passing through when he was captured. So he played dumb.

"What do you mean?" I asked.

"There used to be a goat farm just north of here. The guy that ran the place raised them all organic and shit. Made cheese with their milk and sold it for twenty bucks a pound. When the Outbreak hit, he wanted the little fuckers to have a fighting chance, so he set 'em all free. They went forth and multiplied."

"So you hunt wild goats?"

"Yep. Capture 'em and use 'em for milk, too."

I shook my head and chuckled. "So how did you learn where all the goats came from?"

"Remember the farmer I just mentioned? He was one of the first guys to join up with the Legion back when Lucian took over. We were on a crew together for a while until the Carl over in Western figured out what he could do. Gave the guy a permanent gig making cheese and raising new herds. Lucky bastard."

He took the goat steak off the grill, turned off the burner, and began cutting it up. "You want some of this?"

My stomach lurched, growling loudly. Even with the extra rations I'd been getting lately, I still hadn't been eating much. "I could eat the ass out of a buffalo right now."

Rat-Face chuckled, and scraped some meat onto a metal plate, along with a few potatoes from a mason jar. We sat in silence, eating our meal together.

The irony of the situation was not lost on me.

A short time later, Kasikov showed up with another man whom I recognized as the guard who had caught me talking, and had cracked me in the kidney with his rifle.

"*Privyet* assholes! I am being hungry. Mikhail, be giving me food."

Rat-Face glared at the Russian. "Stop calling me that, or I'll fucking poison you. I ain't no goddamn Cossack."

"And how is being our new friend?" Kas shot me a wolfish grin.

"He is being better now that he's got a full stomach," I said. "This is the first decent meal I've had in months."

"That is being good. There is being more where it is coming from."

"You remember me, right?"

I looked up at the man that had accompanied Kasikov. "Yeah, I do. My back hurt for a fucking week."

"Look man, I was just doing my job. If I hadn't done it, it would have been my ass."

I waved off his apology. "Don't worry about it. I've had worse."

"No hard feelings?"

"Would it do any good?"

He grinned. "Nope. I'm Will Jones, by the way."

"Will is to be joining our crew now," Kas said, whacking him on the back. "He is being good man, you will see."

I sincerely doubted that there was anything good about Will Jones, but I stayed quiet and ate the rest of my food. The other men exchanged chitchat and cleaned their plates. Once finished with his meal, Kasikov belched loudly wiped a hand across his mouth, and reached under his shirt. He produced a length of cord with a set of keys dangling from it. He selected what looked like a handcuff key and handed it to me.

"It is being time for party now, Logan. Go and get our women. Mikhail, find us something to drink. I am being thirsty man."

My heart beat faster in my chest, and I felt cold fingers marching up my back. "Um … which ones are your women?"

Rat-Face gestured to where the female slaves were chained up. "The skinny blond with the big tits, the redhead, and the black chick with a butterfly tattoo on her ass." He pointed a finger at me. "That last one's mine. Keep your hands off her, new guy."

I struggled for a good reason to refuse, to convince Kas I wasn't interested without raising suspicion, but nothing came to mind. Numbly, I muttered acknowledgement and started walking.

When I reached them, the girls all stood up and let their blankets fall to the ground. They kept their gazes pinned downward, their eyes blank and lifeless. All of them were naked, and I wondered if their captors ever allowed them to wear any clothes.

Out of the thirty or so women, Miranda was the only large-breasted, slender blond. The redhead was also easy to identify—she was the only one with red hair—but there were several black women. I asked them to turn around, and identified the one with the tattoo. After unchaining them, I told the three of them to follow me. The others looked relieved to be passed over, and sat back down on their pallets, pulling their blankets around them.

On the walk back across the warehouse, I realized that my fists were clenched and I was grinding my teeth. Taking a deep breath, I forced myself to relax.

Come on, Riordan. Think.

When I got back, Kasikov thrust a bottle of Captain Morgan at me. "Drink, my friend. This is being good day for you. Miranda, you are being with Logan tonight. You are to be doing whatever he wants, *da*?" There was a subtle warning in his voice that made the petite girl shudder.

"Yes, master."

"Hey, what about me?" Jones shouted.

Kasikov seized the redhead by the arm and thrust her at him. "She is having three holes. Two for me, and one for you."

Jones laughed. "That works for me."

The black girl straddled Rat-Face, keeping her head turned away as he began slurping at her breasts. The redhead knelt down in front of Jones and started unbuckling his pants. Kasikov dropped his trousers and pulled up on the girl's hips.

"Be standing up, bitch. The floor is being cold."

She got to her feet and bent over in front of him. Her head started bobbing up and down over Jones's lap. The Russian slapped her buttocks, crouched into position, and roughly thrust himself in. I looked away, but still heard the fleshy slapping sounds.

For a moment, I considered just killing them all right then and there. They were all distracted, and Jones had left his gun belt on a table just a few feet away. I could snatch up the pistol and the knife, stab Kasikov at the base of the skull, and shoot Jones in the heart. The only worry was Rat-Face. I'd have to pull the girl off his lap first, which might give him time to draw a weapon. My hand had just begun to stray toward the belt when Miranda reached out and touched my arm. I looked at her and saw her eyes shining wetly in the dim light of the lantern. Her head shook just a fraction.

Please don't. She mouthed, using the hanging sheet of her hair to hide her face from the others.

I let out a breath I hadn't realized I was holding. Absently, I became aware of the forgotten bottle of rum in my hand. Miranda stepped over to a chair a few feet away from the others and motioned for me to sit down. I hesitated for a long instant, not wanting to do it, fighting down the killing urge. The silent pleading in her eyes finally moved me.

I sat down in the chair, and Miranda took a seat on my lap. Her hand started rubbing circles on my chest, and she leaned her head down to nibble on my ear. I wanted to crawl out of my skin.

"It's okay," she whispered. "I know you don't want to do this. But if you don't, they'll send you back to the mines. It's part of how they test you."

She slid down my lap until she was kneeling on the floor in front of me. Gently, she pushed my knees apart and began rubbing a hand over the front of my pants. Her other hand pushed up my shirt and her lips began tracing a tingling line over my stomach. Even though I didn't want it to, and as much as I hated myself for it, my body reacted.

I remembered a girl I had known back in junior high who had thought that boys only got erections when they were horny. She'd been one of those kids with hyper-conservative parents who had refused to let her attend sex education. I had explained to her that guys get hard-ons all the time, usually for no reason at all. The penis has a mind of its own, and it will react to just about any kind of stimulus, as long as it isn't too painful.

As Miranda's hands and lips did their work, I told myself that it wasn't my fault. I wasn't doing this. It was just the animal that was my body responding to millennia of evolution.

A pretty girl was touching nerve endings that stimulated an involuntary response in my cerebral cortex. A chemical reaction that I had no control over. Nothing more.

Her fingers began plucking at my belt buckle, and I turned my head away. I had a desperate thought to drag her off somewhere in the darkness under the pretense of wanting privacy, but then remembered Miranda's warning. I needed to maintain my cover, and the last thing I wanted to do was get myself killed. But this was too much. Beatings, I could take. Isolation, I could take. Slave labor, and starvation, and being locked up underground, I could take.

But this, letting this girl do what she was about to do, it was more than I could stand. I was not being victimized here. I was the one doing the victimizing. The Legion was making me an accessory to their crimes by forcing me to sit here and let Miranda carry out this act. Realizing that fact, juxtaposed against all the other things the Legion had put me through, their methods were beginning to make a monstrous kind of sense.

I thought of Allison, and her lovely smile, and the soft, glowing warmth that we had shared on so many cold nights together. Something mutual, and consenting, and beautiful. One of the most profound joys of the human experience. Not sordid, barbaric, and filthy like what these men were doing.

I resolved that if I survived the coming fight, I would tell Allison about everything that had happened here. I just hoped she could forgive me.

Miranda was gentle, and skilled from long practice. When she took me into her mouth, I wanted to scream with frustration. My hands gripped the sides of my chair, and I clenched my jaw so hard I thought my teeth were going to break. She kept her hands busy as she worked, and thankfully, it was over quickly.

She wiped her mouth and leaned back. "Is there anything else you want me to do?"

Her eyes were wide, and I saw pity in them. My throat constricted with a barely suppressed sob, and I felt the burning sting of tears as my vision blurred. I stayed quiet, not trusting my voice. Looking at Miranda, I wondered what kind of gentle, forgiving soul could feel sorry for a man who had just forced her to give him oral sex, even if that man had done so against his will. Maybe she thought I was just as much of a victim as she was.

Get it together, Riordan. You've come too far and endured too much to fuck this up now.

I cleared my throat and sat up straight, blowing out a deep breath to relax. "No, that's good enough for now. Go on, fuck off."

I stared at her as I said it to let her know I didn't mean it. She gave me a small smile, and squeezed my knee.

"Are you being sure?"

Looking up, I saw Kasikov still ravaging the redheaded girl. Jones cried out across from him as he came in the girl's mouth.

"She is good, my friend. Well trained." He switched his attention to Jones. "Hey, hand me my vodka."

"Okay, enough bitch." Jones pushed the girl's head away. "Goddamn woman, the thing gets sensitive right after a man cums. Didn't anybody teach you that?"

He leaned over and grabbed a bottle off the floor, then held it out to Kasikov over the redhead's bare back. The Russian unscrewed the cap and took a long swig, then gestured at me. "Go on, my friend. There are many things she can be doing to you. Give it a few minutes. You will be getting it up again."

I opened the bottle of rum and faked a languid yawn. "I appreciate it man, but I haven't had a good night's sleep in … shit, I can't even remember. If it's all right with you guys, I'm just gonna have a few drinks and go to bed."

Rat-Face turned around from where he had the black girl bent over in front of him. "You're fucking lame, Morrison. A goddamn two-pump chump." The others laughed.

"Yeah, yeah. Pick on the new guy. See you tomorrow, fellas."

Their attention went back to the women as I left. Jones called Miranda over and ordered her to pick up where the redhead had left off.

"If the new guy doesn't want to use you, I will ..."

I propped up a pillow, lay down on my bunk, and tried to ignore the sounds coming from the common area.

You had better enjoy yourselves, you sick fucks, I thought, taking a pull from the rum. *Because by God, your days are numbered.*

*****

I awoke from a nightmare in the middle of the night.

It was one of those dreams where in the middle of it you realize you're dreaming, and when that realization strikes home, you wake up. I didn't sit up in my bunk screaming, or anything. My eyes simply snapped open, and suddenly I was awake.

For all the light in the warehouse, I might as well have kept my eyes shut. The darkness was complete and impenetrable. I reached down and fumbled in my pack until I found the wind-up lantern. A few spins of the crank handle charged it, and I used it to find my boots and make my way to the main entrance. A sleepy looking guard stood by the doorway, Kalashnikov in hand.

"Where do you think you're going?"

I motioned toward the door. "I was going to step outside and get some air for a little while."

"Not out here, you're not. This entrance is off-limits after dark. If you want to go outside, you'll have to take the tunnel over to the admin building. There's a courtyard behind it that's invisible from the road. But you'll have to leave your lantern with the guard over there. No lights outside after dark; it's the rules."

"Oh, okay. Thanks."

He dismissed me with a nod and went back to looking bored. I climbed down the hatch to the tunnels and ran into two more guards at the main intersection. One of them yawned and pointed me to the tunnel leading to the admin building. I thanked them, and headed that way.

I emerged into the same basement as the first time I went there, and had to use my lantern to find the stairwell in the darkness. At the rear exit to the building, another set of guards challenged me and took my lantern before letting me outside. As soon as I stepped through the door, the acrid scent of marijuana smoke made me curl my nose. I looked around for the source, and spotted a familiar figure sitting on a picnic table nearby. I moved closer.

"That you, Paul?"

He turned around. "Yeah. Morrison?"

"Guilty as charged. Mind if I join you?"

"Not at all, man. Have a seat."

He scooted over and let me take up one half of the table. We sat on top of it, resting our feet on the bench beneath.

"So how'd you like your first day with the Legion?"

I shrugged. "It started out uneventful and boring, but then I got a shower and a blowjob. Can't remember the last time I had both of those in the same day."

Paul laughed, and I wanted to stab him in the throat for thinking it was funny. "Sounds like you had a good day." He took a plastic baggie out of his shirt pocket and began filling a glass pipe with a swirling purple design embedded in it. “You smoke?”

“Depends. Is that weed?”

“Yep. Grow it myself. One of the benefits of being on Lucian’s staff.”

In the silver light of the half-moon, I could see that his eyes were bloodshot and a little swollen. The odor of marijuana coming from him was enough to make me cough.

“What’s the story with that?” I asked. “I mean, how’d you end up working for Lucian?”

He picked up a butane lighter, lit the pipe, and inhaled deeply. He held his breath, and then blew out a plume of thick gray smoke. “Can’t talk about that. He swore me to secrecy. You don’t break promises to a guy like Lucian.”

Okay, let’s try a different approach. “That’s cool, I understand. But still, that’s got to be a sweet job, man.”

I could only see him in profile, but the half that was visible smiled. “Yeah, it is.” He held out the pipe. “Want a hit?”

I hesitated for a few seconds. I had tried the stuff a few times, but never really cared for it. All it did was make me hungry. But it was an opportunity to gather information and further cement my cover, so I took the pipe.

“Been a long time, man. I’m probably gonna cough like a motherfucker.”

“It’s cool. Just take little tokes. Here you go.” He handed me the butane lighter.

“They let you have this outside at night?” I asked, holding up the lighter.

“The guards know better than to give me shit about it.”

I nodded and lit the pipe, covering the vent hole on the side with my thumb. The dry, smelly buds turn orange, and after a second or two, I took my thumb off the vent and breathed in.

"You look like you've done that before," Paul said.

I nodded, held the smoke in for a few seconds, and then blew it out. I didn't choke, but I did have to cough a few times before I could breathe again. "Yeah, once or twice."

Paul chuckled. "Go on and take another hit, man. I'm pretty baked."

I did, and then handed the pipe back to him. "Gotta take a break. It's been a while, man. Not sure how bad it's gonna hit me. I don't want to get lost in the fucking tunnels on the way back."

Something about that must have tickled Paul, because he spent a good five minutes giggling uncontrollably. I waited while he got himself together, and felt the THC beginning to kick in. His weed was some strong stuff.

"Oh, man. I needed that. Thanks."

"So how long you been with the Legion?" I asked conversationally.

"About a year now, if you count the time I spent in the mines. A patrol caught me as I was heading north from Hollow Rock. Traded a box of ammo for some food there, and then set off for Canada. I'd heard there were a few communities up near the border that were welcoming survivors."

"Doesn't sound like much of a hope to go on," I said.

He shook his head. "It wasn't, but at the time, I had nothing else going. I figured I'd get there, or die trying. Then the Legion came along."

He was silent for a while after that, gazing blankly into the darkness. Just as I was beginning to worry he wasn't going to say anything else, he spoke up again.

"At first I fucking hated it, you know. You've been there, too, you know what I'm talking about. They beat the shit out of me. Starved me. Wouldn't give me any water. For a while there, I just wanted to die. Get it over with, you know? I even begged the guards to kill me, but they wouldn't do it. They told me I'd get stronger. And you know what? They were right."

He went quiet again, his bloodshot eyes hardening. I didn't really care why this guy had sided with people who'd brutalized him, but there was the odd chance that he might let something useful slip. So I decided to encourage him.

"I think I know what you mean, man. That first week was rough, being in isolation. But at the same time … I don't know. I kind of feel like it taught me something."

"That's because it did." He turned to face me, his expression showing a fierceness that hadn't been there before. "You learned the same thing I did; you're stronger than you think. Tougher than you think. You can take a hell of a lot more abuse than you thought you could. You can survive on just a little bit of food and water. You can sleep when you're freezing cold. You can work when you're so exhausted you can barely move. Your body will do whatever your mind tells it to."

He tapped a finger on his forehead, and went back to staring into the blackness of the forest. "When I was in that hole, something changed inside me. The old Paul was weak and stupid. He was still holding on to all the bullshit he'd believed back before the Outbreak. All the lies politicians used to feed people to keep them under control. All the years of indoctrination that had turned me into a sheep, the same as everybody else. I wasn't the man I was meant to be. I'd never been shown what I was really capable of, never had a chance to learn it for myself. Lucian changed all that."

He paused long enough to take a hit from his bowl, then went on. "At first I was just scared. When they took me down to the mines, I literally pissed myself. The work was terrible. My body wasn't used to it, I hurt constantly, and I cried until I ran out of water to cry with. The guards mocked me and kicked me around like a dog. God, I had hated them then. Hated them with a passion. But a few weeks went by and, as much as I didn't want to be, I was still alive. I got used to not eating. Not having enough water. My body adjusted to the workload, and it got easier. I think that was when I first started to really get it, you know? When I first started to understand."

I looked down between my knees and feigned contemplation. "I think I know what you mean."

His head turned, and he put an arm around my shoulders, giving my deltoid a quick squeeze. "Of course you do. You just went through the same thing. It's a fucking harsh crucible, man. But can you honestly say you're not stronger for having gone through it?"

I stayed quiet for a few seconds, nodding slowly and pretending to think about it. "You know, you're right. I hadn't really thought about it that way, but you're right. I think I am stronger now."

He withdrew his arm. "Goddamn right you are. Want another hit?"

I held up a hand and waved the offer away. "No, not right now. Those first two are hitting me hard. That's some good shit, man."

He laughed. "Yeah, it is."

I waited while he took another drag, and then he continued, "I went to the fights every Sunday, just like everybody else. There were some big guys down there with me, so I figured it would be best to wait until they got out before stepping up. After about a month, the toughest guys were gone, and I figured I could take the rest. I almost won it, but I fucked my hand up on the last guy and wound up getting choked out. The guy I lost to is actually on your team. Mike, that rat-looking fucker." He shook his head ruefully. "That was fucking embarrassing. I had to give my hand a couple of weeks to heal, and then I tried again. That time, I won."

A smile crossed his face at the memory. "I can't tell you what that was like, man. I stood up over my beaten opponent and roared like an animal. Everyone was screaming and cheering. It was fucking surreal. Lucian came out to congratulate me, and I gave him a hug. Can you imagine that? He didn't get weird about it, though. He just looked me in the eye, and he said, 'Today, you're a man.' And that was when it clicked, you know? When it all made sense. The old world was soft, and it raised soft people, and it fed them lies to keep them under control. Reality is way fucking harsher than that. Reality doesn't lie, and neither does Lucian. All the shit he put me through, all the beatings, and the work, and the starvation, it was like putting raw metal in a fire. You have to melt it to make something out of it, and in the process, you burn away the impurities. All the things that make it weak. And when you add the right ingredients, and shape it, what you get is something stronger. Sharper. That's what Lucian did for me. He dragged me kicking and screaming into the fire, he burned away all the lies that made me weak, and he showed me what it means to be strong. I'd have never done it on my own, never would have put myself through that. I'm glad Lucian did it for me. Not a day goes by that I don't look at that great man, and think how lucky I am. I'd say I'm grateful, but grateful ain't the word, man. Grateful doesn't cut it. Not by a long shot."

I thought about pointing out to Paul that his logic was as full of holes as the proverbial Swiss cheese. But looking him in the eye, I could see that he was a fanatic. A convert. A zealot. There is no arguing with people like that, no reasoning with them. They're going to believe whatever they want to believe, and nothing you say is going to make a damned bit of difference. I stared at Paul for a long moment, and wondered at the things people become.

"That's fucking hardcore, man," I said, breaking a smile. Paul chuckled, and the hard lines of his face relaxed.

"Yeah, I get carried away talking about that shit. It just means a lot to me, you know?"

"I know exactly what you mean, Paul. Believe me." I leaned back on my elbows and looked at the sky. Now that the world had gone dark, the stars stood out bright and clear, crystalline against the cloudless night sky.

"Just wait until you start training and go on your first raid. That's when shit's gonna get real." He stood up and stretched before tapping the ashes out of his bowl. "I got the munchies like a bastard. I'll catch you later, Morrison. I'm gonna go find some grub."

"All right, man. See you around."

He ambled off, a little unsteady. When the door had shut behind him, I let out a sigh and released the end of the table. I had been gripping it hard, resisting the urge to do something painful and damaging to Paul. When I looked at my hands, they wood had bitten into them and they were bleeding a little. I picked out the splinters and tossed them to the ground, and then I lay back on the table and stared up at the sky.

You're a goddamn evil genius, Lucian. To take a man and turn him into a monster like that. You're going to pay for what you've done, you heartless fuck. You're going to get it back in spades.

I thought about the transponder implanted under my skin. I thought about its range, and the battery that I charged every time I moved. I thought about the satellites swirling up there in space, exchanging RF signals with the little blue sphere below. I thought about Steve, and his little shack with all the radio equipment. He would have my signal by now. Or at the very least, they had it over in the Springs and would be sending an encrypted message to Hollow Rock in short order. I wondered who Steve would send. Great Hawk for sure. Maybe Grabovsky? Gabe? Whoever it was, the Legion was in for a world of hurt.

I thought about all this, lying there in the cold, and I smiled.

Chapter 22

The Journal of Gabriel Garrett:

Beacon of Hope

"We've picked up his signal again," Steve said without preamble as I stepped into his office. He stood up and flipped the map on his desk around so that I could see it, pointing to a spot fifteen miles northwest of Hollow Rock.

"It showed up again here, the same place as where we lost it. He's on the move, headed northwest."

I stepped forward and glanced down at the map. "You sure?"

He nodded. "Positive. Central Command still has plenty of GPS satellites up and running. They can pinpoint his transponder to within five yards, and the signal is one of a kind, unique to his device. It's him."

"How do we know he's still alive? Maybe the Legion is moving his corpse. Or maybe they got overrun by the walkers, and he's wandering away."

"No, if that were the case we'd know it. The transponder is programmed to tell us if his vitals have flatlined. He's definitely alive."

I felt a tension that had been building in me for the last six weeks begin to loosen. "That's good news. What do we do now?"

Steve eased back into his chair and motioned for me to have a seat. The office we occupied at the VFW hall was the same one that General Jacobs had commandeered a few weeks earlier. The old soldier had flown back to Colorado Springs, and was lobbying for us with Central Command for troops and resources. After Eric left, we had hoped to find information he could use to argue our case. A month and a half had gone by, and so far, things had not been going well.

"Now we try to make contact with him," Steve said. "I wish I knew why it took so long for him to resurface. Maybe the Legion changed their recruiting tactics, or something went wrong that kept Eric tied up in the tunnels."

I leaned back in my seat and steepled my hands under my chin. "That's good news for Grayson Morrow. I'm sure he's just as anxious to get word from Eric as we are. Probably more so, seeing as his life depends on it."

Steve's expression darkened. "He's not out of the woods yet. At least not until we contact Eric and find out if his story holds water."

"Let's hope it does, for all our sakes."

Steve nodded again and went silent for a few seconds. He rubbed a hand over his chin, and I got the feeling he was working his way up to what he wanted to say next, choosing his words carefully.

"I had planned to send Grabovsky with Great Hawk for next phase of the operation, but after careful consideration, I think you might be a better candidate for the job, Gabe."

I waited a few seconds, staring him down. "Why the sudden change of heart, Captain? I thought you wanted me to keep my distance from this op. What was it you said, that I was too 'emotionally invested'?"

He accepted the jibe with a shrug. "I've had time to think about it. You know Eric better than anyone else. You know how he thinks, and you can predict what he might do. Beyond that, you're every bit as good an operator as Grabovsky, if not better. And Great Hawk actually *wants* to work with you."

He leaned forward, dropping his voice to a conspiratorial hush. "You should feel special. That guy never works with anyone unless he's ordered to. And even then he has a tendency to take off on his own, the slippery bastard."

"On his own? Do the SEALs not work in teams anymore?" I asked.

"They do. At least most of the time. Great Hawk went from Team Three, where he excelled, to Team Six, where he excelled even more. After the Outbreak, the president tasked General Jacobs with selecting the best operators to assist with the bloodier aspects of the reclamation effort. Guess whose name was at the top of the list?"

I absorbed that, letting out a low whistle. "Jesus. Is he really that good?"

"Yes. He's that good. Honestly, the guy scares me."

Steve leaned back and rolled a short distance from his desk, crossing one boot over his knee. "Of course, you're free to refuse the assignment. I have no authority to give you orders, not that it would do me any good if I did. But I would urge you to consider the danger to our mutual friend, and how you would feel if one of my guys bungled the op."

"Our mutual friend? Is that what you think Eric is? Your friend?"

Some of the animated energy left the Green Beret, and he went still as he shot me a flat glare. "I may not be as close to him as you, but he and I have been through some shit together. He's a good man, and I'd like to see him come home safe. Same as I would any other soldier."

"You realize Eric isn't one of your soldiers, right?"

"He may not wear the uniform, but he does the same job. I wish I had ten of him. We would have destroyed the Legion months ago."

I couldn't find fault with that sentiment, so I stayed silent for a little while, thinking. Steve's logic was dead on. I was the best person for the job, hands down. No doubt about that. But Great Hawk was a wild card. I didn't know him, didn't trust him, and I had never worked with him before, which meant that he was unpredictable. None of that filled me with confidence that he could help me rescue Eric, regardless of what Steve had to say about him.

"Why not just send me? I've worked alone plenty of times. Keep the Apache in reserve, just in case. If anything happens to me, send him in with Grabovsky."

Steve shook his head. "If you don't come back, I'm not sending anyone else in because that would mean the entire mission has gone tits-up, and the Legion figured us out." He cut his hand in a negating gesture. "I need both of you for this. You two are the best I have, and your best chance at success is to work together. I'm sorry, Gabe, but this is a non-negotiable, take-it-or-leave-it offer."

"I could always go on my own." I scowled at him. "I know where to look, and we both know you're not going to stop me."

"That's true," he said. "But you would go alone, with no support, no comms, and no backup."

He smiled then, his yellowish eyes twinkling with mischief. "We can do better than that, Mr. Garrett. Much better, in fact."

He opened a drawer, took out another map, and spread it out on the desk.

"I've been keeping this quiet, but I think it's time to let you in on it." He stood up and began pointing out locations on the map. The paper was laminated, with three symbols drawn on it in black grease pencil. The symbols formed the vertexes of a triangle, each symbol highlighting locations to the north, west, and south of Hollow Rock, roughly thirty miles from the center of town.

"Over the last six weeks, General Jacobs has been quietly moving troops from Fort Bragg to these locations around Hollow Rock, and lining up air support from Pope AFB. They weren't able to spare much; the Springs is preparing for action against rogue factions. But we do have an AC-130 gunship, two Chinooks, and two Apache Longbows that we can call on. Not to mention about two hundred troops."

I blinked at the map a few times, and then looked up at Steve. "So all this time, while you were hemming and hawing about not getting enough support from Central Command, it was just a smokescreen? They were helping us all along?"

He smiled and held up his hands. "Hey, you never know. There could be spies anywhere. I figured it was best to play it safe."

"Holy shit."

Steve's smile widened. "Holy shit is right."

He let me study the map while he sat back down behind his desk. "So what do you say, Garrett? You want in, or what?"

I sat down heavily, and felt a warm tingling run from my stomach all the way out to the tips of my fingers. The Apache attack helicopters by themselves would have been enough to devastate the Legion, if we could only find them. But with a gunship and two-hundred troops at our disposal, this thing was setting up to be a bloodbath.

"When do we leave?"

*****

I had four people to talk to in the next forty-eight hours: Allison Laroux, Elizabeth Stone, Raymond Grabovsky, and Lincoln Great Hawk. Not necessarily in that order.

Elizabeth's office was just down the street from the VFW hall, so I started there. Not surprisingly, she already knew about the troops and aircraft stationed around Hollow Rock, as well as Steve's plan to rescue Eric.

"I know you're the right man for the job," she said. "But I still don't like it."

She stood with her back to me in front of the floor-to-ceiling windows in her office. The pale, mid-morning light framed her curves in a golden silhouette. Looking at her, I felt a stirring in my chest that had been growing harder and harder to ignore.

"It's not just about Eric." I stepped forward and put my hands on her shoulders. "Whatever he's learned, it's going to be invaluable in the fight against the Legion. He's risking his life for the people of this town, people that you've sworn to protect. We have to make sure he gets home safe. The future of Hollow Rock depends on it."

She nodded slowly and leaned back into me, still looking out the window. There were dark circles under her eyes, and her shoulders slumped with weariness. "I know," she said quietly. "But still … I don't want you to get hurt, Gabriel."

She turned around, her arms slipping around my waist. Even though she was tall for a woman, her head barely came up to the middle of my chest.

"Don't worry about me," I said, holding her and stroking her hair. "I'm as tough as old saddle-leather. Those Legion yahoos have no idea who they're fucking with."

She chuckled, and looked up at me, leaning back to meet my eyes. "Just be careful, okay?"

"I always am." I bent down to kiss her, and then said goodbye.

My next order of business took me through the north gate and out to the training camp. Grabovsky was aware that Steve wanted me to take his place on the rescue mission and, from what I had gathered, the G-man was none too happy about it. Since being wounded a few months earlier, the recent skirmish against the Legion had been the only action he had seen. Special Forces operators become Special Forces operators because they *want* to fight. If they wanted a less dangerous job, they could work in supply or logistics. Grabovsky was anxious to get back into the proverbial shit, and me taking his spot on the upcoming operation was likely to cause tension between the two of us. I figured it best to mend that fence sooner rather than later.

When I reached the camp, the recruits were on the Grinder watching Marshall give a presentation about squad tactics. He had dragged a rolling chalkboard out of the instructors' barracks and was describing assault formations like a coach mapping out plays to a football team. Grabovsky stood with his arms folded over his chest behind where the recruits were sitting, and the look on his face was not a happy one.

I stopped next to him, and tried to think of something to say. He kept his gaze on Marshall, not turning to me.

"Fuck you, Gabe." He pitched his voice low, so that the recruits wouldn't hear him.

"Come on, Ray," I whispered. "What do you want me to do?"

"Turn down the offer and let me fucking do it, that's what. I've been babysitting this militia for three months now, and I'm bored out of my goddamn mind. If I don't shoot something soon, I'm gonna fucking lose it."

"You do realize it's a rescue mission, right? The goal is to get in and get out without shooting anyone. You'd be just as bored, except without three hot meals a day and a warm bed."

The G-man glared at me. "You fucking know what I mean."

I sighed, and shuffled my feet. "Look man, it's not that I doubt your skills, okay? Eric is like a brother to me. We go way back. If you were in my place, wouldn't you want to be the one handling the op?"

He glared daggers at me for another moment, then let out a breath, looked down, and shook his head. Some of the venom drained from his tone. "I'm not even in your place and I want to handle it. But you have a point. If it were Wilkins or McCray, I wouldn't want anyone else pulling their asses out of the fire."

The stiffness left his shoulders, and he scratched absently at the back of his head. He obviously wasn't thrilled with the situation, but at least he wasn't going to hold a grudge. I figured that was the best I could expect from him.

"I gotta go talk to Great Hawk. I'll see you around." I turned to leave.

"Hey, Gabe."

"Yeah?"

"If I don't see you before you leave, good luck. Watch your ass out there."

I nodded. "Thanks."

Great Hawk watched the proceedings without interest, his dark-red face impassive. I took a seat a few feet away from him on the podium.

"Looks like we'll be working together after all," I said.

He pinched a toothpick from between his teeth and flicked it into the grass. "Do not worry about Grabovsky. He is not a man to stay angry for long."

I looked out across the field where Marshall had ordered the recruits to their feet. The squad leaders huddled up for a quick meeting, and then fell out with their squads to begin the next exercise. Sanchez and Flannigan were among them. Grabovsky had promoted them after they helped prevent the Legion from stealing our supplies.

"We leave in forty-eight hours. Steve give you the mission briefing yet?"

"Yes."

"Do you have everything you need? If not, you've got full access to the armory."

He shook his head. "I am prepared. Thank you for the offer."

He shifted his gaze to the surrounding forest, his eyes tracking over something in the distance that I couldn't see. "I take it that Captain McCray has explained to you what has been happening?" he asked.

"Yeah," I nodded. "Caught me by surprise. The guy had me fooled; I thought Central Command was holding out on us."

The Apache chuckled. "He understands the value of deceiving his enemies."

"That he does. Listen, we've never worked together before, so I want to make something clear. My priority here is getting Eric home alive and in one piece. Anything else takes a back seat. And that includes any hidden agenda Steve is serving by sending you out with me."

Great Hawk looked at me, and his mouth twitched in the beginnings of a smile. "You do not trust the Captain?"

"No, I don't."

"That is good. I do not trust him either."

*****

On the way home, I passed by the doublewide trailer the Glover family had moved into shortly after we arrived in Hollow Rock. It wasn't far from where I lived, but I didn't visit them very often. My duties with the militia gave me a viable excuse for my absence, but in all honesty, I was avoiding them. Not all of them, really. Tom was still a good friend, and Brian begged me to visit more often every time I saw him. It was just Sarah I didn't want to see. And of course, it was just my luck that as I rounded the bend past their house, Sarah was out in her front yard playing catch with Brian.

Fuck's sake, I thought. *What the hell is she doing home in the middle of the day*?

"Gabe!" Brian screeched when he saw me. The kid was going through puberty, and the change had turned his voice into something akin to a vulture eviscerating a cat. Nevertheless, I couldn't hold back a smile as he ran over to me and threw his arms around my waist.

"It's good to see you," he said, my heavy jacket muffling his voice. "What are you doing away from the camp?"

"Got business out this way." I hugged him back and patted him on the shoulders. "I'm headed over to Doc Laroux's place."

He leaned back and looked up at me, concerned. "Are you sick?"

I chuckled. "No, son, I'm fine. Just work stuff. She takes care of the militia, you know."

"Oh yeah, that's right. Forgot about that." The clouds over his face cleared, and his smiled shined through like the sun. "Got time for a catch?"

It was on my lips to say no, but Sarah chose that moment to wing an underhanded pitch straight at my face. I caught it one handed and winced. Sarah had played softball from junior high all the way through college, and she had a hell of an arm.

"Come on, Gabe," she called out. "We haven't seen you in a month of Sundays. Come visit a spell."

"Yeah, come on." Brian grabbed my sleeve and began dragging me toward their yard.

"Well, I guess I can stay a little while …"

"Great, come on." Brian broke into a run.

I followed him and took up position near the front of the house. The three of us made a wide triangle.

“Heads up.” I threw the ball to Brian, who caught it deftly in his old baseball mitt.

“So, what have you been doing with yourself?” Sarah asked, as Brian lobbed the ball to her. She caught it and side armed it to me, gently this time.

“Same old, same old.” I lied, and tossed the ball to Brian.

“I hear the militia’s getting ready to graduate soon. ’Bout a month from now, right?”

I nodded. “Yep, pretty close to that.” Sarah opened her mouth to speak again, but I jumped in. “How’s the new job treating you?”

The ball came my way again. As I caught it, Sarah absently reached a hand to the gold-plated star on her shirt. “Things are getting tense.”

I flipped the ball to Brian. “How’s that?”

“All of us deputies spend more time on patrol with the security details than we do keeping the peace here in town. Most folks around here are honest enough, but there’s a few that are becoming a problem.”

Brian sent the ball sailing through the air, and Sarah bobbled it in her oversize glove for a few seconds before bringing it in.

“You know how it is,” she said. “When the cat is away, the mice will play.”

I caught the underhand she threw me, and sent it Brian’s way. “There anything I can do to help?”

She smiled at me and caught the pitch Brian threw at her. “Sheriff Elliott has it covered. We don’t need to put the fear of God in them just yet. If we do, though, I’ll let you know.”

“Mom, are you hungry yet?” Brian chimed in.

She folded her glove around the ball and stuck it under her arm. “Sweetie, I was hungry when I got here. I’d be eating lunch right now if you hadn't dragged me outside to play catch."

"Okay, okay." He held up his hands and trotted toward the house. "Can we eat at the picnic table?"

"Sure, honey. Don't forget to bring the water."

The boy went up the stairs in two nimble leaps and disappeared through the door. I watched Sarah as she walked toward me, waiting for the old familiar lurch in my stomach. It didn't show up.

"How's he been doing?" I asked when she stopped beside me.

"Better than before. He had a lot of nightmares after the firefight."

I nodded. "Yeah. My first one hit me pretty hard, too. But I was a grown man then."

"I won't lie to you Gabe; he was bad for a while."

I glanced at her, and her eyes held a depth of sorrow that only parents with damaged children know. "He woke up every night for two months. Not screaming, or anything. Just disoriented. Confused."

She walked over to the picnic table and sat down, still facing me. "Tom had the same problem. I saw some things during my time with the Bureau, so it didn't bother me as much, but the two of them …"

I walked over and sat down beside her. My pulse stayed steady, and my breathing was calm and even. The old desire to reach out and hold her seemed to have left town.

"It gets easier," I said. "Time dulls the sharper edges, and after a while, it almost feels like it happened to someone else."

"Brian seems to have learned to deal with it. Most of the time, he just seems like a normal kid. You would never guess that he killed seven men in a shootout just a few months ago.

But at night, when he's getting ready to go to sleep, that's when it hits him."

I looked down at my hands. At the scars, and the burn marks, and the miles etched into the skin. "That's when it hits all of us, Sarah. In the darkness, and the silences, and the spaces between. When we got nothing else to do but listen to the howling of our own souls. And when you've been through what we've been through, that howling is a mournful sound."

She smiled a sad smile, and leaned over to rest her head on my shoulder. "You're good at that, you know."

"At what?"

"Understanding."

I smiled down at her. "For a friend, I do my level best."

She gave my arm a quick hug, and then sat up as Brian came back outside bearing a picnic basket.

"Care to stick around for lunch?" Sarah asked.

" 'Fraid not, I have to get going." I stood up and started walking back toward the street. "You be safe now, you hear?"

"Bye, Gabe," Brian called, waving.

From the corner of my eye, I saw Sarah watch me walk away for a few moments, and then turn to help Brian lay out their meal.

On the walk to Allison's house, I thought about Sarah touching my arm, and hugging me. A few months ago, it would have left me nearly breathless. Now, I felt the same kind of warm affection as I did for Allison. Or Carmela, the old lady down the street who did my laundry, and sent me home with empanadas when I visited her.

My infatuation with Sarah had been a terrible affliction, and I couldn't help but wonder if I might finally be cured. Maybe the chemotherapy of sharing a bed with Elizabeth had sent that particular cancer into remission.

I smiled at the thought, and felt something let go inside of me.

*****

Allison made tea for us, and even broke out some of Eric's sugar stash. I stayed quiet while she prepared it, sitting at the kitchen table and watching her.

She had been a handsome woman when I first met her, with shining brown eyes, a lithe physique, and thick hair that hung well past her shoulders. But the weeks that had passed in Eric's absence had taken a toll on her. The crow's feet around her eyes were more pronounced, the cold had etched deep, dry wrinkles into her hands, and frown lines had shown up around her mouth that hadn't been there before. The lustrous hair that she had once taken pride in now hung lank and unwashed. She hunched over when she walked, her arms drawn tight to her torso, and she had lost weight, which I wouldn't have believed possible. She had been lean before, but now she was downright gaunt.

"You haven't been eating much, have you?" I said, as gently as I could.

She picked up the kettle, about to pour water into our cups, but hesitated. "It's been busy at the clinic," she said. "Two more women had babies this week. One of them is sick. It's bad, we're not sure if she's going to make it."

"The baby or the mother?" I asked.

She finished pouring the water and set the kettle back on the stove. "The baby."

"I'm sorry to hear that."

She put her back to the counter and crossed her arms over her stomach. "It's been difficult since the Outbreak, dealing with infants. We just don't have the same resources or facilities. Children are dying of illnesses that used to be easy to cure. Simple colds and minor infections can be lethal. It's frustrating."

Her eyes stayed down as she spoke, but I saw the pain and worry written there. I couldn't imagine what it was like for her, trying to take care of people with limited medical supplies and no electricity to power the clinic. Perseverance is the toughest form of strength, which Allison had in spades. But she was wearing down, and it showed.

"Allison, I have something to tell you, but it's not something that I'm supposed to talk about."

She looked up, eyes narrowed. "Okay."

"You have to keep this between us. This is serious."

She nodded, and made a twirling gesture with one finger. "Gabe, I'm a doctor. I know how to keep a secret."

I took the teacup she handed me. "I'm leaving tomorrow on a rescue mission to find Eric. We're bringing him home."

She didn't say anything for a long moment, just stood there staring. "Is he all right?"

"He's alive," I said. "Beyond that, I don't know."

Allison took that in, and sat down at the table. "It's been so long. I was starting to think …"

I reached out and covered her hand with mine. "Yeah. Me, too."

She smiled at me, bringing some of the old light back into her eyes. "So where has he been all this time? I know he was sent to spy on the Legion, but no one will tell me anything else about it."

"You weren't even supposed to know that much, Allison. Who else have you told?"

She shook her head. "No one. Captain McCray and Elizabeth are the only two people I've asked, and they already knew what was going on. They both told me the same thing.

That I wasn't supposed to know about Eric's mission. I'll tell you what I told them. I don't give a damn."

"Allison …"

"No, seriously Gabe. I'm sick of this cloak-and-dagger shit. I've kept my mouth shut because I don't want to put Eric in danger, but enough is enough. I bust my ass to help the people of this town, I do whatever is asked of me, and it's about goddamned time people started giving me some answers."

She leaned across the table and fixed me with an icy glare. "Tell me what's going on, Gabe. Tell me, or by God, don't you ever walk through my door again."

I met her gaze, and felt my will to argue die on the vine. To be honest, she had a point. If there was anyone I could trust on this matter, it was her. No one cared about Eric more than she did, and her loyalty to Hollow Rock was without question. Being that she was a doctor, she knew all about confidentiality.

So I laid it all out for her, as much as I knew, anyway. When I finished, she sat in silence, chewing on her lip.

"This better work," she said, her voice trembling. "This better be worth it, or there's going to be hell to pay."

"You should be proud of Eric. He did a brave thing. Most people wouldn't have had the courage."

"I know." She deflated with a sigh. "And I am."

I walked around the table and looked down at her. It always caught me by surprise, the things people turn into. Doctors, and leaders, and villains, and everything in between. Allison was one of the good ones, and this town was a better place for having her in it.

"I need to head out. You should get some rest, you look tired."

She stood up then, abruptly, and took my hands in hers. Even though her fingers barely made it around the edges of my palms, her grip was strong. She stared at me hard, pulling my arms down so that I had to look at her.

"Promise me, Gabe. Promise me you'll bring him home safe."

I looked away, avoiding her eyes. My mother had always warned me against making promises I couldn't keep—some people never forgive that sort of thing—but sometimes, you just have to be a good friend. You have to tell people what they want to hear, even if you aren't sure if you can deliver on it. Besides, if I didn't bring Eric home, it would be because I had died trying.

"I promise, Allison. If he doesn't come home, neither will I."

Her eyes searched mine for another moment. Finally, she nodded and wrapped her arms around my waist. It occurred to me that women seemed to be hugging me a lot more often lately.

"Be careful, Gabe. I want both of you back here alive."

"I'll do my best, Allison. You can count on that."

I left her house, and made my way back to the camp. It was well after dusk by the time I got there, and the militia was bedding down in the barracks for the night. Quietly, I unlocked the armory and slipped inside, looking for one crate in particular.

I found it near the back of the small building, nestled between two shelves full of ammo and piled on top with boxes of grenades. After working it out from the bottom of the pile, I placed it on a workbench and opened the lid.

Inside, was an LWRC M-6 chambered for the hard-hitting 6.8 SPC. It was more powerful than a standard M-4, but not as bone-jarring and loud as my SCAR. Steve had special requested the M-6 for me from Central Command, and it was perfect for the mission I was about to embark on. I cleaned it, fitted it with a specially designed suppressor, and from a crate containing 2000 rounds, I loaded the twelve magazines that came in the box with it.

From another crate, I retrieved an Aimpoint optical sight, night-vision scope, FLIR thermal imager, and a Crimson Trace laser sight, just in case things got up close and personal. I walked down to the range and put the weapon through its paces, zeroing it and getting used to its feel. It fit me like a glove. I might even have liked it better than my trusty old SCAR. Finished, I cleaned it again, and slung it over my shoulder to bring it home with me.

"Thanks, Uncle Sam." I chuckled on the walk back to town. "This will do just fine."

Part IV

The only reason a warrior is alive is to fight, and the only reason he fights is to win.

-Miyamoto Musashi

The Book of Five Rings

Chapter 23

The Journal of Gabriel Garrett:

Own the Night

One o'clock in the morning is a bad time to be awake, but a good time to set out on a stealth mission.

Captain McCray arranged with Central Command to send an HH-60 Pave Hawk to be our air support during the operation. Designed for spec ops missions in denied areas—which was exactly what we were doing—it was the perfect transport to get us into Legion territory undetected.

It took the pilot twenty minutes of skimming the trees to bring us within five miles of Eric's transponder signal and drop us in an uninhabited patch of forest. Once on the ground, we wasted no time putting distance between us and the LZ.

Great Hawk took point, keeping track of Eric's signal, while I hung back and used my optics to keep an eye on our Six. The goggles we'd been issued were beyond top of the line; I'm not even sure if they existed back when I was in the Marines. They combined thermal imaging with night vision, giving me the option to switch back and forth, run them concurrently, and adjust intensity between the two with a resolution unlike anything I'd ever seen. If any creature living or dead showed up within a kilometer of our position, line of sight providing, I would be able to see them. Steve had admonished me to take care of the high-tech optics, citing that the Army didn't have very many of them, they were in high demand and, in pre-Outbreak terms, they were more expensive than most people's houses. I think he was more concerned about getting his gear back in one piece than he was about me.

Eric's signal was coming from a cluster of buildings just south of Carroll County airport. The Pave Hawk had dropped us off east of his position, which gave us a buffer zone from the nearby town of McKenzie. Most of the people in that town had fled across the Mississippi during the Outbreak, but there was still a strong undead presence in the area. Being that we were moving at night, the risk we were taking on this op was considerable. The only thing working to our advantage was the fact that, for reasons not understood, the undead don't moan at night until they are right on top of you. With our advanced optics, as long as we saw them before they saw us, we could put them down without trouble. Still, if we attracted a horde, we might have to abort. That was the last thing I wanted to happen.

As we made our way toward our goal, ghosting through the woods on silent feet, I couldn't help but be impressed with Great Hawk. He was the first person I had ever met who could move through dense forest as quietly as I could—maybe even quieter. There were times when, after checking our flanks, I had to scan carefully to find him in the darkness. Even with the thermals giving away his heat signature, he was doing a good job of staying hidden. If I had just been using NVGs, I might not have seen him. I decided he would be a bad person to have as an enemy.

Rather than approach our destination in a straight line, we cut a meandering path that would make us more difficult to follow. Our GPS devices kept us on course, and roughly two hours after roping down from the helicopter, we had a visual on our objective.

Calling it a town would have been too generous. It was nothing more than a collection of buildings that straddled the highway. The kind of place that used to scrape out a living selling gasoline and cheeseburgers to commuters. A bastion of the homogenized American way of life. I used to sneer at these places, deeming them feeding troughs for the fat, mindless sheep of our society. Now, I would have killed for a Big Mac.

A deep voice said, “I think he is near the McDonald’s.”

I almost jumped. Turning my head, I saw Great Hawk’s shadowy form crouching beside me. He was wearing a ghillie suit, his exposed skin was streaked with black and gray face-paint, and he was studying a small touch-screen device with a dim, green-lettered display. Like me, he was wearing a pack under his camouflage, which made him look hunched and ungainly. The last I’d seen him, he’d been twenty yards ahead of me.

“Is he moving, or stationary?” I asked.

“Moving. He is awake. You should take a look.”

I knelt down to set up a spotting scope. The scope was even more impressive than my goggles, boasting better resolution and longer range, but those advantages came at a cost—it ate batteries like candy. Consequently, Great Hawk had warned me to use it sparingly. I peered through the lens and spent a few minutes studying the restaurant at the end of the street.

Adjusting the scope to full thermal, I counted six bodies on the roof. Four of them appeared to be sleeping. Two others walked side by side around the edge, no doubt keeping watch. Since his signal wasn’t stationary, one of them had to be Eric.

“Can you tell which one he is?” Great Hawk asked.

“I think so, but I can’t be sure. They’re all wearing balaclavas and heavy jackets. I’ll need to move closer. You take the .338 and stay here on overwatch.”

“Very well. Use your illuminator if you need me to take any of them out.”

He was referring to a small infrared pointing device on my web gear. “Will do. Keep an eye out for the infected.”

“Always.”

I handed him my sniper rifle, checked my M-6, and began working my way closer to the dilapidated restaurant. A short time later, I stopped at the edge of the woods, scanned the tall roadside grass with my thermals and, once satisfied that there were no crawlers lurking, I belly-crawled to the side of the road. Ahead of me were the backs of the drugstore and an auto repair shop across from the McDonald's.

Briefly, I debated what to do. One of the men patrolling was Eric, but the other was a Legion trooper. I needed to get Eric's attention without alerting the other man to my presence. After that, I needed to find a way to talk to him without the others seeing. This was going to be tricky.

Slowly, I crawled out of the weeds and moved to the edge of the drugstore. My ghillie suit was great for woodland stealth, but in the open, without trees or brush around, its rustling would attract unwanted attention. After taking it off, I stashed it, along with my pack, behind a long-dead air conditioning unit. I risked a peek around the corner, and saw Eric and the other man standing at the edge of the building facing away from me. Perfect.

Backing off, I retreated to the far side of the auto repair shop, paused at the corner to make sure no one was looking my way, and then walked across the street. I went quick, but not hurried. When you hurry, you make noise. Worse, you tend to make mistakes. Right then, I could afford neither.

By rolling my steps, and keeping my weight on the outside of my boots, I made it to cover behind a gas station adjacent to the McDonald's without drawing any attention. A quick peek around the corner revealed that the way was clear. Slowly, carefully, I leveled my rifle and turned the corner. Ahead of me were two large A/C units and a rusted-out dumpster. Keeping my profile behind the A/Cs, I crept forward until I was close enough to the dumpster to crouch behind it. From there, I could see Eric and the other man as they made a circuit of the rooftop. At the end farthest from me, they disappeared from view, but for most of their patrol, they were visible.

From here, it was just a matter of patience. I took a small red-lens flashlight from my belt, and keeping it behind the dumpster, I dialed down the illumination to a muted crimson glimmer. Now that I was closer, I was fairly certain which one was Eric. If I could get his attention, I could give him a chance to take the initiative. I held the light at the end of the dumpster, poised my finger over the switch, and waited.

On the first three passes, the two men both faced in the same direction. They took a few steps, paused, looked around, and then continued on a short way before repeating the process. Finally, on the fourth pass, the shorter one turned away and clapped his hands over his face to muffle a sneeze. Eric didn't know it, but he was looking right at me. I tapped the switch, and for just a fraction of a second, the light came to life.

Eric stopped.

The other man was still trying to stifle another sneeze, so I turned the light on again and traced the shape of a G in the air. Through the goggles, I saw Eric nod once, and then continue on his patrol. I had a strong urge to simply light up the man next to Eric with my illuminator, but thought better of it.

Patience, Garrett. Give the man a chance to think.

That's the thing I admire most about my skinny friend. He's got an agile mind, and if you give him enough time, he can figure out a solution to almost any problem.

The two of them made another couple of passes on the rooftop and, on the third, Eric stopped and pointed northward.

"Hey Mike, do you see movement out that way?"

The other man stopped and looked. "Where?"

"There, out past the garage, toward the billboard. I think I see a walker over there."

"Really? I can't see shit."

"Put the binos on it."

The smaller man walked to the middle of the roof and came back with a pair of binoculars. He held them up and peered where Eric indicated. "I still don't see anything."

"I'm telling you, there's something over there."

The Legion troop stepped closer to the edge of the roof. Now that his back was turned, Eric slowly and quietly drew something from his coat pocket that shined in the moonlight. "Morrison, you're being paranoid. There's nothing—"

Eric stepped forward and slammed his hand into the man's kidney. The raider gave a strangled gasp and went rigid. Eric's hand shot around and caught the binoculars as the dying man dropped them, simultaneously grinding his blade around in cruel circles. He let the binoculars dangle from his elbow by the strap, and then clamped a hand firmly over the raider's mouth. His hand came back again and he plunged his knife into the man's other kidney. I winced.

That's a bad way to go, getting stabbed in the kidney. It hurts so bad that your body locks up, your diaphragm seizes, and you can't scream. Rapid hemorrhaging and paralysis ensue, and without immediate medical attention, you bleed out internally. Eric didn't wait for that to happen. The knife came up again and he sawed at his opponent's neck. Unlike in the movies, cutting someone's throat is neither an easy nor a neat process. The tendons and ligaments around the big arteries in the neck are tough, and don't part easily. Eric hacked at them with the knife until he cut through to the big veins beneath. Slowly, he lowered the raider to the ground, blood pouring down his torso.

I stepped out from behind cover and waved. He acknowledged me and motioned me around to the other side of the restaurant. When I had run over there, he made a shooting gesture with one hand, and then a throwing motion. I pulled my nine-millimeter pistol, screwed on a suppressor, and tossed it up to him. He caught it deftly, checked the safety and the chamber, and then motioned me to climb the service ladder to the roof.

Although I tried to be quiet, the ladder was rusty and loose on its bolts. It rattled and squeaked as I climbed up. From above me, a groggy voice said, “Logan, what the fuck is going on?”

I heard the telltale *crack-clang* of the pistol firing, followed by a dull thud. The pistol fired twice more as I topped the ladder and stepped up onto the roof.

“Don’t move.” Eric said.

For a second, I thought he was talking to me, and froze. He saw me from the corner of his eye and gestured impatiently. “Not you, Gabe. Come on.”

Ahead of me, two men lay in expanding pools of blood and another kneeled half-risen from his bedroll.

“Keep your hands where I can see them, Kasikov.”

“What is being happening, Logan?” The voice was deep, and heavily accented. Russian.

“What is being happening, you sick son of a bitch, is I’m taking you prisoner. Now, if you like your kneecaps, I strongly suggest you keep your hands where I can see them.”

The man slowly raised his hands. I leveled my rifle at him and stopped next to Eric. “Who’s this guy?”

“His name is Vasily Kasikov. He’s a sadistic puddle of rotten pig shit.”

“*Go fuck your mother, traitor*,” the Russian said in his native language.

“*You should be more polite. We are pointing loaded weapons at you, after all*,” I replied.

Eric turned his head. “Holy shit. You speak Russian?”

I kept my eyes on the captive. “Focus, Eric.”

Kasikov was staring at me now, and even though I was looking at him in infrared, I could see the surprise on his face. Remembering that I didn’t need the goggles at the moment, I reached up and slipped them off. The world went back to normal, and I felt blinded without the enhanced vision. I placed the optics carefully on the ground, and advanced on the marauder.

"Don't move. Eric, keep this bastard covered."

The Russian's face contorted with hate. "Eric. So that is being your name true name then, little cunt. I will be remembering it for when I am gutting you like pig."

"Kas, insults ain't worth tits on a turtle coming from you. Neither are threats, for that matter."

Eric moved left to keep a vector on the Russian as I stepped behind him. "If he moves, kill him," I said.

"Gladly."

I swiveled my rifle around on its sling to free up my hands. Just as I was reaching back to grab a couple of zip-ties, the Russian sprang up.

The top of his head caught me in the jaw and rocked my head back. My tongue got caught between my teeth and I tasted blood to go along with a jolting shot of pain. Before I had a chance to reach back for my weapon, the Russian had turned into me and slammed a fist into my solar plexus. He was standing directly between Eric and me, and if Eric pulled the trigger at this range, the bullet would go straight through and shoot the both of us.

"Gabe, get down!"

Kasikov grabbed me by the web gear straps on my chest and, before I had time to do anything about it, he shoulder-tossed me straight at Eric. I had time to think, *Christ, this fucker is fast*, and then I slammed into my friend. I managed to get a grip on Kasikov's shirt as he threw me, dragging him along for the ride, and the three of us hit the deck in a tangle of limbs.

Kasikov got back to his feet first and swung a kick at Eric's hand. The toe caught him just below the wrist, and the pistol went flying. He aimed another kick at his head, but Eric got his arms up just in time and cross-blocked it, trapped the Russian's ankle, and lashed out with a kick aimed at his knee. Kasikov saw it coming and turned so that instead of getting his knee broken, it simply buckled from behind and dumped him onto his back.

Between the punch and the throw, I still hadn't managed to draw a breath through any of the exchange. My tongue was a screaming ball of fire in my mouth, and I had to spit out a mouthful of blood to keep from choking on it. I got up to one knee, only to have Kasikov rip his leg free from Eric's grip, pivot around on his back like a breakdancer, and swing a boot into my jaw. My vision exploded, and I toppled over backward, striking the back of my head on the cinder-block false front bordering the roof.

He aimed another kick at Eric, but missed as Eric flipped through the air in a capoeira-style, no-hands cartwheel. Dimly, I wondered where the hell he had learned to do that. Eric landed just next to the Russian, dropped down into the knee-on-belly position, and started raining down punches. Three of them landed before Kasikov could move an arm to block, and then, to my surprise, he bridged up on the back of his neck and did a hip-switch, throwing Eric to the side. That was a fairly advanced technique. Where did this guy learn to fight like that?

Not waiting for the bigger man to mount an offensive, Eric lunged forward in a somersault and popped back up to his feet in a fighting stance. The Russian got up, reached under the back of his shirt, and drew a fighting knife. I recognized it immediately—a Soviet era NR-40 combat knife. I had seen many like it before.

Eric saw the knife, and his eyes darted over to the weapons lying on the ground next to the men he had killed a few moments ago. Kasikov moved to his right, cutting Eric off from getting to them.

"Now, my friend. I am to be gutting you like pig."

Eric's face darkened, and he tightened up his fighting stance. "Bring it on, bitch."

I rolled my eyes. *Enough of this shit.* The illuminator was still on my web belt. I took it out and pointed it at the Russian. "Eric, hit the deck!"

The Russian spun around, surprised. He must have thought he'd knocked me out with that kick. Behind him, Eric dropped. I grinned through bloody teeth, and pushed the button on the illuminator. Kasikov had a half-second to register what it was, and then his chest burst open in a crimson geyser. Gore and bone shards peppered me, splattering my chest and face. The Russian slumped to the ground.

I reached up and keyed the mike at my neck. "Took your fucking time, didn't you?"

"I am sorry." Great Hawk's voice came back. "I did not have a shot until your friend dropped to the ground. Just so you know, I had already pulled the trigger when you activated the illuminator. It was not really necessary."

"Just making sure you knew who was who."

"Who are you talking to?" Eric asked as he walked over to me.

"Great Hawk. He's on overwatch."

Eric helped me sit up and looked over his shoulder. "Took his sweet-ass time, didn't he?"

I chuckled, wincing in pain. "That's what I told him."

"So where is he?"

" 'Bout a klick south of here, set up on a hilltop."

He looked at Kasikov's corpse. "That's a hell of a shot."

"I gave him my .338."

"Ah. That'll do it."

I handed Eric my flashlight. “Would you mind taking a look at my tongue? I bit the shit out of it when that fucker head-butted me.”

He clicked it on and looked. By his expression, I was guessing it wasn’t pretty. “Yeah, you cut a little chunk off the tip there.”

I took the flashlight from him and reached back for a first aid kit. “Give me just a minute here.”

“You okay man?” Eric asked. “You took some pretty bad licks.”

“I’m fine. Just not as quick as I used to be.”

He patted me on the shoulder, smiling. “You did fine. Most people would be dead. That son of a bitch was fast, though. Wasn’t he?”

“You ain’t lyin’.”

I folded a patch of gauze over my tongue and held it in place until the bleeding subsided, then spit it out and walked over to the dead Russian. Eric had already rolled him over onto his back and was checking his pockets.

“Does he have something we need?” I asked.

“There’s a key … got it.”

I checked the other bodies and the backpacks next to them, but found only weapons, food, water, medical supplies, a few baggies of marijuana, and several bottles of liquor. Nothing that revealed any information about the Legion.

“You have any luck over there?” I asked.

Eric sat back on his heels and let out a disappointed sigh. “Nope. Just the key to the women’s shackles.”

Just as he was about to stand up, his eyes shifted to the Russian’s wrist and he picked it up, pulling back the shirtsleeve. “What do you make of this? Looks like some kind of military insignia to me.”

I walked over and knelt down, shining a light. “Holy fuck.”

“What?”

I moved the dead man’s arm so that Eric could see it. “That’s emblem for Spetsnaz GRU. This guy was a fucking Russian commando. No wonder he kicked our asses.”

“Actually, he only kicked *your* ass.”

I scowled at him, and then my eyes drifted over to the pile of Kalashnikovs the raiders had been carrying. Eric followed my gaze.

“You think?” he asked.

“I can’t say for sure. But I don’t believe in coincidences.”

Eric stood up and put his hands on his hips, looking down at the dead marauders. “What the hell is going on here, Gabe?”

I got to my feet and stood next to him. “I don’t know. But I intend to find out.”

Chapter 24

The Journal of Gabriel Garrett:

Assets

I called Great Hawk down from his hide.

Eric and I cached the marauders' weapons in the manager's office of the drug store, then dragged their corpses into the refrigerator of the McDonald's. The reek of moldering flesh would soon join the stench of long-spoiled food, but the seal on the door would trap most of it in.

We set up camp on the roof of the garage down the street and waited for Great Hawk to arrive. Having retrieved my ghillie suit and pack, I took out the satellite phone and called the prearranged number that connected directly to Captain McCray's office.

He answered immediately. "This is Alpha. How copy?"

"Alpha, this is Wolf. Copy loud and clear. Subject acquired, five by five. Three ECs down. AO green."

"Nice work, Wolf." His voice sounded relieved. "Where's Hawk?"

"En route. Will establish comms for subject debrief."

"Very well. Reestablish comms via VTC."

"Wilco. Wolf out."

Eric scooped another sporkful of corned beef hash from his MRE and scarfed it down. "Okay, so in English, what just happened there?"

"I told him we found you, killed three hostiles, and that you're uninjured. We're safe, and the area is clear. When Great Hawk gets here, we'll debrief you via video teleconference."

"So why didn't you just say that? Why all the jargon?"

I frowned at him. "It's called brevity. Getting messages across quickly and concisely, with no confusion. The military does shit the way it does for a reason, Eric."

He smiled at me, put down his food, and leaned forward to throw his arms around my shoulders, squeezing hard. "I can't tell you how glad I am to see your ugly-ass face, Gabe."

I laughed in spite of myself and patted him on the back. "I'm happy to see you too, old friend. Now get the hell off me."

He sat back down and picked up his food. "How's Allison doing? She okay?"

"She's fine. Busy as hell, and worried about you, but fine."

He nodded, his hands slowly falling to his lap, eyes distant. "God, I miss her. I can't wait to get home. I can't believe it's only been six weeks. Feels like forever."

"Just imagine how she feels."

"Yeah." He was silent for a while after that.

I heard footsteps approaching, and looked through my goggles to see Great Hawk drawing near. I climbed down to help him carry up his equipment, and once we were settled, the Apache dug a touchscreen device out of his pack, touched a few icons, dialed a number, and in a few seconds, Steve's face appeared on the screen. Great Hawk propped the tablet on an old roof-mounted A/C unit, and we all sat back far enough for the Army captain to see us.

"Damn good to see you alive, Riordan. Do you need medical attention?"

"No, I'm fine. Listen, Steve, we need to get things moving here. We don't have much time."

Steve's eyes went flat. "What do you mean?"

Eric told us his story, and relayed all the intelligence he had gathered. From start to finish, it took a little over two hours. When he mentioned the supply cache with the Chinese rifles, Russian ammo, and Korean shipping manifests, I saw something flicker across Steve's face.

"What do you make of that, Captain?" I asked, pointedly.

He sat still, his face blank. Several seconds passed. "Gentlemen, you deserve an answer to that question, but right now, there's no time. It would take too long to explain. Furthermore, it's irrelevant to the task at hand. We can discuss it once the Legion has been dealt with, and you're all home safe."

I opened my mouth to argue, but Eric held up a hand. "He's right, Gabe. There's no time. We'll deal with it later."

It was frustrating, but I bit down on my retort and let Eric continue. By the time he was finished, the mood had grown decidedly grim.

"Lucian is the key to all of this," Eric said. "If we can get our hands on him, we can find out everything there is to know about the Legion. Their numbers, alliances, bases, supply caches, everything. He's the mastermind behind their whole operation. And the sooner we get him, the better. He's planning an offensive against Hollow Rock, and there's no telling when he'll leave Central to oversee it. If that happens, we might not get another chance to capture him. We'll be back to square one."

For the first time that night, Great Hawk spoke up. "I do not believe that Lucian is the only leader. The evidence is clear that someone is helping the Legion. There is a larger group, probably the Midwest Alliance, that is giving them troops and equipment. From what you are telling us, their numbers have doubled from what Captain McCray thought they were a few months ago. There is no way they have grown so much by capturing people as they did with you. Also, there is the matter of the Spetsnaz commando. I believe there is a larger game being played."

Steve tried to keep his face blank, but I saw his jaw twitch, and he didn't quite keep all the irritation out of his voice. "That may be, Great Hawk, but again, it's irrelevant to the task at hand. I agree with Riordan; we need to capture this Lucian character, and as many other insurgent leaders as we can. We have assets not far from your location. We need to mount an offensive against that warehouse, and we need to take Lucian and his lieutenants alive. Eric, how long before the Legion starts searching for your crew?"

"We're not expected back for a week, and it took us two days to get here. So a minimum of nine days before the Legion realizes their men are missing."

"Good. That will give us more than enough time to send in infantry and air support. It'll be tricky maneuvering around the Legion's patrols, but there's nothing for it. If we have to engage them, we will."

"Steve, I think you're forgetting something," Eric said.

The captain's eyebrows came together. "What?"

"The hostages. There's more than thirty women being held as sex slaves, and at least forty men working in the tunnels."

McCray nodded. "We'll have to take steps to ensure their safety. But for now, I'll get on the horn and get the ball rolling with the reinforcements. Grabovsky, Wilkins, and Marshall will be airborne within the hour. I'll give them your info and have them contact you. The unit closest to you is a Ranger platoon. They'll be under orders to split in two, with one of our people as liaison to each squad."

“They are not going to like that, Captain,” Great Hawk intoned.

“Right now, I couldn’t give less of a shit what they like or don’t like. I’ve been dealing with the Legion for over six months, and I’m ready to put an end to this mess. Make no mistake, gentlemen, this is a full-court press. I’m throwing everything I have at this, including the kitchen sink. So fuck the politics, and let’s get this done. Agreed?”

“Agreed,” Eric said, speaking for all of us.

Steve turned his head, and I heard the rustling of papers being shuffled off camera. “I think the best way to proceed is to have the two squads of Rangers approach from the north and the east, respectively. They’re closest, so they’ll be in position first. I’ll take charge of the Hollow Rock militia personally, and cover the south flank. Anyone who escapes will be driven west, right into the waiting arms of an entire company from the First Reconnaissance Expeditionary. I know those people; I served in that brigade for eight months. They’re out of Fort Bragg, and every last one of them has seen action. The Legion won’t stand a chance.”

“There’s still the matter of the tunnels,” Eric said. “If we just go at them head-on, then when the fighting starts, a lot of Legion troops will try to escape that way. That will make it difficult to rescue the hostages.”

“Okay. What do you suggest we do about it?”

“We don’t want this to be a slugfest. Too many of the wrong people could get killed. This needs to be a surgical strike. I have a plan, but it hinges on whether or not you can provide me with what I need.”

Steve said, “And what would that be?”

“First, I need these two guys.” He pointed his thumbs at Great Hawk and me. “We’ll also need a few soldiers to help us. Maybe five or six men altogether. Seasoned veterans only, no newbies. They need to have experience conducting operations at night, preferably in an urban environment.”

“That can be arranged,” Steve said. “What else?”

“I know a way in that won’t alert the men in the warehouse, but we’ll have to take out the perimeter watch and a few other guards to make it happen. How many snipers do we have at our disposal?”

He leaned back in his chair and thought for a few seconds. “Each squad, both Rangers and regular infantry, have designated marksmen. But full-fledged snipers? Including you, Great Hawk, and Garrett, that gives us maybe seven or eight.”

“That should be enough. Can we outfit them with the same long-range thermals as these two?” Eric gestured to Great Hawk and me.

Steve grimaced. “We can, but I’ll have to call in some favors.”

“Call whoever you have to. Just get us those scopes.”

“Before I do that, how about you lay out your plan?”

Eric did.

I could tell he had been thinking about it for a while. It was careful, methodical, and detailed. He had thought through solutions to every contingency it was possible to anticipate. As for the rest, we would just have to adapt and overcome. But on the whole, it was a good plan, and I said as much to Captain McCray. He agreed, and Great Hawk offered no objections.

“Lucky for you, the Rangers have a couple of Barretts on hand. Between that, and Garrett’s .338, you should have all the firepower you need. But once you get the hostages out, haul ass. I’m not going to wait long to send in the cavalry. If you can, grab that Lucian bastard while you’re at it.”

“We’ll keep an eye out for him,” I said.

“Very well. I’ll have the Pave Hawk make a supply drop as soon as I can. In the meantime, you three get some rest, and get ready to move out at first light. I want you to get back to the Legion’s encampment and conduct surveillance. Keep me in the loop, and stay in touch with the other operators. I want this to go smoothly, gentlemen. No fuck-ups."

"I have a question," Eric said.

"Go ahead."

"If you're leading the militia, who is going to be coordinating things back in Hollow Rock?"

"General Jacobs is on his way as we speak. He should be here in the next twenty-four hours. He'll be overseeing the operation personally."

"This must be important to the top brass," I said. Steve's eyes shifted in the camera image. "Isn't it unusual for the head of Special Operations Command to personally take part in combat operations?"

"Is used to be," Steve replied. "We live in a different world now. You men have your orders. Update me if anything changes. Any questions?"

No one responded.

"Good. I'll contact you when the Pave Hawk is inbound with your supplies. Good luck, gentlemen."

McCray reached forward, and the screen went blank.

*****

The Pave Hawk caught up with us on our way back to the Legion's central headquarters. It dropped off food, ammunition, and explosives. Additionally, Steve had provided combat gear for Eric—MARPAT fatigues, ghillie suit, web gear, NVGs, a radio, M-4 carbine and Beretta M-9 sidearm (both suppressor equipped), first-aid kit, tactical light, combat optics, laser sights, and an assault pack stocked with MREs. We divided the rest of the new equipment among us. No one was happy about carrying the extra weight, but we were determined not to let it slow us down.

At the bottom of the crate was a black metal box. Eric opened it, and showed it to me with a broad grin. Inside were three stainless steel syringes with short needles and plungers, and a small handbook with detailed instructions explaining what was in them, and the correct way to use them. I didn't recognize the name of the drug. It had about a two dozen letters, and was completely unpronounceable. If I didn't know better, I would have thought it was just a random assortment of consonants.

"I'm guessing that's for Lucian?" I said.

He nodded. "And Aiken, and the engineer in charge of constructing the tunnels."

"Let's hope we get a chance to take them alive."

Eric's grin faded. He closed the box and stashed the syringes in his pack.

We made good time getting back to the warehouse, reaching it in a single day's hard travel. Great Hawk took point the whole way, and set a blistering pace. Eric and I were beat by the time we reached our destination, but the Apache was no worse for wear. I was beginning to understand why General Jacobs held him in such high esteem.

Under cover of night, we set up hides on three hillsides that, between the three of us, gave us 360-degree coverage of the compound. Once set up, we settled down to wait.

Two more days passed before all the pieces were in position. It was a tense time for Eric and me, but Great Hawk seemed to be enjoying himself. Nothing amused him more than having a patrol pass a few feet away, and not see him.

"Do me a favor, Hawk." I radioed to him after watching him ghost three Legion troops for nearly an hour.

"What is that?"

"Don't tie anybody's shoelaces together. We don't want them getting suspicious. And don't slit any throats either."

"I will make you no promises."

I don't think he was joking.

I stayed on the satellite phone when I could, and worried over my dwindling supply of batteries. It was a relief when Steve finally got all the leaders on the net at the same time and we hammered out the final details.

Grabovsky was with the Ranger squad to the north, and Marshall was with the one to the east. Both were dug in less than half a mile from the Legion compound. Neither had been spotted by patrols yet, but the longer we waited, the more likely that possibility became. Captain McCray was leading the Hollow Rock militia straight up the middle from the south, and Wilkins had met the infantry platoon converging from the west. The Rangers would be the primary assault force, with Steve's troops providing reinforcements, and the regular infantry staying put to catch anyone who tried to escape. Their commanding officer wasn't happy about not being in the middle of the fight, but Steve explained to him that we needed seasoned, experienced troops on standby to hunt down anyone who got away. It would be better to herd them in one direction than have to chase them all over hell's creation. The CO hadn't liked it, but he'd agreed. Not that he had much of a choice; General Jacobs had made it clear that McCray's orders were the law.

The two Apache Longbow attack helicopters were standing by and could be on station within a matter of minutes, along with a pair of Chinooks to transport hostages and prisoners back to Hollow Rock. The AC-130 would be in the air shortly after nightfall, but other than helping us track down escapees using their FLIR, I hoped we wouldn't need its services. Gunships aren't known for subtlety.

Per Eric's request, Captain McCray had selected a team of six Army Rangers to assist us with infiltrating the warehouse. Each one had extensive combat experience, including night ops and urban warfare, and had been made aware of the importance of our mission. Two men each had been assigned to Great Hawk, Eric, and me. Steve had sent them the details Eric had provided—maps, diagrams, locations of guards and hostages, and so on—which made briefing them on the mission relatively easy. I told them where to take up position, and then instructed them to wait for further orders. As night began to fall on the Legion base, my radio crackled, and Eric's voice buzzed in my ear.

"Doesn't this seem like a bit of overkill? I mean, two hundred troops, a gunship, attack helicopters. It's like killing a cockroach with an RPG."

"That's an apt comparison. And no, I don't think it's overkill. The whole point of warfare is to win. Why make it a fair fight, when we can attack with overwhelming force?"

He was silent for a moment, then said, "You know, that's a damn good point."

If he had any further commentary on the subject, he kept it to himself.

The sun went down, and the light faded into darkness. At my request, Steve sent out an order to maintain radio silence unless engaged by the Legion, and wait for me to give the order to advance. I waited long into the night, drifting in and out of consciousness. I didn't sleep, really. Just let my mind go blank and floated along numbly through the hours. It was a technique I had practiced extensively in the Marines, and while it wasn't as good as a night's sleep, it was better than nothing. Finally, at just after three in the morning, when I was fairly confident that most of the Legion troops were out cold, I keyed my radio.

"Hawk, Irish, this is Wolf. How copy?"

Great Hawk checked in first. "I am here. Standing by."

Eric keyed his radio. "Ready when you are."

Next, I checked on the Rangers accompanying us. "Charlie One?"

"Ready to go, sir."

"Charlie Two?"

"Standing by."

"Charlie Three?"

"Chomping at the bit, sir."

I smiled. "Charlie Squad, hold position and stand by. Hawk, Irish, let's move out. Alpha Leader, we're going to get this party started. If you don't hear from us in ten mikes, tell my momma I done my best."

There was laughter in McCray's voice when he replied, "Will do, Wolf. Bravo and Echo Leaders, be ready. Make sure your men keep their fingers off the triggers until it's time to kick ass. Am I clear?"

Grabovsky, Marshall, and Wilkins all acknowledged.

"All right then, Wolf. Work your magic."

"Copy. Moving now. Standby."

I lowered the volume on my radio, picked up my .338, and started down the hillside.

Chapter 25

Non-Combatants

While waiting for Gabe's order to start the evening's festivities, I decided that NVGs with thermal imaging capability were the coolest invention in the history of cool inventions. It's a powerful feeling, having goggles that turn night into day, and let you see an enemy that can't see you.

Evidently, Great Hawk had a pair of them as well. I caught sight of him moving through the woods on the northwest side of the compound heading for one of the sentry stations. With his ghillie suit masking his movements, it was hard to track him, even though I could see his infrared signature. The guy was even sneakier than Gabe, and that's saying something.

Slowly, with footsteps more careful and gradual than anything I could ever have managed, he closed the distance to a pair of sentries. They were both facing away from him, sitting on folding camp stools and leaning close to speak to each other. One of them held a small, red-lens flashlight that he occasionally shined at the surrounding trees—the only lights Lucian allowed his men to have outside at night. The lens cover muted the light, and limited the distance from which it could be seen.

Leveling the thermal scope on my rifle, I watched as the Apache stopped barely two feet behind one of the guards. His hands came out from under his ghillie suit, one of them holding a knife, and the other clutching the handle of a tomahawk. He raised the weapons, and like a bolt of lightning, he struck. The knife went into the back of one marauder's neck, while the tomahawk came down and buried itself in the other's skull. Using the handles of his weapons for leverage, he gently eased their bodies to the ground. It was an impressive feat of strength, controlling the weight of two grown men like that. Even Gabe would have struggled with it.

Great Hawk made it look easy.

Retrieving his weapons, he wiped them off on the dead men's clothes and moved at a slightly quicker pace toward the next guard station. As he neared it, he approached the marauders head-on, crawling on his belly with glacial slowness. Every time the guards' flashlight beam swept around the forest, he went still. When it went off, he moved again. Finally, after what felt like forever, he stopped less than a foot from where the doomed men sat. The flashlight swept over his prone body, first to the left, then to the right, the guards barely even bothering to look. When it clicked off, Great Hawk stood up, inch by creeping inch, and then went still as a rock, waiting. The guards sat and chatted, unaware of the towering death standing less than an arm's length away.

The next time the flashlight came on, the guards went rigid with shock. Great Hawk's arms shot forward in a flash, the knife in an upward thrust, and the tomahawk in an arcing, backhanded chop. The two men twitched, and then slumped over. The Apache cleaned off his weapons again, and then set out to intercept a patrol on the other side of the building. His path took him out of my line of sight.

I shifted the scope back to the slain marauders, their heat signatures growing dimmer as their bodies cooled, and wondered what the final seconds of their lives had felt like, especially those last two. One minute they're just sitting, chatting, passing the time until their watch is over, and then they turn on the light and BOOM! Out of nowhere, there's a big, stone-faced killer standing in front of them, weapons in hand. I shuddered, and thanked my lucky stars that Great Hawk was on our side.

A little while later, my radio crackled to life and Gabe gave the order to advance.

Finally.

With my new eyes, avoiding the Legion's patrols on my side of the compound was easy. They always stuck to the same routes after nightfall, not wanting to get lost in the pitch black where the forest blotted out the moonlight. From high up on the hillside, I could see all five of them, their infrared signatures standing out stark white against the charcoal-and-silver background. With the thermal scope on my M-4, I could have taken them out but restrained myself. I had made a promise to the people trapped in that warehouse, and I intended to keep it. The bad guys could wait.

The two Rangers, designated Trident and Gladius, were waiting less than a hundred yards from the back entrance to the admin building. They blended perfectly into their surroundings, and if not for the thermals, I never would have spotted them. I keyed my radio to let them know I was en route and not to perforate me with 5.56mm holes as I came up behind them. Staying low and moving quietly, I knelt down beside the Ranger to my left.

"So which one are you, Trident or Gladius?"

"Gladius," he whispered back. I looked over at Trident. It wouldn't be hard to tell them apart; Gladius was a foot taller, and black. Trident was a lean white guy.

"You must be Irish," Gladius said.

"Only on my father's side."

In the courtyard ahead of me, I saw the familiar figure of Paul Harris sitting on a picnic table and smoking from his pipe. Good. That meant Lucian was still here. Past him, I knew there were two guards posted by the door even though I couldn't see them.

I keyed my radio. "Wolf, Irish. In position and standing by. I just spotted one of Lucian's personal staff. He's the one sitting in the courtyard, smoking weed. If he's here, chances are good that Lucian is here as well."

"Copy. Stay low and quiet. I'll let you know when it's time to engage."

"Roger that."

I lay down flat on my belly and let my ghillie suit drape over me. Settled in, I positioned my rifle and fixed the reticle on Harris.

"Hey, guys."

The two Rangers looked at me.

"When Wolf gives the order, we tandem snipe the motherfucker on the picnic table. Once we're inside, let me take point. I know the layout, and I'm not completely useless in a firefight."

Trident spoke up, just off the train from Brooklyn, "You a spook or somethin'? You don't sound military."

I spoke slowly. "Who I am is not important. What is important is rescuing the seventy or so hostages in that warehouse over there. Let's focus on that, shall we?"

He lowered his face back to his rifle. "Yep. Definitely a spook."

I shook my head, and went back to concentrating on Harris. "Remember, guys. On Wolf's mark, we fire."

They acknowledged. A few minutes later, Great Hawk came over the radio. "Wolf, Hawk. The guards on the northwest perimeter are down. Charlie Three is in position and standing by."

"Copy," Gabe said.

I waited. One heartbeat. Two. Three. Harris picked up his pipe and lit it.

"Charlie One, on my mark."

I took in a breath, let half of it out slowly, and held it. The men beside me did the same.

"Three, two, one, mark."

Five triggers pulled at the same time.

Three of them were from my team, Charlie Two. Harris had his pipe up, the flame bright around his hands as he took a hit. Two splotches appeared on his shirt, center of mass, courtesy of the U.S. Army Rangers. I aimed for the head, shattering the glass pipe in his hand and blowing his teeth out through the back of his head.

As he tumbled to the ground, ten cloudbursts of cement plumed from the wall behind him in rapid succession. High explosive fragmentation rounds, fired from two .50 caliber Barrett long-range sniper rifles, punched through concrete like tissue paper, perforating either side of the door in an expanding zigzag pattern. Contrary to what Hollywood once depicted, thermal imaging does not allow people to see through walls, so the shooters couldn't see their targets. But if you use the right ammo, and enough of it, it doesn't matter where your target is standing when you blast through a barrier. If the frag doesn't get them, the ricochets will. As long as they're somewhere within the blast zone, they're hamburger.

When the report reached us, it was surprisingly gentle, like distant thunder. I doubted the troops in the warehouse heard anything at all. The troops on patrol, however, were a different story. Great Hawk had taken out several of them, as well as the three sentry stations on our side of the complex, but there were still six more sentry stations and three patrols.

"They heard us, Bravo Leader," Steve's voice said over the radio.

"Copy." Grabovsky this time. "Ghost team, Bravo One. Weapons free."

The five Army snipers and twelve designated marksmen positioned around the perimeter didn't bother acknowledging; they just went to work. I stayed still and quiet, listening. Muffled cracks echoed in the darkness, like the sound of sticks breaking. They must have been using smaller-caliber, sound-suppressed rifles. I heard the occasional strangled cry of pain, but they were quickly silenced.

God bless our troops. Especially the snipers.

"Alpha Leader, Bravo One. All targets neutralized. Charlie is clear to advance."

"Outstanding work, my friend. Bravo One and Bravo Two, advance to within one hundred meters of position designated India, and standby. Charlie Squad, proceed on mission."

Gabe's voice crackled in my ear. "Copy, Alpha Leader, Charlie is moving in. Wish us luck."

"Good luck and godspeed, gentlemen."

Gladius stood up. " 'Bout damn time."

Quickly, I dropped my ghillie suit and led the way down the embankment to the door. When I tried it, it was locked from the inside. I motioned to the Rangers.

"Back off a minute, guys." I keyed my radio. "Wolf. We're locked out."

"Copy. Get your men clear."

The three of us ran around the other side of the building. "Charlie Two is clear."

By way of response, Gabe fired his .338 at the offending lock. It shattered on impact, the door slowly yawning open. The suppressed report sounded like a dull, faraway thud.

"Nice shooting, Wolf. Charlie Two is making entry."

We ran back and stacked up on both sides of the door. After adjusting my scope to its close-quarters combat setting, I counted off and we went in. I took point, stepped over the dead bodies of the sentries the Barretts had nearly torn in half, and moved left along the wall. The Rangers flipped down their NVGs and did the same on the other side.

"Clear," I said.

"Clear."

"Clear."

"Which way?" Trident asked.

I motioned to the other side of the building. "Over there. Basement entrance."

Again, we stacked up outside the door and executed a textbook dynamic entry. The stairwell was empty, so we proceeded down into the basement. I took point and tried to sweep as much of the room as I could with my thermals. It was unlikely that anyone was hiding behind the assorted equipment, but I hadn't stayed alive this long by taking dumb chances. Not seeing anyone, I motioned the Rangers forward.

Just as we cleared the staircase, the door to the tunnels opened and a man with a bald head and thick glasses stepped through. I recognized him immediately as the engineer in charge of the tunnels. Gladius raised his M-4, but I held up a hand and motioned him back.

Happy birthday to me.

The engineer pulled a Faraday flashlight out of his pocket and began shaking it up. I crept through the darkness until I was standing within arm's reach of him. Slowly, I moved the barrel of my carbine until the suppressor touched his neck.

"Don't move."

He gasped, and pulled away. I stuck the barrel under his chin and pushed up, forcing his head back. "I said don't move. Do that again and you're dead."

He put his hands up and went still, eyes darting around in the darkness. I'd be lying if I said it didn't make me feel powerful, me being able to see, and him being blind in the lightless basement. With my free hand, I motioned Trident over.

"Gag and cuff this fucker, and get him back to Alpha Leader."

I'd half expected the Ranger to protest, but being the professional that he was, he complied without a word. In short order, the engineer was bound, gagged, and being dragged back up the stairway. Gladius and I moved through the door.

"What about traps?" the tall man asked.

"No traps. These idiots spend most of their time piss drunk, or stoned out of their minds. If the Legion booby-trapped their tunnels, they'd lose half their guys in a week."

Gladius shook his head. "Fucking amateurs."

"Look at it this way; it makes our job that much easier."

The two of us crept slowly down the corridor, moving silently. We crossed the hundred or so yards of tunnel that connected the office building basement with the network under the warehouse. As we rounded a corner, I saw two guards at the main intersection standing under the light of a lantern. They both leaned against the wall, rifles slung over their shoulders, not expecting trouble.

Motioning for Gladius to take position on the left side of the wall, I shined an infrared illuminator on one of the guards and then pointed at my chest. Shifting the illuminator to the other guard, I pointed at Gladius. He gave a single nod, and leveled his rifle. The guards continued chatting, oblivious to the fact that their lives were about to end.

I whispered, "On my mark. Two, one, mark."

I triggered two rounds, and Gladius triggered four. As before, his shots hit center of mass, and mine took my target in the head. Even with suppressors equipped, the clanging of our rifles was uncomfortably loud. We waited a few seconds to see if we'd drawn any attention, ears straining for the telltale beat of footsteps. When we heard nothing, and no one else appeared, we moved out of cover, doused the lantern, and dragged the two bodies off into the darkness. I paused over one of the corpses long enough to remove his hat and his jacket. Lifting my goggles out of the way, I shined a light on him and studied his face. I recognized him from my time in the tunnels; his name was Williams.

"What are you doing?" Gladius asked.

"You'll see."

We went back to the intersection and waited, me covering the hatch to the warehouse, and Gladius covering my back. Gabe didn't keep us waiting for very long.

"Charlie Two, Charlie One. Closing on your position. Charlie Three is with me."

"Copy, Wolf. Did you see Trident on the way in?"

"Affirmative. Alpha Leader sent two men to secure the prisoner. Trident is inbound."

"Great. We're gonna need the help."

Two minutes, and approximately a thousand years later, Gabe motioned to me from the tunnel to the office building. I waved him forward. He gestured a hand behind him, and then the other six men who comprised Charlie Squad emerged from around the bend, all armed to the teeth and equipped with NVGs.

"What's the situation?" he asked upon reaching me.

"We took out the guards stationed here, and we've been waiting on you ever since."

"Good work." He pointed at the hatch. "What's waiting on the other side of that thing?"

"About sixty Legion troops, Lucian, and the female slaves."

He looked at me, his heat signature clear and distinct. By his hesitation, I could tell what he was thinking. "Maybe you should-"

"No." I cut my hand through the air. "We stick to the plan."

The ghostly illumination of his mouth turned down, his lips a thin white line. Behind him, standing out brightly in the darkness, the other soldiers shuffled, looking like chalky paper cutouts come to life. It reminded me of that old movie franchise “Predator.” The one with the murderous, man-hunting aliens that saw everything in infrared. Only instead of seeing the world in oranges, reds, and yellows, I saw it in grays and whites. And the resolution was a hell of a lot better.

“Fine. I’ll take the Hollow Rock tunnel,” Gabe said. “Hawk, you take the Connector Loop, just like we planned. Let’s get this place wired up.”

The big Apache dropped his assault pack and started taking out little black cubes and coils of wire. He and Gabe spent a few minutes placing charges around the small cavern, and connecting them to detonators. The rest of us stood around with our guns trained on the hatch above us, praying nobody tried to come through it.

Finally, Gabe motioned to his men. “All right, the charges are good to go. Eric, you take the switch. You can trigger it from anywhere within a hundred yards, and it should reach the receivers just fine.”

He handed me the little triggering device. It was a small cylinder with a switch on one side, and a little button under a plastic flip-top.

“Depress the switch, flip the top, and push the button. You want to be far away when you do it.”

I tucked the switch into my chest pocket. “Will do. You and Hawk keep an eye out for the guards. When I blow the entrance hatch, they’re gonna come running.”

Gabe nodded. “We’ll be ready. Good luck.”

He slapped a palm on top of my shoulder, then turned to his Rangers. “Let’s go.”

The three of them set off down the Hollow Rock access at an easy trot. Great Hawk paused for a moment before leaving, staring at me.

“For someone who is not a soldier, you fight well,” he said.

“And you, Lincoln Great Hawk, are the scariest son of a bitch I’ve ever met.” I raised a finger and pointed at him.

"Before you go brushing off that comment, consider the company I keep."

The big Apache chuckled. "*Ka dish day*, Irishman."

"Uh … yeah. Back at you. I think."

He laughed, and turned toward the connector loop, breaking into a loping trot. His Rangers took off after him.

I turned to Gladius and Trident. Both men looked tense, but focused. This obviously wasn't their first rodeo. "Okay, guys. Here's what we're going to do …"

They gathered close, and I explained the plan. Even with his eyes covered by NVGs, I could tell that Trident was looking at me as if I had lost my mind. "Irish, that ain't gonna work. Nobody's that stupid. A unit this small, that guard's gonna know you're not one of 'em. Trust me."

I grinned. "That's where you're wrong. These guys rotate out all the time, back and forth between encampments. There are new faces coming through every couple of weeks. In the dark, if I use the right name, they won't know the difference. At least not until it's too late."

Gladius tilted his head at me. "How do you know all this?"

"Sorry, man. That information is need to know only."

Trident looked at Gladius. "Told ya. Definitely a spook."

"Anyway," I said. "Which one of you is better at silent kills? No egos, gentlemen. Be honest."

The two Rangers looked at each other.

Gladius said, "Come on, man."

Trident waved a hand. "Fine, whatever. Your kung-fu is stronger than mine."

"Great," I said. "Come up the ladder with me, but hang back until I distract the guard. When you go, don't hesitate, and don't let him scream. There are a lot of innocent people up there counting on us to get them out of this hellhole."

He nodded, slid his rifle around to his back, and drew a K-bar combat knife from his MOLLE vest. “Roger that. Let’s do this.”

I was starting to like this guy.

Slipping out of my tactical sling, I handed my rifle to Trident, donned the hat and coat I’d stolen from the dead guard, and shouldered one of their Kalashnikovs. Last, I checked myself over as best I could to ensure that I looked the part. Satisfied, I slipped off my goggles and handed them to Trident as well. The world immediately went dark.

My hand was already on the ladder, so I didn’t have to grope around to find it. I climbed up, with Gladius nipping at my heels, until my knuckles scraped on the cement surrounding the hatch. Sliding my hand along the rough metal surface, I found the latch, turned it, and pushed the hatch open.

Calmly and slowly, like a man doing exactly what he’s supposed to be doing, I climbed out. The lack of sudden movements kept the guard standing a few feet away at ease. He turned around casually, seeing only a dim outline in the low-banked light of a single wind-up lantern.

“Everything okay?” he asked.

“Something’s wrong with Williams, man. He’s sick as hell. Started getting stomach cramps all of a sudden. I need to find Doc Klauberg. You know where he is?”

The guard turned his head and pointed. “Over there by the-”

Gladius’s knife severed the guard’s brain stem, ending his sentence mid-note. While I had been talking to him, I’d been gesticulating and moving to my left, drawing the guard’s eye away from the hatch. Gladius had crawled out behind me, quiet as a mouse, and snuck up behind the unsuspecting marauder. With the knife reversed in one hand, and a palm poised flat against the pommel, he thrust forward, stepping into the strike. The guard shuddered and then collapsed, like flipping a switch. I stepped forward and caught him under the shoulders, easing him to the ground.

"What do you want to do with the body?" Gladius whispered.

"Just leave him. We won't be here long, and shift change isn't for another hour. Nobody will find him until then. Besides, we can't risk the noise. Hang out here for a minute, I'll be right back."

I went back to the hatch and motioned for Trident to climb up. Taking off the dead raider's coat and hat, I donned my thermal imagers, and slipped my rifle's tactical sling back around my shoulders. The two Rangers crowded close, and I spoke to them in a hushed voice.

"Okay, next step is to kill the last four guards. There are two at each station, but lucky for us, they can't see each other."

"No radios?" Gladius asked.

I shook my head. "Like you said, fucking amateurs. We'll go to the north side first. That side is the most dangerous because it's closest to the troops' sleeping area. Once they're down, we go to the south side and take out those guards. While you two are doing that, I'll start unlocking the hostages. Let's go."

With deliberate care, we made our way to the north side of the warehouse. We skirted around the large piles of dirt near the hatch, gave the area where the reinforcing materials were stored a wide berth, and crept with aching tension past the poorly lit sleeping quarters. Finally, we reached the north wall and hugged it, staying low and fanning out on either side of the guards. Gladius circled around their front, darting by less than five yards away.

"Hey, did you see something?" One of the guards said.

"Where?"

I stopped in my tracks and, in a quick series of movements, I pulled my pistol and attached the suppressor. Gladius kept moving and took position off to the left of the guards. Trident closed in on the right. One of the marauders reached for his flashlight and, just as he was about to press the switch, the two Rangers gave me the signal that they were in position. Raising the pistol, I took careful aim, one hand poised next to the ejection port to catch the brass as it came out.

My finger squeezed the trigger and the gun fired, the suppressor keeping the noise down to a low thump. The hollow-point projectile hit the first guard in the nose, mushroomed out, and made an exit wound the size of a man's fist on the back of his skull. Blood, bone, and brain matter smacked the wall behind him with a splat. Trident caught his body as it fell.

The other guard barely had time to register what happened before Gladius rushed forward, clamped a hand over his mouth, and rammed his K-bar into the man's kidney. A fraction of a second later, the knife came up and sawed viciously at the guard's throat. Gladius let him slide to the ground.

Nervously, I looked around. The shot from my pistol hadn't been very loud, but in the dead silence of the warehouse, it might have carried far enough to wake someone. If that happened, we were going to have to shoot our way to the hostages. With sixty troops between us and freedom, I didn't like our odds.

My heart hammered in my ears as I looked around. Behind me, the two rangers stood up with their rifles leveled. I held up a hand to keep them from doing anything rash.

Five seconds went by. Ten. Fifteen. Nobody moved. I lowered my hand and let out a breath.

"That was close," I muttered.

If that guard had turned on his flashlight, he would have seen me. While I felt confident that Trident could have handled the kill, I didn't want to leave anything to chance. Gladius had already demonstrated good killer instinct, and I knew that as soon as the first guard was down, he wouldn't hesitate to step in and take care of the second. I had been gambling that the sudden demise of the guard's friend would give Gladius the momentary distraction he needed to do his job, and the gamble had paid off.

The Rangers followed me to the other side of the warehouse, again carefully skirting the area where the Legion troops were sleeping. Halfway past them I paused to look them over more carefully. Fully half of them looked to have passed out where they sat, too drunk or stoned to bother crawling into their bunks. The rest lay under heaps of blankets, breathing slowly. None of them seemed aware of what was happening, or what was about to happen. Regardless of whether or not we succeeded in getting the slaves out, these men's days as marauders—boozing and raping and pillaging—were over.

I stepped closer to the area where Lucian usually hung out. After searching for a moment, I spotted him lying sprawled out on a queen-size mattress, one of his personal slave girls curled up in the fetal position beside him. I reached a hand down to the pouch on my web belt containing one of the syringes Steve had included in my kit.

Gently, step by agonizing step, I moved toward his prone form. I recognized most of his staff lying nearby, excluding Paul Harris, of course, but I didn't see Aiken anywhere. God only knew what that creepy bastard was up to this time of night.

I drew the syringe, removed the cap with my teeth, and slowly lowered my hand toward Lucian's thigh. Taking a deep breath, I counted down three, two, one, and then drove the needle into his leg, depressing the plunger with my thumb.

Lucian's eyes snapped open.

I pressed a palm over his mouth to keep him from shouting while the drug did its work. For just a second or two, he reached up to grab my hand, eyes darting wildly in the darkness, and then his hand fell away and he went limp. The girl beside him stirred. I froze. She moved closer to the warmth of Lucian's body, heaved a sigh, and went quiet.

Letting out a relieved breath, I pulled my knife, held it just below Lucian's eye, and carved a shallow furrow with the tip. Lucian didn't twitch. Smiling, I made my way back to the Rangers. Holding a finger over my lips, I motioned the two of them to back off into the darkness. Once we were a safe distance from the sleeping enemy troops, I motioned for them to lean in.

"That was the leader," I whispered. "He's drugged now, and he'll be out for at least three hours. You two head over and take out the other guards. Be quick, and be quiet. As soon as they're down, signal me so I can start freeing the hostages."

The two rangers nodded and headed for the guards on the south entrance. I moved toward the pallets where the female slaves were chained. Stopping a few yards away, I knelt down and watched the Rangers creep up on the last two guards. The lantern on that side was brighter and cast a pool of illumination that was too broad to allow the soldiers to get close enough for knife work. Stopping just outside the ring of light, they drew their pistols, both nine-millimeters, and both equipped with the same type of suppressor as mine. They took aim, and after a few seconds, fired in tandem. Both guards' heads snapped backward, and they slumped to the ground. I was halfway between the sleeping troops and the Rangers, and I barely heard the pistols. The troops wouldn't have heard a thing.

Miranda's bunk was on the far left side of the slaves' sleeping area. I crept up next to her bunk, and gently shook her awake. She, like most of the other girls, was accustomed to being awakened in the middle of the night. She blinked in the pitch darkness and sat up on her pallet. I took her hand in mine and leaned in close to her ear.

"Miranda, it's me, Logan."

She opened her mouth to say something, but I clamped a hand over it. “You have to be quiet. I’m getting you out of here.”

She reached up and touched my face, her expression growing perplexed when her fingers brushed the thermal goggles.

“Listen, there are two whole companies of soldiers surrounding this warehouse. We’ve got helicopters and an airplane gunship standing by to blow these bastards to hell, but I’ve got to get you and the other girls out of here first.”

I held up the key I’d taken from Kasikov’s dead body, and then unlocked the leg iron connecting her ankle to the floor. Handing her the key, I said, “Go around and unlock the others. Do it quietly, and tell them not to make a sound. Got it?”

She nodded, her confusion replaced by a look of grim determination. She gave my hand a quick squeeze, and then got to work. Quickly, she started moving from one pallet to the next, waking the girls up and whispering to them what was going on. Just as I had done to her, she unlocked the manacle binding them to the floor, but left the other chains in place. Taking them all off would have taken too long, and made too much noise.

The Rangers trotted over from where they had dragged the two dead guards away from the entrance. We fanned out and covered the Legion troops’ sleeping area until Miranda finally got all the girls ready to go. They stood huddled together, blankets wrapped around their naked bodies and shivering in the cold. I motioned to the Rangers to fall back. We gathered in a huddle next to Miranda.

“Okay, Gladius, you lead the way. We’re going out the south entrance. Trident and I will hang back and provide cover. As soon as we’re clear, I’ll radio Alpha Leader to advance and get these women to safety. Understood?”

The Rangers nodded. Miranda said, “What about the men in the tunnels?”

I put a gentle hand on her shoulder. "We've got people on the way to rescue them as we speak. But right now, I'm only worried about you, okay?"

She nodded quickly. I motioned for her and the others to get moving.

The girls stayed close to each other, many of them weeping quietly and holding hands. Some of them looked to be injured, their friends half-carrying them along. My chest tightened at the sight, and I felt a hot coil of anger stirring in my chest, but I forced it down.

Concentrate.

Keeping my breathing steady, I slowly eased back, following the procession. Trident held position a few yards to my left, occasionally checking behind him to look for obstructions. In less than a minute, we were at the door. Gladius pulled a small can of spray lubricant from his web belt and doused the rusty hinges with it, trying to keep the door from squeaking too much. Slowly, he opened it enough for the girls to squeeze through, and started motioning them out.

"Come on, let's go. Run for the highway. No talking," he whispered, over and over again. The girls did as he said, too terrified to argue. The last to leave was Miranda. She had hung back to help keep the others calm as they made their escape. Finally, they were all out the door.

Gladius and Trident followed them, and I stepped out last, pulling the door behind me, but not quite letting it shut all the way. When the two Ranger squads showed up to wreck shop, I didn't want them having to contend with a latched door.

When I turned around, the others were running toward the highway, with Trident and Gladius carrying a couple of girls who couldn't run. I saw another one limping along with two other girls trying to help her as she hopped on one leg. I sprinted over, offered her a hand, and then threw her over my back in a fireman's carry. Reaching up, I keyed my radio as I ran.

"Alpha Leader, Irish. Hostages are secure. You are clear to advance."

"Copy, Irish. Damn fine work. Alpha Company is coming your way to render aid. Bravo Leader, get your men ready to move in on my order."

"Copy, Alpha. We're standing by. Cocked, locked, and ready to rock."

I grinned. Good ol' Grabovsky.

Relief washed over me in waves as I saw the Hollow Rock militia emerge from the cover of the forest and converge on the fleeing prisoners. They ushered them back to the tree line where Army medics waited to begin treating them for their injuries. As they were being led away, Miranda ran back to me and threw her arms around my neck. She squeezed hard, and brought her lips to my ear.

"I knew you were different," she said. "I knew you weren't like them. Thank you so much."

I hugged her back, and then gently pushed her toward a waiting medic. "We'll have plenty of time to talk later, Miranda. Let the medics look you over."

She smiled at me, tears streaming down her face, and waved goodbye. I watched her go, and then turned to the two Rangers.

"Okay, first of all, what the hell are your real names?"

Gladius held up a hand. "Tarique Blakeney. Jackson, Mississippi."

Trident said, "Anthony Toricelli. New York City."

I pointed a finger back and forth. "Blakeney. Toricelli. Got it. Now, I got a question for you. You fellas down for a little more action tonight?"

The Rangers grinned.

"Fuckin' A." Toricelli spoke for both of them.

I keyed my radio. “Bravo Leader, Charlie Two. Don’t suppose you have room for three more, do you?”

Grabovsky came back. “Charlie Two, Bravo One. You know the layout of this place, right?”

“As a matter of fact, I do.”

“Welcome aboard. I’ll have one of my men shine an illuminator. Move to my position. You copy all that Alpha Leader?”

“Copy loud and clear, Bravo One. Charlie Two, let me know when you’re in position.”

A moment later, I saw the illuminator flashing from the tree line a hundred meters east, just at the edge of the highway. I motioned to Blakeney and Toricelli.

“Let’s go. This party ain’t over yet.”

I took off at a run with the two Rangers close behind

Chapter 26

The Journal of Gabriel Garrett:

Lovely Things

As Eric had warned me, the Hollow Rock access tunnel stretched for miles. Occasionally we saw side tunnels, but they only went a few feet into small caverns; storage rooms for supplies and equipment. We cleared them anyway, just to be safe. Aside from railroad ties, hand augers, spikes, and metal bracing brackets, we didn't find anything.

The two Rangers assigned to me were designated Cestus and Spatha. The names were easily memorable, but struck me as a bit dramatic. Whoever designated them must have spent way too much time reading up on Roman gladiators and the weapons they used.

Cestus was average height, medium build, and quite possibly the least remarkable human being I had ever met, aside from the fact that he was an Army Ranger with obvious combat experience. Spatha was Hispanic, maybe five-foot seven with his boots on, and moved with the quick, fluid grace of an athlete. Both men kept the chatter to a minimum, and focused their attention on the task at hand. That was fine with me.

We set a fast pace, trusting Eric's assessment that the tunnels weren't booby-trapped. According to my watch, it took us just over thirty minutes to come within sight of the guards. They huddled around a small table playing cards, while the slaves sat on crude wooden pallets nearby. The Rangers and I slowed to a halt, and then backed off a short distance away.

We had run at least six miles to get where we were, and I didn't want us engaging the enemy until we'd had a chance to catch our breath. Not that we couldn't have done it, we could have. But the enemy wasn't going anywhere, and in a fight, you take any advantage you can get. We had time to rest, so we took it.

Cestus leaned close, and whispered, "How do you want to handle the takedown?"

"Let's keep it simple," I said. "There's enough room for all three of us to fire at the same time if you kneel down in front, Spatha."

The short man nodded. "Fine by me."

"All right then. Let's move up and take position."

My thermal imagers and the Rangers' NVGs gave us far greater visibility than the anemic circle cast by the guards' oil lantern. We spotted them from more than a hundred yards away, their light standing out like a supernova in our highly sensitive optics. The Rangers and I advanced until we were within forty yards of our targets and sighted in. The oblivious troops continued with their card game, unaware that three well-trained marksmen had them in their crosshairs.

"On my mark. Three, two, one, mark."

We kept our shots high, taking the raiders through the upper chests and heads. I only had to fire once, the heavy 6.8 SPC slug pulverizing my target's skull. The Rangers hit their targets three times center of mass, just as the Army had trained them to. The marauders fell to the ground, while the slaves next to them jumped up and shouted in panic.

"Calm down," I called out to them. "We're with the United States Army. We're here to help you."

Slowly, I slung the rifle around to my back and raised my hands in the air. I stepped into the light of the lantern, removed my goggles, and studied the men in front of me. They were all filthy, and what little clothing they had on was threadbare and falling apart. Their hair and beards were long and matted, and most of them bore bruises, cuts, and other marks of abuse. I thought back to Eric's debrief, and the story of how he had spent more than a month amongst these men—starving, dehydrated, and enduring constant beatings and brutally hard labor. Not for the first time, looking at the evil that men do, I felt an ache in my chest.

"It's okay." I continued in a gentle tone. "My name is Gabriel Garrett, United States Marines. These two men with me are Army Rangers. We're here to get you out of these tunnels."

The rest of the slaves got to their feet and slowly pressed forward, trying to get a look at us. Their stared at me with wide, bloodshot eyes lit up with a desperate, forgotten hope.

"What about the Legion?" one of them asked. "If they find you down here, they'll kill us all."

I held up a mollifying hand. "Don't worry about the Legion; the Army is dealing with them as we speak. Now I need all of you to listen to me, okay? In order to get you out of here, I'm going to need your help. How much farther down does this tunnel go?"

"Not far," another man said, stepping forward. He was older, nearly emaciated, and his only clothing was a pair of ragged pants that barely clung to his scrawny hips. He didn't even have shoes. Pointing behind him, he said, "It ends about twenty yards that way. The only way back to the surface is through the warehouse."

I smiled. "Actually, no. It isn't. Which one of you installs the ventilation pipes?"

The same old man raised his hand. "I do."

"How long do you have to cut them to get through to the surface?"

He shrugged. "Not long. About three feet."

I pointed to the ceiling. "Here's what we're gonna do, then. We're gonna dig our way out."

The old fellow looked confused for a moment, and then realization dawned on him. "Son of a bitch. You're right." He turned around, motioning to the other slaves. "Come on fellas, get the tools. Let's get the hell out of here."

"Wait," I said, reaching out. "Let's get those chains off of you first."

I dropped my pack and fished out a pair of bolt cutters. One by one, I snipped the chains binding the men. The manacles were still attached—I didn't have a key to get those off—but that problem could be taken care of later. Without the chains keeping them hunched over and hobbled, the men straightened up and took to their work with gusto.

In a few short minutes, they had knocked a couple of support struts out of the ceiling and began hacking at the earth above their heads with mattocks and shovels. While they were doing that, the ground trembled beneath my feet, and I heard the far off *whump-whump-whump* of the Semtex charges being triggered. The air shifted a few seconds later, blowing by in a strong gale, and then went still. The workers stopped, peering fearfully back toward the warehouse.

"What the hell was that?" one of them asked.

"Don't worry," I said. "That was our people blowing the warehouse access to the tunnels. The Legion won't be able to escape that way. Come on, let's get this hole finished."

As the men got back to work, I pulled Cestus and Spatha aside. "Just in case, fellas, why don't you move back that way a bit and keep an eye out?"

They agreed, and went to it.

After fifteen minutes of frantic digging, with the workers occasionally passing their tools off to a fresh set of arms, the shovels broke through and fresh, cold air drifted down into the cavern. Working with renewed vigor, the men widened out the hole, and piled up the dirt to make it easier to climb out. I had them keep at it until it was big enough for me to fit through, and then called the Rangers back.

I put my back against the cavern wall and interlaced my fingers, boosting Cestus through the opening. He clambered out, and then reached down to help Spatha do the same. The two of them lay down over the lip of the exit and reached down their arms.

"All right, gentlemen," I said, waving upward. "Who's next?"

The closest man grabbed my shoulder and stepped into my hands. His feet were bare and felt like boot leather covered in sandpaper. Lifting him took no effort at all; he was so starved he barely had any meat left on his bones. Cestus and Spatha gripped his arms and pulled him to freedom. The next man stepped up, and we did the same for him. Over and over, we helped them out until only the old-timer with the tattered pants remained.

He paused for a moment, looking up through the hole at the sky above. On his face was a glimmer of childlike glee mixed with the relieved expression of a man waking from a nightmare. Tears streamed down his cheeks, carving muddy furrows through the caked-on dirt. His lips began moving, and I heard him whispering. Although I missed the first part of it, leaning in, I caught the end.

"*... through some small aperture, I saw the lovely things the skies above us bear. Now we came out, and once more we saw the stars.*"

I let him stare for a moment longer, and then said, "Dante's Inferno. Thirty-Fourth Canto."

He shifted his rheumy gaze to me, surprised. When he spoke again, something had returned to his voice as though from a long absence. A steady, cultured tenor came from his depths, a bellows to the diminished fire behind his eyes. "That's right. You've read it?"

"I read a lot of the classics. My mother insisted."

He smiled, revealing missing front teeth and, to my surprise, he stepped forward and gently wrapped his arms around my waist. He smelled like the south end of a northbound water buffalo, but I hugged him back anyway. A few moments passed, and he stepped back.

"I felt Dante was apt, you know? I can't remember the last time I saw the sky, and I have most certainly been through hell."

I smiled at him. "Well, it's over with now. Come on, friend, let's get you out of here. There's a bath, a hot meal, and a warm bed waiting on you."

"Never have more welcome words been spoken to a more grateful ear." He stepped into my hands, and I lifted him up.

Out of the tunnel, he went. And out of slavery.

Chapter 27

Those Who Sow in Flames …

Grabovsky and his squad took point and led the way to the entrance. It stood slightly ajar, just as I had left it.

"Irish, get your ass up here," he said.

I hustled to the front and stacked up next to him by the door. Blakeney and Toricelli followed.

"What are we looking at?"

"Just beyond the door there's a big open area. On the far wall to our right is where the Legion troops are sleeping. I've drugged Lucian already, so as long as we don't shoot the place up too badly, we should be able to take him alive. That has to be our number one priority. Without him, we're back to the drawing board."

"Understood." He keyed his radio and, in five terse sentences, he explained the tactical situation, had Bravo Two cover the other exit, and ordered his men to stay weapons tight unless fired upon. After a round of acknowledgements came in, he hefted his rifle, flipped down his NVGs, and motioned for me to proceed ahead.

Slowly, I opened the door and peered beyond. Nothing moved. I raised my rifle and used the thermal scope to scan around.

"The way is clear. Moving in."

"Copy, right behind you."

I stepped through the door followed closely by the rest of Charlie Two and Grabovsky's fire team. Once we were clear of the entrance, the other Rangers filed in and fanned out, rifles up and scanning for threats. Silently, we covered the vast distance of the warehouse.

The huddle of sleeping marauders stood out bright white against the cold background. The pallets where the female slaves had lain just a few minutes ago had already cooled, their color darkening to a grainy charcoal. I led the way past them to the living area and moved toward Lucian's bed. He lay where I had left him, snoring loudly. Grabovsky and the Rangers covered the surrounding marauders as I approached the girl sleeping next to Lucian.

Not wanting to risk her alerting the other raiders, I took one of the two remaining syringes from my web belt and stuck her in the back of her shoulder. She snapped awake for just a moment and then went limp. I picked her up and handed her off to Blakeney. "Get her back to the militia."

He took hold of her wordlessly and moved back toward the entrance. I backed off to the line of Rangers covering the sleeping Legion troops. The fact that our entrance had not awakened any of the marauders was a testament to the skill of the men around me. Either that, or the marauders were just used to sleeping through anything. Considering how raucous the Legion could be, that seemed just as likely.

Grabovsky motioned to four of his men and pointed at Lucian. "Take this guy and get him out of here, too. He belongs to Alpha Leader. Be careful with him, we need him alive."

The men lifted Lucian with strong hands and carried him out the door. Watching them go, I kept expecting a sense of victory to spring forth. Some elation, or relief, or glowing triumph. Instead, I just felt tired. Too many days with too little sleep weighed down on my shoulders, and I wanted nothing more than to lie down next to Allison and pass out.

"What do you want to do now?" Grabovsky said.

"Why are you asking me? This is your show."

He turned his NVGs toward me. "Because you know these guys. You lived with them, and you know what they've done. If you don't want to make the call, I will. But I think you've earned a say in the matter."

I hesitated. These men had done terrible things, but not all of them had done so willingly. Many of them had been captured and had committed their crimes because it was either that or die at the hands of the Legion. When someone is given a choice between life and death, it's really not a choice at all.

I thought back to Miranda, and having to sit quietly while she allowed herself to be violated to save my life. I thought about the self-loathing I had felt—that I still felt—over what I had done. I thought about Grayson Morrow, and the seething hatred in his voice when he spoke about the Legion, and what they had forced him to do. What acts he had committed to stay alive. There were men here who deserved to die, that was true. But there were also men here who deserved a shot at redemption. While justice demanded that they pay for their crimes, I couldn't bring myself to believe that all of these men deserved death. And even if they did, who was I to mete it out? My hands weren't exactly clean.

Too many times, I had pulled the trigger simply because survival demanded it. No thinking, no hesitation. If I found myself in that kind of situation again, I would do what I had to do to stay alive, but this wasn't like that. Here, I had a choice. Here, there was another way.

"I think there's been enough killing tonight, Ray. Let's take them prisoner if we can."

He kept staring at me, and it was a long instant before he spoke. "You sure?"

I nodded. "It's the right thing to do. If we just slaughter them wholesale, without even trying to sort out which ones deserve it and which ones don't, then we're no better than they are. I don't know about you, but that still means something to me."

He shrugged. "All right then. Whatever you say." He keyed his radio. "Bravo Two, Bravo Leader. I'm sending a team to open the back entrance. We'll be on your left, about fifty meters from your location. Orders are still weapons tight. We're going to try to take these men alive. If anyone goes for a weapon, put him down. If they surrender, cuff-and-stuff 'em, and turn them over to Alpha Leader. Alpha, you copy all that?"

"Copy loud and clear, Bravo One. Irish, I'm assuming Bravo Leader sought your council on this decision?"

"You're a smart man, Alpha. I don't care what people say about you."

As usual, he ignored me. "Care to explain the sudden change of heart?"

I clicked the mike a few times before answering. "Let's just say it's a matter of perspective, and leave it at that."

"Very well," he replied. "Bravo Leader, proceed on mission."

Grabovsky gave everyone the order to back away, take cover, and pick a target. Most of the Rangers had laser designators on their rifles, which Grabovsky ordered them to turn on to enhance our intimidation factor. It made sense; waking up to a host of laser sights bristling from the darkness would be enough to give any man pause. I just hoped the Legion recognized that they were in a no-win situation.

The Rangers had brought a bullhorn along as a form of backup communication, just in case something terrible happened and they couldn't use their radios. Grabovsky held it in one hand as he waited for everyone to get in position. Once all fire teams had reported in, he raised the microphone to his mouth.

"This is the United States Army. We have you surrounded. There is no escape. Step forward with your hands in the air and surrender immediately. If you reach for a weapon, you will be fired upon. I repeat, this is the United States Army …"

He said the message several more times, and the Legion troops who weren't passed out drunk woke up immediately, staring in shocked terror at the laser sights weaving at them from out of the darkness.

A few of them were dumb enough to reach for weapons, and shots rang out in response. The offending marauders went down in a hail of bullets, the Rangers putting them down with short, controlled bursts. My hands tightened on my rifle, expecting the other Legion troops to return fire. My heart sped up as I braced for the bloodbath that would ensue.

It didn't happen.

The rest of the marauders quickly realized what was going on, and got their hands up. Some of the less drunken raiders slowly began coming to, urged by their compatriots to get up and get their hands in the air. Reluctantly, they began stepping away from their bunks and out onto the warehouse floor. Grabovsky gave them instructions to face away from his voice, get down on their knees, put their hands on their heads, and lace their feet together.

Within a few minutes, all but the dead—and a few troops who were too inebriated to emerge from their drunken stupor—were zip-tied and being marched out through the south entrance. The rest were quickly rounded up and restrained, some of them so drunk that they had to be carried out of the warehouse on litters. Once the living were taken care of, more troops came back to remove the dead.

When they were all gone, I stood alone in the middle of the warehouse and stared around. Taking down Legion Central had not been bloodless—far from it. But it could have been a hell of a lot worse. I wondered if the Apache helicopter pilots and the infantry company to the west were disappointed that we hadn't needed them. Then I remembered Lucian, and that there were other Legion bases out there. And while we had just scored a huge victory, the fight wasn't over yet.

I walked back outside to look for Steve.

*****

"So what's next?" I asked.

Steve stood on the highway looking at the ranks of prisoners lined up in the parking lot. They all lay face down on the ground, hands and feet bound, with black bags over their heads. Where the Rangers had gotten all the bags from, I had not the faintest clue.

"Did you blow the tunnels yet?"

"No. Do you want me to?"

He thought about it for a moment, his yellowish eyes wandering toward the open warehouse entrance. "Yes. I don't want anyone else stumbling upon those tunnels and using them."

"No problem." I dug the switch out of my pocket and activated it.

Nothing happened.

"What the hell?" I said.

"You're probably out of range." Steve pointed at the warehouse. "Get closer."

I walked over to the doorway and held my arm over the threshold. This time when I activated the switch, the Semtex detonated in a succession of powerful thumps. The ten-foot section of floor over the tunnels shattered, and the massive piles of dirt surrounding it poured down into the hole.

I walked back over to Steve, smiling. "Got it that time."

"I heard."

"You got an answer for me yet?"

"No. That's why I sent you to blow up the tunnel entrance. I needed time to think."

I was silent for a little while, letting him work the problem over. He looked out toward the treeline where the Army medics were still treating the rescued hostages. His eyes shifted toward the sky, scanning for the helicopters that were inbound, but not yet on station. He sighed in frustration, no doubt remembering how smoothly things used to run back when the U.S. military was at its full, indomitable strength. I felt a pang of longing, thinking about that. It had been nice, once, living in the strongest, most secure nation on Earth. Now, we were just as fucked as everyone else. It was not a good feeling.

"It all hinges on what we learn from Lucian," Steve said, finally. "If he breaks, and his intel turns out to be solid, we can take down the rest of the Legion. If he doesn't, then we'll have to go to work on these guys until we find out what we need."

I looked at the prisoners. "You mean torture them?"

"I mean do whatever it takes to bring an end to this conflict. If I have to break a few bones to make that happen, I'll do it. You got a problem with that, Riordan?"

I glared at him, my good humor dissipating. "I'm not a fucking boy scout, Steve. I've hurt people to get information I needed, and I don't regret doing it. But what you need to understand is that some of those men over there were unwilling participants. Not all of them deserve to be tortured."

Steve squared off with me, hands on his hips. "Eric, I understand what you're saying. Really, I do. But I don't have time for games, and neither does Central Command. If some of these men are innocent, or were coerced into aiding the Legion, we'll take that into account later on. But right now, there's a town full of good, hard-working people who don't raid, or rape, or steal, and they're in danger from people that these assholes are in league with. The Legion operates like a terrorist network, Eric. Just because we have their leader, that doesn't mean we've shut them down. The other cells will carry out the offensive Lucian was planning. And if they do that, even without help from Legion Central, people in Hollow Rock are going to die. Do you understand that? People will die. So no, Eric, right now I don't give a rat's ass about these guys. If I have to string them up by their nuts to save innocent lives, then that's what I'm gonna do."

I stepped forward and got within an inch of Steve's face. "Don't you fucking lecture me about protecting Hollow Rock, you arrogant son of a bitch. You know how I just spent the last six weeks of my life. In spite of that, in spite of everything the Legion did to me, I didn't let it turn me into a monster. I'm no saint, but I still know the difference between right and wrong. Torture Lucian if you want to. Burn him at the fucking stake for all I care. The bastard earned it. But before you go tearing into these troops, you better damned well take a minute to ask yourself if what you're doing is justified. Because if it isn't, then you're no better than Lucian. You're just another murdering bastard twisting morality like a pretzel to justify your own self-serving actions. That's not leadership, Steve. That's laziness, and it's the purview of the petty and the cruel."

We stood there a long time, glaring at each other, neither one willing to back down. The tension broke when our radios crackled in our ears.

"Alpha Leader, Bravo One. Angel is outbound, headed home. Eagle One and Eagle Two are engines cold, but staying on station. Echo Leader is standing down and headed our way to render aid."

Steve turned away, keying his radio. "Copy, Bravo Leader. Any word from Wolf or Hawk?"

"Not yet, sir."

"What about the infected? Any hordes headed our way?"

"Angel spotted a few small ones, but they're not within striking distance. We'll have most of our people out of here by the time they arrive. I'll leave some extra ammo with the guys guarding the prisoners; they can take out the walkers form the office building rooftop. They've got comms if they need additional support, and we can always send the Pave Hawk."

"Acknowledged. Keep me posted."

"Copy that, Alpha."

"So where is Lucian, by the way?" I asked.

Steve let his hand fall away from his radio. "He's being taken to a safe location. We'll start the interrogation as soon as he comes around."

"Good. After everything that fucker's done, he deserves it."

He turned to look at me. "What about you, Eric? Are you still in?"

"What do you mean?"

"I mean, do you still have the stomach for this. You have to admit, you've been through a lot lately."

"Are you fucking kidding me?" I said, offended. "You think I want to quit? Listen, I may not agree with you on everything, but there is no way in hell I'm walking away from this."

"Good. Because I'm going to need you for the next part of the offensive."

"And what's that going to be?"

He let out a breath. "As soon as I figure it out, I'll let you know."

He took a few steps away, his shoulders losing some of their rigidity. I watched him push back the brim of his hat and run shaky fingers across his forehead. Looking more closely, I could see that his eyes were puffy and bloodshot.

"Steve, you look like shit man. When was the last time you slept?"

He yawned, stifling it with the back of his forearm. "About two days. I'm fucking running on fumes."

"You should get some sleep. Let Grabovsky run things for a few hours; he knows what he's doing. General Jacobs is available if he runs into trouble."

"You know, I might just do that. There's not much left for me to do now that we have the prisoners hemmed up."

I looked back at the parking lot, and the Rangers standing guard. "Speaking of, what are you gonna do with them?"

"I'll have Echo Company secure them in the warehouse with those floor anchors."

"That's fitting. Give them a taste of their own medicine."

Steve walked over to the median dividing the highway and lowered himself to it, crossing his feet in front of the curb. He looked much smaller sitting down. To the east, the sky was just beginning to lighten from black to gray, the first tendrils of false dawn flirting with the horizon.

"One of the Chinooks is inbound. They're going back to Hollow Rock. If you want, I can order the pilot to allow you onboard. You should go see Allison and get some rest. If the offensive starts back up, I can send word to have you flown out."

I shook my head. "I'm staying here until we get word from Gabe and Great Hawk."

Steve smiled, and lay back on the median. Stretching his legs out, he crossed his ankles, pulled out his earphone, and turned off his radio.

"Good. Do me a favor, and tell Grabovsky he's in charge until Echo Leader gets here. I'm gonna catch some shuteye."

He pulled his hat down over his eyes and laced his fingers behind his head. Gabe had once told me that after serving in the military long enough, you learn to sleep anywhere. Looking at Steve, and feeling my own weariness pressing down on me, I believed it. If life in the Army was always this intense, it was a wonder that soldiers didn't have nervous breakdowns every couple of years.

Or maybe they did.

I sat down on the curb a few yards away and watched the sky. It would be dawn soon, and after spending so many weeks trapped underground, I had a new appreciation for sunrises.

*****

"Alpha Leader, Bravo One."

I answered, "Bravo, Irish. Alpha is indisposed. He left you in charge until Echo Leader gets here."

"Great. That's just what I need. Is that fucker asleep?"

"That's a-firm-titty."

There was a pause, and I could almost see Grabovsky walking around in a little circle and cursing like an angry, drunken sailor. I decided it would be prudent not to mention that I was the one who suggested that Steve put the G-man in charge.

"Well, when he wakes his dead ass up, let him know that Wolf and Hawk both checked in. The hostages are secure, and a Chinook is outbound to pick 'em up. Some of the hostages are in bad shape, and need to be medevaced to Hollow Rock."

"When you say 'bad shape,' how bad are we talking?" I asked.

"In need of treatment, but not life-threatening."

"That's good news. What about Wolf and Hawk, are they coming here or heading back to town?"

"They're going with the hostages. General Jacobs wants to meet with them personally."

That can't be good. "Any idea what for?"

"You kiddin' me? You think a General explains himself to a lowly peon like me? I'm just the fuckin' hired muscle around here. Nobody tells me shit."

I knew for a fact that wasn't true, but I let it go. "Acknowledged. When the chopper gets here, make sure the pilot knows to let me onboard, will you?"

"Did Alpha authorize that?"

"Yep."

"Will do, then. In the meantime, I need you to meet with some of my guys over in the parking lot and help them identify these Legion troops."

I frowned. "What the hell are we doing that for?"

"Orders came down from General Jacobs. He wants us to start a dossier on each one of these guys."

"Right now? Out here in the field?"

"Yep."

I sighed in irritation. "Fuckin' hell … okay, man. I'll do what I can."

I started moving toward the parking lot. When I spared a glance back at Steve, I noticed his jaw had gone slack and he was snoring. "I know a lot of these guys, but not all of them. They rotate out a lot."

"Just do the best you can. Anything is better than nothing."

"All right then. Can you make sure the Chinook doesn't leave without me?"

"Will do."

"Thanks. I'll see you back in town, Bravo."

"You're welcome. And tell Alpha I said fuck you very much."

I laughed. "I'll be sure to do that."

A few minutes later, a trio of Rangers showed up and began photographing the prisoners. They started a list of names, dates of birth, and any obvious identifying marks such as tattoos or scars. Some of them I recognized, and some of them I didn't. For the ones I did, I told the Rangers whatever I knew about them on a little voice recorder. Just as we were cataloguing the last one, I heard the distinctive sound of an approaching helicopter. Before turning to leave, I recorded one last message.

"All of Lucian's staff and senior lieutenants are accounted for with one exception: Lucian's brother, Aiken. From what I gathered of him, he has some kind of military training, is highly intelligent, and according to his own men, he's a homicidal maniac who likes to torture and dismember women. He should be easy to identify if we find him; he bears a strong family resemblance to Lucian. They may even be twins. I'm not sure what Aiken's role is in the Legion's leadership, but I know he's extremely dangerous. He might have escaped, or he might have simply moved on to another Legion stronghold. That's all I know."

I handed the recorder back to one of the Rangers, and then set off for the Chinook at a run. When I reached it, the interior was nearly at capacity with rescued women and medical staff. True to his word, Grabovsky had told them to save me a spot. I climbed in, took a seat against the bulkhead, and tried to keep my stomach from lurching too much as the helicopter lifted into the air.

*****

It took Allison a few seconds to recognize me.

Between the longish hair, the beard, and the weight loss, I wasn't surprised. When she saw through it, she ran across the clinic's lobby and leapt into my arms. Neither one of us spoke for a while; we just stood there clinging to each other. I pressed her small, frail body against mine and hung on for dear life, my face buried in her neck. Finally, Allison let go and put a hand on my cheek.

"Eric, I'm so sorry, but I have to go."

"It's okay. Go do your job, we can talk later. I'll be home when you get there."

She pulled me down for a kiss that was far too brief, then wiped her eyes, took a deep breath, and pulled back on the mantle of a doctor. When she turned to go back into the clinic, her steps were sure and confident, her back straight, and her hands steady. I smiled, watching her go. She and a few nurses—supplemented by several Army medics—were triaging the influx of patients pouring out of the Chinook. Once the big machine had disgorged all its passengers, the pilot wasted no time getting it back in the air to go pick up another batch.

With nothing else to do, I turned around and started toward home. The streets were deserted this early in the morning, as most of the townsfolk didn't get out of bed until after sunrise. Dawn was just turning red and gold to the east, and soon the streets would be crowded with people opening their businesses, forming work crews, boarding wagons to begin another day of work in the fields, or heading to the sheriff's station to arm up for security duty. For once, I didn't look forward to the prospect of being among the bustling crowd. Right then, all I wanted was a warm bed and some uninterrupted sleep. It had been more than thirty-six hours since I had last slept, and my steps were beginning to weave from exhaustion.

When I got home, I took my boots off on the porch, stripped out of my filthy clothes, and crawled into bed. It had been two months since the last time I had lain in my own bed, and it felt indescribably wonderful. The sheets were clean, crisp from being dried on the line, and smelled like Allison and soap. I nestled down into them, relishing the warmth.

I was out in seconds.

*****

The next thing I knew it was dark outside, and someone was crawling into bed with me. A soft, female body slid under the sheets and rolled over so that her back was against my chest. I put an arm around her, told her I loved her, and went back to sleep.

*****

I've always had trouble remembering dreams.

When I wake up, I can still feel whatever emotion the dream wrung out of me—usually fear—but I can't recall the specifics. Not that I wake up screaming, or anything that dramatic. Mostly I just awake with a start, stare around in disorientation for a few seconds, and then reality takes hold and I relax. It had been happening more and more often lately, and it happened again when I woke up next to Allison for the first time in two months.

She was still asleep, snoring softly, her hair tucked behind her ear and falling gracefully down her neck. I leaned over and kissed her on the cheek, on the jaw, and on the tip of her nose. Her lips curved into a smile and she rolled over onto her back, eyes still closed. Sunlight from the window played over her soft skin, turning it bright gold in the sullen morning haze. One of her hands came up to the back of my neck, her slender fingers sliding through my hair. She pulled me down, and as soon as our lips met, I wanted her. Not just a little, but a lot. A burning, raging need that made my heart pound and my skin feel like it was on fire.

I shifted on top of her, gently sliding her legs apart with my knees. At the same time, I kissed a line down her cheek all the way to her neck. Allison turned her head and arched her back, offering her throat. She was wearing nothing but a pair of panties, and her breasts were firm against my chest, hard nipples pressing into my skin. I sealed my mouth around her neck, bit down just a little, and ran my tongue in slow circles, just the way she liked it. She groaned, and clutched at my back, raking me with her nails. Pressing down with my hips, I could feel her wet heat against my cock and began grinding against her. I leaned back, intent on kissing my way down her chest, her stomach, to the deliciously hot softness between her legs.

Allison opened her eyes to look at me and, with a frightened jolt, I saw that they weren't brown anymore. Her eyes had turned blue. Her hair had lightened to a honey blond color, and her breasts were two cup sizes bigger. My blood stopped in my veins as I realized it was no longer Allison beneath me.

It was Miranda.

Her mouth opened, but there were no words. Just a dark gurgle of blood that sprayed me in the face as her eyes went from the hooded languor of sex to the wide, shocked rictus of panic. She struggled to speak but couldn't get any words around the black fountain gushing out of her mouth. As I watched, her eyes went pale, then gray, and then shriveled into the wasted orbs of a walker. Her skin wrinkled, rotted, and began to peel away from muscle and bone. I sat up, drew in a breath to scream, and then-

I woke up.

Not with a scream. Just a start.

Allison lay exactly where she had curled up next to me hours before. Neither one of us had moved. She was wearing one of my T-shirts and a pair of sweatpants. I stared at her for a moment, making sure her hair was indeed brown, and resisting the urge to pull her eyelids up to make sure her irises were still the color of dark honey.

In a few moments, my heartbeat slowed, my mind kicked into gear, and the biting cold made its presence known on my skin. Before getting out of bed, I leaned over and kissed Allison on her cheek just as I had done every morning before this whole mess started. This time, she did not stir. Her breathing stayed slow and steady, her body small and still under the heavy comforter. She must have been exhausted after working so late at the clinic. I tucked the blanket back around her neck and left her in peace.

Grabbing a set of clothes from the closet, I got dressed in the living room so I wouldn't wake Allison up. On my way to the kitchen to get a bite to eat, I saw something propped up in the corner and stopped. The light in the living room was dim, being that all the windows faced north, and I had to blink a few times to make sure it was really there.

I took a few steps closer, the hardwood floor creaking under my feet, and reached out a hand to pick it up. Smooth, lacquered rosewood met my fingers as I lifted it out of its stand to hold the headstock close to my eyes. At the top, the stylized curves of a Celtic knot formed an A above the tuning pegs. Breakfast forgotten, I sat down on the ottoman, pulled the guitar across my lap, and ran my fingers across the smooth cedar soundboard.

I didn't have a pick, but my fingernails had gotten long enough to pluck the strings. It took me a few seconds to get my stiff fingers to obey my commands, but finally I managed to fire off a scale of basic, one-string notes. The instrument was perfectly tuned, each string vibrating with flawless resonance that echoed effortlessly throughout the room. I had been worried that it was a knockoff, but it wasn't. In my hands was a genuine Avalon premier series. Before the Outbreak, the particular model I was holding would have sold for more than five thousand dollars. I wondered where Allison had gotten it.

The light pouring into the kitchen grew brighter, heralding the start of another day. I sat on the ottoman playing note after note and, once my hands were sufficiently warmed up, I began playing a few chords. As the morning wore on, the chords turned into riffs, and the riffs turned into songs. I didn't think about what I was playing, I just let my mind drift, my eyes drooping shut, and my hands taking over from there.

I thought about the tiger those Legion raiders had killed, how cottony its thick fur had been, and what it had sounded like when it died shrieking in agony. It was still hard to believe that anything living could have made a sound like that.

I thought about the Rottweiler I had shot, and the rest of its pack, and wondered how they were doing. I hoped they were still alive, and finding enough to eat. Maybe they had moved north to McKenzie to hunt wild goats.

Then I thought about the bird that had watched calmly while I sat on a bench surrounded by dead bodies, and cackled like a madman. I wondered if it still remembered me in its little birdbrain.

Distantly, I became aware of soft footsteps entering the room and settling on the love seat across from me. A sweet, throaty contralto started singing, the voice rising and falling with the music pouring out of the guitar. The voice stirred me, opening my eyes and slowly pulling me back down from the rafters. Once my feet were firmly on the floor again, I realized what I was playing—Eric Bachmann.

Allison's voice was like ice on a raw burn, so I kept on strumming the instrument in my hands. She sang on ...

Crescent blushing veiled by rain,

Glowing so the day she came.

Sweet as laughter flowing free,

Nowhere river carry me.

Nowhere river carry me.

I began to drift away again as I played the bridge and she sang along. I wandered back to the warehouse somewhere north of Hollow Rock. There was a bloodstain in that warehouse, lumped in among many others. It was at the edge of a crudely drawn yellow circle, a blotch of darkness in the lightless space. I remembered how Number Four's head had snapped to the side when I kicked him in the neck, and the melonlike crunch as his skull hit the ground. Tears slid out from beneath my eyelids as it occurred to me that I hadn't thought about him since that day. Maybe too much had been going on, or maybe I was too focused on not blowing my cover. Maybe I had grown so inured to killing that my sleeping mind simply glossed over it.

Or maybe I just didn't want to remember.

Wrenching myself out of that minefield, I came back into the room just in time to hear Allison sing the final chorus.

Full moon silver snowfall lay,

Still tonight to light my way.

Though I may drift and I may roam,

She's the one I call my home.

She's the one I call my home.

As the last note faded, I saw Allison staring at me from across the room. She was smiling, but it was sad at the edges. I stood up and put the guitar back on its stand, then crossed the room and sat down next to the woman who had thawed my heart more than anyone I had ever known. Her head came to my shoulder, her arms around my neck. One hand strayed down to my chest and began to rub, back and forth. Back and forth. Sometimes it came up to my face, fingers threading through the growth of beard. Vaguely, as though from a great distance, I became aware of my own voice. I was talking. Relaying in a lifeless monotone the events that had occurred after I stepped foot onto that stealth helicopter two months and a lifetime ago. Allison's head never left the hollow of my shoulder.

At some point, I wrapped my arms around her and drew her close, but I didn't remember doing it. By the time I was finished, the sun had climbed to its tallest perch in the sky, and my beard was wet with tears that had trickled down my face and dripped onto the back of Allison's arm. The room was silent then, and we let the silence sit there for a while. Finally, she raised her face up to mine and put a warm hand on my cheek.

"Eric, I'm so sorry."

I had expected her to be angry. I had expected her to take her hands off me and recoil in disgust. She knew about all the people I had killed. About torturing Mitchell Carson in that abandoned town. About killing Number Four—a man whose name I would never know—to fulfill my mission against the Legion. About forcing Miranda to … do what she had done in order to maintain my cover. She knew all of it, and she was still there. There was no judgment in her steady gaze. No anger. There were tears at the bottoms of her eyes, and an endless, aching pity.

Gently, she pulled me down to brush her lips against my forehead, and then drew my face to her chest. I clutched at her, my shoulders beginning to hitch despite my best efforts to stop them. Loving hands caressed my back and held my neck, and all my carefully built walls came crashing down. I held my woman, my love, my anchor, and I wept into her embracing warmth. All the while, the refrain echoed in my head and my heart, falling like a cleansing rain.

Nowhere river carry me.

Nowhere river carry me.

*****

An hour later, I wasn't quite myself again, not yet. But at least I wasn't a blubbering mess anymore.

I made flatbread sandwiches and held hands with Allison as we ate breakfast in the kitchen. The love of my life made tea, and once two cups were down the hatch, I decided to make something out of my day.

"You feel like coming with me to check on Gabe?"

Allison turned away from the sink. "Do you think he's back in town yet?"

"I think so."

"Okay. Let's go."

She left the dishes where they were and went to the hall closet to get her coat. I smiled, grabbed my jacket, and followed her out the door.

Gabe was in his yard when we arrived, hacking away with a sling-blade at the dead, knee-high grass surrounding his porch. It struck me as odd, watching the big man doing something so tediously normal. I had seen him in action so many times, teeth bared and a blazing rifle clutched in his fists, that it was hard to perceive him any other way. But like anyone else, he was just a person. Just a man getting on into his forties. A man who liked to sit on his front porch sipping whiskey, and who, in the midst of a war where he would soon be on the front lines, still found time for the little things. Like yard work. If the next few days went badly, he might not live long enough to enjoy the neatness of a well-tended yard, but nevertheless, here he was. Thwacking away. It made me smile.

Allison crossed the yard ahead of me and called out, "You know, there are people in town you can hire to help you with that. It'll take you a week to knock all this grass down by yourself."

Gabe stopped working, looked up, and grinned. "Yeah, but I'm old and miserly. I'd rather do it myself and save a nickel."

He propped the blade against the porch and made his way over. "What are you two troublemakers getting into today?"

"Just coming over to make sure you got home in one piece," I said.

"Ah hell, I'm fine. I got in yesterday morning. Spent half the day debriefing with General Jacobs. He wants to see you next time you're free, by the way."

"Why? Didn't he get my statement from Steve?"

"Yeah, he did. But he wants to hear it from you, face to face."

I groaned, and ran a hand across my forehead. "Well, he's gonna have to wait. I don't feel like rehashing that. Not right now, at least."

"You know, he told me to have you report to him at 0800 yesterday. Do you believe that? Like you're his fucking errand boy, or something. I reminded him, none too politely I might add, that you're not in the Army, and he has no authority to go ordering you around. If anything, he owes you a debt of gratitude."

"What did he say to that?"

Gabe grinned even wider. "He goes, 'Shit, I keep forgetting that Riordan's a civilian.' So I say, 'So am I, just in case you forgot. And this is the last time you try to give me an order, understood?' He didn't like that too much, but he kept his mouth shut. I tell you, it's a lot of fun talking shit to a general and getting away with it."

That got a laugh out of me. Allison smiled, and rolled her eyes. Movement caught my eye from the intersection down the street, and I saw a young man in a militia uniform riding a bike toward us.

"Shit." I sighed. "What now?"

The cyclist caught sight of Allison and swerved down Gabe's driveway. His brakes squealed in protest as he slid to a halt a few feet away from us.

"Mornin' Robinson," Gabe said, recognizing the young man. "What do you need?"

He pointed a finger at Allison. "One of the patients fell out of his bed and broke his arm."

Allison's smile disappeared, and the calm, clear-eyed mien of a doctor took its place. "How bad?"

The kid paled a bit, which was impressive considering how dark his skin was. "I could see the bone poking through."

Allison said something decidedly unladylike, and reached toward Robinson's bike. "I need to commandeer this from you."

He hopped off hurriedly. "Yeah, go on. Take it."

Allison climbed on and turned to Gabe and me. "Guys, I'm sorry, I have to go."

I waved her off. "It's fine, sweetie. Sounds like somebody needs you more than we do."

She reached out, grabbed my arm, stole a quick kiss, and then pedaled down the road. Robinson followed her at a brisk trot. When they had gone out of sight over a hill, I turned to Gabe and said, "Care for a drink?"

He sighed, and started walking toward the porch. "Why the hell not?"

Once inside the dark, cool house, Gabe poured two tumblers of Mike Stall's finest and we took a seat in the kitchen. I put my back to the warm sun coming in through the window and looked across the table at Gabriel.

"Listen Gabe, we need to talk."

His eyebrows came together. "About what?"

"Since when do you speak Russian?"

The eyebrows drew down tighter. "The hell difference does it make?"

"I want to know. Your always saying, 'You never asked' when I find out something new about you that you never told me about. So now I'm asking. Since when do you speak Russian?"

He thought about it for a while, ruminating over his drink. He took one sip and put it down. Spun it twice on the table. Another sip. Another spin. If he was trying to wait me out, he was going to have to wait a long damn time.

"Gabe?"

"Why do you want to know?"

"Because you're my best and oldest friend, but sometimes I feel like I don't know you at all. Or maybe I just know a part of you, the Gabe you let out for the world to see. I think I've earned an explanation at this point. You're not being much of a friend by keeping me in the dark."

His gaze flickered as I spoke and, by the end of the last sentence, he had lowered his face to the table.

"Okay then." He pointed a finger toward a bookshelf in the living room. "Go get a book off that shelf for me."

I turned to look at it. "Which one?"

"Doesn't matter. Any one of them will do."

I shot him a quizzical glance, but did as he asked. Returning to the table, I held the book out to him.

"Open it to any page."

I put my thumb in the middle and flipped it open. It had been shut a long time, and the pages crackled as I pulled them apart. Gabe held out a hand, and I gave him the book.

As I sat back down, he started reading. I watched his eyes flitter back and forth as he worked his way down the page. Finished, he handed the book back to me and pointed at the top margin.

"Read along with me." He said, and closed his eyes. Over the next minute or so, he proceeded to recite the page he had indicated.

All of it.

The entire thing.

Word for word.

No mistakes, no hesitation. It was as if he was reading it straight from the book, but that wasn't possible. I was holding the book out of sight, and besides, his eyes were closed. When he had finished the recitation, he gave me a grim smile and said, "Nice trick, huh? Pick another page."

I did, and he repeated the process. For a long moment, all I could do was sit and stare, jaw slack with astonishment.

"Holy shit, Gabe."

He picked up his tumbler and sipped it. "Holy shit indeed."

"You've got a fucking photographic memory."

"Actually, the correct technical term is *eidetic* memory. I'm not limited just to images. I can remember damn near anything, from anytime, even shit that happened decades ago, with a clarity most people will never know."

"That's a hell of a gift, man."

His eyes clouded over. "A gift? Really? You think so?"

He stood up from the table and pulled up his shirt, pointing a finger at a long, ragged scar on his lower abdomen.

"You see that? An RPG did that. Baghdad. It was February eleventh. A Saturday. I had the cookie bar from an MRE for breakfast that morning. When the RPG hit, shrapnel tore open my belly like gutting a fish, and pieces of that cookie bar fell out onto the street. My intestines were dangling down to my knees before I collapsed from blood loss. Imagine what it would be like to relive that memory in vivid detail every time you look at yourself in the mirror. Imagine what it would be like to remember your mother dying of cancer when the passage of time does nothing to dull the memory. Imagine being eight years old, and your father dies under a mountain of rubble in a coal mine, and you can't make that pain go away no matter how much you wish it would. Imagine the feeling of failure when your marriage falls apart because you've turned into a useless drunk. When your wife can't stand the thought of you being the father of her children, and throws you out. Imagine that staying with you, never fading, never getting any easier. You think about that the next time you want to call what I can do a gift. It ain't a gift, Eric. It's a goddamn curse."

My sense of wonder atrophied under the onslaught of Gabe's anger. I fished around for something to say, but pulled back an empty hook. Gabe lowered his shirt and sat back down at the table, leaning forward on his meaty forearms. Neither one of us said anything for a long time. The wind blew outside the window, and the house creaked in response, until I finally worked up the courage to open my mouth again.

"So how many languages do you speak?"

The big man sat back in his chair. "Not counting English?"

I nodded.

"Eight. Russian, German, Spanish, French, Mandarin, Arabic, Japanese, and Farsi. That last one isn't my strongest; I had to learn it on the go."

"Well, that's about eight fucking more languages than I speak."

"I thought you knew Spanish?"

"A little bit. I'm not fluent."

"Oh."

Silence took up residence again, sitting down with us at the table. I completely gave up on trying to think of something to say, my mind too stunned to come up with anything meaningful, and settled for drinking my hooch. When my glass was empty, I filled it back up and didn't feel the least bit guilty about it. At the end of drink number two, just as I was eyeballing the bottle and thinking hard about a third, someone knocked at the front door. Relieved, I stood up and went to answer it.

When I opened it, Grabovsky stood on the porch, grinning. "He broke."

"What?"

"Lucian. Steve broke him. Come on, we've got work to do."

I glanced at Gabe. The big man stood up and strode over to where his vest and weapons hung from the wall. Mine were still at home. I turned back to Grabovsky.

"Give me ten minutes."

*****

"That was quick."

Steve looked at me flatly and handed me a copy of Lucian's statement. "I can be very persuasive."

"I don't doubt it."

I sat down and started scanning the document. It was an inch thick, printed front and back. Thankfully, Steve—or someone on his staff—had included a summation of pertinent facts in the first few pages. Steve handed additional copies to Gabe, Marshall, Grabovsky, Wilkins, and Great Hawk, and then sat down at the head of the conference table next to General Jacobs and Mayor Stone. The general's command center was next door at the VFW, but we had chosen to hold the meeting in town hall's lone conference room rather than crowd everyone into his tiny office.

Jacobs had pinned a large map of western Tennessee to the wall where everyone could see it. The locations of the three remaining Legion strongholds were highlighted in red, along with a rough approximation of the Legion's tunnel network traced out in yellow. There were four long tunnels, and a dozen or so shorter ones branching out from the main corridors. All radiated out from Legion Central.

After giving everyone a few minutes to read over the intel Lucian had provided, Jacobs got up from his seat and shined a laser pointer at Legion Central.

"As you all know," he began, "Legion Central has been captured. We still have a contingent of Rangers there guarding the insurgent prisoners, and eliminating the infected population. We have plans to transport the insurgents to a secure facility in Kansas, but due to our tactical situation and resource concerns, that's on the back burner for the moment."

He shifted the little red dot to a spot west of Hollow Rock, just north of Huntingdon. "This is Legion West. It's a smaller facility than Central, but there are more troops stationed there. They've set up shop in a small business park just off Highway 77. As you can see, the tunnel they call the connector loop runs directly to it. We believe this is the Legion's primary staging area for weapons and munitions."

The dot moved to the east of Hollow Rock this time, not quite five miles from the Tennessee River. "This is the location known among the Legion as Haven. It's a gated community of luxury homes surrounded by an eight-foot security fence. This location is going to be a problem. According to the insurgents we've questioned, there are families and children living here, and a significant number of slaves. Obviously, we'll have to approach this one with the utmost caution."

Last, he indicated another spot south of Hollow Rock, a few miles north of I-40. "And this is Legion South. It's an old valve factory. Thick walls, easy to fortify. Most of the insurgents stationed here aren't Lucian's recruits; they're reinforcements from the Midwest Alliance. There are some three hundred enemy combatants at this location. We're going to make sure they don't bother anyone ever again."

He clicked off the laser pointer and turned to face the room. "I'm a firm believer that the simplest solution to a problem is often the best solution. So I'm going to make this simple. Legion South and West are the two biggest threats, so that's where I'll be directing the most resources. Grabovsky, I want you and the company from the First REU to take down Legion West. You'll have an Apache and a Chinook for air support. If what this Lucian character tells us is true, there's a wealth of weapons and ammunition there, not to mention supplies and equipment. I want it. There are a few thousand people on extermination duty back in the Springs that would love to get their hands on that ordnance. Garrett, Riordan, and McCray, I want you to pick a squad of Rangers and get eyes on Legion South. I'm putting the AC-130 at your disposal. Do your worst. The rest of you will be leading the remainder of the Rangers and the Hollow Rock militia to Haven. You'll have the lion's share of medical staff, the Pave Hawk, the other Chinook, and the other Apache. Well, two Apaches if you count Great Hawk."

The general smiled at his joke, but no one laughed. Great Hawk's obsidian eyes glittered blankly, his expression unmoved. After a brief, awkward moment, Jacobs's smile faded and he continued. "Take as many prisoners as you need to, and keep the collateral damage to a minimum if you can. That said, your priority is to dismantle the insurgency. Period. Anything else takes a back seat, and that includes sparing non-combatants. Is that clear?"

No one spoke, we all simply nodded. There were a lot of things I could have said to that, but in all honesty, the general was right. We would make every effort to minimize the body count, but when the bullets started flying, there would only be so much we could do. If the Legion troops stationed at Haven really cared about their families, then they would surrender peacefully. If they didn't, well ... we would do what was necessary. The people of Hollow Rock had never wanted this fight. The Legion had brought it to our doorstep. Now, we were going to end it.

"All right then," Jacobs said. "You all have your orders. Let's get this over with."

We all stood up and filed out of the conference room. On the way out, I caught Mayor Stone exchanging a glance with

Gabriel. It was brief, only a few seconds, but there was a lot in their eyes as they looked at each other. I wondered if anyone else noticed.

I pedaled my bike home and sat down in the living room. Allison still hadn't gotten home from the clinic, and only a few weakly burning coals remained in the fireplace. I thought about getting another fire going, but decided I didn't have the energy. What little mental fuel I had left, I needed to save for when Allison got home.

She wasn't going to be happy when I told her I was leaving again.

Chapter 28

… In Ashes They Shall Reap

Legion South looked just as abandoned as Legion Central had, but my FLIR scope told me a different story.

There were six sentries on the roof, but they stayed well back from the edge, making them invisible from the ground. Another ten patrolled the perimeter just past the tall grass bordering the treeline. There had been two on the water tower where I was watching from, rotating out every few hours with the other patrols. We had left them alone until word came down to secure the perimeter and get ready for the final assault to begin. Gabe and I decided that the water tower would be a good spot to watch the show, but first, there was the minor problem of the two Legion troops currently occupying it.

My M-110 had solved that problem nicely.

The AC-130 gunship was en route from Pope Air Force Base, but it would be a little while longer before it arrived. In the meantime, Grabovsky and Echo Company had begun their assault on Legion West. They'd encountered stiff resistance, and had lost several men. Grabovsky himself had been wounded as well. Not life-threatening, but he would be out of commission for a while.

The reward for their efforts was more than a hundred dead or mortally wounded Legion troops, a massive stockpile of guns, ammo, and supplies, and documentation revealing the location of all the Legion's supply caches. The price our people paid was six dead and eleven wounded, counting Grabovsky. I couldn't help but wonder if it was worth it.

Maybe it would have been better if we'd said to hell with the supplies, and just bombed the shit out of the place. I knew it wasn't my call to make, but it still bothered me.

At least I didn't have to worry about that at Legion South. As soon as the gunship arrived, it was going to rain death on the Legion as fast as its 40mm Bofors and M102 Howitzer cannons could pour it out. The only concern now was waiting for Great Hawk and Marshall to check in from Haven. Steve had set up our radios to listen in on the satellite uplink the Apache would be calling in on. It had required extra equipment, and extra weight for all of us to carry, but keeping everyone on the same page was more than worth the inconvenience.

My earpiece buzzed, and a slow, resonant voice spoke. "Alpha, Hawk, how copy?"

Speak of the devil.

"Loud and clear, Hawk. Give me a sitrep."

"Something is wrong here, Alpha. Haven has been abandoned."

The radio was silent for a few seconds. I could imagine Steve's face pinching down as he absorbed the news. In the silence, distantly, I heard the drone of the AC-130's engines approaching.

"What do you mean abandoned, Hawk?"

"There is no one here. The houses are all empty, and rigged with homemade explosives. If I had not been here, our men may have walked right into them. I found a tripwire on the first house my team searched, and radioed to the other fire teams to be on the lookout. Every one of these houses was set up to be a death trap. It looks like they left through the tunnels, and then blew the entrance behind them to keep us from following."

The sound of four turboprop engines turning in unison grew louder. A few of the sentries on the roof turned in the direction of the gunship and started motioning to the others.

"Shit," Steve said. "They knew we were coming."

"It gets worse, Alpha," Great Hawk intoned.

"What happened?"

"We found the slaves. They are all dead, shot execution-style. The Legion left their bodies piled in a house they were using as slave quarters. It looks like the people here left in a hurry, and did not want to deal with the slaves slowing them down."

While Steve and Great Hawk spoke, the sentries below realized what was going on above their heads and retreated down the stairwell back into the factory. Through my thermals, I saw the gunship arrive on station and wheel around, presenting its port side, slowly beginning to tip is wings in a pylon turn that would allow it to pulverize the factory with a stream of sustained fire. Gabe activated an illuminator and directed it at the factory, highlighting the target clearly in the aircraft's FLIR.

"Hawk, withdraw your troops and radio the Chinook. Get your people out of there."

"Acknowledged."

Less than a minute after the last sentry vanished down the rooftop access, the door opened again the four men came out, running in pairs. One man in each team was carrying a long cylinder with optical sights mounted to the top. One of the men stopped, brought what looked like a night vision scope to his face, and searched the sky. He pointed in the direction of the gunship and motioned to the others.

What the hell?

Beside me, I heard Gabe curse and key his radio. "Alpha, Wolf, there are two SAMs on the rooftop. Repeat, two SAMs on the rooftop. Radio the gunship and get them the hell out of here."

"What?"

"SAMs goddammit! Surface-to-air fucking missiles! Stingers! Get that plane out of here now!"

The radio cut out as Steve switched frequencies.

"Come on, Eric, shoot the fuckers!"

Gabe dropped the illuminator and picked up his .338. I remembered that I was holding an M-110, and hurriedly raised the scope. Through the crosshairs, I saw both men carrying missiles take aim. I remembered what Gabe had told me about Stinger missiles, how effective and easy to use they were. How they were heat-seekers that could bring down an aircraft as big as a 747.

The gunship was smaller than that.

Gabe's rifle fired next to me, and again, I marveled at how fast he could sight in and shoot. I was coming along as a sniper, but I wasn't at Gabe's level yet. It took me a couple of seconds longer than him to sight in, let out half a breath, and squeeze the trigger.

It was a couple of seconds too long.

Gabe's round hit its target just as he was firing the Stinger. The impact from the powerful slug knocked him forward, and his missile flew straight out over the treetops and detonated a few hundred yards distant, its propellant sending it streaking into a tower supporting high-tension wires. The explosion snapped the heavy wires, causing them to whipsaw through air in a flailing path of destruction that would stretch for miles.

At the same instant that I pulled the trigger on my M-110, the Legion troop on the rooftop fired his Stinger. The missile shot forth from the tube, and then the propellant kicked in, sending it streaking toward the gunship. The man who fired it didn't live long enough to see what happened next—my bullet took him through the heart, and he was dead before he hit the ground—but I did.

The only explanation I could come up with was that Steve hadn't radioed the pilot in time for him to deploy countermeasures. If he had, the white-hot flares would have lit up the night sky and diverted the missile, and disaster.

But that's not what happened.

Instead, the missile careened upward almost faster than my eyes could follow, blazed a trail straight to the gunship, and exploded into one of the port-side engines. Half of the wing on that side sheared away, leaving only a flaming stump behind. The massive airplane rolled over like a huge, bloated bird shot in mid-flight, and plummeted nose-down, spiraling toward the Earth.

As I watched, my heartbeat fluttered in my chest, I stopped breathing, and I felt a sinking sensation, as though I were standing on the gunship's one remaining wing and falling down with the doomed flight crew. It seemed to take forever for the plane to descend, foot by agonizing foot. Lower it fell, closer and closer until finally it hit the ground with a thundering *PHOOM* that set the forest around it swaying, and made the water tower under my feet shudder and heave. An orange ball of fire bloomed into the night sky, billowing upward in an impossibly expanding mushroom cloud. The surrounding forest—bereft of rain for the past several weeks—was dry as kindling and went up like it was covered in gasoline. A few seconds later, even as far away as I was, a blast of heat struck me like the hand of an angry god, sending me shrinking back with my arms over my face.

Gradually, the heat faded and I got to my feet, slowly lowering my arms to stare at the wreckage.

The mushroom cloud dissipated, revealing the remains of the gunship covering a huge swath of blasted ground, and for hundreds of yards in every direction, the surrounding trees had burst into flame, catching and spreading in a furious blaze. All

I could do was stand and stare. Dimly, I wondered how the hell the Legion had gotten their hands on Stinger missiles.

And then, coming to mind unbidden, I remembered the map General Jacobs had shown us. I remembered the tunnel system, and the yellow highlighter marks that traced its path. I remembered looking at Haven and Legion South, and seeing the thin yellow band connecting the two. No side tunnels, no deviations. Just a straight line from point A to point B.

It had been two days since General Jacobs had called a meeting in that room. Two days to get our troops and equipment into position. Two days that Gabe and I had spent reconnoitering Legion South, and chewing on our own impatience.

Two days of warning for the Legion.

Someone had escaped the assault on Legion Central. That was the only explanation. Someone had gotten away, and had made a beeline for Haven. The math made sense. They could have covered the distance, even if they were on foot, in just over a day. It would have been hard travel, but not impossible. That coincided with the amount of time it took for Steve to break Lucian. Then they had another two days to kill the slaves, pack up what they needed for the journey, and high-tail it through the tunnels. But that only left one destination. One connection to that lonely furrow drawn from one spot on the map to another.

Legion South.

And then there was the one person from Lucian's retinue that was still unaccounted for.

Aiken.

He must have somehow evaded the AC-130's FLIR and fled to Haven. Knowing what a sadistic bastard he was, it was probably his orders that had compelled the people living at Haven to execute the slaves prior to escaping.

Which meant there could be as many as five hundred souls in that factory. Men, women, and children, along with any weapons that had been stashed in the tunnels between Legion South and Haven.

Motion on my left distracted me, and I looked over to see Gabe leveling his rifle at the two surviving men on the factory roof. He sent a round downrange, and one of them fell. He worked the bolt and fired again. The explosion must have shaken him up, because that round missed its mark and sent up a plume of dust next to its intended victim. Gabe cursed, cycled the bolt, and fired again. This time he hit his mark.

"Eric, come on, man. Get back in the fight." His hand came up to his mike. "Alpha, Wolf. Me and Irish are okay. How's your team?"

"Wolf, Alpha. We're okay. Alpha Two, report in."

"We're fine. A little shaken up, but otherwise okay."

There was silence for a few moments while Steve pondered his next move. "Command One, Angel is down. Repeat, Angel is down."

General Jacobs's voice came over the net. "What the hell is going on out there, Alpha?"

"Sir, our intel was wrong. They just hit the gunship with a Stinger. It's down, sir. They're gone."

Another silence.

"Alpha, I need you to keep it together, son. This is not your fault. There's no way you could have known they had that kind of firepower. We'll deal with that problem later. Right now, I need you to keep those insurgents from escaping, do you understand?"

"Yes sir."

"Good. I'll get Hawk and his unit headed your way. You'll have air support and reinforcements there in less than twenty minutes. There won't be many troops, just what they can fit onto the Chinook and the Pave Hawk. Have your men cover all of the egress points and fire on anyone that tries to come out. Do you copy?"

"Yes, sir, I copy."

"Make it happen."

Steve said, "All right, there are five exits. Two on the north side, two on the south, and the main entrance on the east side. I'll take Alpha One and cover the north side. Alpha Two, you take the south doors. Wolf, Irish, do you have eyes on the east exit?"

"Affirmative," Gabe said.

"Good. Shoot anything you see coming through that door."

"Can do." Gabe shifted his weight and settled into a more stable firing position.

"How many rounds do you have for that thing?" I asked, sitting down and leveling my M-110.

"Only about fifty or so. How about you?"

"A hundred 7.62 rounds, and a hundred-eighty 5.56."

Gabe shook his head. "My six-eight can't reach that far, so there's no way in hell your NATO rounds are gonna get there. Once we're dry for the big guns, we'll have to move to a closer firing position."

I looked around, seeing only trees. "Like what?"

"I don't know. Maybe we'll climb a tree or something."

I glanced at him, hoping he was joking. He wasn't. "Well, we're not at that point yet. Let's just make every shot count, okay?"

"I always do. Now listen, I want you to cover the front door. I'm going to keep an eye on the roof. When people start coming out of those doors, Alpha squad is going to fire on them. Pretty soon, the Legion's going to get tired of that, and send people up onto the roof to take them out. Remember what I taught you about fighting an enemy that's firing on you from an elevated position?"

I thought about the twenty-four Army Rangers and one Green Beret deployed around the factory. That was a lot of space to cover and not a lot of people to do it. "Yeah. I remember."

"When that happens, I'm going to suppress their fire for as long as I can. Sooner or later, they're gonna figure out where the shots are coming from, and return fire."

I swallowed. "Gabe, is this supposed to be helping?"

"I'm just making sure you know what we're gonna be up against. If they have long-range weapons, we'll have to abandon this tower. It they just have the Kalashnikovs, they won't be able to hit us at this range. You might hear a few rounds bouncing off the struts underneath us. Just ignore it."

"Yeah, sure. Great idea. Ignore the bullets. Got it."

Gabe shot me a frown, and then turned back to his rifle. "Just stay focused."

I took a deep breath to clear my head, adjusted my grip on my rifle, and waited. As I sat there, it occurred to me that the Legion might have installed additional exits in the tunnel to Haven. If they had, we wouldn't see anyone coming out of the factory. They would all go that way.

"Alpha, Irish."

"Copy Irish."

"Do we know where that tunnel is? You know, the one from here to Haven?"

"We know what Lucian told us. At this point, I can't trust that intel anymore. Why?"

"Because if we don't see people coming out soon, that means they have another escape route somewhere in the tunnels."

"Believe it or not, Irish, that did occur to me."

"Copy. Just making sure."

I sat and waited. My breath formed a fog in front of my face and, after a few minutes, the cold began seeping into my limbs. I resisted the urge to squirm around and get some blood flowing, and kept my attention on the door. No one showed up. Another minute went by. Still no one. I was starting to think things were about to get much more difficult.

And then I felt a thump.

Not like the one I'd felt when the gunship had gone down, but still pretty powerful.

"Gabe, did you feel that?"

"Yeah, I did."

"What the fuck was it?"

"Hell if I know. Felt like an explosion. I don't see anything, though. You?"

I scanned around. "Nope. Nothing."

"Hmm. Weird."

I put my eye back on the scope just in time to see the front door open. A body appeared in the doorway. I fired, the round crossing the distance in a blink and hitting the figure in the chest just as he cleared the door. Another appeared behind him and I gave him the same treatment. Then more came. I got two of them, but they were coming faster now, fanning out and running in a serpentine pattern toward the treeline.

"Goddammit, I can't get all of them."

I kept firing until I ran out of ammo, and had to pause to reload. As I did, more Legion troops emerged and ran for cover.

"Just keep at it, get as many as you can," Gabe said.

Steve's voice sounded in my ear. "We've got contact."

From the north side of the factory I heard the staccato crack of rifles firing on the fleeing marauders. I kept up my end of the bargain and got as many troops coming out of the east entrance as I could, but it was like swatting mosquitoes in a swarm. The rest of the squad had better luck, probably because they were in three-man fire teams, and I was all by myself.

"This is Alpha One. The bad guys on our side retreated into the factory. How are you doing over there, Alpha Two?"

"Same story. We dropped a dozen or so, and they stopped trying to come out."

I keyed in. "Great. Mind sending some guys over to the east side? I'm getting my ass kicked over here."

The Ranger in charge of Alpha Two keyed in. "Roger, en route."

A few seconds later, his squad appeared, moving through the forest toward my position. In short order, he had his men fan out and begin picking off the Legion troops. It didn't take the ones inside long to figure out what was happening to their friends, and they vanished into the darkness beyond the door.

"Okay, Alpha, looks like we got 'em hemmed in," I said.

"Copy Irish. Keep your eyes peeled."

"Now here comes the fun part," Gabe said.

"What?"

"Just wait."

As he said it, the rooftop access door slammed open and men began fanning out on the rooftop, heading for the areas where they had taken fire.

"Holy shit."

Gabe's voice was fearful.

Gabe's voice was never fearful.

This was not good.

"What?"

Rather than answer me, he clicked his mike. "RPGs! They've got RPGs!"

"Copy Wolf. Take 'em out."

I shifted my aim and saw what Gabe was looking at. Several troops on each side of the roof carried those evil, pointy cylinders that all Americans, inundated with decades of television depicting terrorists, have grown to dread.

Five of them were pointed right at us.

Staring at those wicked little rockets, a familiar feeling began creeping up on me. It began as a cold ball in my chest that grew and expanded, turned liquid, and flowed outward into my arms, my hands, and up to my face. I could hear my own heartbeat. My vision narrowed, going gray at the edges. Sounds acquired sharpness and clarity, my sense of touch became acute, my nerve endings booming their messages in thundering flashes. I could smell the sharp, acrid scent of wood smoke on the air as the nearby forest fire whipped itself into a frenzy. The rough texture of the trigger grated against my finger like sandpaper. The weld of my rifle stock against my cheek was achingly cold. Each breath I took rasped in my ears like an amplified respirator.

Down on the rooftop, my enemies moved with glacial slowness. The crosshairs on my scope lined up with the first one as though moving on their own. I felt a thump, and realized that it was the stock bucking backward against my shoulder. The marauder in my scope fell, and before he hit the ground, I was sighting in on another one. Another thump. This time, the round slammed through the center of his face and blew a fist-size hole out the back of his head. I didn't wait to see him go down, I was already picking my next shot.

A blast of wind came from my left. The noise that followed told me it was Gabe firing his weapon.

Twice more my hands moved. My eyes followed. I didn't think, I just went with it. The last marauder aiming a rocket at me fell face-first to the rooftop.

And then the world came back in a rush.

It was as if someone had flipped a switch, canceling out whatever strange calmness had come over me. My vision re-expanded, the coldness inside of me receded, and I could hear and feel things normally again.

All five marauders on our side of the roof were down. On the north and east side, several others had gone prone at the precipice, aiming their rockets in the general direction where the Rangers had taken cover.

"I'll take the ones on the east side," Gabe said. "You take north."

"Got it."

I shifted my aim and began firing, but not before two of them fired their rockets. The warheads streaked out into the night and blasted into the forest close to the Rangers' infrared signatures. Being the trained professionals that they were, they had gone flat to the ground behind cover to avoid the explosion and the shrapnel that came with it. When the smoke cleared, all but one of them were back on their feet, firing their weapons. The one who stayed down wasn't moving.

Goddammit, Riordan. Get to work.

Gabe had already put down three more on his side, but I'd only accounted for one. I adjusted my grip, took a single, steadying breath, and fired. Got one. Another breath, another pull of the trigger. That was two. Then three. Four.

The ones who weren't dead or dying realized they were being sniped, and withdrew from the edges of the roof. One of them pointed his launcher at the water tower and, before I could get a bead on him, he fired.

Faster than the blink of an eye, it seared a trail straight toward my position. For a brief, heart-stopping instant, I thought I was done for. I thought I was going to end my life, after everything I had survived, in a ball of fire while sitting on the catwalk of a water tower in middle-of-nowhere Tennessee.

I needn't have worried.

RPGs are not precision weapons. They are heavy, tough to aim, and not terribly accurate at long range. Hitting anything with them at distances over three hundred yards is like trying to shoot a bird in flight with a bow and arrow.

Gabe and I were more than four hundred yards away, and it was our saving grace. The rocket careened off to my right, missing the water tower by at least twenty yards. Beside me, Gabe calmly swiveled his rifle and fired a single shot that blew the offending marauder's heart out through his spine. His few remaining compatriots witnessed his demise and decided that discretion was the better part of valor. Gabe and I kept up a steady stream of fire as they retreated, taking out two more of them before they disappeared down the roof access stairway.

"Alpha Two, Alpha One. What's your status."

"One man down. The rest of us are okay. How about you."

"No casualties. Wolf, Irish, you okay up there?"

I answered, "I about shit my pants when that RPG went by, but other than that, we're fine."

"That was damn good work, you two. You saved our asses."

"Anytime amigo."

Gabe tapped me on the shoulder. "Hey, look at that."

The fire caused by the crashed gunship was growing with incredible speed, leaping hungrily from tree to tree. I had heard stories about how quickly forest fires could spread, but had never before seen it in person.

It was, in a word, terrifying.

In the short amount of time that went by while I was concentrating on the firefight, the inferno had crossed the distance between the AC-130's wreckage and the field around the factory. As fast as it was moving, it would reach Steve and the Rangers in just a few short minutes.

"Alpha, Wolf. I don't know if you can see it from where you are, but there's a big goddamn fire headed your way. You have to get your men out of there right now."

A few seconds went by. No answer.

"Alpha, do you copy?"

"I copy," Steve said tersely.

"Move your men toward the water tower and get climbing. There's not much foliage on this hill, we'll be out of the fire's path. It's your only chance."

A few more seconds. "Actually, no it's not."

Gabe and I looked at the fire, then at each other, confused. "Alpha, there's nowhere else to go, believe me. I've got a hell of a view. You have to get moving, right now."

"Negative, Wolf. Alpha Two, do you still have your LAW?"

"Affirmative, Alpha One."

"Relocate to my position. We're going to make our own entrance, and we're going straight at these motherfuckers."

"Copy, Alpha One, on our way."

The little white dots that were Alpha Two began running for Steve's side of the warehouse. I blinked a few times, not quite believing what I was hearing.

"Alpha, what the fuck are you thinking?" I said. "You're outnumbered God knows how many to one. This is suicide."

"Don't underestimate me, Irish. I've taken on a hell of a lot worse odds. We have plenty of ammo, grenades and, most importantly, night vision and radio comms. It's pitch black in that warehouse, and the Legion doesn't have radios. We'll have the advantage. Besides, like you said, they might try to escape through the tunnels. I can't let that happen, not now. It's time to end this. You two stay on overwatch and advise Great Hawk and his men when they get here. We're going in."

"I hope you know what you're doing, Alpha."

"Watch and learn, my friend. Watch and learn."

I watched.

Alpha Two reached Steve's men. One of them kneeled down, hefted a LAW canister to his shoulder, and fired. Even from half a kilometer away, I felt the thump when it hit the factory, leaving a gaping hole where a door used to be. Steve ordered his men forward. In seconds, they were all inside, and I lost sight of them. From here, all Gabe and I could do was listen in on the radio.

"Alpha Two, contact. Thirty meters, straight ahead."

"Copy, moving to flank."

I heard guns firing.

"Clear, Alpha One. Moving up."

"Copy, right behind you."

Another voice, someone I didn't recognize. "Alpha One, something's wrong."

"What is it?"

"I'm up on one of the service ladders on the west side. All the enemy troops are crammed together near the south wall. There's only a couple of dozen of them. Aren't there supposed to be-"

Another voice broke in. "Shit, Alpha, we gotta get out of here, the whole fucking place is wired!"

"What?"

"I'm near the east wall. I just found a bomb on one of the support struts, and spotted another one near the roof. Look around, man, they're fucking everywhere."

A moment's pause. "Shit, he's right. Alpha Squad, fall back, fall ba-"

It was the last thing he ever said.

Dozens of charges detonated all at once, spread out around the periphery of the factory, lashed to each of the support beams. The noise was horrendous. The roof and walls collapsed in on themselves, sending up a gigantic cloud of dust and debris. The wind created by the fire blew it up and over the treetops, swirling and mingling with the smoke.

"Oh my God," Gabe whispered beside me.

I couldn't speak. All I could do was stare.

"Alpha, Wolf, do you copy?"

Silence.

"Alpha, Wolf, are you still there?"

Nothing.

He tried again. Same result.

"They're gone, Gabe."

He looked at me.

"They're gone, man. No one could have survived that."

Down below us, the factory had gone flat, as though stomped down by a giant foot. Heaping tons of rubble tumbled and rolled. Steel I-beams stretched up toward the sky like dead fingers.

"What the hell?" Gabe breathed.

"Lucian."

"What?"

"Lucian," I said again. "He fooled us. That son of a bitch. He set us up, and we fell for it."

Gabe looked at me again, and as understanding took hold, his face went blank. The fire raged on unabated, glowing orange behind a thick veil of black smoke. It surrounded the factory, came together like a lava flow on the other side, and moved on, consuming everything in its path.

Gabe and I watched, stunned into silence.

*****

Whoever had built the water tower, however long ago, had cleared away the trees around it in a circle that stretched over a hundred yards in all directions. Only tall grass stood below, growing scruffy and thinning out near the hilltop.

It was the only thing that saved us.

As the fire surrounded the tower, Gabe and I had to tie our headscarves around our faces and pull our shirts up over our mouths. The smoke was all-pervading, smothering and choking us. Even from more than a hundred yards away, the heat was intense, blown by its own wind. It was like standing in the maw of a giant hair dryer on its highest setting.

Our goggles warded off the worst of the smoke, but some still made it through. We huddled against the metal tank breathing as shallowly as we could and squeezing tears out of bloodshot eyes. Even if I could have opened them, I wouldn't have seen anything. Smoke had turned the world black.

Distantly, I heard a Chinook approaching. Faint at first, then louder and louder. It circled the wreckage of the warehouse a few times, and then came to hover over our heads. A cable came down, and harnessed to that cable was Great Hawk. He retrieved Gabe first, then came back for me. Before the winch had even drawn us up to the door, the pilot wheeled around, gained altitude, and flew us away from the blaze.

Once inside, I leaned my head against the bulkhead and forced my hurtling thoughts into order. I pushed my grief and anger back as far as I could, put them in a box, and closed the lid. Slow and steady, I breathed. One breath, then another.

Just keep breathing, I told myself. *Just keep breathing*.

Below the chopper, smoke swirled and rose. The fire feasted greedily upon the dry forest. Eventually, we outran it, but it was close on our heels. Headed north.

Headed toward Hollow Rock.

Chapter 29

The Journal of Gabriel Garrett

Embers

General Jacobs came to see us at the clinic.

Eric and I had a room to ourselves. We were just down the hall from where Doc Laroux was keeping some women we had rescued from Legion Central.

Everyone on the Chinook had disembarked with the exception of Great Hawk and Marshall. They'd wanted to go back and make sure all of their troops got home safely. I wished them luck, and then Eric and I propped each other up on the walk across the parking lot.

Doc told us we were lucky. The smoke inhalation wasn't too bad, and covering our faces had kept the ashes out of our lungs. She made us stick around for a little while to make sure no other symptoms developed. She said she was worried we might have inhaled toxic fumes.

I think she just wanted to keep Eric close by.

I debriefed with Jacobs and two of his staff. They came in armed with notebooks and digital recorders. They took a statement from me, but Eric didn't have anything to say. When one of the staffers tried to tell Eric that giving a statement wasn't optional, he gave the man a sharp look and drew his pistol. Jacobs stepped between them and told his man to go wait in the hallway.

Later, after they had finished with me, Jacobs decided to give it another try with Eric. My friend had sat still on his bunk during the debrief, staring down at his hands. When the old soldier started talking to him, Eric had raised his head and blasted him with a desolate glare. The general's words died on his lips, and I understood why. The look on Eric's face was the same one I've seen on hundreds of other people. Soldiers, Marines, et cetera. It's the look of a man who has hit the wall. Who has given all he has to give, and has no more reserves to call upon. The general looked down, nodded a few times, and got up to leave. I had a feeling he knew that look, too. Maybe he'd even been there himself.

On the way out, he said, "For what it's worth, men, I'm sorry about Captain McCray. He was a good man. A good soldier. I don't know what I'm going to do without him. We lost a lot of people today."

I didn't say anything. Jacobs looked old, and pale, and damn near used up. I knew the feeling. He shot me one final, broken glance, and left.

The next day, the first winter storm came in, and it couldn't have picked a better time. The forest fire that started at Legion South had grown and spread until it was only a few miles away from Hollow Rock. On the morning the snow blew in, the sun emerged red and angry over the horizon, and a steady rain of ashes had turned the town an ugly shade of charcoal. By noon, the first gunmetal leviathans had invaded the northern sky. By sundown, they hung fat and heavy over most of Kentucky, Tennessee, and the Carolinas. By nightfall, the drifts had piled up nearly a foot high, and a freezing wind was sweeping southward. I shivered in its cutting onslaught, and thanked my lucky stars it had shown up. By the next morning, most of the fire was out. Smothered under three feet of snow.

It was the first time I could remember being grateful for a blizzard.

*****

It was two weeks before the dust settled.

General Jacobs sent his men around to gather Eric and me. He wanted to have a sit-down with us. Explain everything that happened. I went. Eric stayed home. I didn't blame him.

Jacobs chased his staff out of the office and motioned for me to sit down in a chair. He had made tea on a hotplate in the corner, and offered me a cup. I took it, and nodded toward a report on his desk.

"That for me?"

He sat down and stared at it for a moment. "Yes. I assume I can trust you to keep this information confidential? This is still a federal matter."

I nodded, and held out an impatient hand.

The militia, and all of the troops Central Command had sent us, had spent the last two weeks out in the field retrieving the supplies and equipment we'd seized from the Legion, and trying to figure out what the hell happened at the factory. To that end, some of Jacobs's men had found a heavy equipment rental facility, requisitioned a fuel shipment from Pope AFB, and had gotten some excavation equipment up and running.

It took several days of working around the clock to clear enough rubble to investigate and, along the way, they discovered the bodies of Captain McCray, the Rangers with him, and about two dozen Legion troops. They also discovered not just one, but two tunnel entrances. One of them, the Haven section of the connector loop, was still intact. A search of the tunnel had revealed nothing but dirt, mud, and a trail of objects that the people fleeing from Haven had decided weren't worth carrying anymore. The other had been blown, sealed at the entrance with explosives. It took another couple of days of digging to get the tunnel open again, but by then, the last remnant of the Free Legion was long gone.

Everything that happened at Legion South, the sentries, the Stinger missiles, the RPGs, the staunch resistance, the bombs, all of it had been a front. A ruse to keep us occupied while they got the women and children away safely. Something close to a hundred troops had stayed behind to cover their retreat. They had sacrificed themselves to ensure that the others would have enough time to escape. They knew what was coming their way. They had to have known what the Army was going to do. But they stayed anyway. And as much as it galled me to admit it, they had acted bravely. They were still a bunch of thieving, murdering bastards, but I could no longer think of them as cowards. Not after what they had endured at our hands. Even criminals have families. Even marauders have people that they care about. People they love. Wives. Children.

I wasn't sure where that left me.

As I read on, it became clear to me that Eric was right. Lucian had fucked us over something fierce.

The bastard had fed us enough good intel to string us along. He knew someone was going to get back to Haven. He knew what their worst-case scenario procedures were. He knew what they would do once their location was compromised. He knew how we would deal with Legion South. He knew, and he had used it against us. And now there were more than three hundred enemy combatants floating in the breeze. We had no clue where they were, and all of our air assets had been called away by Central Command. Without the helicopters, and their FLIR imagers, we had no way to search for them.

Probably, they had fled. Probably, they were headed north to join up with the Midwestern Alliance. Probably, they were running with their tails between their legs, terrified that we were going to catch up to them. I wasn't sure how I felt about it. Although I wasn't happy that so many Legion troops had escaped, I couldn't help but think about their women and children. I finished reading the report and tossed it back onto Jacobs's desk.

"What about Lucian? What are we going to do with him?"

General Jacobs paused, and put his cup down. "Officially, he's in federal custody at an undisclosed location. That's the word, if anyone asks you. Understood?"

I nodded. "And what's the unofficial story?"

"I can't make a statement about that. But if I did, I would mention that Lucian was diabolically clever."

"Was?"

"Was. If I were to make an unofficial statement, it would include some mention of how one of our interrogators got sloppy. It would mention that after a round of questioning, he couldn't remember what he'd done with his glasses, but didn't say anything to anyone. It would also mention that Lucian sharpened one of the lenses from those glasses on the floor of his cell, and used it to cut his own throat. But of course, none of that happened. Officially."

I met his eyes, and it was a long time before I looked away. I thought about everything that had happened over the past few months. All the people killed on both sides. How many resources had been used up. How much effort the Legion had gone through just to harass one little town. None of it made sense.

"So what was the Legion's end game here, Phil? What were they trying to accomplish with all this? They didn't need Hollow Rock. It doesn't add up."

General Jacobs shook his head and sat back in his chair. His chin sank to his chest, and he rubbed at his eyes. "I'm not supposed to talk about this, but I think you deserve to know."

I stayed quiet and waited.

"We don't know the whole story, but here's what we do know. The Midwest Alliance has declared itself an independent nation, and it is claiming territory. Out west, the Republic of California is doing the same thing. Until about four months ago, the leadership back in the Springs wasn't too worried about it. We had our hands full just getting Colorado, Nebraska, and Kansas under control. Restoring food production, getting an oil refinery online down on the Gulf Coast, that sort of thing."

"So what changed?"

Jacobs opened a drawer on his desk and removed a file folder. He shuffled through it, pulled out a glossy 8x10 aerial photo, and handed it to me. It showed a massive flotilla of ships approaching a harbor.

"Where is this?" I asked.

"California. Humboldt Bay."

My stomach began to twist up.

"Where are these ships from?"

"We're not exactly sure. Some of them are from China. A few others from Russia. But we believe most of them are North Korean."

I let out a breath and dropped the photo in my lap. "How many of them are there?"

"That picture there, it's just a fraction. There are hundreds, possibly over a thousand ships. Almost all of them freighters, but a few warships as well."

I remembered Eric telling me about the Legion supply cache. The Chinese rifles. The Russian ammo. The Korean shipping manifests.

"This is a problem, Phil."

"Yes, it is."

The weight on my shoulders that had been lightening up the last couple of weeks suddenly grew heavy again. More pieces started falling into place.

"So the Midwest Alliance is in cahoots with the Republic of California. Enemy of my enemy, and such. They're both making a land grab, with Colorado dead in the middle. This flotilla shows up with guns, and food, and ammo, and God knows what else, and they set up shop in Humboldt Bay. They're sending weapons and munitions to the Alliance, and in exchange they're getting …"

I held out a hand to Jacobs.

"Food," he said. "The Alliance is in prime farming country. Much like Hollow Rock, they have more abundance than they know what to do with. On top of that, they're slowly beginning to bring electricity and manufacturing capacity back online, however limited."

"Aren't we doing that as well?"

"We are, especially now that we've secured the Hoover Dam."

I reached up to scratch my beard, only to find that it wasn't there. I let my hand drop. "So what does all this have to do with Hollow Rock and the Legion?"

"It was a power play. War by proxy. The Alliance wanted us to know what they're capable of. How far they're willing to go. They wanted to capture Hollow Rock for no better reason than the federal government offered this community its support. Agents from the Alliance found an easy ally in the Free Legion and started helping them ramp up their operations. They wanted to cut this town's head off, put it on a pike, and stand it up outside their gates. The subjugation of Hollow Rock was to be a warning to the President to stay off their doorstep, or suffer the consequences."

"But it didn't work out for them."

"No, it didn't. You played a big part in that."

I dismissed the comment with a wave. "And what did it cost them? The Alliance, I mean."

Jacobs didn't answer. His gaze shifted away.

"They won, Phil. They didn't get Hollow Rock, but they go an AC-130. They got Steve. They got quite a few soldiers. Every plane we lose is one we can't use against them. Every bullet we shoot at cannon fodder like the Free Legion is one we can't shoot at them. Every one of our soldiers that dies is a soldier we can't send to fight them. That's what they're doing. They're chipping away, bit by bit. You ever heard that old joke about how to eat an elephant?"

Jacobs chuckled, but it was bitter and without warmth. "One bite at a time."

"Guess what, Phil. We're the elephant."

Jacobs stood up and walked to the window. The blinds were shut, and he reached out a hand to open them. Light filtered in through the slats and cast streaks of shadow over the old soldier's face. His crow's feet and frown lines stood out in stark relief.

"This is just the beginning, Mr. Garrett. The first salvo in what my gut tells me is going to be a long battle. The Alliance, the flotilla, the Republic of California, they're not just going to go away. Sooner or later we're going to have to deal with them."

He turned and looked at me. "We're going to need all the help we can get."

The weight on my shoulders pressed down harder.

"So for now, where does that leave us?"

Jacobs straightened up and walked back to his desk. "For now, we finish mopping up. The Ranger company has been called north to Kentucky, and most of the First Expeditionary is going with them. I'm headed back to Colorado, and I'll be taking Great Hawk, Grabovsky, and Wilkins with me. Marshall will stay behind to help you finish training the militia. I pulled a few strings with Central, and they're letting me leave a few dozen men here to help see Hollow Rock through the winter. More importantly, now that the Legion is gone, this town will be getting a facilitator."

I kept my poker face on. "What's a facilitator?"

“Oh, that’s right, I haven’t told you about them yet.” He went over to a safe on top of a file cabinet, keyed in passcode, and took out a file folder. On the front, in bold black letters, it read: PHOENIX INITIATIVE: TOP SECRET.

“Phoenix Initiative?”

Jacobs brightened. “That’s right. You didn’t honestly think the federal government didn’t have a backup plan in case of a mass extinction event did you?”

He handed me the file, smiling. I spent a few minutes flipping through it and scanning the pages. As I read, for the first time in longer than I could remember, I started getting excited.

“Is this for real?”

The general laughed. “Of course. I couldn’t make that shit up if I tried.”

I handed the folder back to him. “You’re trusting me with an awful lot of classified information, General.”

He heard the suspicion in my voice, and held up a hand. “You’ve proven yourself, Gabriel. I have no reason not to trust you. And the way I figure it, if I want your help in the future, I’ll need to keep you in the loop.”

I stood up. “You figure right.”

Jacobs smiled again, got out of his chair, and held out a hand. I shook it.

“I can’t thank you enough for everything you’ve done, Gabriel. Same goes for Eric. Let him know for me, will you?”

“I’ll do that. You take care, Phil. If you need me, you know where to find me.”

I left his office and stepped outside into the driving wind. A pair of ski goggles kept the snow out of my eyes as I walked home. I thought about Captain McCray, and how I had treated him. Constantly suspicious of his every action. I thought about how I’d always given him a hard time, always assumed he was working toward his own ends. I still wasn't sure if I was wrong about that, but whatever else Steve had done, he had died a brave and loyal soldier. He had pledged his life to protect what was left of the United States, and he'd kept that oath. For that, if for nothing else, he had earned my respect.

When I got home, Liz was sitting by the stove in a terry-cloth robe reading a novel.

"How'd it go?" she asked, looking up.

"Jacobs told you about the facilitator, right?"

"Yes, he did."

"How are you not bouncing-off-the-walls excited?"

She laughed, her voice musical in the chill air. "Who says I'm not?"

She stood up and walked over to me. Her arms went around my neck, and I pulled her close, squeezing and pressing my lips to her cheek. I ran my hands over her back and realized she wasn't wearing a bra.

Or a shirt.

My hands drifted further down, and discovered an absence of panties. Elizabeth's fingers slid up my neck, bringing out the goosebumps. I leaned back just far enough to tilt her face up and press my lips to hers until they parted, and I felt her soft tongue against mine. I took my time and did a thorough job of things. Her hands kept moving and she let out a soft moan.

I came up for air. "I hate this robe. It looks terrible on you."

She giggled, and snuggled closer. "Maybe you should take it off me."

That was exactly what I did.

Chapter 30

Welcome Faces

It always surprises me how quickly people move on with their lives. Whatever the event, through any tragedy, the survivors always find a way to carry on.

We lose a loved one. We have a funeral. We spread the ashes, we hold each other and say comforting things, and then we get on with the business of living.

A house burns down. We sift through the charred remains and salvage what we can. We carry off the wreckage and make plans to build a new home. And then we get on with the business of living.

We suffer trauma, and lose our way for a while. We mope silently around the house for a few days. We get drunk. Being drunk feels better than the hurt, so we get drunk again. Finally, we get a stern talking-to from our significant others telling us that while they know we're hurting, drowning our sorrow in a bottle isn't going to make things any better. Then that significant other kisses us gently, and something breaks loose, and then we're crying like a baby again. Later, when all the tears are wiped away, we feel better. Stronger.

And then we get on with the business of living.

*****

In late December of one of the best and worst years of my life, I attended two events. One of them a month late, and the other far too early.

The first was the graduation ceremony for the Ninth Tennessee Volunteer Militia. Or as they jokingly called themselves, the Bloody Nine. At first, I thought that whoever named them must have been a big fan of Joe Abercrombie's *The First Law* series. But apparently, that was not the case. Some of them said it was because they had seen combat and taken casualties before they had even graduated from basic training. Some said it was because of their unit patch, a crimson 9 on a plain green circle. Whatever the case, either name sounded better than simply "the militia." At least their unit was now important enough to warrant capitalization.

In the spirit of naming things, the Bloody Nine's training facility, formerly known simply as "the camp," was renamed Fort McCray. Mayor Stone even commissioned a plaque in Steve's honor, and in honor of all the brave men and women who had given their lives in defense of Hollow Rock.

I think Steve would have liked that.

Sanchez, Flannigan, and two others were promoted to NCO and assigned one squad each. Marcus Cohen gave up his deputy's star, accepted a field commission from General Jacobs, and took the helm as the Bloody Nine's commanding officer. He was a good man for the job, but he wasn't the general's first pick.

That had been me.

Needless to say, I turned him down. I can barely hold myself together most days, much less a militia. I told Jacobs as much. He had smiled sadly, patted me on the shoulder, and let the matter rest.

The second event was Steve's memorial service. It had taken the Army a while to recover his remains, and the remains of the men who had died with him. The remains had been transported back to Hollow Rock, cremated, and the ashes either sent back to families, or buried at a nearby cemetery. Steve had no family left, so in Hollow Rock he remained. It was nice to have him close by; I could go and talk to him if I wanted to. Maybe he could hear me, maybe he couldn't. There was only one way to find out, and while my enthusiasm for life had dimmed somewhat, I hadn't sunk that low just yet. Someday, maybe. But not now. Not while I still had Allison in my life. And Gabe. And the Glovers. And all the other friends I had made along the way.

On my way home from the memorial service, I stopped by the clinic to check in on Allison and see if she had any work for me. Now that the Legion was gone, I had a lot of free time on my hands. I spent most of it at the clinic helping out where I could. Washing sheets, emptying bedpans, sterilizing instruments, having hot, steamy monkey sex with Allison in the supply closet. You know, the basics.

My heart and soul stood in front of the clinic with a couple of nurses, all of them watching a bustle of activity up the street at the VFW. I stopped beside her and bumped her with my hip. She smiled and bumped me back.

"What's going on down there?" I asked.

"Remember Gabe saying that the Army was leaving a few troops to ride out the winter with us?"

"Yeah."

"Well, they arrived today. The mayor is putting them up in the VFW hall."

"Hmm. Maybe I'll go introduce myself."

She swatted me on the butt. "Maybe you should."

I strolled up the street and turned into the small courtyard the VFW shared with the town hall. It was covered in over a foot of snow, but someone had shoveled the walkways clear. Townsfolk were hustling back and forth setting up cots, carrying in supplies, and building outhouses in the field behind the building. I approached a group of soldiers standing just inside the entrance. They were huddled in a cluster, sipping instant coffee and trying to stay out of the way. One of them laughed at something a tall, blond fellow standing beside him said, and turned where I could see his face.

I stopped in my tracks.

His beard was gone, and his hair was cropped short. He had lost weight, maybe about twenty pounds. He looked leaner. Denser. His face was sharper around the edges, and more weathered than I remembered. The eyes were the same, if a little darker from hard experience. But the smile was what gave him away. I would have recognized that shit-eating grin anywhere.

I called out, "Don't you have anything better to do than follow me around?"

The men stopped talking and looked at me. Their faces were a mixture of confusion and hostility. Their hands began straying toward weapons.

All but one of them, that is. He just stood there looking shocked.

"Eric? Is that you?"

The tall blond man looked down at him, and then at me, and I recognized him as well. He was a lot different than I remembered. He was bigger, more filled out, and looked ten years older even though it hadn't been nearly that long.

I smiled at the two of them and walked closer. "What's the matter, Ethan. Aren't you happy to see me?" I clapped Justin on the shoulder. "You too, man. It's been a long time."

Ethan Thompson, my old friend from Alexis, North Carolina, broke free from shock and swept me up in a bear hug, laughing.

The rest of his men just stared.

*****

Ethan and Justin came over for dinner that night, along with Gabe and Elizabeth. We ate, caught up with each other's lives, and generally enjoyed being in good company. After dinner, Justin pulled a laptop computer out of his pack and showed us the portable solar array he used to power it. The battery had a full charge, enough to last five hours. So we opened a bottle of Mike Stall's finest, huddled around the small screen, and watched movies until the batteries died.

At one in the morning, the womenfolk called an end to the night's proceedings, and informed us menfolk that it was time for bed. I proposed that our guests crash the night in the spare bedrooms rather than brave the cold on the way home. I didn't get any arguments.

Swaying a little drunkenly on his way to one of the guest rooms, Ethan stopped, walked over to me, and threw his arms around my shoulders. He was just as bull-strong as I remembered.

"It's damn good to see you again, man. I wondered what happened to you. Andrea's gonna fucking freak when she hears you're still alive."

I smiled and slapped him on the back. "I'm happy to see you too, man. Now let me go. I can't breathe."

He released me, allowing my ribcage to expand, and then punched me on the shoulder and ambled off to bed. As he shut the door behind him, I thought about all the trouble we had gotten into back in North Carolina. I thought about how far he'd come to be here, and how much he must miss his family back at Fort Bragg. I thought about the time he'd told me about his father, and how he still didn't know what had become of him. Mostly, though, I thought about how people drift in and out of our lives, and the legacy they leave.

I went to my own bedroom and curled up next to Allison. Time passed, the wind blew outside, and although Allison was soon snoring softly, I lay wide awake, staring out the window at the moon.

Restless, I got out of bed, pulled on some warm clothes, and stepped out onto the porch. As I came through the door, Gabe's voice startled me.

"Couldn't sleep?"

I rounded on him. He was swaying slowly back and forth on the porch swing. I hadn't heard him come outside. That was Gabe for you. If he didn't want you to hear him, you didn't hear him.

"No. I couldn't."

He gestured to the wall in the distance. "Feel like going for a walk?"

"Sure. Why the hell not?"

We grabbed our rifles just to be on the safe side, and walked to the nearest watchtower under a clear, starry sky. The bloated snow clouds had drifted away a few days ago, but they had left their damned howling wind behind. It blew strong and freezing over Hollow Rock, cutting into exposed skin and grabbing words and laughter from people's lips before they could reach their intended ears.

We reached the wall and began walking a slow circuit. Along the way, we exchanged short, respectful greetings with the guards we ran into. Everybody knew us now, and understood what we had done for the town. Gone were the suspicious stares and low whispers behind cupped hands. Now we got handshakes, and invitations to dinner.

At the southwest corner, the wall climbed a low hill before turning east at the apex. There, it fell away on the other side and revealed a gently rolling vista of fields and little copses of trees that stretched away toward the Ozarks. Gabe and I stopped, put our backs to the wind, and stared for a while.

"Shame about what happened to Steve," he said.

I nodded. "Yeah."

“I feel bad, you know? I was always so standoffish to the guy. I never really trusted him, and I made sure he knew it. I always assumed he had his own agenda.”

“Maybe he did,” I said. “If so, it doesn’t matter now.”

The wind picked up, and I had to lean in to hear what Gabe said next. “Gonna be a rough winter.”

I looked up at the sky, and at the ribbon-like, striated little clouds speeding across the full moon. “Gonna get worse before it gets better, I think.”

“You could say that about a lot of things.”

I glanced at him. His flint-gray eyes were nearly as pale as the snow.

We stood for a little while longer, watching the wind howl over the frozen fields and drive streamers of snow across the expanse of flawless white. I closed my eyes and leaned back into the wind, letting it support me. I tried to imagine what my future was going to be like. What storms the coming years were going to bring. Nothing that came to mind pointed to a brighter, happier tomorrow.

But that’s why people work. Why they prepare, and hope, and dream, and strive to grab the future’s delicate threads and pull them in with steady hands. We all strive, and we all fail. And with that failure comes the monster, born of fear and fed on uncertainty, that lives in each and every one of us.

The wind curled around me, and I imagined a dark ball, deep down in the center of my chest. Black, and undulating, and streaked through with red. I imagined it boiling from within, sending out heavings of orange along its surface like flares erupting from the sun. I imagined my body going pale, then translucent, and then invisible. The ball of anger, and hurt, and sorrow the only thing left of me.

I imagined the wind swirling around it, each molecule reaching out and stealing away a little portion. Bit by tiny bit, I imagined that ball growing smaller and smaller, eroding away under a sandstorm of winter breath. I imagined that blackness being born up by the wind. High over the wall, across the frozen distance of Tennessee, over the Ozarks, and out into the far, wide plains beyond. When it was gone, I opened my eyes.

I was still there. Still alive.

I decided that was a good thing.

Despite all I had been through, despite the pain, I was grateful that I had another day ahead of me. That I had love, and light, and warmth in my life. And no matter how tough things got, no matter how dark, I vowed to myself to always remember that.

Eventually, the chill became annoying, and Gabe and I stepped down from the tower. We turned down the road and started back toward where our two houses, and our two lives, sat comfortably close to one another.

Walking together, we went home.

About the Author:

James N. Cook (who prefers to be called Jim, even though his wife insists on calling him James) is a martial arts enthusiast, a veteran of the U.S. Navy, a former cubicle dweller, and the author of the "Surviving the Dead" series. He hikes, he goes camping, he travels a lot, and he has trouble staying in one spot for very long. Even though he is a grown man, he enjoys video games, graphic novels, and gratuitous violence. He lives in North Carolina (for now) with his wife, son, two vicious attack dogs, and a cat that is scarcely aware of his existence.

Printed in Great Britain
by Amazon.co.uk, Ltd.,
Marston Gate.